TRUE LOVE NEVER BLEEDS

ROBERT W. BARKER

Also By Robert W. Barker

The Devil's Chosen, *A Search for Understanding*
(Decision processes of the Holocaust)

Nuclear Rogue
(First of the Peter and Maria Thrillers)

Lucifer's Gold
(Second of the Peter and Maria Thrillers)

TRUE LOVE NEVER BLEEDS

iUniverse books may be ordered through booksellers or by contacting:

iUniverse
1663 Liberty Drive
Bloomington, IN 47403
www.iuniverse.com
844-349-9409

Cover art by Justin Barker-Detwiler

The author thanks his friends who assisted him with his Spanish. They will, however, remain anonymous, to ensure they are not faulted for any of the author's errors.
iUniverse books may be ordered through booksellers or by contacting:

ISBN: 978-1-6632-1749-3 (sc)
ISBN: 978-1-6632-1750-9 (e)

Print information available on the last page.

iUniverse rev. date: 01/27/2021

CHAPTER 1

The sound of semiautomatic gunfire has died away, replaced by the moaning of the wind and the rattling of the snow-covered mass of young balsam fir trees. The temperature is well below zero. Peter Binder removes his skis. He is acutely aware of the sharp squeak of his footsteps in the snow as he steps out of his ski bindings. He moves deliberately, only when the gusts of wind cover the sound of his steps in the snow.

Where the hell is Maria?

He fights the urge to attack.

Slow down. Do this right.

A light, wind-blown snow still falls, and the wind blows some of the snow off the needles of the trees. The clouds are thinning, but the moon provides only a dim light. It is enough. He maneuvers through the tight growth of trees, and as he moves, the snow from the trees coats his parka. He barely notices. Still hidden by the trees at the edge of the clearing around his cabin, he stops.

Headlights from a parked car, engine running, illuminate the door to the cabin, and flames flicker on one wall. Peter ignores the flames. They are not an immediate danger to the log cabin.

Two men, armed with assault rifles, stand in the cold, facing toward the cabin. They appear to be completely unaware of his presence behind them. They stamp their feet as they watch the door and talk softly to each other. Peter can't make out the words. Both men hold assault rifles, but Peter sees no heavy weapons. A third person is faintly visible in the driver's seat of the car. Peter considers the odds.

Manageable, he thinks. *Are there any more? Anyone hidden?*

He looks closely at the cabin. Interior steel shutters cover the windows, and the door is still intact.

Is she still inside? He shakes his head. *Have to find her first.*

He carefully moves back through the trees to his skis. He shrugs off his pack, pulls out the shotgun he took from the dead policeman at the end of the road, and turns away from the cabin. As quietly as possible, he pumps a round into the chamber and leans the shotgun against his pack.

In the dim light, he searches for the opening to the escape tunnel from the cabin, but, as he bends down to dig through the snow with his hands, the snow beneath his hands begins to move.

Christ!

Peter steps back, grabs the shotgun and moves behind the opening. Anyone climbing out of the short shaft will initially face away from him.

He waits. His breathing is deep and strong, nearly silent, but he is acutely aware of both his breathing and his beating heart. He stands in his own small cloud of water vapor, from his breath and the heat of his dash through the woods, but the gusty wind quickly blows it away. He pushes back against the adrenaline surge.

Hold it! Hold it!

His body and his mind are already moving into combat mode. He feels, hears, sees his surroundings with a familiar intensity. The sound of the wind is almost painful, and he works hard to control himself. He is still close to the cabin, but he can no longer see it or hear either the men or the car over the sound of the wind.

Still have to be quiet.

The hatch cover to the escape shaft squeaks faintly.

The glove on the hand holding the hatch looks familiar. It's too dark to be sure.

Peter maintains his hold on the shotgun and watches as the person silently lowers the cover onto the soft snow. He smiles as he sees a paisley parka.

"Maria!" he whispers hoarsely.

Maria Davidoff jerks her head up and around. She inhales sharply as she sees him in the gloom.

He puts his finger to his lips.

Maria raises one finger and silently disappears down the ladder into the shaft.

Peter focuses again on what he can hear. He tunes out most of the natural sounds. He listens hard for the men at the cabin, but he cannot hear them.

They don't know.

Peter flexes his hands. Once more he pushes back against his urge to attack.

We've got plenty of time. Time to be calm. Time to be cold.

He props the shotgun against his pack again and steps over to the shaft as Maria appears a second time.

"Here," she says softly. "I brought your toy, fully loaded. One round in the chamber." She hands up his .460 Weatherby Mark V rifle.

Peter nods. "Thanks," he whispers.

He takes the rifle with his left hand and reaches down with his right to help Maria out of the shaft. Once she's standing on the ground, she hands him five extra cartridges.

"I wasn't sure I'd see you again," Peter says, as he pockets the cartridges.

"Yeah. I was pretty sure you were already dead." She steps back. "You scared the hell out of me."

This is crazy, Peter thinks. *What's happening to us?* He breathes deeply. *Been here too many times.*

"What happened?" he asks.

"Right after you left, the gate alarms sounded. They were cutting the gate with a welding torch. Didn't look friendly. I covered all the windows and barred the door and I waited."

Peter looks toward the cabin. They are too far into the dense woods to see anything, but he listens.

"The shooting?" he asks.

"Random shots into the walls, around the door, into the steel shutters over the windows."

"Didn't last long."

"Some got into the cabin. I got out."

"They're trying to burn it down," Peter whispers.

"That's the other reason I left."

Peter shakes his head. "Log cabins are hard to burn."

"How'd they get past the cop at the end of the road?" Maria asks.

"Shot him," Peter says, still staring in the direction of the cabin.

"He was just a kid."

"Yeah," Peter says. "I called it in. The cops won't be here for at least fifteen to twenty minutes. Probably longer."

We need to make our move now, Peter thinks.

"You take the shotgun," Peter says. "There's a round of buckshot in the chamber." He pauses for a moment. "Let's get closer."

"You sure?" Maria asks.

"They don't know we're out here."

Without another word, they weave their way to a large, snow-covered log at the edge of the trees. They crouch low to the ground as they move slowly, deliberately. They lie down in the snow behind the log. The light snow has stopped, but the clouds still filter and diminish the light from the moon.

Peter looks over the log. He sees that the garage door is open. One of the men has taken the ladder from the garage and placed it against the cabin's roof. He goes back to the garage and returns with a five-gallon can of gasoline.

Peter takes a rough inventory of what they are facing. One assault rifle leans against the cabin by the ladder. A second man watches the cabin door with another assault rifle. The third man is still in the car, presumably armed.

Surprise and darkness are on our side. Reasonable odds, too, but is there a hidden lookout?

He lies back down to the right of Maria. "I don't want to do anything," he whispers, "but it looks like they're ready to pour gasoline down the chimney into the stove."

Peter takes another quick look over the log. The man with the gasoline makes sure the ladder sits solidly on the ground beneath the snow.

Peter whispers to Maria. "Let's see what happens when I yell at them."

"I'll take the guy watching the door," Maria says.

"I'll handle the guy at the ladder and the one in the car."

Peter looks over the log and then rises to his knees. He peels the glove off his right hand and brings the rifle to bear on the man with the gasoline. His target steps on the bottom rung of the ladder. He tests it to make sure it's steady, holding the gas can in his right hand.

Peter yells, "Hands up!"

The reaction is not encouraging.

The man at the door turns. Suffering night blindness from the headlights, he searches for a target he cannot see. He fires ten or twelve pointless shots into the night.

The shotgun blasts on Peter's left.

The man at the ladder drops the gasoline can and grabs his rifle. He turns and fires half a dozen shots into the darkness.

Peter presses his rifle firmly against his shoulder. He fires once and absorbs the harsh kick of the rifle. It rocks him back, and the muzzle jumps up about a foot and a half. The sound of the shot from the Weatherby is as loud as the shotgun, perhaps louder. Peter immediately works the bolt action.

Peter's shot hits the man by the ladder in the chest. He falls heavily against the wall of the cabin, shooting several times into the air before he drops his rifle into the snow. He slides down the wall, and slowly falls to his side in the fluffy snow at the edge of the cabin.

Maria pumps a round into the shotgun. Peter glances quickly at the man she shot, the one who had been watching the cabin door. He lies on his back in the snow, motionless.

The car door opens. Peter focuses on the driver, who has stepped out of the car and stands behind the driver's door. The driver opens fire in their direction. He can't see his target either, but he's seen the muzzle flashes. Peter hears the snap of one of the bullets as it passes much too close to his head.

Peter fires one shot at the driver, through the window of the driver's door.

The glass explodes, and the door quivers but remains open. The glass only makes the massive round from the Weatherby a bit flatter and more deadly. The driver drops onto the ground behind the door.

With two more shots, Peter snuffs out the headlights. Only the dome light remains, dimly glowing in the interior of the car.

Peter reloads and fires one final shot into the radiator. A cloud of water vapor begins to engulf the front of the vehicle.

The flames on the side of the cabin flicker out. Suddenly Peter hears the sound of the wind again, the soft chattering of the tree branches as the wind slaps them against each other, and the sharp snapping of the Canadian flag on its pole beside the cabin. The hiss of the steam escaping from the car's radiator is accompanied by some ominous clanking sounds from the engine.

Peter takes a deep breath. Then a couple more.

The entire action has taken less than half a minute.

"Jesus Christ!" Maria says in a whisper.

"You think that's it?" Peter asks.

"I saw four at the gate."

"Probably a rear guard, up the road. Let's sit tight. He'll have heard the Weatherby, and he'll show up pretty quickly."

"Lovely," she says. "Glad I dressed for the cold."

Peter works a fresh round into the chamber of the rifle. Then they wait in silence. Having raised a sweat on the trail, Peter begins to feel the cold.

The car's engine rattles off a few more strange noises and dies. The cloud of water vapor from the radiator begins to subside. After ten minutes, between the gusts of wind, the silence becomes deep and cold.

A few minutes later, Maria whispers, "There he is."

Peter watches as a dark shadow materializes in the road. Dressed in black, the newcomer is barely visible. He moves slowly and cautiously.

"Wait. See what he does," Peter whispers back.

The shadow becomes more distinct as it approaches the car.

Well armed, just like the others. And no night vision problems.

The shadow sees the driver lying in the snow, and he pokes at him with his foot. Then he steps around the side of the car and looks at the other two bodies. He hesitates. He looks all around, searching, his assault rifle at the ready. He slowly backs up to the driver's door, looks around one more time, and then he turns to get into the car.

Peter fires one shot at the driver's door. The roar of the shot fractures the night, and the car door swings shut with a loud bang.

The shadow man jumps back. He stands in the darkness, motionless, facing the closed door.

Now that's control, Peter thinks. *This is no amateur.*

Peter works the bolt action of the rifle. The implications of that distinctive sound are not lost on the man standing beside the car.

Peter and Maria wait in silence. Slowly the man bends down, places his rifle on the hard-packed snow by the car, stands up, and clasps his hands over his head.

"Good boy," Peter mutters. He stands up, and Maria stands beside him.

As he continues to watch the man, Peter says to Maria. "Let me have the shotgun." She gives it to him, and he hands her the Weatherby. "Head back to the cabin the way you came out. Make sure the lights are off. Open the door and cover me from anyone else coming down the road. Try not to shoot any cops."

"Yeah. Right. And you?"

"I'll try to make sure our buddy doesn't do anything stupid before the cops show up."

"Okay, then. See you in a bit."

Maria makes her way back through the thick trees. Peter hears the hatch shut with a soft clank.

The man at the car begins to lower his hands.

"No!" Peter shouts.

The man jerks his hands back to the top of his head.

Peter steps over the log and stands at the edge of the clearing that surrounds the cabin. Though the snow has stopped, there is still very little light. Peter is glad to have the shotgun. This is close work, and he likes the shotgun for that.

He hears Maria open the cabin door, and he slowly walks toward the man and the car, each footstep squeaking in the snow.

The man by the car wears a black parka and a black, knit cap. The hood of the parka is laid back, off his head. Peter's memory jerks back to the two shinobi who attacked him and Maria in Kyoto last year.

Unlikely, he thinks.

Even through the parka, Peter senses that the man tenses as Peter gradually approaches him. When Peter is twenty feet away, he swings the shotgun up and aims it roughly at the center of the man's back.

"Okay, buddy," Peter says. "We're going to wait quietly for the police to arrive. Turn around, slowly."

Peter keeps the shotgun trained on the man's torso.

The man turns, slowly. Later, Peter would say that the man had no expression whatsoever on his face, though that seems impossible. And in the dim light, how could he tell?

When the man fully faces Peter, he stands motionless for a long moment. Then he makes a movement that must have taken years to perfect. In the darkness, Peter senses the movement, more than he actually sees it.

In less than a second, the man's right hand reaches to his collar to retrieve a long slim knife. His hand whips forward to throw the knife.

Before the knife leaves the man's hand, Peter shoots. The round of buckshot hits the man squarely in the chest. He attempts to complete the throw, but the knife misses its target. It bounces with a soft clink on an errant piece of gravel in one of the hard tire tracks.

The man staggers. He wavers unsteadily, but still he stands.

Peter pumps another round into the shotgun and shoots a second time. The soft thud, when the man hits the ground, is lost to a gust of wind.

As the echoes of the shotgun blasts die away, Peter hears Maria say, "Jesus Christ!"

Peter lowers the shotgun. He closes his eyes for a moment. When he opens his eyes again, Peter looks at the man on the ground in front of him.

"You stupid, stupid man," he says.

Peter walks over to him. He takes a small flashlight out of his left pocket and shines the light on what is left of the man's face. The man looks Japanese. He checks on the driver. Dead. Japanese.

Peter examines the man who had been watching the front door. He stoops down and looks at his face for a long time before he stands up.

That doesn't surprise me.

The last one, at the ladder. All four men are dead. All Japanese.

"Lovely," he says, turns, and heads for the open door to the cabin. He stands in front of Maria for a moment. They look at each other. Neither one of them speaks.

Finally, Peter says, "Let's go inside. It's getting cold out here."

Peter shuts the door and turns on the lights, including the flood lights in front of the cabin and the garage. He leans the shotgun against the wall next to the door. Then he steps over to his desk and picks up the VoIP telephone. He punches in a number.

"Ontario Provincial Police. How can I help you?"

"This is Peter Binder. I called earlier on the radio, about an officer shot and killed at the end of the access to my cabin."

"Yes, sir. Two cars should be arriving in the next ten to fifteen minutes."

"Tell them it's a mess. We've got five bodies here, counting your officer."

"Is it an active shooter situation?"

"Not anymore."

"Where are you located?"

"I'm at my cabin, with Maria Davidoff."

"I'll notify the patrols."

"You might want to notify the RCMP. These guys are all Japanese, and I happen to know one of them."

"With you, we always notify the RCMP. Standing orders."

"Lovely. We'll be waiting inside the cabin."

"I'll tell them."

Peter puts the phone down and turns to see Maria staring at him.

"All Japanese?" Maria asks. "And you know one of them?"

"Yes… You remember Akihiko Uehara, that well-dressed Japanese thug we met at the bank in Zürich?"

"Yes, I remember him. He's one of these guys?"

"He's the body in front of the door."

"Jesus!" Maria says. "I don't believe this."

"Believe it," Peter says. "Our Japanese friends have paid us a visit."

She stares at him. "That's really bad news."

"Actually," he says, "it's fantastically good news. We survived. They didn't."

CHAPTER 2

Peter puts the Weatherby away in the bedroom closet, and he makes sure the entrance to the escape tunnel is closed and well covered. As he strips off his coat, hat, gloves, and boots, he takes the P229 pistol, in its holster, out of the large, right-hand pocket of his parka. He hesitates, before he straps it onto his belt.

When he returns to the cabin's main room, Maria raises her eyebrows at the pistol, but she says nothing about it. He sees that she has raised the steel shutter over the front window.

"I thought we should let the cops see us sitting in here," she says, "assuming we've seen the last of our Japanese friends. But it's going to get pretty cold in here with all the broken panes of glass."

"We can tape some plastic bags over them. That should hold us for tonight, at least."

Maria helps him with the temporary repair job. Peter throws some logs into the stove, and they sit down at the rough-hewn dining table, each with a cup of coffee.

Peter puts his head in his hands.

"You okay?" she asks.

"I think so." He looks up. "I just feel sick. How about you?"

Maria says nothing.

Peter watches her. She isn't looking at him, and her face seems to hold no emotion at all. He's seen it before. *I have no idea of where the hell she is.*

"That last one was a suicide," Peter says. "Almost a ritual suicide. He would not accept failure. I think it was because I mentioned the cops. I should have kept my mouth shut."

Maria remains silent.

Peter looks slowly around the cabin. "You know, I love this cabin."

"I know," she says flatly.

"It's been good for us, too. Every time someone comes after us here, we've survived."

"Yes," she says. "We have."

"The bedroom's nice," Peter says with a smile.

"And a few other places, too." Maria returns his smile.

That's better, Peter thinks.

He drinks some of his coffee. "I always thought our defensive options were good enough here, and they have been." He puts his cup down and looks at Maria. "I don't think we should stay here anymore."

"Everyone does seem to know the way to the front door," Maria says. This time she has a smaller and somewhat enigmatic smile, almost slipping back to her blank expression.

"Someone will figure it out."

"Peter, there's a hundred ways to kill us here. You've said it before. These guys really aren't too bright." She turns to him, serious, frowning. "Walk through the woods, for Christ's sake. Don't just drive down the stupid road. If you have any brains, you should know, or at least suspect, there must be alarms and cameras. If they walked through the woods, they could blow us to hell before we'd even know they were here. If they were quiet about it, the cop at the road wouldn't know anything either."

"I don't think they're stupid," Peter says. "They're overconfident." Peter drinks more of his coffee and nods at Maria. "Like me."

They both look out the window as the lights from two police cars come into view. They have all the flashing lights running on both cars and stop behind the disabled vehicle.

"Christ!" Maria says. "Real subtle. They could sneak right up on someone."

Peter stands where he can see better what is happening outside.

"They don't want any surprises… on either side," he says.

Still watching the police, Peter says, "We've got plenty of money." He turns back to her. "I've been talking to some security geek friends of mine in Washington."

They hear the doors slam on both cars as the officers get out, their Glock 17M sidearms in their hands. They immediately begin their first examination of the scene. Maria stands beside Peter. They wave at the officers. The officers each raise an arm, very briefly, in acknowledgment.

"What do your security geek friends say, Peter?"

"They say they can help."

"Their type always says that," she says. "Sometimes they're overconfident, too."

"Yes," he says. He looks out as the police begin to move towards the cabin.

"You remember what Bentley, the FBI Director, said to us?" she asks.

"Yes. We'll never be able to relax. That this is our life."

The two police officers continue their slow walk to the front of the cabin.

"There are ways we can make it better," he says.

Maria frowns and shakes her head. "There's no place any better. Face it. This is the way it is, wherever we live." The flashing lights of the police cars dance on the snow and the branches of the trees. "Anyway, let's talk about it some other time. I think our dance card's pretty full tonight."

"Yeah. I think you're right," Peter says.

They head back to the table, sit, and face the door. One officer knocks at the door. The second officer stands by the window.

"Come on in," Peter says. "It's unlocked."

"Just the two of you?" comes the muffled voice at the door.

"Yes," Peter says loudly.

"Please put your hands where I can see them," the officer says.

Peter and Maria put their hands flat on the table in front of them. The man at the window turns toward the door and gives a thumbs up.

The door opens slowly, and the first officer enters cautiously, holding his service pistol in front of him. He kicks the door shut. He's heavy-set, probably in his forties, and the winter gear does nothing to slim him down. His round face is quite rosy from the brief exposure to the wind and cold.

"I'm Inspector Hugh Jones," he says. "OPP. Responding to your call."

After he stares at Peter and Maria for a moment, Jones scans the entire room before turning back to them.

Peter and Maria sit quietly at the table, watching.

"You armed?" Jones asks.

"Yes," Peter says. "P229 pistol."

"Please remove it from your holster, slowly, and place it on this side of the table, butt toward me."

Peter doesn't move. "I'd rather not," he says softly.

It takes Inspector Jones a moment to react. "What? That's not a request, Mr. Binder. That's an order." He raises his pistol and aims it directly at Peter's head.

Peter remains completely still. He stares fixedly at the muzzle of the pistol in the officer's hand, and at the face behind it. "You in contact with Commissioner Branch?" he asks.

"Yes."

"Call him. Tell him what you requested and my response. I'll keep my hands on the table. I won't move. Maria won't move either, will you, Maria."

"Under the circumstances, that's a reasonable expectation," Maria says.

"That means she won't move," Peter says.

Inspector Jones shakes his head as he slowly lowers his pistol. "Blake!" he shouts. "Get your ass in here!"

The second officer, a younger, thinner man who had been watching through the front window, steps into the cabin, closing the door behind him. "What's up?" he asks, as he pulls off his black, knit cap. He puts his hand on the butt of his pistol, but it remains in its holster.

"I've got to go back to the car and call Branch, but I want to do a quick search of the cabin first." He keeps his pistol in his right hand and gestures in the direction of Peter and Maria with his left. "Watch these two. Make sure they keep their hands on the table. Especially him."

"Got it, sir."

Jones looks at Blake. He opens his mouth but snaps it shut again. He turns, taking in the whole main room of the cabin, walks down the short hallway, pokes his head into the bathroom, the laundry room, and the bedroom. He is inside the bedroom for several minutes. Finally, he checks the small loft area over the main room.

He stands for a solid minute, looking at Peter and Maria. "I know you have a permit for the pistol, Mr. Binder. Something about death threats due to heroic service to the country, or some such bullshit. Now, I'm going to talk to Commissioner Branch, as you requested." He pauses. "Hero, or not, make sure you behave yourselves for Sergeant Blake while I'm gone."

"We'll be good," Maria says.

Jones turns to Blake. "He's armed with a semi-automatic pistol. If he moves his hands off the table, shoot him. Is that clear?"

"Yes, sir," Blake responds, but he still doesn't draw his pistol.

Jones scowls and shoves his pistol into his holster. He turns and marches out the door, slamming it behind him.

Blake looks at Peter and Maria. "I'm Sergeant Richard Blake," he says. "You must have pulled rank on old Jones. He doesn't like that."

"Just trying to make sure I stay alive," Peter says.

Blake smiles. "From what I hear, plus what I've seen outside, that seems to be a fulltime job."

"Sometimes it does feel that way," Maria says.

"Well, you two get some pretty special treatment from the brass in this organization, I can tell you that… though I suppose I shouldn't."

Nobody says anything for several minutes. Sergeant Blake continues to look at Peter and Maria with a small smile of amusement, which Peter thinks is a bit out of place.

"You have a habit of littering the countryside with dead bodies." Blake says. "What happened out here tonight anyway?"

"Is this an interview?"

Sergeant Blake raises his eyebrows and shrugs. "Sorry. Only trying to make conversation."

"Yeah. Well, I'm sorry, too," Peter says. "I'm not particularly interested in carrying on a conversation at the moment."

Blake makes a sound that is something between a grunt and a laugh. "I'm not surprised."

They fall into silence again. Peter looks out the window. He can see Inspector Jones heading back to the cabin.

"Your buddy's coming back," Peter says.

Blake shakes his head. "Definitely not my buddy."

Peter isn't sure how he would describe Inspector Jones' entrance. It's as if the door wasn't there. Yes, he does open it, and he does close it, but it seems to Peter that his entrance is instantaneous. And he isn't smiling.

Maria says, "Any luck?"

Jones ignores the question. He stares fixedly at Peter for half a minute.

"Okay," he says finally, quite slowly. "Here's what we're going to do. You two will stay in the cabin for the night. If you're armed, Maria, I'd like to know it."

"Not at the moment, but I do have a pistol like his back in the bedroom."

"Okay. And you, Peter? Any other weapons lying around?"

"I'm sure you noticed a shotgun and a rifle in the closet in the bedroom."

"I did."

Peter points to the shotgun next to the door. "That shotgun is from the cruiser at the end of the driveway. I was out skiing when all this began. That's how I came across the dead policeman in the car and called in on his radio. I thought I'd better borrow the shotgun."

"I wondered about that," Jones says. "I'll take a brief, preliminary statement from both of you shortly. Commissioner Branch will come up tomorrow morning by helicopter."

"Not until tomorrow?" Maria asks.

"A bit tough by helicopter at night in a snowstorm." Jones opens and looks at a small notebook. "Anyway, you're attracting quite the crowd out of Toronto."

"Really," Maria says flatly.

"Yes, really." Jones consults his notes. "I think it's three or four cars plus the helicopter. Let's see… Chief Forensic Pathologist and a couple of others from his office. Deputy Chief Coroner, in charge of special projects and an assistant." He looks up at Peter. "Our best crime scene investigation team is heading out of Toronto right now. Depending on road conditions, they should be here by…" Jones looks at his watch. "Maybe a little before midnight."

"Does that team include John Maitlan?" Peter asks.

Jones raises his eyebrows. "You know John Maitlan?"

"Don't really know him, but he's been here before. Seems like someone who knows what he's doing."

"Well, he ought to. He's head of the whole bloody unit. You're getting the best of the best."

"Good," Peter says. "It does sound like a crowd."

Peter's comment elicits a faint, partial smile from Inspector Jones. "I've barely started. Tomorrow morning, along with Commissioner Branch, the OPP helicopter will bring Bruce Richards out of the Toronto office of the Canadian Security Intelligence Service, the CSIS, and Superintendent Lois Bruce, who heads the Integrated National Security Enforcement Team for the RCMP, also out of Toronto."

"Good God!" Maria says.

"And still one more," Jones says, raising a finger, "Murray Jackson from the National Security and Intelligence Review Agency, one of their national security experts. He'll come up with the rest of the crowd on the helicopter."

"Christ!" Peter says. "That's most of the security apparatus of Canada."

"Well, when your names pop up on our computer screens, there are lots of asterisks after them." He looks back at his notes. "There's probably one more. I think Murray Jackson will bring one of his associates along."

"I'm surprised that the Prime Minister isn't showing up," Maria says.

Jones looks at her. "He already knows about this situation, and he has expressed a strong interest. He has ordered that we keep him completely up to date on developments."

"Lovely to know so many people are interested in our welfare, isn't it, Maria?" Peter says. "Can I get up, Inspector?"

Jones looks at Peter for almost half a minute, before he says, "Yes. You can get up."

Peter stands up. "I think I need something stronger than coffee." He walks over to the counter and picks up a glass and the bottle of Ardbeg Scotch. He pours half a glass and says, "You can tell the pilot that there's a helipad at the end of my dock, but I suspect he may already know that. My MD 500 is sitting there right now, but I'll move it for them and get the snow off the pad. They can use the flag by the cabin as a windsock."

Jones looks intently at Peter. "Make sure one of us goes with you when you move your helicopter."

Peter smiles. "I can give someone a quick aerial view if they want."

"That might be useful," Jones says. Then he turns to Sergeant Blake. "You, Sergeant, have the job of securing the crime scene and making sure no critters decide to snack on the bodies. Be sure to tape off the footprints that head into the woods."

Peter sits down at the table again, next to Maria. "If you get to my skis and poles in the woods, maybe you could bring them back to the cabin. And if you want to tape off my ski tracks, you'd better have a few miles of tape."

"What about Prescott and the car?" Blake asks Jones.

"Once you secure the crime scene here, and I get a quick, preliminary statement, I'll drive up there and keep watch by the road."

"Okay. I'd better get busy." Blake shrugs on his parka, gloves and cap, and heads out the door.

After Blake leaves, Inspector Jones turns to Peter and Maria. "Commissioner Branch asked me to get a preliminary statement from the two of you, a quick review of what happened." He pulls a small recorder out of his pocket. "I'll record it, and we can transcribe it later." He sits down, across the table, turns on the recorder, and places it in front of Peter and Maria.

Peter glances at Maria before he says to Jones, "I don't think we want to do that."

Jones raises his eyebrows in an exaggerated look of surprise. "And why not?"

Peter sets his glass of Scotch back onto the table. He reaches out, takes the recorder in his hand, searches for a moment, and turns it off.

He looks up at Jones. "We've gone through questioning before, without any lawyer." He shakes his head. "Not this time."

"What the hell? What's different this time?"

"You guys are bringing in this a huge bloody team, from Ontario, from the federal government, anti-terrorism and intelligence experts. Everybody but Jesus Christ himself. We're just... us." He gestures to Maria and himself. "We're a couple of ordinary mortals. This looks a bit like a 'cover your ass' exercise on your side, and that makes me more than slightly nervous. I at least want a lawyer on our side."

Peter looks at Maria. "You agree?"

Maria shrugs.

"We need your impressions now, when they're fresh," Inspector Jones says.

Peter hears a distinct note of frustration in his voice.

"Look, I understand your frustration," Peter says, "but I want a lawyer present for any interview."

"Where will you get one? There's none around here."

"None of the people coming up here on your side are 'around here' either, but you'll manage to get them here. We don't even need the lawyer physically present. He can be present on a video link, or just by telephone, but I want the lawyer present, real time, for any interview."

"I'm going to repeat myself, but details get lost if you don't record them right away," Jones says. "We need a statement from you now, right now, when everything is fresh in your mind."

"And you'll get one. A written statement. We're not going anywhere, and we'll prepare the statement as soon as we talk with Patrick Balakrishnan in Toronto."

"The criminal defense lawyer?"

"Yes. This is a crime scene, isn't it?"

"You haven't been charged with anything," Jones says.

"Yet," Maria says.

Jones says nothing.

Peter takes a sip of the Scotch. "We'll write up a statement of what happened right away, run it past Patrick, and give it to you hopefully in the next couple of hours. You'll get it by nine or ten tomorrow morning at the latest. We'll have Patrick present one way or another for any follow-up interviews. Reasonable?"

Peter carefully places his glass back down on the table. He continues to stare directly back at Jones. Peter doesn't return the recorder. Instead, he drops it into his shirt pocket and picks up his glass again.

Jones looks from one of them to the other. Then he says, "I guess I don't have much choice in the matter."

Peter says softly, "No. You don't."

CHAPTER 3

Inspector Jones closes the door slowly and quietly when he leaves. Peter and Maria sit silently as they watch him go to his car, sit behind the wheel for a few minutes, turn off the blinking lights, turn the car around, and head back to the highway.

"He's not happy," Peter says.

Maria looks at Peter. "You play some of the most dangerous games I've ever seen. You've challenged that guy, seriously, two or three times already, and he hasn't been here an hour."

"I know."

"You're lucky he didn't blow your head off."

Peter drains his drink. "Well, we're not black, which is a big advantage, and if we have so many damned asterisks after our names, I might as well use them to get us a little protection."

"What? You're getting a lawyer to listen in on the interview? What good is a lawyer? And why bait a cop anyway?"

"The lawyer will be a witness, and I wasn't baiting Jones. I'm trying to make sure we're treated fairly. Besides, the risk was low. I'm pretty sure those asterisks say to protect us, not kill us."

"You're crazy."

"Yeah, I know," Peter says. "But even if I'm crazy, we're still alive, and we've got a lot of work to do." He smiles briefly at Maria and stands up. "What do you say we get over to the desk and get started. I'll call Patrick, and you can start writing up your part of the story."

Maria stands. "You never told me you knew Patrick Balakrishnan. He's the one who represented me after I… when my husband fell off the balcony of my apartment. How did you get to know him?"

Peter locks the cabin's door again. He walks over to his desk and retrieves the VoIP phone. "I know he was your lawyer. Your case was a big deal. Patrick loved the TV cameras, as I recall."

Maria rolls her eyes. "Okay. Fine. You read the newspapers, and you watched TV, but how did you get to know the man?"

He scrolls down the list of contacts on his cell phone and finds Patrick's number. "Goes back to graduate school," he says. "I was friends with a guy by the name of Jim Baker, who was studying mineral law."

"I thought you told me you didn't have any friends in graduate school."

Peter laughs. "I didn't have many. I was pretty screwed up at the time, but Jim…" Peter shrugs. "We'd go out to have a couple of beers once in a while. Sometimes we didn't talk much, and he didn't seem to mind. He was easy to be friends with, even for me back then."

He picks up the VoIP telephone. "Jim introduced me to Patrick, and I kept in touch. I figured he was a potentially useful contact. Besides, he's a really interesting guy, and after my mental health improved, I discovered his wife is a fantastic cook."

Peter enters Patrick's number in Toronto. As he waits for him to answer, he says, "And besides, he warned me about you."

"Shit!" Maria says.

Peter laughs.

"Balakrishnan here."

"Patrick," Peter says. "Peter Binder. Sorry to call you this late. I'm at my cabin with Maria Davidoff, and we need a little help here."

"Serious?"

"Rather."

"Okay. Fire away."

"You remember that story I told you? A few months ago? The one about the mine with no gold, and the gold bars in the Swiss bank?"

"You and Maria," Patrick says. "Yeah. I remember. Pretty crazy story."

"I told you about a Japanese thug, and a couple of encounters with his enforcers in Jakarta and Kyoto."

"I remember. Not the details, though."

"Don't need the details," Peter says.

"Let me guess. He showed up, with a small army, and tried to kill you, but you destroyed them all."

Peter grunts. "You're too good, Patrick, though I think they were after both of us. Look, it's a royal, bloody mess. I called it in to the OPP. They're involving the top brass from Toronto, along with the CSIS counter terrorism, the RCMP national security, and the NSIRA. And they all want a statement, and they want it right now."

"Have they charged you with anything?"

"No," Peter says. "I don't expect they will."

"Why not?"

"Well… It was all self-defense."

"With no witnesses, right?"

"No witnesses, but it's pretty obvious."

"Could get ugly," Patrick says.

"We've got some good friends in high places who owe us a lot."

"You may need all of them." Patrick pauses. "They want a statement. Right away?"

"I told them I wouldn't give an oral statement unless you were present, at least by telephone. We want to give a written statement first, but I want you to review it before we give it to them." Peter pauses a moment. "I have a tendency to say too much."

"One of your more charming failings," Patrick says, "though not so much when I first knew you. When do you need to give this statement to them?"

"By midnight tonight would be good, but it could wait until nine tomorrow morning. They'll probably be looking to interview us sometime late tomorrow morning."

"Get it to me tonight. Call me at my office at nine tomorrow morning. When you write it, stick to the facts and only the facts. Don't give any insights, inferences, conjectures, or conclusions. None of that. Clear?"

"Yep. We'll do our best, but that's where we need your help," Peter says. "We do appreciate it. Thank you."

"Thank me when we're done, when you're not in jail, and after you get my bill."

Peter laughs. "Bye!"

He puts the phone down and looks over at Maria. "How's it going?"

Without looking up from the computer on the desk, she says, "I'm just starting, obviously, but I don't think this will take all that long. I'm putting down bullet points and the basic information." She looks up. "What did he say?"

Peter shrugs. "Basically, that we should do exactly what you're already doing. He said we should stick to the facts. Period."

"Glad to hear it."

A little before midnight, they complete their written statement, and Peter sends it as an email attachment to Patrick.

Peter sits back in his chair. "Well," he says, looking at Maria. "What do you think?"

"Not many secrets left," Maria says. "They'll know about all your defenses now."

Peter shrugs and stands up. "I suspect they already know. I have a feeling the RCMP, at least, has been up here a couple of times when we've been away. This place has been searched, top to bottom."

"You sure?"

"No," he says. "I couldn't prove it. Assuming they were actually here, they were pretty careful, but it's what I would do if I were them. It makes sense, even if they have to stretch the legal niceties a bit. If they did a thorough search of the cabin, they'd never miss the tunnel system."

Maria frowns. "I've never liked people screwing around with my life that way."

"This isn't the first time." Peter gets up from his chair at the desk and stretches.

"Doesn't mean I have to like it."

"I'm willing to bet there have been others, too," he says. "Like the CIA… or maybe some of your old Russian buddies, the ones who moved over from the KGB to the SVR."

Maria remains silent.

"Maybe someone thinks they still own you."

Maria looks up at Peter. She doesn't laugh, but she shakes her head. "Maybe they still do own me. I don't think so, but maybe they really do."

Peter raises his eyebrows. "You've got to be kidding me."

Now Maria smiles. "I assume I'll be the first to find out."

Peter shakes his head as he looks at her.

"Don't worry," she says. "You'd be the second. I guarantee it."

"And everybody tells me not to trust you."

Maria stands. She puts her arms around Peter's neck and clasps the back of his head. "I know they do, but you trust me because you love me." She kisses him.

Peter feels her tongue pressing, searching, and he meets it with his own. *I really am in love.*

She pulls away. She holds her eyes on his. "And I love you, too, you crazy, crazy man. But…" She hesitates.

"But what?" he asks.

She hesitates again before she answers. "I worry about us. Too many people seem to want a piece of us, or all of us. It's not how we should be living."

Peter looks away, toward the table by the kitchen area. "Let's go over to the table, where we can see when someone is coming," he says.

"Seems to me," Peter says, after they sit down, "we've eliminated a couple of major threats. Rostov and his rogue Russians are gone." He gestures at the door. "And tonight takes care of Uehara and his bunch of Japanese thugs. The ring leaders of the cabal in Washington are all in prison or dead. Who wants to kill us now?"

Maria frowns. "You think there aren't any Russians to replace Rostov? You think we didn't piss off a bunch of pretty powerful people in Washington this past year or two? You think their allies are all locked up or dead? People are still out there, my happy, naïve lover, wishing we never existed."

"Well, there is that, but you have to admit we also have some pretty powerful protectors in Washington, and here in Canada for that matter."

"Peter, your country just elected a fascist pig, Helmut Wisser, as your president. You think he has any interest in protecting you? Or me? You think Canada can protect us from his goons? Really?"

Peter sighs. "Maybe not. But we do have some strong support from the ranks of civil servants. They're the ones who really run the government anyway, at least the US government. They won't forget what we did to protect the United States. They know. They understand, and Wisser can't do anything without their help."

"Dear Peter," she says, "sometimes you can be so bloody innocent. It is a beguiling, if dangerous, characteristic of you Americans. That honorable corps of civil servants? Helmut Wisser can destroy it by signing his name. Once. That's all it takes. One signature. I've seen it happen. And allies? Even when you think you know their soul, Wisser can turn them into your enemies in a heartbeat."

"God, you're depressing."

They sit in silence for several minutes.

"I can't argue with you," Peter says. "We've got to change how we live. I don't want to, but we have to live like the super-rich, or celebrities that everybody knows and wants to meet... or stalk... or murder."

He looks up as the headlights of three police cars come into view. Once again, they have their flashers on, but they turn them off as soon as they stop.

"Looks like our friends from Toronto have arrived."

"Round two," Maria says.

Peter and Maria watch as the men and women get out of the three cars. Sergeant Blake meets them at their cars. There is much gesturing. Peter and Maria can hear voices, but they cannot make out any words.

"Guess I'd better unlock the door," Peter says and smiles at Maria. "I should be friendly, right?"

Maria shakes her head as Peter gets up. "You should be friendly."

He steps over to the door, unlocks it, and returns to the table.

After fifteen minutes of discussions in the cold, Inspector Jones and the new arrivals carefully make their way to the door of the cabin. They knock on the door.

"Come on in," Peter says.

Five people pile into the cabin, led by Inspector Jones. Several of them try to stamp or kick some snow off their boots before they enter.

He points to the extra chairs around the table. "Have a seat, if you want. One of you will have to grab a chair by the desk."

John Maitlan sits across from Peter and Maria. He reaches out his hand to Peter. "A few more bodies this time," he says. He turns and holds out his hand to Maria. "And Maria."

"Do we have a written report?" Inspector Jones asks.

"It's done. It's with Patrick," Peter says. "We'll talk tomorrow morning at nine. You should have it by ten, I hope."

Jones frowns but says nothing.

"We'll start our work tonight," Maitlan says. "It would be helpful if you could give us a bit of guidance." He pulls a small notebook and pen out of his shirt pocket.

Peter glances at Maria. She shrugs her shoulders.

"We can give you a quick summary," Peter says. "I was out on my regular cross-country ski run. That's when I found Jack Prescott."

"Did you touch anything?" John asks.

Peter opens his mouth to respond, but he shuts it again. He turns to Jones and speaks slowly and deliberately. "Inspector, I understood that we had agreed that we will not participate in an interview without our chosen lawyer being present, by telephone at a minimum."

Jones frowns. With a small gesture, he says to Maitlan, "I've talked with Branch. They'll say what they want to say. You'll get the details tomorrow."

"Give us what you feel you can," Maitlan says.

Peter provides an abbreviated version of the events of the evening. He concludes, "You'll find his knife on the packed snow, where it landed about a foot from my feet. After that, we left everything alone, went back into the cabin, and waited for Inspector Jones and Sergeant Blake to arrive."

It takes a while, in the silence after Peter finishes, before John Maitlan says, "That's it?"

"It's the basics. You'll get the details tomorrow morning." Peter turns to Maria. "Can you think of anything fundamental that needs to be added?"

"Just one thing," she says. "When they first arrived, they tried to break down the door. When that didn't work, they started shooting at the door and a couple of windows. They fired a lot of rounds before we confronted them, and before they fired directly at us. You should find lots of bullets freshly embedded in the outside walls of the cabin, and a lot of brass from their assault rifles scattered around out there. None of that belongs to us."

John Maitlan leans back in his chair and shuts his eyes for a moment. When he opens them again, he says, "Okay. My team has plenty of work to do. We'll get started." He looks around the cabin. "Doesn't look like much space to sleep."

Peter smiles. "There are two roll-away beds up in the loft with clean sheets and blankets. The sofa is comfortable, and the two large chairs aren't bad, but I have no blankets for either the sofa or the chairs. I'm not offering the bedroom."

"We won't sleep much anyway," Maitlan says.

Peter stands. "If you don't mind, Maria and I are going to bed. You might keep some wood in the stove. I have a propane furnace if we need it, but I'd rather heat as much as I can with wood. There's more wood outside, around the back of the cabin."

"Would you mind giving us access to the internet and let us use your phone?" Jones asks.

Peter lies alone in the bed, waiting for Maria to return from the bathroom. He stares at the rough, planked ceiling. He thinks about the pain he felt when he built the cabin. Every time he hit a nail with the hammer, he tried to kill the guilt and raw pain he carried home from Afghanistan. He can still see the deep imprints of the hammerhead in the wood. The pain was fresh then, and raw.

"Still raw," he mutters.

The bad dreams are gone, the voice says.

"You're back," Peter says. He's annoyed to hear the voice again. Sometimes it speaks to him in his dreams and comes with a vision, some sort of fuzzy and wraithlike version of Merlin.

The dreams are still here. You're a dream. The others are hiding for a while. Peter is as silent as the insistent voice in his head.

The dreams are gone, but the warrior remains.

The warrior will leave, too, Peter says.

Leave what?

This life.

The voice is silent for a long time. Then, faintly, Peter hears, *You can't.*

I can.

Still fainter, Peter hears the annoyed reply, *Suit yourself.*

Peter takes a deep breath as Maria comes into the room and closes the door behind her. She slips out of her bathrobe, switches off the light beside the bed, and crawls under the covers. He feels her turn toward him. She reaches and lightly touches his chest with her hand.

"You okay?" she asks.

"I think so... but, God, I'm tired."

They lie there in silence for several minutes. Peter inhales deeply. "I'm really tired of this garbage. I'm tired of my life. I've got to get out. I can't..."

Maria says nothing. She continues to caress his chest. She moves her hand down across his hard stomach, and he begins to respond to her touch.

Peter rolls onto his side. He puts his arms around Maria and rolls back with her above him. They kiss.

"Help me," he says.

Maria sighs. "I can help you now. This minute. But long term? Not so sure."

"I'll take the now… for now," he says, and kisses her again.

It does help, for a little while. Of course it does. It helps him forget, but Peter still can't sleep. Not right away. He lies on his back, in the darkness, as Maria drifts out of consciousness. He can hear her measured breathing. Occasionally he hears the men speaking in the front of the cabin, but he ignores them.

You're a fool, the voice says.

Perhaps.

She said it herself. She cannot help you.

I heard.

There's only one way to leave the life you chose, and you know it.

I refuse to believe that, Peter answers.

You will die. That is your only escape.

I am not ready to die, and I have no intention of entertaining the possibility.

Prepare yourself, the voice replies.

You are becoming as annoying as the ghost of my great-grandfather.

With that, the voice is silent, and Peter lets it rest. The edges of his lips turn upward into a modest smile. He has insulted his ghost. Being a trifle petulant, the ghost has swiftly left the scene.

He closes his eyes. There is no change in the depth of the darkness, but with his eyes closed he can see Maria beside him. Without touching her he feels her physical presence, her warmth, her sex.

He whispers softly, into the darkness, "I love you, Maria."

He enjoys the lingering residuum of sexual pleasure.

"I do love you," he whispers again.

He closes his eyes. The usual silence is broken this night by the propane generator, forced into service to supplement the solar power system.

They should turn out the lights.

He falls asleep.

CHAPTER 4

Peter's eyes snap open. He can hear voices from the living room. He looks at his watch. 5:30. *They're up early… or they didn't go to sleep.*

In the darkness, he swings his legs out of bed and stands up. The room is cold, and he shivers. He quickly pulls on his pants and shirt, steps into his insulated boots and tucks his pants inside.

He stands at the bureau, turns on his laptop, and checks his email. He has nothing from Patrick, but he sees one from Alden Sage, a senior advisor to the previous president of the United States, President Pelton.

I wonder what he wants.

Peter opens the email.

> *Peter,*
>
> *I hear that you and Maria have had a bit of trouble with some old Japanese friends. You should be fine, from what I hear from my Canadian sources. I still have some pretty good connections with Canadian intelligence services.*
>
> *When things quiet down, and you have a little time, give me a call. I do some consulting in the UK these days. I plan to be in Toronto Wednesday and Thursday. Can we get together on Thursday, late morning or afternoon, for at least a few hours? Somewhere private. I'd like to talk with you about your time in Afghanistan.*
>
> *I also know some people who want a geologist to look at a copper deposit in Peru.*
>
> *Stay well. For that matter, stay alive.*
>
> *Alden*

An escape? Perhaps?

Then Peter thinks about Endang, the gold mine with no gold.

That was no escape.

He turns as he hears Maria moving in the bed. She turns on the light.

"You're up early," she says.

"Yeah. Got to shovel off the helipad and move the helicopter to make room for our visitors. And I don't want to be late calling Patrick." He laces up his boots and points at the window. "Looks like it cleared off during the night, but I bet it's cold out there."

"It's cold enough in here," she says. "You should get the cops to do the shoveling."

"Don't worry. I'll get help if I need it. I'll turn up the heat for you." He looks at his laptop, hesitates, closes it, and picks it up. He stops by the door on his way out and adjusts the thermostat. "Give it a few minutes."

"Have fun shoveling," she says and pulls the covers up. "I'll get up around seven."

Peter latches the door behind him and heads down the short hallway to the living room.

John Maitlan is busy at Peter's desk, with two of his assistants. Inspector Jones and Sergeant Blake, seem to be missing.

Peter walks over to his safe file and locks his laptop inside it.

"Already writing your report?" Peter asks.

John looks up. "Not yet. Getting our notes organized and waiting for your statement."

"I need to shovel the snow off the helipad for the mob from Toronto. Any problem with that?"

"Shouldn't be a problem," John says. "We've picked up out there. We towed the dead car, and the bodies are in the back of the van. We'll do one last search for shell casings and such when the light gets better, but if you stay in the area of packed snow, you should be fine. Please stay away from any flags or marked areas in the snow."

Peter takes his jacket off a peg by the door and shrugs it on. Before he opens the door, he turns back to Maitlan. "Jones and Blake leave?"

"Yeah. They didn't have anything more to do here. Commissioner Branch and I will take your statement."

"Jones is a bit of a pistol," Peter says.

"That he is," Maitlan says with a frown. "You know, you should be more careful with people like him."

"He told you?"

"Oh, yes. He was not at all happy."

"So I gathered," Peter says at the door. He turns back to Maitlan. "And should I be worried about him?"

"No." Maitlan shakes his head. "He doesn't hold grudges, and he doesn't look back. Just be careful when you're dealing with people like him."

Once outside, without a breath of wind, the cold of the morning grips him like a tightening fist. Peter looks up at the flag above the cabin. It hangs limp and lifeless.

The brightest stars are still visible in the sky, but the faint, first light of dawn, along with the outdoor lights, are more than enough to guide his shoveling. The floodlights illuminate the numerous bits of marked evidence and flags that decorate the packed-down snow in front of the cabin. The exchange of gunfire left a sea of evidence for Maitlan and his assistants.

The scene looks strangely empty, with the bodies and dead car removed. He picks up the snow shovel by the door. Once he steps out of the crime scene tape and reaches loose snow, he begins to clear the path to the dock. It has snowed about eight inches since they last flew in, four days ago. He has already plowed the road, but the light, fluffy snow is untouched on the path and the dock itself.

He works steadily, enjoying the physical exertion, and he soon clears the snow from the dock and two of the twelve drums of fuel along one side of it. Then he clears the attached helipad.

From the beginning of the dock, he shovels another pathway to a point on the lake, close to the shore but a little over a hundred and fifty feet from the helipad. This is much tougher going. The wind has packed the snow from earlier storms, and it resists shoveling. He doesn't bother to shovel down to the ice.

He thinks about shoveling out a large area where the helicopter could land, but he dismisses the thought. *Too much damn work.* With the aluminum pads bolted to the skids, his helicopter snowshoes, he can land on the snow without a problem.

He returns to the dock, puts the shovel down next to the helicopter, and picks up the one empty drum. He adds it to a number of others behind the garage. Back at the helipad, he removes the fabric cabin cover, the doghouse cover that protects the engine intake and main rotor control system, and the tail rotor cover. He unfastens the tiedown straps that attach the skids to the recessed metal hooks in the wooden platform. After a moment contemplating the calm air, he also removes the tiedown straps for the main rotor. He throws all the covers and ties into the cargo hold, walks around the helicopter, doing a visual check, and removes some of the snow that fell from the covers.

When he's done, he throws the shovel into the back seat and returns to the cabin. It's a little past seven-thirty, and the dawn shows every indication of progressing to a beautiful, crisp, clear, and windless winter day.

As he enters the cabin, the smell of cooking bacon greets him. Maria is cooking, and John Maitlan and his assistants sit at the table eating bacon, eggs, and toast. They mostly talk hockey and joke about the antics of some of the Canadian politicians. They are at ease with the peculiarities of their work, and they find it easy to relax. Peter feels a little envious.

"Sit down," Maria says. "Your breakfast is ready, and you might as well take advantage of my sudden burst of cooking enthusiasm." She holds out a plate for him with two eggs, over easy, four pieces of bacon, and two slices of buttered toast.

Peter takes the plate and smiles as he sits down. "We must have guests this morning," he says.

"Annoy the cook at your peril," Maria replies.

"Yes, ma'am," he answers. As he eats, he listens to the eb and flow of the light-hearted conversation at the table.

When he finishes, he carries his dishes to the counter and turns back. "Sorry to interrupt this serious discussion," Peter says with a smile. "I have to move my helicopter to make room for our visitors. Now's the time, John, if you want a quick aerial view of the area."

When they climb into the helicopter, Peter hands a helmet to John Maitlan. "This is extra-large. I hope it fits."

"You really think I need this?"

"Probably not, but it provides some extra safety if we run into problems, and it makes communications easier when we're flying. The microphone is voice activated."

As Peter starts the helicopter, he asks, "Anything particular that you'd like to see, John?"

"Show me the path of your cross-country ski run last night, where you turned off the lake, and how you approached the police car."

"No problem."

Peter lifts off with an abundance of care. Even with all his shoveling, the main rotor blades blow loose snow into the air, making for poor visibility close to the ground. *The landing will be worse.*

As they fly along, Peter points out various aspects of his usual skiing trail, and John asks a few questions.

At the end of the tour, Peter lands at the helipad, turning to face the cabin. "You can get out here, John. Easier than where I'll land on the lake. If you want to see anything else, now's the time to say so."

"No. That's good for now."

"Just keep your head down when you leave the helicopter."

Peter watches Maitlan walk down the dock toward the cabin. Two of his assistants are outside, completing their final search for evidence. They pause to speak briefly with him as he passes them. Peter waits until Maitlan is almost at the door before he takes off. He moves the short distance to the end of the pathway he shoveled out onto the lake and turns to face the helipad. The rotor wash raises a lot of snow, and Peter lands more by feel than by sight. Even with the over-sized snowshoes, the helicopter settles nearly six inches into the snow.

He stops the rotor blades and waits for the engine to cool down. After about ten minutes, he gets out, puts the covers back on, and ties down the main rotor blades again. He grabs the shovel, jumps into the snow, and shovels his way to the pathway he had cleared earlier.

Back in the cabin, John Maitlan is sitting at Peter's desk again, already adding to his report.

"When's the Toronto gang arriving?" Peter asks.

"Should be here around ten," Maitlan responds. "You have your report ready?"

Peter reaches down and picks up the telephone. "I'll call the lawyer right now. Should have it in your hands shortly before everyone shows up."

Peter punches in Patrick's number and waits.

"Balakrishnan here."

"Hi, Patrick. Peter Binder. What do you think?"

Patrick suggests removing one paragraph and a few other minor changes. Peter questions one of the changes, but in the end, he agrees and summarizes the changes on a notepad.

"I've set aside three hours," Patrick says, "starting at ten this morning. Call me when you want me."

"Okay."

They end their call. Peter returns the phone to the desk and retrieves his laptop.

"Ready to give us your report?" Maitlan asks.

"If you let me use my desk, you'll have it in ten minutes or so. How many copies?"

"Ten or fifteen, I guess."

After John Maitlan moves to the kitchen table, Maria sits down next to Peter. "What did Patrick say?" she asks.

"Not much," Peter says. He shows Maria his notes. "You have any problems with those changes?"

Maria quickly reads his notes. "Nope."

Five minutes later, Peter gives fifteen copies of the statement to John Maitlan.

Peter picks up his laptop, turns to Maria, and says, "Come with me. I've got something I want to show you."

Maria raises her eyebrows, but she says nothing and follows him into the bedroom.

Peter sits on the edge of the bed, clicks on the email from Alden Sage, and gives the laptop to Maria. "Take a look."

After reading, Maria looks up. "What do you plan to do?"

Peter raises his hands. "Call him."

Maria glares at him. "You never learn, do you."

"What? That Peru's more dangerous than the people who keep trying to murder us at my little cabin in the woods? I don't think so."

"Oh, come on. Surely you don't think Alden is consulting for some little exploration company, do you? He's probably working for MI6, or some other governmental agency. It's probably MI6 who wants you to look at the copper deposit. Our last governmental assignment started off as a geological excursion in Indonesia. You think that was safe?"

"No. Endang was an unholy mess, but in this case we know nothing of what the man wants us, or me, to do."

"Bullshit!" Maria says. "For Christ's sake, just say 'No!'"

"Nope. I'm going to call him, and I'll meet with him. He's a good guy, and I owe him that courtesy."

"You owe him nothing."

Peter sits silently, not looking at Maria. Finally, "You've made your point, and, I admit, it has some validity. However, it's based on a lot of assumptions. I'm going to offer to pick him up in Toronto, fly him up here, and meet with him. You can join us or not. Your choice."

Maria glares at him. "Jesus! You are a stubborn man, and in this case, I would add, not particularly smart."

"Well, you have no obligation to be involved with any of this, if that's what you want."

"That's not what I want, and you should know it. I know you don't want my opinion, but I don't think you should touch this with a ten-foot pole. I want you alive, not dead. Please! Don't agree to work for Alden Sage."

Peter closes the laptop and stands up. He looks out the window into the dark green and bright white of the surrounding forest. Without looking at Maria, he says, "Whatever one of us does, the other lives with it, I suppose… or dies by it."

Maria doesn't respond. Peter hears the sound of several car-doors slamming shut. "More guests arriving," he says.

As they walk back to the cabin's main room, they hear the police helicopter arriving.

After a round of introductions, the morning turns rather intense for Peter and Maria. With Patrick Balakrishnan on the speakerphone, they endure a long and intense question session. They repeat the details multiple times. They deflect any questions regarding Uehara's motives.

During a break in the questioning, Peter sends a quick reply to Alden Sage.

> *Alden,*
>
> *I'll come down and pick you up at 10:30 AM on Thursday, if that works for you. Go out to the little Billy Bishop airport in downtown Toronto. Go to the StolPort FBO executive lounge. That's the general aviation area. I'll land there, and we can fly up to my cabin. It's as private as you can get. I can get you back any time late Thursday or the next day, if you want to stay over. Plenty of space. Plenty of whiskey. Plenty of quiet, most of the time. The weather promises to be excellent.*
>
> *Let me know. At the moment, I'm entertaining most of the Canadian national security staff in my cabin, but they should be leaving soon. I can call later tonight if you want.*

By three in the afternoon, all the high-level visitors have seen all they want to see, and they're ready to return to Toronto.

As they pack up, Bill Branch stands beside Peter. "Let's go for a walk," he says.

"Not many places to walk to," Peter answers with a smile.

"Let's go look at your helicopter. How about that?"

"Sure," Peter says. "Let's go."

They walk in silence to the dock, step down to the shoveled pathway, and walk toward the helicopter.

Without looking directly at Branch, Peter stops and says, "I'm sorry about Officer Prescott. He was a nice guy, and way too young to end his life that way."

"Thanks. It's part of the job, but it's never easy."

"It makes me sick… literally. He died because of us, and that really bothers me."

"Peter, he died because I underestimated the risk. The Prime Minister believes Canada has an obligation to protect you and Maria, because of what the two of you have done for Canada, the United States, Russia. I agree with him."

They walk the rest of the way to the helicopter.

"Just so you know," Bill says, "there are no plans to charge you with anything."

"Speaking for yourself or everyone?"

"Speaking for the Prime Minister."

"Can I get that in writing?"

Bill makes a sound, something between a grunt and a laugh. "You know the answer to that one."

"I got an email from Alden Sage offering me a job," Peter says. "Something about a copper mine in Peru. You know anything about that?"

"Yes."

"That's all you're going to say?"

"Pretty much. I'll let Alden speak for himself."

"What's his position these days? He can't be working for Wisser. He says he's doing some consulting in the UK. Is he working for MI6?"

"Working for them? Probably not. Probably better to say that he's working with them. There's a group in Canada and Britain, and very quietly a few people in the United States, trying to maintain some global sanity in the face of Wisser's madness and stupidity."

Peter feels Bill's eyes on him. They seem to penetrate his skull.

"What I just said, Peter, is absolutely top secret. For your ears only. Understand?"

"I don't like the sound of this."

"I want you to talk with Alden. We need you. And you need to find some way to speak with him... confidentially... and alone. Maria is not to be a part of this discussion, at least not now."

"I've offered to pick him up at Billy Bishop and fly him up here for a few hours. This is as private as it gets."

"And Maria?"

"I can land at a lake on the way if I have to. We can have our private talk there."

They stand silently beside the MD 500E. "A nice little machine," Bill says. "I've always liked them."

"Fun to fly," Peter replies.

"To change the subject," Bill says.

"Yes?"

"You and Maria?"

"How much do you know?"

"Enough."

Peter sighs. "It's fine, but she's not happy. She doesn't want me to even talk to Alden Sage, and she sure as hell doesn't want me to go to Peru."

"You're still in love?"

"Yep. Still in love."

"Love can change a dangerous game into a fatal game, for a person in your position."

"Yeah. I probably underestimate the risk," Peter says. "Like somebody else I know."

Bill smiles. "While we were here, we swept your cabin, helicopter, truck and garage for listening devices."

"Find any?"

"Yes, we did. One. In the cabin. Very sophisticated and well hidden. We removed it. Someone took their time getting it into position. Probably tied in somehow to your wireless internet when you have it on."

"Do you know the origin?" Peter asks.

"Not for sure. Not yet. We think it might be Russian, but we don't know for sure."

"What could it hear?"

"Probably everything in the main room of the cabin."

"Bloody lovely."

"I'm concerned that we may have missed something," Bill says. "I don't think so, but be careful of what you say… anywhere. Trust no one."

Peter looks away from Bill and out over the lake. "I understand what you're saying."

"You do?"

Peter turns back to face Bill. "Yes, Bill. I do understand what you're trying to say."

The police pilot yells that he's ready to go.

"Looks like I've got to go," Bill says.

Peter sticks out his hand, and they shake hands. "I'll talk to Alden," Peter says. "I won't promise anything more than that."

"Nor should you." Bill begins to walk toward the dock and the helipad.

"And thanks for your help," Peter calls after him.

Bill stops. "It's our job, Peter. Just be careful, and find a more secure place to live."

"I'm working on it."

"Good."

Peter stands next to his helicopter. He can't help but think of when he was a little boy, and his father gave him advice. Peter didn't want it then, and he isn't sure he wants any fatherly advice from Bill now. He watches as the police pilot goes through the start-up procedure for the larger Eurocopter.

The takeoff blasts him with snow, and he turns his back to the larger machine. The MD 500E shudders in the wind. Once they're gone, Peter removes the doghouse and tiedowns, and starts the machine. He takes off, flies out over the lake and surveys the area around the cabin. Then he flies along his regular cross-country skiing trail, along the road, and down the access to the cabin.

He hovers over the first gate.

Got to weld a patch on that, he thinks. *Maybe a couple of lengths of chain and some good padlocks will do for now.*

Back at the helipad, as he shuts down, he considers his pending meeting with Alden Sage.

Do I work for him now? And if I do, what the hell am I getting into? Who can I trust? Who can I talk to? Pelton?

He laughs softly. The thought of contacting the previous president is amusing.

He gets out, pulls on the covers for the helicopter, and ties down the main rotors. He doesn't bother to tie the machine down to the helipad. The weather forecast predicts a calm night.

CHAPTER 5

About half an hour after Peter returns to the cabin, John Maitlan and his two assistants are packed and ready to leave. Peter shakes John's hand.

"Thanks, John, for making the time to be here yourself."

"Well, I do have a little history with this place, and that always helps."

Peter reaches into his pocket and pulls out the recorder he took from Inspector Jones. "Could you get this to Jones? He left before I could give it back, and before I could apologize for being such an obstreperous ass when he first got here."

"Like I told you before, he doesn't carry grudges," John says as he pockets the recorder. "I'll tell him you apologized. He'll appreciate that. In our profession, you don't get many apologies."

"He deserves it." Peter pauses. "I assume Prescott was married. Would it be possible to get his address and his wife's name? I spent a lot of time with him, and I'd like to send her some kind of note."

John looks at Peter, the surprise showing in his eyes. "I'll dig out my laptop and give you the details right now."

John opens the door to the back seat of the car, pulls out his laptop, and sets it on the hood. A moment later, he says, "Yes. He was married. His wife's name is June." He gives Peter their address.

"Any children?" Peter asks.

"Yes. One. A boy named Peter, like you. He's two and a half." John closes the laptop and puts it away.

"It's going to be awful for her."

"Yes. It will be," John says. "Survivor benefits are okay, but they're no substitute for a husband." John is silent for a moment. "I understand they were very much in love." He looks at Peter. "Be kind. I know you will be, but she'll be very fragile for a while."

A moment later John starts the car. His two assistants pile in. He waves and heads down the track to the main road. Peter watches the car disappear, and he thinks about Jack Prescott and his family. He closes his eyes against the intense sense of sadness. The tears surprise him a little, and he blinks them away.

It never ends. He shakes his head. *I didn't kill him, but I might as well have.*

He touches the edge of the intense sadness and shudders. It begs to transform itself into sullen anger and rage. *No. You can't go there. I will not let you into my life again.*

He takes a deep breath, turns, and enters the cabin.

Maria is busy cleaning the kitchen.

"You're looking very domestic," Peter says.

"Don't press it. I'm so goddamned wound up, I can't sit still."

"This is not a Tuesday I will soon forget."

"Or Monday, either," Maria says, as she hangs up a towel. She turns and glares at Peter. "We're alone now, just the two of us, and I want to know. What exactly are you going to do about Alden Sage?"

"I don't know yet. I plan to talk to him. That's all."

"When? Where?"

Peter stares at Maria for a moment. "You really are wound up. If you give me a minute, I'll look at my email and see if I have an answer from him."

"Please."

Peter heads over to his desk, looks up his email, and finds a seven-word response from Alden.

Peter,

I'll be there. I'll stay the night.

Alden

Peter walks back to the kitchen. He opens a cabinet and pulls out a glass and a fresh bottle of Glendronach Scotch Whiskey. He begins to peel back the metal on the cap.

"You want some?" Peter asks.

"Jesus Christ, Peter! Will you please tell me what the hell you're going to do with Alden Sage?"

Peter pulls out the cork. He feels cornered, and he's wary of his emotions. He answers Maria quite slowly.

"I'll fly down to Toronto on Thursday and pick up Alden at Billy Bishop airport at ten-thirty in the morning. We'll fly up here, and we'll have a nice quiet conversation about what he has in mind."

"Lovely!" Maria says.

Peter pauses. "He says he'll stay the night. We'll have dinner, a couple of drinks, and we'll talk about how to solve all the troubles of the world. Then you and I will decide what to do."

Peter pours himself a good two ounces of the Glendronach.

He holds up the bottle. "You haven't answered my question. You want a drink?"

Maria glares at Peter. "Yes, I do want a drink. I could use a frozen vodka, but we don't have any. Your smoky Scotch will have to do."

"Feeling a bit Russian, are we?" He pours a glass for Maria.

"No. I'm not feeling Russian. I'm really pissed at you. You've been whining about how you want to change your life, and now you're ready to jump right back in. You'll make your decision after talking with Alden. Sure! Sure! Will I have any real input into that decision? No. Then you'll ask me if I want to come along for the ride. What should I do? Wait here to see you come back in a box? Maybe you figure I'd prefer to sit in my rocking chair, cinch up my babushka a little tighter, and knit a nice sweater for you." She glares at him. "Jesus! You drive me crazy."

When she has finished talking, Peter hands the glass of Scotch to her. She drinks nearly half in one gulp.

This is getting serious, Peter thinks.

"Maria, neither of us has any idea of who he's working for, or what he wants me to do, if anything. He says he wants to talk about Afghanistan. Fine. He says he knows someone who needs a geologist. Fine. I think you should cool your jets, maybe a little bit."

"I know you, Peter Binder. And I know your buddy Alden Sage. He's not coming to see you because you're a great geologist, and he's not coming to shoot the breeze about Afghanistan. No. He's coming to see you because he wants someone who's good at killing people, blowing things up, and surviving at the end of the day."

"I'll let him tell me that," Peter says softly.

"And if he does, I can already hear you say, 'Sure, Alden. I'll do it. When can I start? Tomorrow? Great.'"

Peter says nothing.

"I'm right? Aren't I?"

Peter looks at Maria and cocks his head to the right. "Let's sit down."

They take their glasses, and they sit down at the table, on opposite sides. They stare at each other. Both sip at their drinks. Neither says a word for maybe two minutes or more. Peter speaks first.

"There is some truth to what you just said."

"Duh!"

Peter looks down at his glass and has another drink of the Scotch. He closes his eyes. When he opens them again, he says, "Look, the life I'm living is a bit like being addicted to crack. You should know that better than most. I know I should quit… but it's hard, and some people don't want me to quit. To be honest, some aren't about ready to let me quit."

He looks up at Maria. "I look at the long term. I'm getting older, and this game of chasing up nasty bastards all over the world, being quicker and better than they are, playing chore boy for the CIA, is a game for the young. I know I have to quit, but I also know I can still do it. For a while. Then along comes Alden, and I say, 'Of course I'll do that little job you have for me.' I know you disagree, but I think I owe him. That's my life, Maria. It's what I'm addicted to. You can be part of it or not. It's your choice."

"Goddamn you! It's not that easy, and you bloody well know it. We're living our lives, right here, right now, together. Remember? We're supposed to be in love. We're not living in different centuries on separate planets."

Peter shrugs. "I can't help what I am. What can I say?"

"You can listen for a change, damn it. I want nothing to do with this discussion you're having with Alden. You could walk away from what we both know he's going to offer you, if you really wanted to, but, no, you've already made up your mind. Again. You want the thrill. You want that kick of adrenalin. My participation in this discussion is a waste of my time."

For a moment, Maria just glares at Peter.

"I'll fly down to Toronto with you," Maria says. "I'll say hello to Mr. Sage, and I'll disappear. Maybe I'll check in on some of my old friends. You and he can fly back up here and have your little conference without me. Sit here, around this table, just the two of you, and talk to your heart's content. When you get around to it, you can let me know what you plan to do… and whether or not you want me to come along with you. And then… I will decide, not you, exactly what I am going to do."

Peter looks at Maria. He tosses down the remainder of the Scotch and gets up from the table. He steps over to his coat beside the door and shrugs it on.

"Where are you going?" Maria asks.

"We've got two wide open gates. I'll get some chain and a couple of padlocks from the garage. It'll have to do for tonight."

He steps out into the cold. The thought crosses his mind that, at this moment, some things are just as cold in the cabin.

In the garage, he grabs an eight-foot tow chain from the truck and cuts it in half with his small cutting torch, throws the pieces in the back of his plow truck, and heads up the track to the gates. As he goes, he clears off what show has not been packed down by all the visitors.

He turns around at the main road and hesitates where the young policeman was shot in the head.

I promise you, Jack Prescott. Whatever I do with the rest of my life, I will look after your wife and son.

He takes a deep breath and heads back down the track to the cabin, locking the two gates behind him.

Peter prepares dinner that night, and they eat mostly in silence. Though Peter tries to make conversation, Maria remains sullenly quiet. Peter gives up. He's not in the mood to push too hard. He cleans up the kitchen by himself. At ten, he says, "I'm headed to bed. You coming?"

Maria looks up from her computer. "No. I'll stay up a while. Catch up on my email."

Peter watches her. She is already focused on her computer again. "I am sorry," he says softly.

She doesn't look up. "I know you're sorry. I know you think there's nothing you can do about it. I disagree, but you have to live your life the way you choose. You need to understand that I've got to live mine… the way I choose." After a pause, "I'll sleep in the loft tonight."

Peter stares at the back of her head. "Let's both be sure that we actually choose."

He watches her for a little longer, but she says nothing, and he can think of nothing more to say. He turns and walks down the hall to the bedroom. He is angry, frustrated, depressed, and he can feel Maria slipping away. To where, he isn't quite sure. *I'm pretty sure it's not a good place for me.*

When Maria is sure that Peter is in bed, she moves to the other side of the kitchen table. She opens an email account, hidden behind three layers of security. Whatever she sends on this account will be heavily encrypted, and her computer will retain no record of it. She taps at the keyboard. When she finishes the lengthy email, she reads it carefully and makes a few minor changes. She signs it: *Victoria S.*

Maria closes her eyes.

"Damn!" she mutters.

I'm trying. What more can I do?

She opens her eyes. Her finger hovers over the mouse. She taps it, and the email is gone. She severs the connection to the email account, closes the laptop, and puts it away in her briefcase.

She stretches and climbs the stairs. She lies down, fully clothed, on the bed in the loft. She feels a sense of regret slipping into her thinking, but she pushes it away.

No regrets allowed. No regrets allowed, ever.

Ten minutes later, her breathing is measured and quiet. She is already sleeping soundly.

When Peter comes out of the bedroom in the morning, after a long and restless night, he finds Maria already drinking coffee and working at her computer. When she sees him, she closes her computer and stands up.

"You want some coffee?" she asks.

From the sound of that invitation, last night's differences are not forgotten, Peter thinks.

"Yes. Thanks."

They sit down facing each other, and Maria returns to her computer. Peter drinks his coffee and watches her. She looks up once, expressionless, and quickly returns to her work.

"You're busy," Peter says.

"In case you've forgotten, I'm still on four boards for four different exploration companies," she says. "Over the last few days I've been neglecting my duties."

Peter goes to the refrigerator and pulls out two eggs, cream, and some ham and swiss cheese. "I'm making myself a small omelet," he says. "You interested?"

"No thank you," Maria says without looking up.

Peter cooks his omelet, adds a few slices of avocado to the top, and sits down to eat. Halfway through, he says, "Our sparkling conversation is going to make for a very long day."

Maria sighs, shuts her eyes for a moment, and then looks up at Peter. "Okay. You said last night that there's nothing you can do to change this. Fine. I'll accept that for now. I'm not happy about it, and I'm not happy about how I get shut out of your decisions. But I can live with it." She pauses. "Just give me a little space for myself right now."

Peter hesitates. "We don't know anything until Alden and I talk."

"Right." She doesn't look up from her work.

Peter watches her for a while longer. He is uneasy and apprehensive with the sharp edge of Maria's anger, and he doesn't like what he is thinking.

He gets up from the table, puts his dishes in the sink, gets his coat, and heads outside without another word. He throws his cutting torch and tanks into the back of his plow truck and drives into town.

After an hour, Peter is back at the first gate with a borrowed arc welder, a few welding rods, and a piece of steel.

He welds the gates back together and welds on some additional pieces of steel to reinforce the repairs. It's slow work.

By a little before eleven, he shuts down the welder at the second gate and looks at his handiwork. He shakes his head at the ugly welds.

"No welder should be afraid of you stealing his job," he says, "but it's good enough for this job."

After he returns the welder, locks up the gates, puts the truck away, and locks the garage, he returns to the cabin. Maria is in the loft.

"You've been out for a while," she says.

"Fixed the gates. Had to borrow a welder in town. You had lunch?"

"Yes."

Peter makes a sandwich for himself and sits alone at the table to eat, staring out the window to the frozen lake. It is another beautiful day. Bright. Sunny. A light wind buffets the trees occasionally, creating small, localized blizzards of snow.

"You want to head down to Toronto this afternoon?" he asks.

"Possibly," she answers from the loft.

"Don't worry. I won't stay. I'll come back up here."

She doesn't respond directly to his comment. "It seems like a lot of flying for you."

"I think it'll be easier than both of us staying here, not talking, and trying to keep from stepping on each other's toes. I'll drop you at Billy Bishop and fly right back. You'll have your apartment to yourself. Just be careful while you're there."

"I think my apartment's safe enough, as long as you're not living there with me."

Peter does not respond.

"Okay," she says. "When do you want to leave?"

"Right now?"

"Give me twenty minutes."

Peter hears her close her laptop, come down the stairs, and head into the bedroom. He puts on his coat, hat and gloves, and heads out to the dock. He rolls one of the fuel drums out and stands it up beside the helicopter. He transfers twenty gallons to the helicopter using the manual pump. He has taken the covers and tiedowns off and is rolling the half drum of fuel back to its place, when Maria steps onto the dock.

"You lock up?" he asks her.

"Yes." She holds out her hand. "Take the keys."

He hesitates at the finality of the gesture, but he stretches out his hand and takes them. They fly down to Toronto in silence. Peter glances at her several times, but she stares straight ahead. He doesn't try to talk to her.

There's nothing I can or should say, he thinks.

He attends to air traffic as he approaches Toronto and calls ahead for fuel.

When they land, and before he is fully shut down, she turns to him and extends her hand. He is confused for a moment. They shake hands.

"You know where I am," she says. "Call me. Let me know."

"Sure."

She turns, opens the door, and steps out. She grabs her bag from the back seat. He watches her walk across the tarmac to the StolPort facility and disappear. When he is fully shut down, the fuel truck heads in his direction. He gets out and waits.

The driver stops beside the helicopter. "Fill it?"

"Yes, please."

"On your account, Mr. Binder?"

"Yes. I'll get myself a cup of coffee while you're fueling."

"Enjoy your coffee. I'll find you."

By the time he lands back at the cabin, the daylight is fading. He sits for some time in the helicopter, listening to all the little pops and snaps as the engine cools. He had landed pointing away from the cabin, and he watches the boundary between land and sky begin to fade into darkness. Gradually, a deep silence settles upon him.

He waits a bit longer until the rising moon is well above the trees, and the black and white moonlit world gains clarity once more. Strangely, he finds himself at peace. He almost feels guilty. *I should be wallowing in self-pity*, he thinks. *I'm alone again.* He frowns. *Perhaps it's time for a change. Perhaps it's time...* He doesn't want to complete the thought.

He takes a deep breath, gets out, preps the helicopter for the night, and walks up to the cabin. He stokes the remaining embers in the stove with kindling and small logs. He takes pleasure in that simple task. Soon, the fire is burning fiercely, and it quickly warms the main room of the cabin. He makes a simple dinner, and when he is done sits down at his desk. He plays with a pencil for a while, before he calls Patrick Balakrishnan's cell phone.

"Balakrishnan."

"Hi, Patrick. It's Peter Binder."

"Everything okay?"

"Yeah, I'm fine. Still a bit wound up. Feeling a bit morose, I guess." He looks down at the pad of paper on his desk. He has been drawing a picture of a small boy.

"Listen Patrick. A young cop was killed trying to protect us. He has a wife and a young son, a boy named Peter. I'd like to set up a trust account for the boy, maybe a half a million, and I'd like to give her a gift of the same amount. If I send you the details, as best I know them, can you shepherd it to the right lawyer in your firm?"

"You sure you want to do this? You might want to hold off for a while, until your emotions settle down."

"I'm fine, Patrick. Besides, I'm sure it'll take a while to get this together. I can rethink it before I sign all the papers. Remind me to do so."

"Okay. Send the information to me. I'll pass it along."

"Thanks. And thanks for all the help yesterday."

"Only doing my job, Peter."

"I know, but thanks all the same."

After he finishes the call to Patrick, he looks up a real estate offering. It's a 156-acre farm, not far from Ithaca, New York, owned by Viktor Sidorov. Peter knows the land well. It hugs the western shore of Lake Cayuga, though Viktor has sold a few lots along the lake. It lies within the still-developing terroir that hosts a number of moderately successful vineyards.

When Peter was a young man, his parents sent him to upstate New York to help his grandfather on his farm. He'd worked for Viktor as well. Gruff as Viktor might be, Peter liked him.

Viktor's farm shared a property line with his grandfather's farm. The two neighbors also shared a Russian background, though Peter's grandfather was a rabbi's son, and Viktor was a Cossack. Both had moved on from the hardships and hatreds of their early lives. They found common ground and friendship. Now, Peter's father has inherited the farm from his father. After years of visiting only in the summer, Peter's father retired a few years early from his highly profitable legal career in New York City, to return to his boyhood home. He has already planted fifty acres in grapevines. He is building a winery from scratch.

On a lark, when he was in college, Peter mapped the geology in great detail on the two, adjacent farms. Both have rocky soil with good drainage. Half of each farm is underlain by shale, and the other half by a limey shale or marl. Ideal soils for vineyards. Most of the land on Viktor's farm lies on a modest, east-facing slope. Half of his grandfather's land slopes gently to the southeast. The other half slopes to the northwest. Good exposures and easy to cultivate.

Peter scrolls through the photographs provided by the real estate listing for the Sidorov farm. Not much to look at, the farm is mostly planted in hay these days, a crop that Viktor finds easy to manage. Viktor still runs a small farm stand in the summer and sells Christmas trees in December. Families come from Ithaca for a small winter adventure to cut their own tree. In the summer they come for what are actually quite beautiful vegetables.

I wonder what Maria would think of this. He knows that this is not a good time to tell her about it. *It never will be.*

Peter calls his lawyer in Ithaca and directs him to make a full price offer, plus two percent, for the Sidorov farm. The lawyer will hold the property, under confidential contract with Seneca Holdings, Inc., a private company Peter established for that purpose. The offer is good for forty-eight hours. Viktor and his wife can lease ten acres around the house for a dollar a year and live there as long as either of them wish. The buyer will commit to continuing the land in agricultural uses for a minimum of fifty years. Anyone trying to find out who is buying the farm will reach a dead end at his lawyer's name. Peter smiles at what he knows will be his father's frustration.

He gets up, goes to the kitchen, takes down the bottle of Ardbeg, pours himself a drink, takes a sip, and laughs out loud. He returns to his desk and sends Patrick the details of Jack Prescott's family.

He types in another address and sends a short, encrypted email to Jeremy Pritchard, reporting on developments over the last few days. He also requests a secure and reliable, high-level contact in the Peruvian military. Once he sends it, he deletes it from his files. He waits to see if there is a quick reply from Jeremy. There is not.

Peter pours some more Scotch into his glass, puts on his coat, and goes outside to the deck. He brushes the snow off one of the Adirondack chairs and sits down. He contemplates the moonlit and snow-covered lake, and he thinks about Maria.

"It had to happen eventually," he mutters. But he knows this isn't just a breakup of two lovers. This powerful reaction was immediate, all related to Alden's email, and clearly exacerbated by Peru. Peter shivers. He doesn't know why he shivers. He isn't cold.

"I love her," he says softly. He loves Maria, the sensuous and lustful woman he sleeps with, the woman who has saved his life so many times. He loves her, unconditionally. But there is always that other side, the woman who admits she was once a Russian spy, who admits that she was once directed to kill him. He can imagine her, the star pupil of the KGB, seducing unwary western businessmen and diplomats. She would have been very good at it.

"She still is," he says.

He smiles in the darkness and shakes his head. "No. That's not what it is."

Once inside the cabin again, he checks his email one last time. There is a short reply in plain English.

> *Keep us informed, after you talk with AS. Back to you later on the general.*
>
> *JP*

"Bloody useless," Peter mutters. He taps out a reply.

> *We need to talk. Find me a secure phone and a secure room at the Consulate in Toronto. Friday afternoon. 1:00 PM.*
>
> *PB*

He closes the computer, secures the cabin, and goes to bed.

CHAPTER 6

Peter awakens quietly as the night peacefully slips away. He dresses quickly and heads into the kitchen. As he prepares breakfast, he takes a certain pleasure in the quiet, broken only by the snapping of the pine wood in the stove, and the light sizzling of bacon and eggs. He feels the emptiness of the cabin, but he has been alone, both physically and mentally, many times since his last tour of Afghanistan. This time, it feels like a healthy alone. He does not mind it.

He sits, eating slowly and sipping his coffee, looking out over the frozen lake. He thinks about Alden and Maria. He will work this one time for Alden, and he understands why. He also knows he must tell Alden and the CIA that this is the end, no matter what the job entails or how it ends.

And what about Maria? Somehow, he thinks, *I don't know why, but Peru has the answer.*

Just the same, he feels a little inept.

He has more than two hours before he needs to leave for Toronto. He checks his email and finds a reply from Jeremy Pritchard.

> *Secure room and phone at US Consulate in Toronto confirmed for 1:00 PM. Friday. Go to the back, 225 Simcoe, to small security window. Guard will let you in. If a long line, go to the large window by the vehicle entrance. They're expecting you.*
>
> *JP*

Peter notes the time and address.

An email from his lawyer informs him that Viktor Sidorov and his wife accepted the offer. He is now the proud owner of a farm in southern

Seneca County in New York. He instructs his lawyer to conclude the deal with the real estate agent and to hold the property in the lawyer's name until Peter exercises his right to transfer the ownership to Seneca Ventures, Inc.

A few minutes later, he is on the lake with his cross-country skis, headed south along the east shore. The air is still. The sun is bright, but the cold is sharp and biting.

He stops and tightens the hood and its fir strip more closely around his face. He skis a bit farther down the lake than normal, before he skis off the lake onto the road that leads to the fishing lodge. He stops a few times to warm his nose, before he heads along the side of the main highway back to the narrow entrance to the bush road to his cabin.

He pauses at the entrance. He thinks there might be fresh tire tracks on the road. "I'm starting to see ghosts," he mutters.

He decides to ski down the road to the cabin, rather than his usual run on the trail through the woods. When he approaches the bend, before the first gate, he hears a thrashing sound from around the corner.

Sounds like a moose.

He pats his parka pocket. He feels his pistol and almost laughs. It's of little use against an angry moose, but this is not mating season.

Even a bull should be relatively mellow this time of year.

Peter quietly continues around the corner.

They see each other at the same instant, and both stand still and silent. Only the sound of their breathing breaks the silence of the forest.

The moose snorts.

Peter stares at the moose. It stands in front of the gate, a little over seventy feet from him. It isn't so much the size that startles Peter — though this is one of the largest bulls he has ever seen. Yes, it's huge, but it's the color that's surprising. The moose is pure white, an albino. He almost disappears into the snow that surrounds him. Even his new antlers, which he has only begun to grow, are covered in nearly pure white velvet.

Peter presses his poles into the snow. He will wonder later why he does it, but he slowly raises his hands. He places them together in front of his face. Still facing the majestic animal, he bows. Twice.

To his amazement, the huge bull nods his head twice in response.

They both stand silently, staring at each other.

Peter bows once more, and yet again the moose moves his head down and up.

"Be well," Peter says softly.

The moose stands still for a moment longer, then he snorts once, turns, and, in that dignified, if somewhat ungainly gait of a large bull moose, disappears into the woods.

Peter realizes he has been holding his breath. He takes several deep breaths. He knows the old stories, some of the native beliefs, that albino animals are visiting spirits, or perhaps ancient ancestors. He has never seen this moose before, nor has he heard any stories of an albino giant in the area. This majestic animal would be hard to miss.

Peter stands silently for another moment. Then, with a deep breath, he continues on his way to the cabin.

When Peter lands at the airport in Toronto, he again requests fueling service from StolPort and walks over to the lounge. He is a few minutes early, but Alden Sage is already waiting.

Alden seems to pop out of his seat, as some small men do, and almost bounds across the floor to Peter.

"Good to see you, Peter."

"And good to see you, Alden," Peter says. They shake hands. "We have to wait while they fuel the helicopter. They have pretty good coffee here, and I'd like a cup before we head back."

A few minutes later, they sit at a small table, facing each other, each with their coffee.

"I thought you'd fly up to your cabin in a small plane on skis," Alden says.

Peter smiles. "I could, but I don't own a plane. I do own a helicopter. So that's how we're going."

"And how long have you had a helicopter pilot's license?" Alden looks at Peter over the top of his glasses.

Peter smiles. "If you want an experienced pilot on this trip, you're out of luck. But the weather's supposed to be excellent over the next couple of days. Even with this inexperienced pilot, I think you'll survive."

"What about the cabin itself? After what just happened there, you think it's safe?"

"That's a good question," Peter says. "I didn't expect this latest attack, but we seem to have taken out the immediate threat. It's probably as safe as anywhere else around me, at least for now."

Alden arches his eyebrows. "Around you? That's a pretty large qualification. I'll take your word for it, but I suspect it's a good thing I don't still work for the White House. The Secret Service would have a fit."

"Speaking of that," Peter says, "how was the transition exercise with Wisser?"

Alden sighs. "Awful."

"I can imagine."

"No. Unless they were there, I don't think anyone can imagine the level of stupidity and simple lack of interest, overlain by a massive and incredibly dangerous level of arrogance, ego, and grand larceny. It staggered me. I still find it impossible to believe." Alden pauses. "And that's part of why I'm here."

"And I suppose we need to find somewhere else, a little more private, to discuss that," Peter says.

"Yes."

"And of course, I do have a few questions for you, like who do you work for these days, and precisely what you want me to do." Peter smiles slightly. "And maybe why?"

"All good questions."

"Okay," Peter says. He looks out the window at his helicopter. "Looks like they finished the fueling a few minutes ago. I'll sign for it, and we'll be on our way." He looks at Alden's small bag. "I don't suppose you have a heavy parka in there?"

"No."

"We'll manage," Peter says. "Maria has some heavy parkas that should fit you."

"Will she be there?"

"No. She's in Toronto for a while. I'm afraid we've had a bit of a disagreement." Peter frowns. "It seems to have something to do with your visit."

"Sorry about that, but I'm glad we'll have the place to ourselves," Alden says.

The flight is smooth and uneventful. Peter points out some of the sights along the way. He also prods Alden on Wisser. Alden is not shy in his comments.

"How's President Pelton doing?" Peter asks.

"As you can imagine, he's pretty upset. Wisser is doing his best to destroy everything President Pelton accomplished, everything Pelton thinks is important."

"So I've noticed," Peter says.

"Looks like he'll pardon most of those bastards you helped us put in prison."

Peter frowns, but Alden is not watching him. "Yeah. I have a personal interest in that. A lot of them probably don't like me very much, and I seem to attract people who want to exact some kind of revenge."

"Yes, that's something I've noticed, too," Alden says.

Peter looks at his GPS. "We're about ten minutes out. When we get closer, I'll fly along the main road, look along my little track down to the cabin, and along the shore of the lake. It's my normal routine. I look around to see if there's anything obviously out of place."

Alden, finally, turns and looks at Peter. "Sounds fine to me."

When Peter lands at the helipad, he turns the helicopter to face away from the cabin. They take off their flight helmets as he begins the shutdown procedure.

"There is one thing you should know, Alden, if you don't know it already. When most of the Canadian national security apparatus visited me a couple of days ago, they swept the cabin and the helicopter for listening devices. They found one in the cabin and removed it. Anybody tell you about that?"

"Yes, they did. They're pretty sure it's Russian. I suppose it could be CIA, but that doesn't seem logical in your case."

"In the last few years," Peter says, "a lot of things happened to me that weren't strictly logical."

"True."

"I'll leave the decision up to you, Alden. I'm reasonably confident we can talk in the cabin now without fear of being overheard, but it is a little unsettling to know that someone cares enough to place a sophisticated listening device in this remote location."

"Any thoughts on when or how someone put it there?"

Peter turns to Alden and raises his eyebrows. "Lots of possibilities. People come to the lake to fish. There's a campsite less than a quarter mile from here. The cabin's unoccupied… a lot. I lock it up pretty tight, but people break into bank vaults, for Christ's sake. Placing the device would be easy. Lots of opportunities. Any number of people could do it."

"The Canadians think someone placed it there quite recently."

Peter sighs. "Well, it's tougher in the winter. There aren't many people around this time of year. I always check the area, at least around the cabin, for anything unusual, like strange footprints in the snow. I haven't seen a thing this winter." After a pause, "There's no use checking now, though. That mob from Toronto tramped all over the place. There have to be a couple of thousand footprints in the snow around the cabin."

They sit a while in silence. Then, rather quietly, Alden asks, "And the obvious candidate to place the device?"

Peter unbuckles his seat belt. He cracks a reluctant smile. "Let's get out. I'll unlock the cabin, open the shutters over the windows, and we can put some lunch together. It's a nice sunny day. Once you get a warm coat on, we can brush the snow off the chairs on the deck and sit outside. Should be safe to talk there. We can even light a fire, if you'd like. I'll put the helicopter to bed later."

Over a simple lunch of sliced corned beef and swiss cheese on rye, Peter asks, "So… what are you doing these days? You say you're consulting. Are you working for the British Secret Intelligence Service, or as most of us like to call it, MI6?"

"I'm not exactly welcome in Washington at the moment. My long association with Pelton paints me as poison, as far as Wisser's bunch is concerned, and I don't actually blame them for being concerned about me."

"He's certainly cleared out anyone with any progressive leanings, or any intelligence, as far as I can tell."

Alden laughs. "I think he'd like to gut me like a fresh-caught trout, but I'm trying to stay out of his reach."

Alden exhales and stands up. "You don't happen to have a beer to go with this sandwich, do you?"

"Sure. In the fridge. Nothing fancy. Mostly pretty tasteless light beer."

Alden finds himself a beer and sits down again. He leans back in his chair and takes a long drink. "There are quite a few people in the US, and scattered around the western allies, who are positively horrified by Wisser and his apparent agenda, if he has one. He's an extremely destructive force. Because of some damning Russian 'kompromat', which I cannot discuss, he is, and presumably will continue to be, a constant aid to the Russians."

"This is not exactly breaking news, and it still doesn't touch on what you're doing these days. Or what you want me to do."

Alden smiles. "I'm getting there." He looks around the interior of the cabin.

He's assessing the security of this place, Peter thinks.

Alden eats the last of his sandwich and finishes his beer, before he says, "I think we ought to move to the deck about now."

They shovel the snow off much of the deck, sweep off the second Adirondack chair, and clear off the large brazier that serves as a raised firepit. Peter retrieves an arm-load of logs and kindling and starts a fire.

"Strange to see you in that paisley parka," Peter says.

Alden looks at it and smiles, "Actually, I thought I looked quite dashing."

Peter laughs. "Let's go back to what you're doing and what you want me to do." He pokes at the fire. "I think you're trying to avoid answering my questions."

Alden closes his eyes and takes a deep breath. "You work for the CIA, and you want to get out. Right?"

"That's right, but they're holding me to my contract. It runs two more years."

"It has something to do with an incident in Afghanistan?"

"There were some unanswered questions," Peter says. "Where is this going?"

"Bear with me." Alden opens his eyes and looks at Peter. "I'll understand if you're reluctant to talk about it, but it's important. One of my sources told me that some people accused you of murdering your entire platoon."

"That's one accusation. There were others."

"What do you think happened on that hill in Afghanistan?" Alden asks quietly. "You were the only one left standing, literally."

"I, and all the shrinks I've seen over the years, have tried to answer that question, without notable success."

"Tell me what you remember," Alden says, so softly that Peter barely hears it.

"Why should I tell you any of this?"

"Because… I think I can give you some relief. But I need you to tell me what you remember."

Peter gets up and throws two more logs on the fire. He doesn't want to think about Afghanistan, but it all comes back anyway. He turns back and looks down on Alden, who looks back up at him, expressionless.

Why should I tell him anything? He can't possibly understand, and for the telling I will surely dream badly again tonight.

But he feels drawn to Alden. He knows he's been silent for too long, and for reasons he doesn't completely understand, he realizes that he does want to talk about Afghanistan. It is as if Alden has some sort of power over him.

He sits down, and he begins to talk.

"We were a full platoon. Sixteen of us. They ambushed us. They outnumbered us, maybe five or six to one. I'm not sure. My ego probably makes me overestimate. The weather was atrocious. Air support was not available, and we were out of reach of any artillery support." He pauses. "No one will admit it, but we shouldn't have been there."

Peter looks at the fire. "We were in a terrible defensive position, but we held them off. They had cut off our only escape. We called for reinforcements, but the nearest of them would take an hour to arrive. Gradually, they whittled away at our numbers. The few of us who were left alive, and able to fight, ran out of ammunition. They swarmed us. Shooting. Beating. Kicking. Knifing. Biting. Blood everywhere. Someone behind me hit me on the head. A rifle butt, I think. I went down. Out cold."

Peter stops talking.

Alden says nothing. He waits patiently.

After a few minutes, Peter continues. "When I came to, I was naked. Every other SEAL was dead, and they, too, were all naked. They knew I was the lead officer. They tied my hands behind my back. Tied my ankles together. Pulled a rope tight around my neck and dragged me to my feet. While one held me by the rope around my neck, they took turns beating

58

me. I knew they would beat me to death. They particularly enjoyed kicking me in the nuts."

Peter gets up and walks across the deck to the railing. He leans on it heavily.

"Surprisingly, the beating didn't last long before, suddenly, they were gone. To my amazement, I was still alive. My thinking was a jumbled mess. It seemed to me at the time that they simply disappeared. They took most of the platoon's equipment. They left one rifle. Mine. No ammunition, of course."

Peter turns to face Alden.

"That's how they found me, the two platoons sent to relieve us. Standing there, naked, covered in blood, puke, and covered with darkening bruises. I stood dazed, with a useless rifle in my hands. Someone told me that tears were streaming down my face, but I don't remember that. They also told me, much later, that I shot every other member of my platoon, in the back of the head. That every single bullet came from my rifle."

Peter continues to look at Alden. He waits for the look of disgust, but it never comes.

Alden says, "They never took you to court-martial, did they?"

Peter shakes his head. "I was sure they would, and I was equally sure the outcome would be a very long prison sentence. The lawyer they provided for my defense was a young kid, younger than I was. Earnest, but not very experienced."

Peter throws another log on the fire.

"In the end, they said they'd let it go, let me leave the force honorably. Maybe it was my war record. I don't know. The one condition was that I had to make myself available to the CIA." Peter sits down again.

"I don't want to ask the question —"

Peter interrupts. "You don't have to. There's one thing I know for sure. I would never execute my family. Period. Those men were all my brothers." Peter takes a deep breath. "But... there's a big blank spot in my memory. I can't prove anything, not even to myself."

They sat for a minute or more in silence.

Alden asks, "Do you want to know the real reason they never put you through a court-martial?"

"You really think you have to ask that question?"

"Here's the simple answer. They couldn't prove anything either. All those *coup de grâce* shots? None of them could be positively traced to your rifle." Alden continues more emphatically. "There is absolutely no proof that you shot any member of that platoon, and plenty of evidence to the contrary."

Peter closes his eyes.

"You were good friends with Admiral Davis, right?" Alden asks.

It takes a while for Peter to open his eyes and respond. "No. Not good friends. Not really. I knew him. His son and I were in training together, and we became good friends. After we completed our training, he invited me home. I met the Admiral then."

He stares at the fire. "Later, his son and I served together. His son was standing less than three feet from me when he was shot and killed."

Alden gives Peter's last statement the respect and space it deserves before he says, "Davis never believed any of the accusations related to your behavior on that mountainside in Afghanistan. He was convinced leadership was trying to cover up their own bad decisions. He pushed for a special investigation of the incident. He kept pushing, and he finally got it.

"I have a copy of the report with me. Davis wanted me to give it to you, and you, conveniently enough, have a high enough clearance that you can read it. It absolves you of all accusations that the military leveled against you. He also yelled, shouted, and pounded his fists enough that the CIA finally agreed to let you cancel your contract whenever you wish. And I have that document with me as well."

Peter leans back in his chair. He closes his eyes. He feels…. He doesn't know quite how or what he feels. Mostly he feels numb. He stands up to put two more logs on the fire. He has an urgent need to do something. Anything. He can't stand still.

Without a word, he steps off the deck, and he walks through the snow to the dock.

Alden makes no move to follow. He sits in silence, and Peter does not look back.

Almost in a daze, Peter impulsively wraps up and ties down the helicopter. To do… something.

That done, he stands at the end of the dock. He doesn't know how to handle the information Alden has given him. His emotions are a wild mix of anger, relief, and disgust.

I can't just walk away, he thinks. *They have to admit their fault.*

He hugs himself with his arms across his chest. He looks out across the lake and stands there, unmoving, for a long time. He tries to wrap his mind fully around what has happened on the deck behind him. He can't do it. Eventually, he sits down at the edge of the dock, closes his eyes, and lets his mind slip away.

When he opens his eyes again, Alden is standing beside him and he points silently to the left.

Peter turns to see the albino moose eating the small branches of the willow bushes along the edge of the lake. When Peter stands up, the moose turns to look at him.

Peter puts his hands together and bows.

The moose nods his head and turns back to his rough, winter meal.

"Did you... bow to each other?" Alden asks softly.

"I like to think so," Peter says. "I've decided to believe the native stories, that he's a powerful spirit, maybe one of my ancestors. Probably my great-grandfather." Peter turns and looks at Alden. "I'm almost positive that he's a good sign for me... maybe for you, too."

CHAPTER 7

By the time they return to the deck, the fire has burned down to embers, and Peter gathers some additional wood and kindling from the woodpile behind the cabin. With a little attention, the fire quickly leaps back to life. Peter sits down again, next to Alden. Only faint hints of the fading daylight persist in the west. The stars are quickly gaining their dominion in the night sky.

"I don't quite know what to say to you," Peter says. "Somehow, 'Thank you,' doesn't seem sufficient."

"Wait until we finish here. Then you can decide whether I brought you a blessing or a curse."

"Well, at the moment I'm still a little numb, and I'm completely surprised that you gave me the gift before the ask."

"I want you to do a certain job because you want to do it, not because you will receive a gift for doing it."

"Like the old guy used to say on the radio," Peter says, "let's hear the rest of the story."

"Paul Harvey. I haven't heard anyone reference him for a very long time." Alden pauses. "Let's start with President Wisser. He's dangerous and unpredictable, which is one worry. He's also wedded to Russia and destructive of the western alliance. That's a much bigger worry for many of us, though the two together are truly frightening. A few governments have decided to build a clandestine exercise to try to establish some guardrails around the US Administration and to try to blunt the effects of some of Wisser's worst impulses."

"Let me guess," Peter says. "Canada, because we're next door. The UK because they speak English, have the Commonwealth connections, and probably still have one of the best intelligence services in the world. France because of their African connections. Germany because of their economy, their intelligence service, and their position versus eastern Europe and Russia. Maybe Japan and South Korea, maybe even China, if you have an Asian perspective to your plans." Peter looks at Alden. "Close?"

Alden laughs. "You want to tell the story?"

"No," Peter says with a shake of his head. "Just trying to help."

"You're close enough," Alden says, "and let's leave it at that. This loose association, along with some of the career professionals at the CIA, is actively working on many things, like maintaining support for Ukraine, or trying to help Iran feel secure without nuclear bombs. Most of all, we're trying to contain the worst actions and intentions of Russia."

"And your place in this?" Peter asks.

"Well, as you guessed, I'm associated with MI6 in London. My job is to look at Russian activities around the world, things that seem strange or inexplicable, considering what we know about Russian actions in the past and their current objectives. In these cases, their actions aren't necessarily and obviously confrontational, but we can't figure out why they're doing this stuff. My experience with Russia is that something unexplained transforms into unacceptable, or terrifying, rather quickly."

"Maria told me right away that you'd be working for British intelligence," Peter says. "I'm not sure I like the direction of your little narrative."

"You jump to conclusions," Alden says.

"Sometimes that's how I stay alive."

"I suppose." Alden sighs. "I haven't lived your life. I don't really know how you actually do manage to stay alive. Here are the basics. You've heard about a deposit in Peru, the Cerro Nublado copper deposit?"

"Yeah. It's right up on the border with Ecuador, where the boundary is a bit fuzzy, and near where Peru had a mini-war with Ecuador over a small oil field a few years back. A friend of mine, Carlos Bellido made the discovery. Another friend drilled it out and made a pile of money selling his little exploration company to Minera Russo-Perú, part of a huge Russian mining company." Peter shrugs. "Right up your alley, I guess."

Alden says, "Perhaps. Maybe you could tell me a little about the history of the project? There's been a lot of protest activity against it, some quite violent."

Peter looks up at the cold, cloudless sky, partly to organize his thoughts. *The stars will be spectacular tonight*, he thinks.

He looks back down and turns to Alden. "You warm enough to continue out here?"

"Let's put some more wood on the fire."

After they tend to the fire, Peter begins. "Carlos worked for a company that did a helicopter stream sediment survey in the mountains of northern Peru. They found a copper anomaly. It was a little brazen to follow up on that anomaly. Peru has long prohibited foreign ownership of land, even mining interests, along the border with Ecuador."

"How did they get around that?"

"I don't know all the details. They hired a fast-talking attorney. He had to get approval and a signature from the president of Peru, Fujimori himself, and in those days that meant that he had to go through Vladimiro Montesinos, Fujimori's fantastically corrupt and evil spymaster. I don't know what the lawyer promised. Maybe, in the end, he bypassed Montesinos. In any case, not long after Fujimori signed, the lawyer fell off a cliff while riding his mountain bike. He died instantly. The investigators called it a tragic accident."

"Interesting. So the company got the land."

"They had to find the copper deposit first. They sent Carlos on an expedition up the river. No trails. No local knowledge. Virgin wilderness. I doubt even the Inca had been there. It's in what we call a cloud forest. The Peruvians sometimes call it *Ceja de Selva*, the eyebrow of the forest. I like that, but it says it all. It's rugged, mountainous, and damned tough country to get around in. To make matters worse, the Peruvian maps looked nice, but they were totally mythological.

"In the end, it took Carlos two tries to get to the discovery outcrop." Peter looks at Alden. "Still warm enough?"

"No problem. Keep going."

"It's a little hard to describe. There were no communications, and Carlos was dependent on what they could carry. At one stage, someone stole all the food. On the second try, Carlos got to the discovery outcrop at the side of Cerro Nublado. A small bit of water ran down the outcrop. The rocks were bright green from the oxidation of the copper.

"The river canyon has very steep sides. It can be dangerous. Rising water trapped them one night, but they survived. They sampled the outcrop, and went back to the office in Lima."

Peter stands up and adds another log to the fire. "They knew they had made a discovery, but it wasn't clear that it was significant or large. The company mapped and sampled the project, and they recognized the potential for a large copper deposit. They partnered with a larger company to do the first round of drilling."

"Carlos must have gotten a nice bonus," Alden says.

Peter laughs rather ruefully. "Success has many fathers, Alden. Carlos got some verbal credit for the discovery, but some felt that maybe others deserved as much or maybe more credit. Almost any discovery like Cerro Nublado is a team effort. As far as I know, Carlos got no big bonus. Most large companies don't give out any discovery bonuses. Like a lot of people who make discoveries, in the end, the company gently pushed him aside."

"Sounds familiar," Alden says. "When did the opposition begin? And when did Minera Russo-Perú get involved?"

"At first, as I said, this was wild, empty country. There's still no road to the property. The locals from the nearest villages were friendly and supportive. In Peru, recent laws have empowered the local communities, and mine development requires local acceptance. When it became obvious that this could be a huge mine, a whole chorus of dissenters came out of the woods.

"The area has a lot of coca, and the drug cartels don't want mine development. It brings the police and the military, and things can get hot for the narco traffickers. The local priests can tend toward liberation theology, and many locals lean far to the left. A huge development, and it's high-paying jobs, makes a mess of simple, communal living.

"Then there's the environmental issues. This mine would likely have a lot of high-sulfide waste. That waste, unless it's very well managed, can cause major environmental damage. That brings out all the environmental NGO's. This was, after all, a very special, pristine environment.

"A lot of that's gone now. People have moved in, slashing and burning to clear land, farming, living near the discovery. All these different interests, and the potential of real money, stirs up the local communities. They want a say in the development."

"But it got violent, didn't it?" Alden asks.

"Yes. It's hardly surprising. With coca there are always guns around. For some reason, one group got angry enough to attack the camp. They burned parts of it and killed one person. Some other group kidnapped a crew working with the local villagers. There were beatings, in some cases torture. It was a mess. It's calmed down lately, but it's still a powder keg."

"So, it could still explode," Alden says. "With all this opposition, all the violent protest, do you think the current owner can permit and develop this mine?"

Peter pokes at the fire, and a small shower of sparks fly up into the cold, night air. "I doubt it. This is a multi-billion-dollar investment. At least, I doubt a US company could do it. The foreign corrupt practices act makes it difficult to pay money 'under the table' for official approvals. Some sort of bribery may be the only easy way to succeed in this case.

"But the Russians?" Peter continues. "They're more comfortable with bribery and corruption. I suspect they think they can pull it off, but it won't be easy."

They sit in silence, watching the fire. Finally, Alden asks, "If the project is so difficult, why do the Russians want this particular copper deposit so badly?"

"Maybe all they want is a reliable copper supply," Peter says. "This is a huge deposit. Once in production it's a long-life mine. It would be a good copper supply for the next twenty to thirty years, at least. Maybe they're taking the long view."

"I don't think so," Alden says. "They seem to want it right now. Already they've signed a contract for North Korea to smelt and refine the concentrates. They want to fast track development. Why the urgency? Why the contract with North Korea?"

"Those questions are more in your area of expertise, Alden. They're sure as hell not in mine."

"I disagree," Alden responds. "We think there's something we don't quite understand about this situation, and we think it's something geological, or mineralogical, something about the deposit itself." He smiles at Peter. "And that's why I'm here talking to you about Cerro Nublado."

"You, and by extension MI6, want to hire me as a consulting geologist to examine the deposit?"

"Well," Alden says, "the small exploration company, Mandrake Minerals, London based, wants you to do the review for them. Conveniently, I'm on the board. The board tasked me to ask you. Mandrake still holds thirty percent of the project. They're beginning to think that Russo-Perú knew something that Mandrake didn't know, that they illegally withheld that information during negotiations, and that they didn't pay nearly enough for the property."

"Great. The last time I did something like this, a whole bunch of people tried to kill me, actually me and Maria, at least a half a dozen times. And Cerro Nublado has as many, probably more, bad actors hovering around it." Peter pauses. "I suppose MI6 expects me to sign on with them?"

"Nope. Straight consulting contract with Mandrake."

"I do know your CEO," Peter says. "How much does he know about the reasons for your interest?"

"Nothing. Julius Grant thinks an outside review is appropriate, and, unprompted, he actually brought up your name."

Peter pushes the logs together. It's getting too cold to stay outside much longer. "The Russians know who I am. They'll assume I still work for the CIA. They'll shoot me, or drown me in the river, as soon as I show up on the property."

Alden stands and stretches. "They also know why you were working for the CIA. They will know, because we'll make sure of it, that you are no longer working for the CIA. We'll also ensure that they know that there's no love between you and that organization. That changes the entire risk matrix."

Peter also stands. "You can say that, if you want, but it all depends on what they believe."

"MI6 is very good at deception."

"Yeah. That's the problem. Russia will expect deception. They may well not believe the truth when they hear it."

"I have thought about that," Alden says as he stands up.

"And?" Peter asks.

"You should tell Maria about the resolution of the incident in Afghanistan, and the release from your CIA contract. Show her the two documents. Tell her the contract with Mandrake was a result of my contacts in the UK."

"And you think she'll believe it? You think it'll get to the Russians that way?" Peter asks.

"Yes."

Peter doesn't respond immediately.

"You are getting close to ending this conversation," Peter says softly.

"Peter. Please. Don't be naïve."

"You're getting closer."

Alden is silent.

"My relationship with Maria is my business," Peter says. "I might do exactly what you suggest, but it will be entirely my decision. I know the risks here, but if you cannot handle the relationship as it is, do not ask me to do any work for you."

"I'm not asking you to work for me."

"That's a technicality. If I go to Peru, I will want assurances of support from MI6. You or I will also have to bring in the CIA."

"You still working with Jeremy Pritchard?" Alden asks.

"Yes."

"You can be honest with him," Alden says.

"Good."

"I would suggest, rather strongly, that you contact no one else in the CIA on this matter."

With slight edge to his voice, Peter says, "You don't have to worry about that. After someone assassinated Watson MacDonough, I don't have any other contact."

Both men stand silently, staring at the dying fire.

Peter says, "Let's go in. We can have supper, an after-dinner Scotch, solve all the other problems in the world, and then get some sleep. We can talk again tomorrow morning. Okay?"

Peter wishes he could see Alden's expressions as they talk, but in the dying light of the fire he sees nothing.

"Sounds good," Alden says.

As they step off the deck to find the front door in the darkness, a wolf howls, quite close.

"Jesus!" Alden says.

Peter laughs. "Ah! That's an old friend. He's around all the time, but he never bothers me. I've never had a good look at him. He shouts at me once in a while, at night, particularly if I'm doing my ski run in the dark. Sometimes he stalks me. He's reminding us who's the real boss around here."

Peter opens the door, steps inside, and flips on the lights.

Alden strips off his paisley parka and hangs it on a peg by the door. "I think," he says, "between moose and wolves, I'm probably more comfortable in a nice Hilton Hotel in the city."

"It's all what's familiar."

They walk over to the kitchen, and Alden sits down at the table.

"How does a steak, a few mushrooms, a salad, and some home-made rolls sound?"

"And you're the chef?" Alden asks.

Peter makes a show of raising his hands and looking around the cabin. "Don't see anyone else. You want a red wine with your steak?"

"Sounds good."

"There should be a nice Barolo in a box with a few other bottles, in the closet in my bedroom in the back. You can grab that while I get started here."

In half an hour, they sit across from each other, enjoying their meal. Alden swirls the wine in his glass. "It's a nice wine." He looks around the cabin. "I understand this cabin has some unique characteristics."

Peter looks up at the walls. "When I got out of the SEALS and built this place, I was a screwed-up mess. The unique aspects are the result of a very frightened and paranoid man being the builder." He takes a moment before he continues. "I've learned to live with it. I'm mostly past it now."

"How did you get there?"

"Lots of counseling, lots of analysis, but mostly it's the result of living with Maria Davidoff." Peter looks away from Alden. "You see, no matter what you and your friends think of Maria, no matter what you see when you look at her, no matter what you think she really is, she saved my life. Literally. Many times. I'm pretty sure I understand the risks, but I also owe my life to her, and we are in love."

"I understand," Alden says.

Peter shakes his head. "I seriously doubt that."

Alden laughs lightly, perhaps a bit nervously. "You're probably right." He raises a glass. "Here's to love that is truly life sustaining."

They touch their glasses and drink. Peter pours more wine. He shifts the discussion to President Wisser, and the world stage. They continue to talk well into the night.

As they head off to bed, Peter to the bedroom and Alden to the loft, Peter says, "We'll talk again in the morning. Then I'll get you to Toronto. When do you need to be there?"

Alden nods. "I need to be at the main airport, Pierson, by three in the afternoon."

"No problem," Peter says.

"Let me give you those two reports." He steps over to Peter's desk and takes two large envelopes out of his briefcase. "Here are your tickets to your next life. Handle them carefully. You can discuss them with a lawyer, of course, but they should hold them under close attorney-client privilege."

"Thanks," Peter says. He pauses for a moment. He wants to say something more to Alden, maybe say another word of thanks.

No. I don't know if I should be thankful or not.

Peter simply turns and walks down the hall. Once inside the bedroom, he stops and listens. He hears Alden climb the stairs to the loft. He shuts the door to the bedroom, strips off his clothes, and turns off the light. He slips under the covers.

The bed feels large, cold, and empty. He sighs and pulls the covers higher, until only the top half of his head is exposed. His mind continues to tumble through his conversation with Alden and the gift of freedom he brought with him. And the gift, or curse, of one last chance at the game, and all the implications that come with it.

He finds no satisfaction in the mental exercise. He can come to only one conclusion. *I cannot accept one without the other, and tomorrow morning... I will still be the fool.*

"Alden Sage," he mutters, "you are one classy son of a bitch."

CHAPTER 8

Peter awakens early, well before the dawn. He hears Alden banging around at the stove. "He wants a fire, I suppose," Peter says softly.

Let him do it himself.

Peter gets out of bed and turns on the lights. He sees the two manila envelopes on the bureau, and he opens them. Still naked, and shivering in the cold, he quietly reads the summary, conclusions and recommendations of the review of the Afghanistan action. It amounts to a detailed exoneration of all charges. The report includes an attached statement of findings, signed by the Rear Admiral and current commander of the Navy SEALs. Peter puts the report back in the envelope to read more fully later.

He pulls the CIA document out of the second envelope. The document is intensely legalistic and ten pages long. A quick scan appears to confirm that he can now choose to terminate his contract at any time, so long as he agrees to confidentiality, non-disclosure, and no legal action. He will receive a one-time severance payment of one million dollars. The Director of the CIA signed the cover letter and copied Jeremy Pritchard.

"Bullshit," Peter says. He thinks about the violent and bloody wreckage of the last two years of his life.

There's not even an apology. The million dollars is neither an admission of anything nor an apology.

Peter returns the document to its envelope. The requirement for no legal action does not sit well with him.

I want an apology, and maybe a payment big enough that it hurts. And I may need their support in Peru.

"Not an easy combination," he mutters.

And somehow Maria has to know I'm quitting, when maybe I'm not. At least not yet. And the Russians, too.

"Jesus!"

Peter steps across the hall to shower and shave. Once dressed, he finds Alden at the desk working at his laptop. The main room is already warm.

"You were up early," Peter says. "Thanks for getting the fire going."

Alden turns with a smile. "Not really used to doing that, but my old Boy Scout training came in handy."

"Breakfast?"

"Sure."

"It'll be pretty basic," Peter says. "Scrambled eggs with some sausage, toast, coffee. There's orange juice in the fridge if you want it."

"Good enough for me."

As Peter begins to put breakfast together, he asks, "You said you needed to be at Pierson International by three this afternoon?"

"Right."

"Well, I don't like to land there. It's too big an airport, and they hate helicopters at an airport like that. I'll take you back to Billy Bishop, downtown, sometime between noon and one. You can take a cab up to Union Station and take the train out to Pierson. You can cab the whole way if you want, but it's cheaper and usually faster to take the train."

"Okay."

"You don't need to worry about personal security, do you?"

Alden laughs. "Not in Canada. Nobody knows me here."

When breakfast is ready, Peter puts the two plates on the table and pours two cups of coffee. They sit down across from each other.

After a few minutes, Alden says, "Good breakfast, Peter."

"Thanks. I do want to thank you again for bringing the two gifts. I scanned them this morning. They should let me live my life on a different level."

"Glad I could help."

"Considering how these actions totally screwed up my life for years, for no reason whatsoever, and considering that they must have known that all along, I'm… you might say, I'm a little annoyed. Neither the Navy nor the CIA offer an apology, and neither accepts any blame."

"Always tough to get an apology."

Peter pours more coffee into his and Alden's cups. "I might talk to a lawyer, but I'm not sure there's much I can do. I won't sign the CIA document, not the way it's written."

"If you're thinking lawsuits, they'll almost surely fail," Alden says, "particularly with this president in the White House."

"I'd like someone to say, 'Sorry. We shouldn't have done that.'"

"A lawsuit might also get you a bullet in the head, rather than an apology. Wisser and his ass-kissing acolytes will not appreciate it, even if they can blame it all on previous administrations. They're unpredictable, never embarrassed, and prone to condone murder without so much as a second thought."

"You may be right," Peter says.

"I'm not a lawyer, but if I were you, I'd press the CIA for a much larger payout, accept that as an apology, sign the agreement, and move on with my life."

"Very practical advice," Peter says. "I might actually heed it. Maybe you could recommend a lawyer in Washington?"

"Sure. Jack Mitchoff. You can look him up. His firm is Mitchoff, Barns, and Blackwood. He's easy to find."

They sit in silence for a while, drinking their coffee.

"You mentioned Wisser being able to blame previous administrations for… for the accusations I faced. How much did Pelton know about my personal history?"

"He knew about the charges. He thought you were doing penance. He also knew about Admiral Davis' push for an investigation. He encouraged it. Pelton likes you. A lot."

Peter says nothing.

"Shall we talk about Peru?" Alden asks.

"We should," Peter says. "I suggest we put the dishes in the sink, put our coats on, and go back outside."

Once outside and on the deck, Peter retrieves some kindling and logs, and lights the fire. When it's blazing, they sit back in the Adirondack chairs.

Peter looks out over the frozen lake. "First question. Why have me do this work? I could name any number of people who could do a great review of this property. They could likely do a better job than I can."

"First of all, we don't know what we're looking for or expecting. Something's going on that we don't understand, something special that piques Russian interest. It can't be anything obvious, or Mandrake, or the other companies who worked there, would have already recognized it. The connection to North Korea only adds intrigue, and perhaps urgency, to the question. It's not a job for a geologist, Peter, it's a job for a geological detective. From what we've seen, we think you're the best in the business. You have a good eye for the invisible and improbable."

"Maria says you want to hire me, not because I'm a good geologist, but because I'm good at killing people, blowing things up, and surviving at the end of the day."

"Maria does like to be blunt, but in this case, she's wrong."

"Really?"

"Yes, really," Alden says. "Your work at Cerro Nublado will not be without risk. Where the Russians are involved, and where they're trying to hide something, there is always risk."

"I have my own reasons for wanting to do this job in Peru," Peter says. "Assuming I agree to do it, how do we proceed?"

"I'll tell Julius that you accepted, and that you'll call him in a day or two to arrange the schedule, reservations, your fees, and the details of your contract. You take it from there."

"I need a little more than that, Alden." Peter rubs his forehead. "I'll need something from MI6, something in writing, that assures me of appropriate emergency backup in Peru, extraction if needed, and a small weapons list with ammunition and the permits to carry the pistols in Peru. Also, until I am officially no longer employed by the CIA, someone there will have to know I'm doing this work."

"Peter, Peter. Really? What do you need this stuff for? You're doing a geological study."

Peter turns away from looking out over the lake to look directly at Alden. "Let me tell you why I need them. First, you're worried about what Russo-Perú is hiding. I'm more concerned about what the Russians might do if they think I'll discover, or even stumble upon, their precious secret, if there is one. Second, when the Peruvian military beat back the Sendero, many of the Sendero soldiers moved smoothly into the business of security for the narco traffickers. The narcos, at least up to now, have not been happy about this mine, and their security forces are direct descendants of one of the most vicious little revolutionary groups in South America. They're not nice little boys and girls. Third, money buys many things in Peru, and one of the most important things it can buy is compliance of the military and the politicians. Those are three reasons. I could list a few others if you want."

Alden throws up his hands. "Fine. I'll get the document from MI6. You give me the list of items you think you need. You need to deal with the CIA yourself, and you'd better hold off a while if you want their help in Peru."

Peter smiles. "Yes, I suppose you're right. However, if your unofficial group, the one putting guardrails around Wisser, includes some in the CIA, maybe I can work for them and not work for them at the same time."

"Perhaps. That's your puzzle to solve."

"Maybe," Peter says. "I think I'll start by having Patrick Balakrishnan talk to your friend Jack Mitchoff in Washington. At least I'll have a better understanding of what's possible. In any case, having Mitchoff begin negotiations will be a logical excuse for delaying signing."

"I leave that to you," Alden says. "I think we both have a little work to do. Are you formally accepting this job to review the Cerro Nublado project for Mandrake? Assuming MI6 meets your conditions?"

Peter looks directly at Alden. "Yes. You get the commitments from MI6, and I'll contact Julius at Mandrake, but I don't come cheap. Two thousand a day plus expenses in the field, and one thousand a day writing the report at home. I don't know how Julius will feel about that."

"I'm pretty sure he knows your price. What about Maria? She going with you?"

"Don't know yet," Peter says. "I have to get all this in place first. I'll find out what Maria wants to do after that." Peter glances at his watch. "I'll see if I can meet my lawyer when I take you to Toronto. After that, feel free to use the phone and my desk."

"I think we can go back inside," Alden says.

Peter smiles. "I suspect you're right."

Peter places the call to Patrick Balakrishnan. Fortunately, he has an opening at two in the afternoon. It's only half an hour, but Peter thinks it should be enough time. "We should leave in about an hour," he says to Alden. "That'll give you plenty of time. I'll fuel up now, and we'll be ready to go any time you want."

They fly down to Toronto in bright sun. A glorious day.

"The weather has been just as you promised, Peter," Alden says.

"It's supposed to get ugly tonight, but not 'till late."

"What do you do if the weather closes down completely?"

"Well, if I'm at the cabin and I have to get out, I always have my truck. Right now, I think I'd like to have a few days to myself anyway. I've got to get up to speed on conditions in Peru, for one thing, and recent developments at Cerro Nublado. The CIA's another delicate matter. For time to think and plan, a big snowstorm at the cabin is about as good as it gets."

"Your communications hold up?" Alden asks.

Peter turns briefly and looks at Alden. "Pretty much. They'll shut down occasionally in the worst of the big storms, and if snow piles up on the satellite dish."

When they land at the Billy Bishop airport, and after Peter shuts down the helicopter, he and Alden part company. Peter secures the helicopter and walks over to the StolPort facility. He asks for fueling services and walks outside to pick up a cab. In a few minutes, he steps out at the US Consulate, at 225 Simcoe Street.

There is a long line at the small security window, next to a barred entrance that the guard controls. Peter steps over to the larger window.

"You should use the other entrance," the guard says.

"My name's Peter Binder. I have a secure room and phone reserved for my use here."

"Identification?"

Peter puts his passport into the metal tray as it opens toward him. The guard opens it, flips through the pages, and studies the main identification page. He scans it into his computer, taps a few keys, and returns it to Peter.

"Please go to the first door to your right. A guard will let you in."

"Thank you," Peter says, puts the passport back in his pocket, and steps over to the door. A woman lets him in.

"Mr. Peter Binder?"

"Yes."

"Please show me your identification."

Peter hands the woman his passport.

After she compares his face to the photo, she hands it back. "Please empty your pockets, take off your shoes, and put your backpack on the belt. Walk into the scanner. Put your hands over your head and stand still, please."

After the security check, the woman leads Peter to an unmarked room in the basement. She points to a phone in the middle of a conference table. "That is connected to an outside line. Please dial direct. Do you need to use a restroom?"

"No. I'm fine," Peter answers.

"Please do not leave this room without an escort. Please wait before you make your call. There is someone who wishes to speak with you before you call. When you are finished, please press the call button next to the door. Someone will come and escort you back to the entrance."

"Thank you."

"No problem at all," the woman responds, and she softly closes the door. *Who wants to talk with me here?*

Peter walks around to the other side of the table and sits, facing the door. He hears a knock at the door.

"Come in."

When the door opens, Peter laughs. "I guess I don't need the telephone."

"No. Probably not," Jeremy Pritchard replies. He shuts the door behind him. "We do need the room, though."

"Now I'm really getting worried," Peter says.

Jeremy sits down. He reaches across the table, and they shake hands.

"Alden briefed me this morning about your discussions. As a result, I don't think we need to talk too much about Cerro Nublado, except to discuss any specific support you might want or need in Peru. We have a few assets there, more than MI6, but they do have some excellent native assets. They could probably give you one for a driver and an interpreter, mostly if you run into a lot of Quechua speakers."

Peter has never been quite sure how he feels about Jeremy. He is two or three years older than Peter, and the product of the connected and wealthy upper classes of New England. One of the "elites" that so many complain about in the United States. His great-grandfather and grandfather made all the money for the family, mostly building wooden ships. His father was in the State Department for many years, rising to Ambassador to France late in his career, an unusual posting for a career diplomat.

Jeremy followed his father to Exeter Academy and then to Harvard, where he graduated second in his class and captain of the squash and golf teams. Always thin. Always tan. Smart as they come, and always perfectly dressed for the occasion. Today it is dark gray pants, a nicely tailored blue blazer, and an open-necked, striped, oxford-cloth shirt.

Peter always thinks he should dislike Jeremy, that he should be a spoiled scion of privilege. But Peter has watched him work a room, charming everyone in it. If he meets you once, and he meets you again five years later, he will still remember your name, and the names of all your important family members and friends. You will be sure that he cares deeply about your welfare, and the welfare of those around you.

Peter also knows that, if Jeremy wishes to do so, he can drink beer with construction workers, and work his charm on them as well. He can even disappear into the background, if circumstances require an invisible presence. He is no Watson MacDonough, Peter's former CIA keeper, no veteran spy from the Cold War, but Jeremy Pritchard can work magic.

Peter smiles. "Always good to see you, Jeremy, but I'm a little surprised by the in-person visit."

"Too many layers of deception here. We have to make sure we get this right. If we blow it… we could easily be in prison or dead." Jeremy looks directly at Peter. "You do plan on continuing to work with me, correct?"

"You mean, do I intend to sign the termination of my contract?" Peter shakes his head. "Not yet."

"Why keep going?"

"Not easy to quit."

"I don't think that's the real reason."

Peter shrugs. "I have some personal issues to deal with, and until I do that, leaving is its own risk."

"And those issues are?" Jeremy asks.

Peter ignores the question. "I'm asking a lawyer in DC to negotiate some of the details of my departure from the CIA."

"What's his name?"

"Jack Mitchoff."

Jeremy grimaces. "That'll take a while."

"That's part of the idea," Peter says. "Who should he talk to at the CIA?"

"Tell him to talk to me."

"You do have to understand that this will be my last rodeo. After this job in Peru, one way or another, I'm done."

"And what will you do when you're finished?"

"Finished? I don't like that word. I'm not sure yet. Disappear? Maybe I'll become a farmer. Good honest work, that."

"Let's see if I remember," Jeremy says. "'... and they shall beat their swords into plowshares, and their spears into pruning hooks... neither shall they learn war anymore.' When you produce your first great wine, let me know."

Peter laughs. "I'll have a better chance of having a good crop of hay."

Jeremy cocks his head to the left. "Somehow, I don't think you're a man content to grow hay. Anyway, I'll do what I can to help you, if you want to disappear. The rest is up to you." He smiles before he continues. "Now, let's talk about Peru."

"Let's."

"As black operations go, this is as black as it gets. It's on nobody's official book in the CIA. No one but you and I can know about it, not even the Director. As far as the CIA is concerned, this is an operation that does not exist. This discussion we are about to have will never exist. You cannot contact anyone in the CIA other than me about any aspect of your Peruvian adventures. Period."

"Oh, goody. I'm getting less enthusiastic by the minute."

"I don't think you should be," Jeremy says. "Aside from sorting out Cerro Nublado, this should provide a good avenue for you to depart cleanly and completely. But you have to understand something from me. I am in an untenable position. I can offer no overt support."

"Great."

"I will, however, be in close communication with Sir Richard Purcell of MI6. He's your main contact for Peru, and he's your conduit to me." Jeremy pushes a sheet of paper across the table to Peter. "Here are Sir Richard's contacts. You should not call me directly unless it is an impossible situation, and you can't reach Sir Richard."

Peter tucks the sheet of paper into his backpack. "I assume, then, that Wisser and his mob know nothing about this exercise?"

"I sure as hell hope that's the case."

"Me, too," Peter says.

Jeremy grunts. "Between Sir Richard and myself, we should be able to provide any backup assistance you may need, Sir Richard more directly than I can. If we're careful enough, you shouldn't need any assistance with regard to Cerro Nublado."

"Fair enough," Peter says. "We have to convince the Russians that I'm not working for the CIA anymore. They have to convince Minera Russo-Perú of that. All that's part of the reason to involve Mitchoff. At the same time, I don't want to burn any connections, particularly to you, until I'm back from Peru."

"Tell Mitchoff to take his time. That shouldn't be a problem for him. You and Alden, and presumably Sir Richard, are working on convincing the Russians that you're no longer working for the CIA. Right?"

"Right."

"Good. Now, Peter, talk to me about Peru. How are you going to make this work?"

Peter and Jeremy talk for the next twenty minutes, quickly sorting through the obvious pieces and parts, and setting up encrypted and deniable communications procedures. If he feels it is needed, Peter can use a code name for himself, Robert Steinbauer. The project code name will be Point Clovis.

When they reach a basic understanding, Jeremy says. "There is one other thing."

"What's that?" Peter asks. "I'm almost afraid to ask."

Jeremy pulls a photograph out of his jacket pocket and lays it on the table. It shows a middle-aged man, slightly portly, dressed in khaki pants and a light brown, short-sleeved shirt. "This is a guy from Colombia. He works for the drug lords. Mostly, he's the buyer for coca for an area that includes Cerro Nublado, and he is one ruthless son of a bitch. He goes by the nickname of El Come Huevos."

"Egg Eater. How nice," Peter says. "I suppose it's not chicken eggs?"

"Uh, no. You can only see a portion of both of his known tattoos." Jeremy points with a pencil. "One, here on the right side of his neck, is an eagle in flight. The other is on his upper left arm, on the outside. It reads 'El Come Huevos', appropriately enough."

Peter grimaces. "I hope I don't get close enough to use them for identification."

"They might be useful to confirm identity once he's dead," Jeremy says. "He's tortured and killed a couple of undercover drug enforcement people. If you encounter him, and bring him in, dead or alive as the old saying goes, or provide adequate proof of his death, there's a nice payment waiting for you. Ten million, US dollars, to be exact."

"Well, nice to know he's in the area, but I think that's a commission I'd prefer to avoid."

"He's a player you should be aware of," Jeremy says. "He may be working with the Russian owners of Cerro Nublado these days. Hopefully, you won't encounter him."

"Hopefully," Peter says. "I asked about a high-level contact in the Peruvian military. You have anything on that?"

"I'm afraid we can't help you on that matter. Maybe Sir Richard?"

"Really? You have no contacts?"

"We have contacts, but the reliable officers don't want to work with us, and we don't want to work with the unreliable ones. MI6 may have some better connections. I don't know. Probably best to avoid any dependence on the Peruvian military in this exercise."

"Okay. I'll see what Sir Richard has to say on the subject."

"Anyway, as you fill out your plan, please keep me informed."

"How do you explain this meeting?" Peter asks.

"Oh, that's easy. I've been discussing how you're going to leave, and trying to dissuade you from employing Jack Mitchoff. I met with failure." Jeremy smiles. "So, have a good day."

They stand, and Jeremy reaches across the table to shake Peter's hand.

"Give me a minute or two before you press the call button." He holds Peter's hand a little longer than Peter expects. "Enjoy your geological detective work. I'll be interested to learn what you discover."

"Me, too."

CHAPTER 9

As Jeremy turns and leaves the room, Peter looks down at the picture of El Come Huevos.

True evil. What crazy bunch of devils created you?

He's known too many men like this one. With a sigh, he carefully puts the photograph into his backpack and pushes the call button.

Moments later he's on the street. Peter briefly studies the crowd waiting at the entrance, and he looks at his watch. Quarter to two. He grabs a cab and heads to Patrick's office on the thirty-first floor of the BMO building at King and Bay. It's almost exactly two when he speaks with the receptionist at the law offices.

"I'm Peter Binder, to see Patrick Balakrishnan."

"Oh, yes, Mr. Binder. Nice to see you again. He's expecting you. He's still in the same place, and you know the way."

"Yes, thanks."

Peter turns and walks down the hallway to his left, turns the corner, and comes to Patrick's office. The door is open, and he knocks lightly on the doorjamb.

Patrick stands up. "Peter. Come in." He indicates a chair. "Have a seat. Do we need to shut the door?"

"Yeah, I think so," Peter says and pulls the door shut.

"It will be a day or two before we have the documents for the wife and son of the slain policeman. But what can I do for you today?"

Peter hands Patrick an envelope from his backpack. "There are two items there. You don't need to look at them right now." Peter takes a deep breath. "I never told you the details of my departure from the SEALs."

"No. And I didn't ask."

"And I appreciate that," Peter says. "The military accused me of some pretty awful stuff. To my surprise, they let me go with an honorable discharge, so long as I agreed to work for the CIA. They kind of... held me prisoner. One document in there absolves me of all those crimes. The other is a separation agreement with the CIA. I don't want to sign it. Not right now."

"Why not?"

"It's a little complicated. First of all, I may need their help in a job I'm taking on, not really for the CIA, but... in some ways, it is for them."

"You're still working for them?"

"Sort of, but we don't need to go there," Peter answers. "The real reason I don't want to sign right now is that they offer no apology. They offer a million-dollar severance, as long as I don't litigate and keep everything confidential. For what they've done to my life in the last few years, I want either a clear apology, or a large enough payment that it hurts a little more than one million dollars. The larger payment is probably the easier course of action."

"What do you want me to do? This is a little out of my wheelhouse."

"I want you to talk to a lawyer named Jack Mitchoff in Washington, DC, with the law firm of Mitchoff, Barnes, and Blackwood. He's supposed to know how to handle something like this. Do a little investigating. Make sure you think he's the person for the job."

"I can do that," Patrick says as he notes the names.

"If you think he's the right guy to handle this," Peter continues, "give him a copy of these two reports. Explain what I want. Keep this all very confidential."

"Naturally. When do you want his detailed comments on the best approach to all this?"

"Probably a couple of months from now." Peter shrugs. "I have some business to attend to, and I won't be able to devote much, if any, time to this before then."

"So... plenty of time. Anything else you need from me?"

"There is," Peter says. "I'm going to be signing a consulting contract with a little junior company in London, run by an Australian. I'm going to try to use my standard contract, using Canadian law as the reference point, with any litigation based here in Canada, but I'm not sure that'll fly. Can you, or one of the other lawyers, call on some British contacts to make sure any contract I might sign will work for both British and Canadian law?"

"I don't do contract law, but we have plenty of people here who can handle this. Shouldn't be tough. How soon do you need this?"

"A couple of days. Is that possible?"

"I think so. Email me your most recent form contract, and I'll work from there. What you're asking for from Mitchoff isn't going to come cheap, you know. Those DC attorneys know how to charge for their services."

"I know. See if you can get a rough estimate for both matters. I don't need anything more than that."

Peter zips up his backpack. "That's all I need for now, Patrick. How's your wife and family? Haven't seen them for a while. I think you have one more kid since the last time, don't you?"

"Yes." Patrick laughs. "My wife swears it's the last one. She says six is enough, and it probably should be. I don't suppose you could come to dinner tonight? She'd love to see you, and Maria."

"Oh, man, that is tempting. Maria and I are on the outs at the moment. I'd love to, but I should get back north. The weather is supposed to get ugly tonight, and I don't want to be flying back to the cabin in a snowstorm."

"Oh, that's right. You have that crazy helicopter now." Patrick shakes his head. "I think you're nuts. And what's this about you and Maria?"

"I'm not entirely sure. It all started when I suggested that I might take on a job in Peru. She thinks I'm getting too old to be battling international terrorists, that I should dial it down a bit. As far as I can tell, though, this job looks to be a simple geological exercise."

"Your jobs are never simple," Patrick says. "You should listen to Maria, and maybe stop flying that helicopter, too."

"Don't think that will happen right away. Anyway, it's better than a motorcycle this time of year."

Laughing, Patrick says, "Yeah. Well, maybe you ought to sell the motorcycle, too."

"I'm not in a rocking chair yet, Patrick."

They chat for a few more minutes before Peter stands up to leave. He is not one to happily pay hourly legal charges for too much small talk.

"I'll be in touch on these two matters," Peter says. "I should have email contact most of the time while I'm away, but nothing's guaranteed. You should assume that any connection I will have is at least semi-public, and not appropriate for sensitive information."

"I'll let you know the basics, but I won't send anything detailed. We should leave that for a face-to-face meeting, I think."

"You're right," Peter says. They shake hands, and Peter finds his own way out of the office.

Once on the street, he decides to walk to the airport. He heads down Bay Street to Queens Quay and turns west along the water. He takes his time, taking the walkways through the little parks and along the shore where he can.

He is about half-way to the airport, on a deserted sidewalk by one of the small, snow-covered parks. He realizes that two men in ski masks are stalking him.

"Dammit!" he mutters. *Peter Binder, you're getting blind, dumb, and lazy.*

At a turn in the pathway, he sits down on a bench and assesses the two.

They stop and eye him in a jerky, nervous fashion. On first examination, Peter doesn't think they look too impressive.

Goddamn mugging. Just what I need. Probably high on something. Then he catches himself. *Don't be stupid.*

Peter isn't sure, but even without seeing their faces, he thinks he may have seen them earlier.

At the consulate? In the line? Maybe.

Without a weapon, Peter looks around and searches for an advantage. He decides the two stalkers most likely have knives, but no gun. He's close to the corner of a building.

I'll give them a choice, he thinks. *They can give it up, or come after me.*

He stands up and looks at the two men. They stare back and begin to move toward him. They are a little less than fifty feet from him, when Peter turns abruptly and runs around the corner of the building.

He flattens himself against the wall of the building. He can hear the pounding of their shoes as they race to catch him.

The first one runs around the corner. He holds a double-edged, stiletto knife in his right hand.

"Hey!" Peter yells, as loudly as he can.

The shout startles the man. He tries to stop, but he's off balance.

Peter kicks him in the balls. He goes down with a grunt. As he falls, he stabs himself in the ribs, about half-way up his right side. He is surprisingly quiet.

Peter doesn't have the time to be amused by the man's determination to kill himself, before the second man races around the corner at full speed. He tries to slash Peter with a hunting knife, but Peter steps back, out of his reach.

The man trips over the legs of his companion, and he heads to the pavement, face first.

Peter jumps and lands hard on the man's back, with his right foot just above his hips.

The fallen man screams.

Peter bends down and, with his gloved hand, picks up the man's knife.

The first man has overcome his silence. "I'm fucking dying," he shouts. He keeps shouting. He turns over on his back. His own knife sticks out from the side of his chest. He tries to kick Peter's legs out from under him.

Peter stamps on the man's left knee.

The man screams.

Peter reaches down and yanks the knife out of his side.

"You're not dying, you dumb ass. Now shut up."

He continues to scream and shout obscenities.

Peter kicks him in the head. A loud crack. The man is silent. Still breathing, but silent.

Peter looks down at the two men. He takes a couple of deep, slow breaths to calm himself. He drops the knives into a pocket in his jacket and pulls out his cell phone. A few people are starting to gather nearby, drawn by the shouting and screaming.

Removing his glove, Peter calls Bill Branch, his contact with the Ontario Provincial Police.

"Hello, Peter. Nothing urgent, I hope."

"Bill, I'm down on the south side of Queens Quay, in a little park walkway, a bit west of Bay Street. A couple of punks tried to mug me. They're in pretty bad shape. Can you get someone down here, along with an ambulance?"

"Okay. I'll call the locals, and I'll get there myself as quick as I can. What did you do to them?"

"I broke one guy's back. The other one stabbed himself as he went down. I think I broke his right knee. Maybe his jaw."

"Jesus! You're a chore, man. I'll get you out of there. The officer responding will know that I'm coming to deal with you."

"I'll be here."

"I should hope so."

Both men are still yelling. Peter can't understand the first one. He's holding his jaw with one hand. The second one keeps yelling that he can't move his legs.

"Shut up! The ambulance is on its way, along with the cops. You'll get more attention than you want." Neither man stops yelling.

Peter stands beside the head of the first man. The man tries to grab Peter's legs.

Peter jumps back and aims another solid kick to the man's head. He passes out again.

The growing crowd edges closer. They are clearly sympathizing with the two men on the ground.

Peter can already hear sirens.

He shouts to the crowd, "Someone please flag down the cops and the ambulance when they arrive."

The crowd hesitates and pulls back a bit. Someone runs back to the street.

Taking advantage of the momentary lull, Peter pulls off the unconscious man's belt and uses it to tie his hands together. Then he ties his bootlaces together. Peter doesn't think the second attacker is in any shape to get up and run away.

Reaching down, Peter pulls the ski mask off the unconscious man's head. He raises his eyebrows.

Why am I not surprised?

Peter steps over and does the same with the second attacker.

On closer inspection, neither man is a skinny, hopped up punk. They both look more like hardened criminals, perhaps in their thirties.

Professional hitmen? Pretending to be punks?

Peter can hear the police come to a stop on the street. Six cop cars quickly coalesce on the side of Queen's Quay, followed by two ambulances.

Peter puts his hands on the top of his head as four police officers, three men and one woman, jog over to him. They all appear to be Toronto Police.

The first one stops in front of Peter. "You Mr. Binder?"

"Yes, sir," Peter replies, keeping his hands on the top of his head.

"You can put your hands down, Mr. Binder. I'm Superintendent Petersen. Please stand against the wall until Commissioner William Branch of the OPP arrives."

"I have the two knives I took from them in my pocket," Peter says.

"Perhaps you could hand them to me?" Petersen says.

Peter reaches into his pocket with his gloved hand and slowly withdraws the two knives. He hands them to the officer handle first. "The one with the chest wound fell on his own knife, the little stiletto."

Peter watches as the paramedics begin their work on the two men. He keeps his mouth shut. The two men still yell and swear loudly, and the man with the broken jaw is a little more intelligible now. He loudly accuses Peter of attacking them. The police handcuff the two men and let the paramedics attend to them.

Some in the crowd angrily accuse Peter of attacking the two men and loudly insist on telling the police their version of the incident.

After about ten minutes, Peter sees Bill Branch arrive. Bill talks to Petersen for a couple of minutes, before he comes up to Peter.

Bill shakes his head. "You're supposed to behave yourself when you come to Toronto."

"I was. My mistake was to walk from my lawyer's office to Billy Bishop airport. I think I saw these two earlier, at the US consulate, but I didn't realize they were stalking me until just before this happened."

"Willing to give me a statement?"

"Sure. It's pretty simple," Peter says.

Bill Branch records a quick statement as Peter describes the attack. He points to a few locations. One of the other officers quickly marks them.

"At first I thought it might be a couple of hopped-up punks, but... I don't think so."

"Any idea as to who they might be?" Bill Branch asks.

"Not really, but I'd start with the assumption that they might be from the US."

"Any reason for that?"

"Mostly their vocabulary. They swear like Americans."

"That's it?" Bill asks.

"It's a guess, but that's about it," Peter says. "They look like professionals to me, and I'd love to know the name of their employer."

"I don't know," Bill says. "We've got some pretty hard-ass muggers around here."

Peter looks at the two men. "I don't think so."

Bill sighs. "You may be right. I assume you're headed back to the cabin?"

"That was the plan."

"Okay. I have your preliminary statement. I'll take you to the airport, and you can fly home. Let me know if you plan to leave the cabin, particularly if you plan on leaving the country. Okay?"

"That's fine by me. I'm probably stuck there with the storm for two or three days anyway. My communications might suffer a bit."

"Well," Bill says. "We'll be in touch if we need anything, one way or another."

Bill drops Peter off at StolPort.

Peter sits in the helicopter for a few minutes, doing nothing. He focuses on calming down. The adrenalin rush is largely gone, and he shuts his eyes. Eventually, he starts the helicopter and calls air traffic for permission to depart. As soon as he receives clearance, he takes off.

Because of the attack, he departs Toronto later than he planned, and he approaches his cabin with only the bare remnants of twilight remaining. He turns on his landing light to help in flight orientation.

A few flakes of snow are already falling, the first sign of the incoming storm, and they are beginning to reduce visibility. Peter cannot see the lights on the helipad, or the floodlights on the front of the cabin until he is less than a mile away. "Cutting it a bit close tonight," he says to himself.

After he lands, he ties down the main rotors and puts the covers on the helicopter. He also ties the skids to the recessed hooks in the helipad. He will take no chances with the incoming storm.

Need to get groceries.

He gets his truck out of the garage for a quick trip to the little grocery store in town. He has barely enough time before it closes. By the time he gets back to the cabin, puts the groceries away, and closes up the garage, there are already two inches of fresh snow on the ground. The sound of the wind begins to rise to a low howl. He carries in a large pile of wood for the stove.

"All set for a long winter's night," he says.

He locks and secures the cabin door with the metal bars, but he leaves the metal shutters open. *Close them when I go to bed*, he thinks. He begins to take off his parka, but he looks at the broken panes in the front window. The quick fix of taped-on plastic bags is still in place, but with the rising wind they won't last. *Have to do better than that.* The wind also whistles into the cabin through a few bullet holes adjacent to the door.

He unlocks the door, and walks through the blowing snow to the garage. He returns with several small sheets of quarter-inch plywood, a circular saw, a few small nails, and a hammer. He rummages around in a cabinet below the sink and digs out a caulking gun and a tube of caulk. He pumps some caulk into the bullet holes. He listens and runs his hand over the wall beside the door. He finds another hole and fills that.

He cuts several pieces of plywood to size and nails them over the window panes. *Good enough for now.* It is much quieter, and it does a good job of keeping out the cold. He cleans up the sawdust and leaves the tools and the leftover plywood beside the door. Then he secures the door again for the night.

The storm has knocked out his internet connections to the outside world. Even the radio connections to the warning systems at the gates are weak and unreliable due to the heavy snow. He is cut off from the world. He is alone. He has everything he needs.

He sits at the table and pours himself a large drink of Ardbeg and listens to the wind moaning and whistling around the corners of the cabin. He has spent a lot of time at the cabin in the winter, and he knows, no matter how ferocious the weather might be, with a little care and maintenance the log cabin will stand firm, unbothered. Somehow, the storm seems appropriate.

He thinks about Alden and his gifts.

Freedom. At a price.

He thinks about Maria. He shuts his eyes. All he feels is loss and pain.

Peru. Peru will resolve this relationship. Somehow. He doesn't know how, but he knows it will.

He thinks about Jeremy and Sir Richard.

Getting too complicated. Jeremy's written me off, but Sir Richard? Sir Richard is still an unknown.

Then Peter focuses on the two men who attacked him along the shore of the lake in Toronto.

Is it old news? Is it Peru? It seems too early to be Peru. But…

He gulps down the remaining Ardbeg and slams the glass down on the table. The sound echoes in the empty room.

"Christ almighty!" he says aloud. "What the hell is going on?"

CHAPTER 10

Peter awakens from a restless night. The noise of the wind did not bother him, but the events of the attack in Toronto kept running through his mind and inhabited his dreams. The more he thinks about it, the more convinced he is that somehow this attack relates to Peru.

Not good that someone knows about it so soon.

Through bitter disappointment, Peter has learned to trust almost no one, not even his friends and lovers. Now, if he wants his freedom, if he wants what he believes Peru will bring him, he knows he must trust only himself. Peter doesn't want to get out of bed and face the day of decisions.

The room is frigid. He throws back the covers and jumps onto the floor. He feels like his body contracts and shrinks. He grabs his clothes and dresses as quickly as he can. When he gets his boots on, he stands up and still shivers.

The hallway and bathroom are both warm to prevent frozen pipes. He forgoes the shower.

No need to impress anyone today.

In the main living area, he crumples up some newspaper, throws in some kindling and a few small logs, and starts the fire in the stove. He makes the morning coffee.

The wind has died down as the worst of the storm moves on, leaving more than two feet of snow. Snow still falls with small flakes that do not hold the promise of a quick ending. He looks at the thermometer. Minus 22 degrees. He puts on his parka and gloves, grabs a broom, and goes out to sweep the snow off the satellite dish.

Once back inside, he throws three more logs on the fire in the stove. He pours himself a cup of coffee and sits down at his desk.

He checks the video cameras at the gates. All he sees is trackless snow. He checks his email. Twenty-five new messages scroll up.

"Christ!"

He checks down the list, deleting most of them. Nothing from Maria. That surprises him a little. One from Bill Branch. He opens it.

Peter,

You were right. US. They made one call to an unlisted number in Washington, DC. A couple of heavy-duty lawyers popped up, demanding their immediate return to the US. Not likely to happen.

Call me.

Bill Branch

Peter reads it again.

Interesting. Is the US government attacking me?

Peter walks over to the kitchen. He pours himself another cup of coffee and puts a frying pan on the stove. He cooks his simple breakfast and sits down to eat.

What do I do next?

He eats his breakfast slowly and looks out the window, through the snow. The helicopter at the end of the dock looks like a giant, frosted Easter egg. Peter smiles. *That'll take a bit of work to clear off.* No need to do it today, though. He has no place to go. Not yet.

When he finishes his breakfast, he heads back to his desk. He finds the contacts for Sir Richard, and he looks at his watch. Early afternoon in London, on Saturday. He picks up the VoIP phone and calls Sir Richard's cell phone. The phone rings six times before it goes to messaging. There is no identification of the person or number.

"Please leave a message."

"Point Clovis. Robert Steinbauer." Peter gives his phone number and hangs up.

Peter sits back and waits. It's less than two minutes before his phone rings.

"Yes."

"Steinbauer?"

"Yes."

"Richard Purcell here. Glad you called. Wasn't sure how to connect with you. You realize you created a bit of an international incident in Toronto?"

"You know who they are?"

"Not entirely sure," Sir Richard says. "Nobody's claiming them. On the face of it they appear to be hitmen, but we don't know who's paying them. Someone in Washington? Probably unofficial, but maybe peripheral to the White House?"

"That's not much to go on."

"Well, we do know it's someone who really doesn't like you, or what you've done, or what you're planning to do. A long and varied list, I suspect."

"You think it's old stuff, or Point Clovis?"

"I think," Sir Richard says flatly, "for planning purposes, we must assume it's Point Clovis."

"If you're right, I need to ramp up my security… a lot. Can you help me on that?"

"Yes… But I think it's best if we stay in the shadows. You need to use some private group as your main, or visible, security."

"Well, I can use On Guard Security here in Toronto. I recently looked up La Seguridad Ejecutiva Peruana, a Peruvian group. They looked okay, but that's all I know. I won't be able to charge all of that to Mandrake. My lawyer is drafting a contract with Mandrake, but I need something from you. Will you cover the extra security costs?"

"Yes."

"Please send me some sort of agreement for my relationship with your group. And can you give me some feedback on Seguridad Ejecutiva?"

"I'll check on them," Sir Richard says. "Have you made any plans yet?"

"Hell no. I was a little preoccupied yesterday. I plan on calling Julius Grant of Mandrake today. I also need to check with a few of my contacts on the status of Cerro Nublado. I haven't heard of much activity there in the last year or so. I suspect it may be waiting for a good reason to blow up again."

"I'll check on Seguridad Ejecutiva and get back to you. We'll plan on backing up your security in Peru, but we'll stay in the shadows as much as possible."

"Thanks," Peter says. "I would like to meet you before I head to Peru. Do I have to come to London?"

"Actually, no. I'll be in Ottawa on Wednesday. We could meet there, or we could meet in Toronto that evening. We have a house we can use in the York Mills area."

"Toronto's easier for me. What time?"

"Let's plan on six." He gives Peter the address.

"Good. I'll have to arrange for a room overnight and some security. I need to talk with Maria Davidoff anyway."

"And what is her status?"

"Good question. I have no idea."

"Plan on dinner with me at the house. I'll set you up with a room there. Easier, and it will give us plenty of time to talk."

"I should have my plans more or less in place by the time we meet."

"Talk to you then."

After the call, Peter sits back in his chair and closes his eyes to think. He sits up again and begins a list of people he needs to contact.

Carlos Bellido is the Peruvian geologist who discovered Cerro Nublado. He and Peter worked together briefly, and they have remained good friends. Tall and light-skinned, Carlos maneuvers easily with the powerful families of Lima, but his practical and empathetic approach to life allows him to work effectively in the tiny communities of rural Peru.

Henry Nomas, a Canadian geologist living in British Columbia, has a lot of experience in Peru. Though he stands out in Peru, with his pale skin and light blond hair, his fluent Spanish has helped him work well in Peru. Peter smiles as he remembers the story of villagers chasing Henry out of town, mistaking him for a mythological and evil albino spirit.

John Webster is an investment banker, also located in Vancouver. He helped raise money for Mandrake. Before he was a banker, John worked as an exploration geologist. Now a buttoned-down banker, he is capable of evaluating projects and companies on a technical as well as a financial basis.

Finally, Peter adds Julius Grant, CEO of Mandrake Minerals, to the list. Julius is a self-confident, garrulous, out-going Australian. He currently calls Brisbane home, but he's constantly on the move, raising money and looking for new projects for Mandrake. He's always the life of any party, and never turns down an invitation. In spite of his self-confidence, he is a careful evaluator of risk and is no fool. He is always willing to take on difficult projects, turned down by many others, but only if he determines that the potential reward is worth the obvious risks. Some would say he tends to overstate the potential of a property, but his views usually turn out to be correct. He shovels off the risk to his investors, and his decisions almost always make his investors happy at the end of the day.

By noon he has completed calls to everyone but Julius Grant. He sits back to review his notes and consider what he's learned.

"As far as I'm concerned, the Russo-Perú bunch is as dumb as a fence post," Henry says. "They think they can walk in there, buy a few governmental officials, maybe a few elected officials, and get what they want. Won't work."

"Why not? It's happened before," Peter says.

"Sure, and it will again. But how much money does it take to buy the Catholic Church, a big chunk of the coca production, and transportation for the Colombian cocaine sales into the United States? In this game, I'll bet the Narcos have more money than the Russians."

"The Russian company does seem to be super eager to put Cerro Nublado into production. Like right now."

"Yeah," Henry says. "That does seem to be the case, and I do not understand that at all. It's nothing more than a copper mine, for God's sake. Russia has pretty good copper production of its own. If they want to develop something outside of their country, there are a lot of other targets with less drama and resistance."

"That's a bit of a puzzle," Peter says.

"Why are you interested in Cerro Nublado anyway?"

"I've been asked to complete a review of the property."

"You mean," Henry asks, "someone wants to buy it off Russo-Perú?"

"Maybe."

"Good luck to them! And to you, too! It's a freakin' mess. If you want to know just how bad it got… You remember Mary Marlowe?"

"I've met her a couple of times. She still in the community relations business?"

"I think she's retired, but she was working on Cerro Nublado. Someone kidnapped her and her team. I don't know who it was, maybe the old Sendero, acting as security for the Narcos. Maybe the local *ronderos*, the local militia that Fujimori first armed. Who knows? They roughed up the men on her team pretty badly. She could give you a good accounting of the players there, when things started to go sour. You have her number?"

"I do. Thanks."

"Give her a call, then. She can give you an ear-full if she's willing to talk about it."

Peter thinks about Mary, born in France, cultured, and smart as any woman he knows. To his knowledge she speaks at least four languages, has a doctorate in anthropology, and has an uncanny ability to understand human relations and resolve complicated conflicts. He calls Mary, but she doesn't want to talk about her experiences in the community relations efforts at Cerro Nublado, or any other aspect of the project. He doesn't blame her. Her memories are still too sharp, too painful. Peter knows a lot about those sorts of memories, and he wishes her well.

John Webster is blunt and to the point, as always. "The Russians are crazy. Who the hell will give them money to develop that property? No one I know of. No one in their right mind."

"Russo-Perú has plenty of money themselves," Peter says. "They have the backing of the Kremlin. They don't need bankers like you."

"If that's the case, they ought to know better," John says. "I don't know what they think they're doing, but neither you nor I will see that project developed in our lifetimes. Too much money. Too much risk. It's a copper mine, and it's not all that high grade. It's a long-term payback in a high technical, security, and permitting risk environment. I tell you; it's going to be an orphan project. In the end, nobody'll want it, not even the dumb-ass Russians."

"I'm not so sure Russo-Perú is as dumb as you seem to think they are."

"Well, can you give me one good reason they'd want to develop this project?"

"Nope. At least not yet."

"It's all bullshit, Peter. All bullshit."

His call with Carlos surprises him. Peter had expected the same rant about the dumb Russians, and the impossibility of developing the project any time in the next twenty or thirty years.

Carlos, it turns out, has a very different take on the situation. Besides that, Carlos' reaction to hearing from Peter is a surprise. Actually, it's not a complete surprise.

"Peter! It's good to hear from you my friend. I heard you were dead," Carlos says.

"I'm very much alive."

"I am so happy!"

Peter laughs. "So am I. The reason I called is that I want to talk to you about Cerro Nublado."

"Ah! An unhappy project. Very messy situation."

"I don't see how anyone can develop the mine," Peter begins. "I mean, there are so many forces arrayed against it. The communities. The NGOs. The environmental activists. Even the Catholic Church and the Narco traffickers. They may be strange bedfellows, but, as long as they're on the same side, they present an overwhelming opposition."

"Sure," Carlos replies, "and it's high risk on many, many fronts. But, let me tell you, Minera Russo-Perú really wants Cerro Nublado in production. I think people underestimate them. There's something at Cerro Nublado that they desperately want."

"Okay," Peter says. "It's a very large, but relatively low-grade copper deposit. It's a huge capital investment, with a long time to payout. It has gigantic technical, permitting, community, and environmental risks. It makes no sense that they want to fast track the thing into production, and that they actually seem to think they can."

"There's a reason, Peter. We're not smart enough to see it. And people forget one thing. This is Peru. This is poor, rural Peru. Money can be very persuasive, and there's a lot of money sloshing around in the communities close to Cerro Nublado. The coca trade. The Russians. The NGOs. Even the government. Maybe even the church. I don't know, but money can buy many things, even an NGO or two, a few judges, a whole host of politicians. Properly applied, it can certainly help acquire needed permits."

"But still," Peter says, "you have the money of the narcotics, the coca trade, in opposition."

"Peter, you know as well as I do, enough money can buy off even the coca trade. With backing from the Russian government, Russo-Perú might have enough money even for that. It won't surprise me if they don't already own the coca trade in that part of Peru. And what does that mean? Who do those old, hard-ass, Sendero veterans work for now? And the *ronderos*? Do they all work for Russo-Perú now? What does that mean for the future of the project?"

"Does it mean that the property actually can go into production?" Peter asks.

"Maybe. I'm not sure. If they succeed and develop the mine, it will be one ugly, nasty, and possibly bloody scene," Carlos says. "Why are you so interested in Cerro Nublado anyway?"

"Someone asked me to do a property review."

"You going to do it?"

"Maybe. Trying to decide," Peter says.

"Be very careful. It's quiet now, but it has been a very dangerous place. It could easily be so again."

"I won't be there long," Peter says. "I'll be in and out before anyone knows I'm there."

"When you come down to Peru, make sure you give me a call. I'll give you any updates I can. Either coming or going, we should have a nice dinner. You can come to the house, or we can meet somewhere."

"Thanks, Carlos. I'll call when I get in."

"Watch your ass on this one, Peter. There are some powerful forces at work at Cerro Nublado, and a whole heap of money. Get in the way of the Russians, and they'll chew you up and spit you out, without even a hiccup."

"Yeah. I know."

Peter sits back and thinks about the results of his calls.

I think the Russians just want a copper deposit in Peru. They want to be international players with mineral production in South America. They think they can throw their weight and money around and bully their way to production. It's that simple, and they're probably right.

As he gets up to make lunch, he realizes that he hasn't called Bill Branch. He sits back down, punches in his number, and waits.

"Bill Branch here."

"Hi, Bill. Peter Binder. You asked me to call."

"You saw my email?"

"Yeah. They some kind of hitmen from the US?"

"That's the current consensus. The Prime Minister is not happy."

"Not surprising," Peter says.

"We're getting all sorts of legal action to repatriate them. Complaints that they were innocent victims of a vicious attack. They're not going anywhere. The doctors think they can patch them up. The guy with the broken back has a good chance of walking again, though probably not very well."

"I think I overreacted. I should have been a little less violent with them."

"Peter, they were trying to knife you. They're lucky to be alive."

"I haven't looked at the news today. Is this all over the newspapers? Do they identify me by name?"

"Yes, it's in the newspapers and on the news networks, and no, you won't be identified. What do you think this is about?"

"Hard to say. There are lots of people in the US who don't think kindly of me. It isn't clearly official, like CIA operatives, is it?"

"No indication of that... yet," Bill says.

"You know what I'm getting into."

"You've agreed?"

"More or less," Peter replies. "Still negotiating the fine points. They're telling me to assume this was in response to this new exercise. I'm not so sure, but I'm ramping up my security. I'll be using On Guard Security in Toronto. Car service and a bodyguard or two when I think I need them."

"I was going to make a suggestion along those lines. We'll also be around, but you should have private security as your first line of defense. It'll at least make people think twice before they jump. Call me if you run into any trouble. And keep us informed of your movements, okay?"

"Anything you need from me? Like another statement?" Peter asks.

"No, but you may need to testify 'in camera' sometime in the future."

"For your information, I'm going to be in Toronto this Wednesday. I'll stay the night somewhere."

Bill is silent for a moment. "Things are getting a little nasty, Peter. Watch yourself. There are too many agendas at work here."

"Oh yeah. Like I said, I'm already hiring extra eyes and bodies."

"Call me with your visit details when you have them."

"Will do."

After the call, Peter sits back in his chair.

What's the possibility that Wisser and his crowd are the real mob behind these two punks?

"Someone wants me to retire early," he says. There is an advantage, he supposes, if it's the CIA. If that's the case, once he does retire, the risk should be over, or at least minimized.

"Possibly," he says. He doesn't think it was the CIA. Meanwhile, best to avoid the US as much as possible.

Maybe it's time to ask for a Canadian or United Kingdom passport, and maybe some other identity.

Peter shakes his head and almost laughs. He gets up and steps over to the kitchen to prepare his lunch. The snow is still falling. Another three inches has fallen since he got up in the morning. The storm is forecast to end in another hour or two.

"Got to plow around the cabin and out to the dock, at least," he says.

He's still thinking about what Carlos had to say about the security situation at Cerro Nublado. He has a lot of trust in Carlos' judgement.

He's so damned convinced.

CHAPTER 11

After lunch, Peter returns to his desk and calls Julius Grant. There's no answer, and Peter leaves a message.

Where the hell is he? If he's not home he's in Europe, Canada, or Peru.
Peter checks the time.
Good timing if he's anywhere but home in Brisbane, Australia.
If he's back home in Brisbane, Peter knows he won't get a call back for at least another six hours. The lack of an answer suggests he's in Brisbane.

Peter taps out an email to Maria.

Maria,

I'm coming to Toronto on business on Wednesday. You'll be happy to know that I'm making some progress on Peru. It really does look like a simple property review.

Alden brought a couple of gifts for me. As a result, I'm negotiating my departure from the CIA.

We should talk, and I need to pick up some decent clothes from the apartment. Could we meet somewhere around 3:00 PM on Wednesday? Mitch's Pub would be good. Maybe a corner table where we can talk relatively privately.

You want me to pick up my clothes before or after we talk?

Let me know.

Peter

He waits to see if there's a quick reply. There isn't. He's bored, and a little restless. The snow has stopped, along with the wind, and the sun is breaking through the clouds. He puts on his parka and gloves, starts his truck, and plows in front of the cabin and down to the dock. Even with the heavy snow, it's quick work.

Before he puts the truck back in the garage, he starts his snowmobile and parks it in front of the cabin. A black, Backcountry XRS Ski-Doo, it's perfect for the deep snow, and a quick trip into town in a nasty snowstorm.

He shovels the dock and the helipad and sweeps the snow off the helicopter. It's still cold, but the clouds are dissipating, and the sun feels good. He removes all the covers, main rotor tiedowns, and removes the ties from the skids to the helipad.

Might as well check it out. Not much else to do until I hear back from Julius.

He completes a ground inspection, gets in, and starts the helicopter. He takes his time, letting the helicopter warm up before he gingerly lifts off. As he leaves the helipad he stays close to the ground, to make sure that the helicopter behaves normally. He gains a bit of altitude and quickly flies his regular inspection circuit. Nothing but snow and a few animal tracks. No sign of his albino moose. He lands, satisfied that the helicopter is working properly, ties down the main rotors, and takes the covers into the cabin to dry them off.

The exercise to clear the snow felt good. He sits at his desk. Maria has sent a reply.

Peter,

Done. Back corner table. Mitch's. 3:00 PM. Wednesday. Clothes after.

Maria

Peter sighs. *Looks like our conversation could be a little short.*

He's feeling sad, which he understands. There is something else there, though, and he isn't sure yet that he knows its name.

It will be a few hours before he should call Julius again. He pulls his snowmobile outfit off the peg by the door, pulls it on, and zips it up. He goes out the door, locks up, starts the snowmobile, puts on his helmet, and heads down the lake to the fishing lodge. He wants to see the caretaker there and ask him to look in on the cabin while he's gone for most of February. John Williams is older than Peter's father and a veteran of Vietnam. His service left him a bit messed up. He and Peter have a lot in common.

The clouds have cleared, and the sun is shining brightly. Peter opens up the throttle of the big snowmobile, and it nearly flies down the relatively flat snow on the lake. He keeps close to the shore, where he would typically be on his skis. As much as seeing John, this trip is designed to pack the snow for his cross-country ski runs.

He turns off the lake onto the road to the fishing lodge. Hopefully, the lack of tracks in the snow on the road means that John hasn't left the lodge since the snow began. Peter accelerates again on the three-mile run to the lodge, pulls up to the main building, and shuts down. He pulls off his helmet, just as John appears at the front door.

"Hey, John. How are you doing?"

"All right, I guess."

"Well, you going to invite me in for coffee?" Peter asks.

"I guess so," he answers and disappears into the building.

Peter knows this is as cheerful and spontaneous an invitation as John will ever manage. He wades through the snow to the front porch, stamps the snow off his boots, and brushes the snow off his pants. Peter finds John in the kitchen, with the coffee pot already heating up.

John points at a plate of homemade muffins. "Have a muffin. Just made them. Chocolate chip."

Peter takes a muffin and sits down at the counter. "Had any visitors lately?"

"Nope. Heard you had quite the ruckus a few days ago." John looks at Peter. "Serious?"

"Fairly. Had a bunch of cops visiting later on."

"I noticed." John brings two cups to the counter and sits down opposite Peter. "You're crazier than I am," he says.

Peter laughs. "Probably."

"You gotta change your business, you know."

"Yeah, I know." Peter takes a sip of the strong, hot coffee. "To change the subject, have you ever seen a huge, albino bull moose around here?"

"Nope. You?"

"There's been one hanging around my place. We bow to each other."

John says nothing for a bit. "You know Vic, the skinny little Algonquin guide who works here?"

"I've met him."

"He'd call that 'big medicine'. He says they're spirits, sent to warn you of danger. Or… maybe a wonderful change."

Peter drinks about half the cup of coffee. "Damn, John. Can you make coffee any stronger?"

"You didn't ask for swamp water."

"How do you tell the difference?" Peter asks.

"What do you mean? Coffee and swamp water?"

"No," Peter laughs. "You tell me that Vic says the moose could be warning me about danger or opportunity. How do I tell the difference?"

"Might be both."

"So it might." Peter puts his cup down. "At least I'm wide awake now. You'll be around in February?"

"Yep."

"I expect to take off around February second for most of the month. You willing to look in on the cabin while I'm gone?"

"Of course."

"I'll be back late in the month," Peter says. "I don't want to winterize it, so I'll leave the furnace on at about fifty-five degrees."

"I'll check in once a day."

"I'll be by with the key before I leave."

"How's Maria?"

"Mad as hell. She split back to Toronto."

John frowns. "Maybe that's what the moose is about."

"Could be."

"Good or bad?" John asks.

"Maybe both? Hard to tell."

John Williams says nothing. He just shakes his head and smiles.

Peter runs the snowmobile back up the lake in the same tracks he had just made coming down to see John. He thinks about the moose, Maria, and Peru.

"Hocus pocus garbage," he says, regarding the moose, but he isn't sure he believes that either.

When he gets close to the dock, he pulls off the lake into a swampy area of stunted trees. With some difficulty, he manages to connect with the trail that parallels the long driveway. He uses the snowmobile to pack down the snow to make it easier when he's on his skis. At the gate nearest the road, he turns around and runs the snowmobile back to the cabin. By the time he gets there, the sun is quite low on the horizon.

In the cabin, he strips off the snowmobile suit and helmet, and sits down at his desk and begins work on one of several lists for his project in Peru. He doesn't need much field gear for this job. His jungle clothes and boots, the basic geological tools of hammer, hand lens magnifier, notebooks, recorder, camera, sample bags, and a few simple tools for mineral identification.

Peter looks at the calendar. It's Saturday, January 23. The timing is ideal for field work in Peru.

I'll need three or four days to review all the critical reports properly.

He also has to decide on which drill holes to examine and sample, and which outcrops, if any. He sketches out a schedule.

First, the review of the critical reports, starting on Sunday, January 24. Head down to Peru twelve days later on Friday, February 5. Spend the weekend in Lima. Five days in the camp. Back to Toronto on February 17. One or two weeks for assay results. Deliver the report the end of February or early March to Sir Richard and Julius Grant. Altogether, start to finish, it's about a full month of his time.

It won't be cheap for Mandrake Minerals. All in, his estimate is $35,000.

He looks at his watch, 4:15 PM. Still a little early in Brisbane, but time to try Julius again.

"Hello?" Julius sounds as if the phone call woke him up.

"Julius. Peter Binder. If this is too early, I can call back later."

"Peter! Yes. Glad you're calling, but I had a long night. Give me a couple of hours."

"Sure. I'll call you back in two or three hours."

"Thanks. I appreciate that."

"Talk to you then," Peter says.

Peter quickly covers the helicopter for the night and returns to his desk to work on planning for Peru. He finds that he can take AeroMexico, with a long layover in Mexico City, and avoid any stops in the United States.

After an early supper, at a little after 6:00 PM he calls Julius again.

"Hello, Peter. Much more civilized hour."

"Must have been quite a party last night."

"We aren't all monks, you know," Julius says. "Did you talk with Alden Sage?"

"Yes, and I'm willing to do the job. You know I'm not cheap. It'll be about $35,000 all in."

"Bloody hell. You're a robber."

"As long as you don't need a report for the stock exchange, you can pay half of it in stock."

"That's a pile of stock," Julius says.

"Bullshit! You've got enough stock out. That's a drop in the ocean."

"That's cruel, mate."

"Whatever," Peter says. "That's my estimate, all inclusive, expenses and analyses included, and a completed report in your hands by the middle of March at the latest."

"We'll live with it," Julius says.

They spend the next half hour talking schedules, expectations, and support. Julius agrees to send all the critical reports electronically, and courier hard copies of all the large maps and sections to Maria's apartment.

"I don't want to give you any detailed progress reports, Julius. It's too dangerous. You're asking me to look for something we don't know is there. You can get into a lot of trouble with the exchange if information leaks on something material to stock price that isn't borne out by the facts later on. I want to hold back on any discussions and provide the full report by the middle of March, signed, sealed, and delivered."

"That's fine," Julius says. "Just make damn sure your delivery date doesn't slip past the middle of the month."

"It won't, Julius, unless something really strange happens."

"And what would that be?"

"I have no idea. Isn't that part of what I'm supposed to find out?"

"I suppose." Julius pauses. "I might come into the camp with you."

"I'd rather you didn't," Peter says. "I'd rather not have anyone looking over my shoulder while I'm working. Besides, wouldn't you be a bit of a lightning rod for trouble?"

"Why should my visit cause trouble?"

"You are the CEO, for God's sake. And there's still a lot of people and groups upset about the potential development of the mine. Your presence alone could encourage an ugly incident."

"I still own thirty percent of the bloody thing. I should be able to visit my own bloody property."

"Julius, I can't stop you," Peter says, "but I think you're adding unnecessary risk to an already, potentially difficult situation."

"Yeah. Well, I'll see you in Lima. We can make the final decision then."

"I'll be in touch if I need anything," Peter says.

"I should be home until I head over to Peru."

After he completes the call, Peter sends a short email to Maria to tell her about the package of maps and sections.

He sits back in his chair. *It's done, and it's time, maybe overdue.* "And I'm done for the day," he says quietly.

He turns on the satellite television and checks the news stations. Wisser, the crazy US President, is up to his usual outrageous lies and illegal pronouncements.

He thinks about Alden Sage and Sir Richard, and how they're trying to contain the damage that the massively corrupt and immoral president is wreaking on the world stage.

What about the national stage? Who's saving the United States?

Peter quickly tires of the news and hunts for an old movie. He settles on Gary Cooper in High Noon.

Brainless entertainment.

When the movie ends, he goes to bed. He'll start on the reports tomorrow. He'll get the maps and sections from Maria when he goes to Toronto on Wednesday. At least he hopes he gets them then.

He isn't sure about what else he might get from Maria.

CHAPTER 12

Peter fills the next three days reading the technical reports. He calls Julius several times each day with minor follow-up questions on some of the details. As Peter makes his way through the reports, he gradually comes to the conclusion that Cerro Nublado is a relatively normal, large copper deposit. No obvious, big surprises or anomalies. Late black veins, identified as iron and manganese oxide, cut through the copper mineralization, and parts of the iron sulfide halo around it. They appear to have no noticeable impact on the copper grade, the metal recovery, or the economics of the deposit.

Peter considers the modeling inadequate for the distribution of trace elements and precious metals, but that's not surprising. He expects to collect 100 to 150 small samples from the drill holes. He will develop his own understanding of the geological architecture, the trace element chemistry, and the major technical issues of the deposit.

He identifies ten recent drill holes as his major focus. Records and samples of some early drill holes were lost when the camp was largely destroyed and burned. The more recent holes, Julius assures him, are all well preserved and available at the camp for inspection and sampling.

On Wednesday morning, Peter writes out a summary of his plan for his own reference. He receives an email with a signed copy of his consulting contract, as adjusted by a lawyer in Patrick's firm. He signs and sends a scanned copy to Julius Grant.

He has an early lunch, packs for overnight in Toronto, locks up the cabin, and heads down to the city. At StolPort he arranges for hanger space for his helicopter for most of February. Fifteen minutes before three, On Guard Security shows up with a car, with Theo, the bodyguard, and drives him to Mitch's Pub. Maria is already sitting in the back corner. Theo comes in after Peter and sits by the door.

When Peter joins her, Maria asks, "How was the storm?"

"Deep," he says. "About two and a half feet. Nice to see you, by the way."

"Yeah. Likewise." She jerks her thumb to the door. "You got someone watching your back these days?"

"Actually, yes. Someone tried to mug me last time I was in town."

"Was that down on Queens Quay?"

Peter nods his head.

"I wondered. That sounded like you. They're refusing to identify the, quote, victim."

They sit in silence. A waiter comes to the table. Peter orders a light beer and some French fries, Maria a Coke.

"I do have four map tubes for you," Maria says. "DHL delivered them this morning."

"I'm glad to hear that," Peter replies.

"So tell me, what did Alden bring you?" Maria asks. "You said you're negotiating a departure from the CIA? Is that true?"

Peter pauses a moment before he says, "I never told you the whole story about Afghanistan, but the military accused me of some awful stuff. The worst of it was that they accused me of murdering my entire platoon. Alden brought me an official report that absolves me of all those accusations. I don't think you want to read it, but I'll give it to you if you really want it." Peter hands her a sheet of paper. "This is the summary. It should be enough."

Maria reads the summary and looks up. "Why didn't you tell me about this?"

She's calmer about this than I expected.

"I don't know. It's a big part of why I was so screwed up. I have a big chunk of memory that seems to be lost, and I could never prove, even to myself, that I was innocent."

"So… What does this have to do with the CIA?" Maria asks.

"It was part of my discharge from the SEALs. I had to work for the CIA as long as they wanted me. It's a little crazy, but now that the Navy absolves me of any dishonorable activity in Afghanistan, the CIA doesn't have a hold on me." Peter pulls out a copy of the severance agreement and hands it to

Maria. "I'm negotiating some of the issues in this, but this is the agreement they propose. Alden brought this with him, too."

Peter watches as Maria reads the entire agreement, spending some extra time on a couple of sections.

The waiter arrives with the fries and drinks.

She finally looks up. "You're really leaving?"

"Yeah."

"I find that hard to believe."

"Believe it," Peter says.

"What will you do with yourself?"

Peter laughs. "I don't think you believe I can change my line of work."

"You're right. I don't."

"I think I'm going to become a farmer."

Maria nods her head. "Oh, yes. Of course. As a segue from that ridiculous comment, perhaps you can tell me about the job in Peru."

"It's pretty simple," Peter says. "Alden's on the board of Mandrake Minerals. I know Julius Grant, the CEO, and they want an independent review of the feasibility study and development plans for the Cerro Nublado project in Peru. Julius Grant proposed me to do the work, and he asked Alden to bring the proposal to me."

Maria looks intently at Peter. "Are you kidding me?"

"Sorry." He shrugs. "It looks pretty straight forward to me."

"You do realize that a Russian company owns the damn thing, don't you?"

"Yes."

"You don't think they'll drown you in the river the minute you show up?"

Peter eats some French fries and finishes his beer. He signals to the waiter and asks for another beer.

"Why should they bother me?" he asks. "I'm leaving the CIA. I'm making no secret of that, and they probably know it already. My contract with Mandrake is to do what I'm good at as a geologist. I've seen the feasibility reports. They look good. Well done. Should be a piece of cake."

Maria reaches over for a few French fries. "I don't think I believe you."

"I didn't think you would, but you should." He eats most of the remaining fries. "Anyway, I'm planning on heading down on the third of February. You want to come to Peru with me?"

"Not sure I have much interest in spending time at another exploration camp."

"You don't have to come out to the property. Stay in Lima. Visit Lake Titicaca, or maybe Machu Picchu."

"That sounds a little more interesting," Maria says.

"I've set aside the first weekend in Lima for being a tourist and recovering from the flight down," Peter says. "There are plenty of nice restaurants in Lima that I think you might enjoy, and some interesting museums, too."

"I'll have to think about it." Maria pauses a beat. "Let's get one thing straight, though. Right now, we're not a couple. If I come to Peru with you, it's separate rooms."

"That's not a problem. I assumed that was the case." Peter finishes his beer. "Now, can I go to the apartment and pick up some of my better clothes and the field gear I need for Peru?"

"That's fine, but, please, I'd rather you didn't spend the night."

"I won't." The left side of Peter's mouth turns up slightly, forming a half smile. "I have a late meeting today, and I have a place to stay the night. I'll head back to the cabin tomorrow morning."

"Okay. Let's pay up and go."

Peter asks for the check, pays in cash, and gets up to go. "You want to ride," Peter asks, "or do you prefer to walk with an escort?"

"Let's walk."

They catch up with Theo at the door. Peter says to him, "We're going to walk to the apartment. I'd like you to walk with us. Tell Sander to wait at the apartment. I'll be getting some clothes, field gear, and four rolls of maps. I should be done there in an hour or less."

"I'll take care of it, Mr. Binder."

They start walking, slowly, and Theo quickly catches up to follow a few paces behind them. Maria shakes her head in disbelief. "I didn't think I'd ever see you using a bodyguard. Such a blow to your pride."

"Ah… We talked about this at the cabin. I just want to be able to relax, and the last time I was in Toronto I relaxed without someone like Theo, and the result was not pleasant. It's the first step to my new life."

"Well, maybe I'll have to start believing you," she says.

"Maybe," Peter says with a smile, "but I won't press it."

When they arrive at the apartment building, Frederick, the doorman, smiles and greets them effusively. "So good to see you again, Mr. Binder. I trust you have been well?"

"Couldn't be better, Frederick. How about you?"

"Oh, the usual aches and pains, nothing serious."

On the elevator, Maria says, "I think Frederick misses you."

"Old buddies. Did you know he was in the Suez campaign with the Brits?"

Maria laughs. "Veterans. Telling stories."

Peter loads a suitcase with some dressier clothes, along with his traveling shaving and toiletries kit. Maria watches him as he packs a backpack with the field gear he wants. It isn't all that much. He packs a notebook, pens and pencils, hand lens, hammer, Brunton compass, a few scales and protractors, and a mapping case with gridded paper. He hesitates at the small pocket radiation detector, but then he adds it to the backpack. He throws in 200 small sample bags, duplicate sample tags, field clothes, boots, and rain gear. He's finished in about fifteen minutes.

He changes into black loafers, gray, pressed pants, a light blue, open-necked dress shirt, and a blue blazer. He sets aside a black coat and gloves and combs his hair.

"Is your date young and beautiful?" Maria asks.

Peter chuckles. "No. It's a man, and though I suspect he will be smartly dressed, he will be neither young nor beautiful."

"You could have fooled me," Maria says. "You know, I'm always amazed at how fast you can pack."

"Too many years of practice." He zips up the pockets and the main opening for the backpack. "I think I'm good to go," he says. "Do you mind if I leave the rest of my clothes here for now?"

"Peter, I haven't kicked you out. Like I told you the other day, I just need some space for myself for a while."

Peter says nothing.

"Let's give our relationship a bit of a time out," she says.

"Yeah," Peter says. *I'm in one of those positions where a man should just shut his mouth.* "I'm ready to go. Let me know if you want to go down to Peru."

"I'll do that."

Peter takes two trips to get everything down to On Guard's car.

Maria and I are done. Maybe?

There's something more going on. He's beginning to guess the details, but he's not at all sure about them.

She'll come to Peru. I know she will. And we will resolve this.

He drops off the suitcase, field equipment, and maps at the helicopter, locks it up, and directs the driver to the address for Sir Richard in York Mills. Because it's the peak of the rush hour, he arrives a few minutes late. He reminds the driver to pick him up at nine in the morning, and he asks him not to leave until someone lets him in the front door.

The house is modest, compared to some of the mansions in York Mills that sell for well into eight figures. It looks to be about six thousand square feet, maybe five or six bedrooms. Before he gets to the door, a young woman, with long blond hair and a simple, tailored black dress, opens the door.

"Good evening, Mr. Binder. I'm Julia Gladding."

She has the voice of a contralto, and speaks with a smooth and softened British accent. She holds out her hand, and Peter takes it in his. He is surprised at the firmness of her grip.

"I'm glad you could join Sir Richard tonight," she says and gestures for Peter to enter, and he does so, carrying his small overnight bag.

"Sir Richard is in the library. I can take you there now, or to your room if you'd like to freshen up first."

"I'm happy to see him directly, but I need a notebook from my bag. Perhaps someone could take my bag to my room?"

"No problem at all. Remove what you need, leave the bag by the table, and I'll make sure it gets to your room."

When he has his notebook, she says, "Follow me, please." She has a firmness about her stride and a sense of force about her.

What else does she do, besides greeting visitors at the front door? Peter wonders.

They walk straight ahead from the entrance, down a short hallway, past two small rooms, one with a conference table, the other with numerous chairs and small tables, suitable for a modest cocktail party. They enter a hallway across from a large dining room, set with a table that could accommodate at least thirty to forty guests. Turning left, two doors down, she stops, knocks on the door, opens it, and says, "Sir Richard. Mr. Binder is here for you."

"Thank you, Julia. Send him in."

She gestures to Peter. "Please."

Peter has no idea of what to expect. The room itself is a library, two stories tall, with one of the classic ladders on a runner that can be moved along the shelves of books. The furniture is oak. It has an appearance of being comfortable and well-worn. The whole room looks as if someone picked it up, intact, as a small reading room at one of the colleges at the University of Cambridge in England.

Sir Richard rises from his chair at a small, round table to meet him. He is tall, broad shouldered, but quite thin. He has a full head of sandy hair, cut close to the head, and a modest mustache. He wears sharply creased, brown pants and a tweed jacket, with a cream-colored shirt. No tie. Peter guesses his age at fifty to fifty-five. His ramrod-straight posture matches what Peter knows is a lengthy military background, a background that provided him his knighthood.

"Ah, Mr. Binder. Good to meet you."

They shake hands. Sir Richard's accent is certainly British, but very polished. He's either from the upper levels of British society, or he's gone to all the right schools to sound like it. Peter never can tell one from the other.

"And you as well, Sir Richard."

"Yes." Sir Richard gestures to the table. "Please have a seat. I think we should move to first names, don't you?"

"Good idea," Peter says as he sits down, "particularly since we'll be working with each other." He looks around at the room. "Lovely room, this. I was thinking that the builder might have stolen it from the University of Cambridge."

"Yes, it is rather… traditional. Probably a bit small to have come from Cambridge, but I like it. In our crazy world, a place like this gives one a sense of permanence. I find it very peaceful."

"Lately, I could use a little 'peaceful' in my life."

"So I understand," Sir Richard says.

"Not to rush our discussion, but I have been wondering," Peter says, "what creates the interest in this property in Peru for your agency, SIS, or MI6 as we tend to call it."

"You've talked with Alden, and you know his thoughts. He's pretty well convinced SIS that something is amiss here, and that we need someone like you to tell us what it is."

"I've looked at the feasibility study, and a bunch of other reports," Peter says. "They're all done by reputable and well-qualified groups and individuals. Nothing looks out of place. It looks like a large investment by a Russian company to develop a long-term copper source in South America. At this point, I can't see anything questionable, except that most of my sources suggest that development will be nearly impossible. I tend to agree."

"Perhaps just a foolish investment?"

"On the face of it, Richard, I would say yes." Peter pauses. "But... some investments only look foolish, because you don't know all the reasons behind the investment."

"I agree that it looks like a stupid investment," Sir Richard says. "It looks like a lot of other cases I've seen, where a company decides to become an international player for the first time. They don't understand the rules in the new country, and they're in a hurry. They can make terrible decisions, like trying to develop a business where the opposition is too great, the environmental hazards are too large, or the land and title security are too shaky. Lots of western companies have made those mistakes in Russia and China."

"But I gather your concern is that we can't see the obvious at Cerro Nublado, and don't understand what's really going on there."

"Exactly," Sir Richard responds.

"I guess I want to emphasize," Peter says, "that nothing strange jumps out at me. These reports are from good, experienced consulting companies, good geologists and engineers, all solid and professional. Cerro Nublado comes across as your standard copper deposit. The only exceptional characteristic is that it's larger than many, though it's certainly not the largest in the world."

Sir Richard smiles. "What you're telling me is that after you spend a pile of Mandrake Minerals' money, you may tell us that there are no surprises, and everything looks normal."

"That's a distinct possibility."

Sir Richard steeples his hands together and says, rather pensively, "There is the contract with North Korea."

Peter gestures. "It's a contract to refine a copper concentrate that hasn't been produced, from a mill that hasn't been built, for a mine that is neither permitted nor developed. Unless Russo-Perú produces a rather large miracle, it will be many years, if ever, before the mine produces concentrate for a refinery in North Korea."

"True. That seems obvious, but why the contract with North Korea at all?" Sir Richard asks.

"Maybe they're the lowest bidder? The Russian company doesn't have any refineries that I know of on the Pacific coast," Peter says. "Shipping the concentrate from the coast to one of their refineries in central or western Russia might be cost prohibitive. Maybe it's only an effort to lock in low costs."

Sir Richard shuts his eyes. "North Korea. It doesn't make sense. What does North Korea get out of this?"

"Hard currency?" Peter suggests.

Sir Richard opens his eyes. He looks skeptical. "Russia has had no interest in helping North Korea. Until now. There's something special here, and we can't see it." He smiles at Peter.

Peter says nothing.

Sir Richard stands up and collects a few papers from a side table. "Come. Let's get something to eat. I think they have prepared a small beef Wellington for us tonight."

CHAPTER 13

Peter follows Sir Richard down the hall to another modest room. While they are walking, he notices that Sir Richard has a slight irregularity to his step. He can't remember any mention of a major injury in the information he had collected on the man.

The dinner is quiet and very well done, with a mature Bordeaux wine. For a while, their conversation focuses on world affairs, hot spots, and the complications presented on an almost daily basis by President Helmut Wisser in the US.

As they pour out the remains of the bottle of wine, and await a chocolate mousse dessert, Sir Richard says, "Alden told me about some of your more recent exercises, and your release from the CIA. I had not heard anything about your work in northern Canada, and I thought what you did in the case of the gold mine that had no gold was magical. Now you can retire. Why do this job?"

Peter shrugs. "In one respect, I owe a lot to Alden Sage. Honestly, though, it looks pretty simple. I think all of you are reaching a bit in this case. I see nothing alarming in all the reports I've read, and all the studies appear to be well done."

"You have different eyes, a different experience base, and a different perspective. I think Jeremy Pritchard refers to you as a geological detective. I like that."

"It's easier being a successful detective if you know there actually is a crime," Peter says.

"Oh, there's a crime here, Peter. I'm certain of that. We just don't know what the devil it is."

"Anyway, I like Peru," Peter says, "and I like the Peruvian people. I have a lot of respect for the people who live in the Altiplano. They live a tough life, but they have hopes and dreams, just like everybody else, and most of them are not only tough, they're smarter than most people are willing to recognize."

"Speaking of the Peruvians, I'll set you up with one of our best operatives in Peru to be your geological assistant."

Sir Richard looks through the papers he brought with him and hands Peter a small color photograph of a man's face.

"He's not a big man, but he's as tough as they come. He's smart, quick, and well trained in the martial arts and most hand-held firearms. He's fluent in Spanish, of course, English, and Quechua. He also has a passable understanding of spoken Russian. He took a few geology courses at university. He can pass as your assistant, but he's been working for us in various capacities for a few years.

"His name is Omar Vargas," Sir Richard says, "and, unlike either of us, he can disappear in the Altiplano. Literally. He looks like a farmer plucked from the fields of the Incas themselves."

"He sounds like someone I will really like," Peter says.

"Oh, as long as you are not his enemy, you will like him. If you run into trouble at Cerro Nublado, he will likely save your life, at least once."

"I can't wait to meet him," Peter says. "And I do mean that."

Their dessert arrives, and they fall into silence.

"Excellent mousse," Peter says. "Not that hard to make, but most people do manage to make a mess of it."

Sir Richard smiles. He drinks the last of his wine and pushes back a bit from the table. "You still plan on using La Seguridad Ejecutiva Peruana in Peru as your visible security?"

"I was thinking of them, but I know very little about them."

"I did check them out. They're fine. Your real security will be yourself, and Omar, when he's with you, and while you're in Lima we'll provide some additional backup security, well hidden. I will be in Lima, and I will give you emergency contacts, but Omar will also have them. I understand you require some sort of written arrangement, and you have a list of certain items you require for the field."

Peter opens his notebook and hands Sir Richard a single sheet of paper.

Sir Richard looks at the list, nods his head a couple of times, and places it on the table. "No problems with any of this. I'll need about six, colored passport photos to get the permits and the passport."

"I have plenty of them in my small suitcase. I can get them now, or, if we're having breakfast together tomorrow morning, I could give them to you then."

"Breakfast is fine. It'll be at half-past seven, by the way." Sir Richard looks back at the list. "One of your ammunition requests is a bit peculiar."

"Yes. Well, I'd appreciate it if you can manage that. It's rather important," Peter says.

"Oh, no problem at all. You sure you want the same pistol for Maria? You sure she's coming with you?"

"Yes, to your first question. Is she coming? Not completely settled, but close, I think. I doubt she'll come to the exploration camp, but I'm not sure of that either."

Sir Richard frowned. "A bit risky, wouldn't you say?"

"I don't think so, but then most everything in my life is a bit risky at the moment."

"You're willing to take on an added risk to end some of the other risks?"

"Yes."

"Good luck on that." Sir Richard frowns. "It's a difficult task, extraction from our particular careers. However," he punches the paper with his forefinger, "though I don't want any clarification on your side exercise here, I can read between the lines. I suspect it has a good chance of success. It also has almost as good a chance of killing you."

Peter is silent a moment. "Resolution. One way or the other."

"True."

"Now," Peter says, "there is one other issue that Jeremy Pritchard mentioned, a gentleman referred to as El Come Huevos. Apparently, he's in the area and may be involved in some way with the Russian company that holds Cerro Nublado. He sounds like a lovely piece of work. Jeremy says there's a major bounty for his hide."

"He's not our objective in any way, but he's a huge complication if he shows up. If you see him, if you can, kill him on sight."

"Not always an easy thing to do."

"True, but if you have the option, do it. Don't hesitate. He's a ruthless little bastard, and you simply cannot have him lurking around. If he shows up, it's most likely he's there to kill you, though he'd prefer to torture you first. He likes to castrate his victims, fry up their testicles, and eat them in front of them before he slowly kills them. A delightful guy."

Peter says nothing.

"Now," Sir Richard continues, "regarding our commitment to you. There's a letter. Five pages. It's in your room. Look at it tonight and let me know tomorrow morning if it's satisfactory. Mostly, you have to rely on my keeping my word to you. I will support you in any way I can, and I will not abandon you. You have my most solemn word on that."

"Thank you," Peter says. "I presume there is no compensation from MI6, as Mandrake Minerals is paying me."

"Not exactly. If you discover some aspect of the deposit, which explains the extreme Russian interest, you will receive a one-time bonus payment of five million dollars."

"Interesting. Who's the judge?"

"I am," Sir Richard responds with a smile. "Alden Sage might have some input."

"If I don't find anything, isn't that a real incentive for me to be creative?"

"Yes. That is true. You have to trust me to watch your back in this exercise, and I have to trust you to be an honorable and truthful person. I firmly believe both of us are in good hands."

Peter grins. "Neat."

"Yes, indeed," Sir Richard says. He stands up and turns to a side table. "There's a decent brandy here." He returns with the bottle and two glasses. "I suggest we drink a toast to our mutual satisfaction in the outcome of all our ventures in Peru."

He pours the brandy, hands one glass to Peter, and they lightly touch their glasses together.

Sir Richard shows Peter to his room and says goodnight.

Peter stands next to the small desk and looks down at the letter of commitment from Sir Richard. He is feeling a bit fuzzy around the edges from the wine and brandy, but he forces himself to review the letter. As Sir Richard indicated, it is five pages, single-spaced. It contained lots of assurances of best efforts, but it carries no promises.

Peter grunts when he finishes the document. He didn't expect much. After all, he is not a full time or career employee of the British SIS.

Best efforts at support and extraction are about as much as he expected, considering the nature of the beast.

Peter carefully removes his clothes, brushes his teeth, and falls into bed. He is asleep almost instantly.

He awakens to his alarm at six in the morning, showers, shaves, and dresses. He makes a few notes regarding his discussions with Sir Richard. When he arrives for breakfast, Sir Richard is already there, reading a newspaper with a cup of tea. He folds and puts the paper aside as soon as he sees Peter.

"I trust you slept well," Sir Richard says.

"Absolutely." Peter hands an envelope to Sir Richard with six passport photos. "I also reviewed the Letter of Understanding."

"And?"

"It's about what I expected," Peter says. "Lots of best efforts but no promises. I don't ask for promises. There are none in this sort of business. I just want some assurances that people will do their best to have my back in a pinch."

Julia Gladding appears. "What would you like for breakfast, Mr. Binder? We have a fresh bacon and mushroom quiche, if you'd like that."

"The quiche sounds good, but I think I'll have two, soft-poached eggs, whole-grain toast, buttered, and sausage. A glass of orange juice and coffee would also be nice."

"I'll have it right out for you Mr. Binder. Sir Richard, you would like the quiche and some fresh fruit?"

"Yes, Julia, and you can bring me a fresh tea, English Breakfast this time, if you please."

"Certainly."

After she leaves, Sir Richard pushes his empty teacup to the side and says, "I don't think we need to talk much more about Peru, but there are a few things I'd like to review. I will have the items you requested set up for you. Omar will provide them for you and will meet you at your hotel. I suggest that if Maria accompanies you that you have separate, and not adjoining, rooms."

"That's not a problem," Peter says with a small shrug. "At the moment, we're not a couple, and separate rooms are required. Still, I want her to come to Peru. I want to try to sort out some personal issues between us."

"Yes. Well, I don't plan on getting involved with those personal issues. I have enough problems trying to manage my own. I'll get things started in Peru, based on what you've already given me, but I'll need your final schedule and itinerary at least three or four days before your flight to Lima. I need that much time to finalize my side of the bargain."

"I'll try to get all that in place by Friday night."

After breakfast and after Peter calls for his car service, Sir Richard waits with him in the front hall.

"Thank you for coming to Toronto to meet me," Peter says. "I do appreciate it."

"Not a problem. I need to speak with a few people here anyway, and we really did need to spend some time together. I'll fly back to London this evening. Keep in touch, and good luck on everything."

The weather has changed, as Peter heads back to the cabin. The sky is overcast, and the next snowstorm is already stirring up a few flurries. He lands in the field behind the small grocery store in town and buys some meat and fresh fruit and vegetables. When he approaches the cabin, he decides to change his routine. He flies to the north end of the lake, down the lake to look at the cabin, and finally around to the driveway. He sees nothing out of place. He lands back at the cabin at a little after eleven.

Once he's settled back in the cabin, he opens his computer and sends a short note to Maria.

Maria,

I'm finalizing my plans for Peru tonight and tomorrow. I plan to fly down on February 5, return on February 17. Please let me know if you want to go by noon tomorrow. It would be nice to have you along in Lima, even in separate rooms. You'd enjoy Machu Picchu, and I can set that up for you.

I'm well compensated for this job. I'll stand the business class airfare (the best that's available) and hotel rooms.

Peter

Peter goes to the kitchen table and unrolls the large surface map of the deposit, and the more important vertical sections through it. The sections show the drill holes, metal distribution, geology, and all the details of the deposit at depth. The distribution and relationships of these features will be the major focus of Peter's attention.

After he has laid out the maps and sections, he makes himself a light lunch and thinks about Maria in Lima. He frowns.

That scene will work itself out. I just need to be alert to what she's thinking. He grimaces. *Easier said than done.*

He has more important things to consider. Will the Russians leave him alone at the site? Maybe if Julius comes along it will be a good thing. What about El Come Huevos, the egg eater?

Omar better be good about getting close to the local workers. That's the only warning we'll get if things are about to go to hell in the proverbial handbasket.

The storm settles in. It isn't particularly fierce, just a light snow. The winds stay relatively calm, but the snow does continue for a full three days, piling up another foot or more on top of what the last storm left behind. Peter hardly notices, though he misses his regular cross-country ski runs.

Maria emails him that she will go to Peru, but not to the exploration camp.

Peter makes all the needed reservations. AeroMexico airlines, through Mexico City with a long layover, is not his preferred carrier or route, but it conveniently avoids any US landing. DoubleTree by Hilton in Mira Flores. A junior suite with a kitchenette for Maria, and a king suite for himself with a little extra space and a table for private meetings. The DoubleTree is well located in Mira Flores, has a couple of restaurants, a good bar, and a pool, in case Maria decides to stay in Lima while he's in Cerro Nublado.

He informs Sir Richard and Jeremy Pritchard of his plans and reservations.

He works steadily, only taking time off to eat, and in the evenings to catch up on the news. He calls Julius often, discussing various details of the deposit. Julius informs him that he has definitely decided to accompany him to the exploration camp at Cerro Nublado. Peter also talks at length with the consultants who prepared the feasibility study. By the end of his review, he still doesn't think he will find anything surprising when he gets to the property.

By Tuesday, the weather has cleared. He plows the snow around the cabin and shovels his way out to the helicopter. Then he runs his snowmobile down to the fishing lodge, to give John Williams the key to the cabin.

In his packing, Peter adds several new acquisitions. He packs three close-fitting T-shirts, with V necks, with pockets for two flexible armor inserts, one for the front and one for the back. Next is a navy-blue sports coat, also with flexible armor. They will provide good protection against knife and pistol attacks.

Another storm is forecast for the early evening on Wednesday. He decides to fly down to Toronto Wednesday morning, a day earlier than he planned. He'll have Wednesday night to himself in Toronto.

I should get together with Jim Blakestad.

Peter has known Jim for a long time. He works for one of the better international executive protection services. His specialty is helping companies work safely in areas of drug smuggling and competing drug cartels, mostly in South and Central America and southeast Asia. Another US veteran living in Canada, Jim is a tall, imposing and ruggedly handsome man, almost a caricature of a Special Forces veteran. He even has a two-inch scar on his left cheek, courtesy of a special project in Somalia.

Unlike Peter, who did his service with the SEALS, Jim spent his time with the US Army Special Forces. Sometimes, with their experiences so similar, the two of them can have a conversation with almost no words. There's a lot of mutual respect between them.

Peter smiles, picks up the phone, and makes the call.

"Yes?"

"Peter Binder, Jim. You have a minute?"

"For you, yes."

"I'd like to buy you dinner tomorrow night and pick your brain a bit," Peter says. "That possible?"

"Depends. You planning on a good Bordeaux? None of that cheap shit?"

"Damn." Peter says with a laugh. "We macho guys are supposed to drink beer and whiskey. What's this wine stuff anyway?"

"Well, a good Scotch or two might also be on the menu before the night is over."

"You order the wine. Just keep it within reason."

"Deal," Jim says.

"How about seven? At Michelli's? I'll see if I can reserve one of their small, private rooms."

"Sounds serious."

"Not yet," Peter says, and they end their call.

That will be an interesting conversation.

CHAPTER 14

Wednesday morning dawns bright, clear, and crisp, and Peter's first waking thoughts are about Peru.

I'm close. It will work.

Peter looks out the window toward the lake as he prepares his breakfast, surprised to see the albino moose again. He had thought the moose had moved on, but it's bedded down, in the snow, at the edge of the lake, about fifteen feet to the south of the dock.

"You'd better be a good-natured spirit," Peter says. There's no loading the helicopter without walking closer to the albino giant than most moose would tolerate.

Peter retrieves his camera from his pile of equipment and opens the door. The moose looks at him, but he doesn't move. As Peter raises the camera, the moose turns his head, as if posing, to give Peter the full profile.

Peter spends the morning reviewing his planning and lists, finalizing his packing. Julius assures him that he will find copies of all the reports, maps, and sections at the property. Peter sends a few emails to update his contacts with his final itinerary.

After lunch, he heads out to the helicopter to remove all the covers and tiedowns. He's cautious when he walks by the moose for the first time. He stops and speaks to the animal. "I don't want to disturb you, but I do have to load the helicopter." The moose stares at him. Peter almost laughs.

As Peter fuels the helicopter and walks by the moose several times with his baggage, the animal simply turns his head to watch. Otherwise, he doesn't move. He does snort a couple of times, but most of the time he remains silent.

Finally, when Peter is ready to leave, he turns to the moose. He says, "Thank you for being so tolerant of me," and he bows his head. He watches with some trepidation as the moose slowly gets to its feet and bows its head quite deeply.

Amazing.

He climbs into the helicopter and begins the start-up process. The moose remains standing and doesn't move, even as Peter goes to full power and lifts off. Peter looks at the majestic animal for a moment, turns, flies out over the lake, and turns again to head to Toronto.

At Billy Bishop airport, Peter lands on a large, wheeled dolly by StolPort's hanger, and StolPort's crew pulls the helicopter into a back corner of the hanger. He finds his ride with On Guard Security and heads to the Hilton just off University on Richmond Street.

Peter has a few hours before he has to be at Michelli's. He lies on the bed and closes his eyes. He grapples with all the different technical, security, and personal pieces of his trip to Peru. "I have to be lucky," he says, and he falls asleep.

Peter awakens in a panic in the dark, sure he has overslept. He turns on a light, looks at his watch, and sees it's not quite six. He relaxes. Plenty of time.

When he dresses, he inserts the flexible armor in one of the tee shirts, and pulls it on. The rest is standard business casual.

The restaurant is only five blocks away. He evaluates the level of risk and takes the elevator to the lobby, steps out onto Richmond Street, and turns to walk south on University Avenue.

The wide street is nearly empty. As Peter approaches King Street, a lone man appears out of the shadows.

"Hey, man, can you spare some change?" the man asks.

Homeless, skinny, and shaking, Peter thinks. *Probably an addict badly in need of his next fix.*

"Sorry buddy, not tonight," Peter answers and continues walking.

Peter senses, rather than hears, the movement behind him. He whirls around.

The man thrusts a sizeable knife into Peter. It's a clumsy attack, but it's so quick that Peter cannot avoid the knife. He feels a sudden pain.

Peter grabs the man's knife arm and uses what's left of his momentum to flip him onto his back. The man exhales sharply as he lands on the cement.

Peter steps on the man's wrist and pulls the knife free. He rolls the man over and kneels on his back with one knee.

"First things first," he mutters, and he rips open his coat. He sees no blood, just a gash in his coat, his sports coat, and his shirt. He realizes that the body armor stopped the blade.

The man on the ground is squirming under his knee.

"Lie still," Peter says loudly, and he completes a quick and rudimentary search of the man's clothing. Skinny. Nothing but bones and gristle. Shaking like a leaf in a hurricane. Nothing of any consequence in his pockets.

"What the hell do you think you're doing, man?" Peter asks. "You knife people on a regular basis?"

"No! No! Don't kill me. Don't kill me."

"I'm not going to kill you," Peter says calmly. "You in bad shape? You need a fix that bad?"

"Oh, God, I'm dying. It's really bad, man."

"I know. Believe me, I do know what it's like. What is it? Rock? Horse?"

"Crank."

"Meth? You poor bastard."

I do not want to call the cops, Peter thinks. *Too much drama. He doesn't need it.* The man starts to squirm again.

"Lie still," Peter says. "Don't give me any trouble."

"No trouble. No trouble." The man lies still, except for his involuntary shaking.

Peter thinks for a moment. "Okay," he says. "I'm taking your knife, and I'm walking away. If you want, I'll make a call. I'll see if I can get some help for you. You want that?"

"Shit."

"Yeah," Peter says. "I know what you mean. I'll make the call. You decide if you want to stay here or not. Up to you."

Peter helps the man to his feet. He looks at the man's dirty coat. "You're a mess man. You really need help. I'll do what I can. Stay here."

Peter wants some distance between him and his attacker. He backs up to the corner, waits for the light to change, and walks across University Avenue. Once on the other side, he looks back. The man is still standing on the sidewalk. Peter takes out his phone and calls Bill Branch.

"Hello, Peter. Hope you're doing well, for a change."

"There's a broken-down junkie on the northeast corner of University and King. He tried to knife me. He was not successful. He needs some help. Right now, he's standing there. He might wait for someone. I told him I'd try to get him some help."

"You're kidding me!"

"Sorry to bother you on this. I'd appreciate it if we could handle this on a relatively low-key basis."

"You are something else."

"I know what he's going through. He can't think straight, and I didn't want to call the locals. They'll come with the whole cavalry, lights blazing, sirens screaming, probably with their guns drawn."

"Please get off the street, Peter. I'll see what I can do."

"Thanks."

Peter puts his phone back in his pocket. He waves at the man across the street, and he waves back. Peter turns and walks to the west on King Street.

After Peter washes his hands at Michelli's, the maître d' leads him to the small private room at the back of the restaurant. Jim Blakestad sits at one of a group of small tables, set for two, with a bottle of wine and two filled glasses.

"You're late," Jim says with a smile. He stands up, and they shake hands.

Peter sits down. "Sorry. On my way, somebody tried to mug me. He actually attacked me with a goddamn knife."

"You okay? No damage?"

"I've got a few holes in my clothes." Peter sticks a finger through the hole in his sports coat. "Nothing serious."

"That looks well-placed. It ought to be serious."

"Oh, I've been having a few problems, maybe related to a job I'm taking on, so I'm wearing some light body armor."

"So, this is business related?"

"No. At least I don't think so," Peter says. "He's a poor junkie, badly in need of a fix."

"Can he walk?"

Peter laughs. "When I left him, he was standing on the corner, wondering what the hell just happened. I called for somebody to try to give him some help."

"Man, you're getting crazy in your old age. Is this 'job' you're having problems with the one we're talking about tonight?"

"Yeah."

"I should have ordered a more expensive bottle of wine after all. Maybe it'll take two bottles tonight."

Peter reaches for his glass of wine and tastes it. "Not bad." He looks at the bottle and nods his approval.

The waiter knocks on the door and enters the room. "My name is Brian," he says. "Welcome back, Mr. Binder. I will be happy to serve you tonight. Do you have any questions about the menu?"

"You have any specials tonight?" Jim asks.

"We have two, actually, osso buco and beef short ribs braised in red wine."

They order sautéed mushrooms and spicy sautéed squid to share as appetizers. Peter orders veal scaloppini and a Caesar salad. Jim orders a rib-eye steak with grilled asparagus

"I hear from my friends that the CIA is cutting you loose. Is that true?"

"God! News travels fast," Peter says. "It's true. An in-depth review made all the charges from Afghanistan disappear. I'm getting too old for front line work anyway. I want to get out, and the CIA no longer has any hold on me."

"What the hell are you going to do with yourself?" Jim asks.

Peter laughs. "Everybody asks me that. I'm going to be a farmer."

Jim nods his head. "Right, and I'm going to sprout wings and become the angel Gabriel."

"That's a sight I'd like to see."

"But before you buy your hoe and tend to your potato patch, you've got one last job for the firm?"

"No, MI6."

"You're kidding," Jim says.

The waiter arrives with the appetizers.

Peter takes another drink of the wine after the waiter leaves. "Let me explain the situation to you," Peter says, and he provides a ten-minute summary of the key players and issues as they eat the appetizers.

"It looks pretty simple," Peter says. "The reports are all done by highly qualified people. Everything looks the way it should. It ought to be a simple geological review of the deposit, which I am very good at, and which is supposed to be my primary job."

"What do you see as the major risks?" Jim asks.

"If Russo-Perú is really hiding something, it presents a huge risk. The Russians know who I am. But I don't see anything out of line here, and so long as there's no secret, or they don't think I'll find their secret, I should pose no threat to them. I think the risk, at least at first, is minimal."

"I think you're too optimistic," Jim says. "They know you, and they know how thorough you are. I think they'll take you seriously. They may know you've left the CIA, but they'll assume you're working for someone else. They may already know it's MI6."

"I'm pretty sure they're arrogant enough to assume I won't find anything, even if there's actually something there to be found, and I'm pretty sure I don't believe that they're hiding anything."

"Don't get overconfident, bud. Don't underestimate the risk they present."

"Okay, I take your point," Peter says. "What most concerns me is this guy, El Come Huevos. For me, he's a total unknown, but he's right down your alley. If he's tied up somehow with the Russian company, and still doing his work with the coca supply chain? The implications of that are truly frightening."

"I do know about this guy."

"I figured you might. Got any advice?"

"Sure," Jim said. He leans forward. "You see him? You kill him. And if you survive, which is a big 'if' when he's around, say a prayer of thanksgiving to whatever deity suits your fancy."

"That seems to be the universal recommendation."

"It ought to be. Kill him, or he'll kill you. Of course, he won't kill you until he cuts your nuts off, fries them up, and eats them right in front of you."

"That part of the story," Peter says, "sounds like a serious case of overacting."

"Listen, Peter. I've seen his work. That's his cute little calling card." Jim sits back. "If you get the chance, kill him, take the bounty, and run like hell to the bank."

"And watch the whole Colombian drug cartel come running after me."

"I don't think so," Jim says. "Even the cartel's a little bit afraid of this guy. That's one of the reasons they banished him to the jungles of Peru." Jim shrugs. "But when you finish this job, and you've killed that miserable piece of shit, that black-hearted son of a mongrel bitch, and you find that farm you're looking for… let's say, if I were you, I wouldn't advertise my whereabouts."

Peter smiles. "Jim, I don't think I've ever heard you talk so fondly of anyone."

"I mean every word of it. You've seen pictures of him? You'll recognize him if you see him?"

"Yes," Peter answers.

"Well, from what you're telling me, Omar's your lifeline, but you already know that."

"How many people does El Come Huevos usually run with?"

"His reputation makes him, alone, like ten men," Jim says. "He runs a pretty tight group. Three or four well-armed men. In rural Peru, if you're vicious enough, that's enough to control a huge area of poor, rural farmers."

"You're saying, though, that he doesn't have a small army, right?"

"Yes," Jim answers, "but just the same, don't underestimate his killing power."

Brian and his assistant interrupt them, removing the appetizers and setting out the main course and accompaniments.

After they leave, and Peter and Jim begin to eat again, Jim says, "You don't have to answer, but I have to ask. You haven't said a word about Maria."

Peter puts down his fork. "She's split. Sort of. This Peru job has been the ostensible reason, but I'm not sure it has anything to do with it. She says she's tired of me taking on jobs like this one. We have to sort ourselves out. I hope we can manage to do that on this trip as well."

"You're adding a layer of distraction, at a minimum. I might say rather needlessly."

"You might," Peter says.

"Don't let your emotions cloud your vision, my friend, or distract you from the obvious risks of this work in Peru."

"Sometimes easier said than done."

"Truer words were never spoken," Jim responds.

They eat for a while in silence.

"How are Brenda and the kids?" Peter asks.

"Brenda's fine. Still putting up with me. The kids are wonderful hellions, but I'm away too much."

"You think of quitting?"

Jim raises his hands. "I don't know what else I could do. I'm pretty much out of the field work now. Mostly I'm doing training and holding hands of timid executives. The trouble is that I was so good in the field that, when things get totally out of control with a nasty kidnapping or hostage taking, they always want me to straighten it out."

"Nice to know you're wanted," Peter says.

"Maybe, but I'm learning to say 'No!' a little more often."

They finish their dinner with the conversation veering from current US politics to old friends, alive and dead. Far too many are dead. When they finish the wine and dessert, they both have an after-dinner Scotch.

"We should get together more often, Jim, but maybe a bit lighter on the alcohol. You're about the only one I can talk to about this stuff. I appreciate your comments and feedback." He raises his glass. "You're a true friend."

They click their glasses together, and Jim says, "You've spoken truth to me when I needed it most. It's the least I can do for you."

Jim insists on walking with Peter back to his hotel.

"I don't want my friend to get mugged a second time in one night, and he's had too much to drink."

"So have you," Peter says.

"True, but two of us, slightly drunk, probably equals one of us completely sober."

"A sobering thought," Peter says.

Jim groans.

They part at the hotel, and Peter goes directly to his room. As he lies down in the bed, he thinks about Jim. He realizes that he's a little jealous of Jim's life. Jim has a job he loves. He has reduced the physical risk of the work. He has a loving family. He has a whole support group around him at work.

And me? Peter asks. *What do I have?*

He's not sure he wants to answer the question.

CHAPTER 15

Peter takes a long shower in the morning. After his mugging last night, he puts on the layer of flexible body armor again. Once dressed, he has breakfast in his room and watches the Canadian national news.

Even the Canadian reporters find themselves compelled to report on the antics of the US president. It's another typical day of Wisser and his allies doing everything they can imagine to dismantle years of progress in every area of governmental assistance and regulation. To Peter, it appears that nothing is safe, not even child welfare or the park system. It's frustrating to watch from a distance, but he's sure it's worse close up. As Alden said, no one can truly imagine how bad it is unless they are there, in the middle of it.

He calls Bill Branch.

"Peter. Please tell me it's too early for you to be in any trouble this morning."

Peter laughs. "Don't worry. How did it work out for that guy last night? Did he hang around for any help?"

"He did, and he's in rehab right now. He still doesn't believe what happened. I'm surprised he can remember anything."

"I'm glad he agreed to rehab."

"He wants to thank you," Bill says, "personally. He asked me to give you his name and where he is."

"It'll have to wait until I'm back in town," Peter says. "Send me the information, and tell him that if he sticks to the rehab, I will certainly come to see him."

"You're a crazy man, Peter, but mostly it's a good kind of crazy."

Peter calls Patrick Balakrishnan next.

"Hello, Peter. How are you?"

"I'm great, Patrick. Have you made any progress on my CIA departure and the money for the widow and son of the policeman?"

"The papers for the widow and the boy, were finished late yesterday. If you want to review them and sign them, we can contact the widow."

"I'm in town. Send me an email with the documents. If I'm happy with them, I can drop by and sign them. When do you need the money?"

"No big hurry. She has to sign the agreements."

"I'll do a wire transfer to your trust account," Peter says. "You can handle it from there."

"That's fine."

"This is all anonymous, correct?"

"Yes," Patrick answers.

"Good," Peter says. "I'll see you this afternoon. What about the other issue? My retiring from the CIA?"

"I've made contact with Mitchoff. It's going to take a while. Maybe the end of the month?"

"That works."

"You want to come by the house for dinner tonight?"

"I will not turn you down twice, Patrick. Of course I'll come. How can I pass up a chance to enjoy your wife's cooking? It's been way too long. It's not a problem for her?"

"Not if I tell her now. Is there any possibility that Maria will come with you?"

"No. There's no change on that front, I'm afraid. We're not exactly a couple at the moment," Peter says. "But, really, Patrick, I will love it."

After the call with Patrick, Peter walks the short distance in the labyrinth of underground passageways and shopping in downtown Toronto. He's happy to avoid the streets and the wet snow that's still falling. He stops at the Harry Rosen clothing store and picks up a replacement shirt and blue blazer for the ones damaged in the stabbing. No time to have them tailored for a better fit, but they will do for the trip.

Back at the hotel, Peter approves the documents from Patrick and sets a time to come by the office at half-past four. He transfers money to cover the wire transfer. He confirms the hotel reservations in Lima and the AeroMexico flights and heads to the hotel gym for a short workout. Later, he sends an email to Sir Richard to confirm that all is proceeding as scheduled.

At four, he walks along the underground passageways to Patrick's office. He signs the two documents. By that simple action, and the wire transfer, he establishes his support of Jack Prescott's widow and young son.

Peter looks up at Patrick. "That's way too easy, and somehow it's entirely insufficient. The guy died trying to protect me and Maria. How do I compensate his wife for that loss? Or his son?"

As Patrick collects everything into a legal folder to hand off to his colleague, he looks across his desk at Peter. "Sometimes, Peter, I don't know who you are. You operate in some of the darkest corners of the world. I'm sure you don't hesitate to kill when you think it's needed, but I also know it troubles you deeply. Still... You do it." He raises his hands off the desk in a gesture of disbelief and lets them fall back again. "Then you do something like this. I don't know who you are."

Peter closes his eyes. After a moment of silence, he opens them and says, "I don't know who I am either, Patrick, but I do know who I want to be. I'm heading to Peru for the very last job of what will soon become my former life. I don't ever want to have this feeling again, this sense of guilt... helplessness... I don't want anyone to feel like they have to die, just so I can live."

Patrick shakes his head. "Go out and have a seat in the reception area. I have to make three phone calls, one for what you just signed. It shouldn't take more than half an hour. Then we'll head home for dinner."

Peter stands. "Thank you, Patrick."

"Just my job."

"No, I mean for everything you've done for me over the years, all the times you've listened to me, helped me, even way back at University. You've been a wonderful friend."

Patrick looks at him for a moment. Then he says, "Get out of here before we both get too sentimental."

Peter enjoys the commotion of Patrick's large family. The six children range in age from a toddler to early teens. They are all curious. Patrick tries to keep them from bothering Peter, but Peter waves him off. "Relax," he says. "I don't mind."

Once the initial excitement has faded, the oldest boy, Christopher, sits on the sofa beside Peter. He's just over twelve years old, and it's clear that there's something about Peter that holds particular interest for him. Peter steers the conversation to school and sports, but Christopher turns it back with a question.

"Have you really killed people?" the boy asks.

"Christopher," Patrick says. "You know better than to ask a question like that."

"I'm sorry," Christopher says, and he lowers his head.

Peter shakes his head. "An honest question deserves an honest answer. You know that I was a soldier in a war?"

"Yes. Papa told me."

"Since then, I have worked where there are some very bad men, sometimes women, too. They want to hurt or kill innocent people. My job is to stop them from doing that. In many ways, I am still a soldier, and still at war."

Christopher looks up at Peter again. "The answer then... is yes?"

"Yes."

Patrick watches and listens to the intimate conversation, but he does not intervene a second time.

"Do you like the job? Being a soldier?"

Peter looks at Christopher for a moment. "Do you want to know if I enjoy killing?"

The boy blushes and glances at his father. "Yes," he says softly.

"That's a fair question." Peter pauses. "When I was a younger man, I loved being a soldier. I was very good at it. Maybe I was too good at it. Because of the killing, I grew to hate being a soldier, and it nearly destroyed me. In about a month, I will no longer be a soldier. Do you know why?"

Christopher looks intently at him. "No."

Peter looks briefly at Patrick before he turns back to the boy and answers. "Because the killing can destroy a man's soul."

Looking at Christopher's face, Peter sees the face of a boy, but with eyes that return his look with an unexpected directness and intensity. "Do you understand what I am saying?"

"I think so, but I will ask papa about it."

Peter smiles. "I think that's an excellent idea. Your papa is a very wise man."

At this point, Patrick interrupts, clearing his throat. "Dinner is served," he says loudly, and all the children, including Christopher, noisily head to the dining room table.

Peter stands with Patrick for a moment, before he says, "You have a smart boy, who is wise beyond his years."

Patrick looks at his children, who are finding their places at the table. "Yes, I know," he says. "Sometimes it is a little frightening."

When the On Guard car drops him off at the hotel, he reminds Sander to pick him up at six in the morning. Peter is still feeling the warmth of Patrick's family. *It's what I want for myself*, he thinks.

He sleeps soundly, but not for much more than five hours before he hears the alarm. As is usually the case when he travels long distances, he shifts his brain into automatic. All the last-minute issues of packing and preparing for a long flight happen without much conscious thought.

The security service picks him up promptly at six, and he meets Maria at the business class check-in line at the airport. The flight leaves on schedule, in spite of the weather, which is now mostly rain. They spend most of their three-hour layover in Mexico City in the airline lounge.

They arrive at the Jorge Chavez International Airport in Lima a little after midnight. Peter has a text message from Omar Vargas, his MI6 assistant, that he will come to Peter's hotel room at three in the afternoon. Another from Julius Grant that he will arrive early Sunday morning and wants to meet Sunday afternoon.

I'll have to arrange for Maria to go to a museum or two on Sunday. Maybe go with her for the one in the morning.

While they wait for their baggage, Peter says, "Looks like people want to meet with me this afternoon and again on Sunday afternoon."

"Takes away some of the tourism, doesn't it?" Maria says.

"Yeah, but I don't think we want to do too much this afternoon anyway, and we're set for dinner at La Rosa Nautica, down on the water. We can go to a museum together Sunday morning, have lunch, and you can go to another alone that afternoon if you want."

"Visiting two museums in one day is about my limit," Maria says.

Peter laughs. "Mine, too, but the two I have in mind are very different. I reserved a table for us at La Huaca Pucllana for Sunday night, probably with Julius Grant. It's right by the old pyramid they're excavating, and it serves some more traditional Peruvian food. I'm pretty sure you'll like it."

"I think I'm in your hands."

"Not really," Peter says. "You should feel free to do whatever you choose."

Maria looks at Peter. "Thank you. I think you really mean that."

Peter shrugs. "I do."

"You may not like my choices."

Peter remains silent.

"You're also learning the value of silence," Maria says.

"Maybe."

They sail through immigration, baggage claim, and customs without delay. Peter finds the driver from La Seguridad Ejecutiva Peruana, who, as instructed, holds a sign with the single letter, B. At the DoubleTree by Hilton in Miraflores, they check in and go straight to their separate rooms.

Peter puts out the "Do Not Disturb" sign as he enters the room. Though he slept some on the way to Lima, he falls asleep immediately when he lies down on the bed. He has no intention of rising early.

Peter sleeps well until about six. He tosses and turns after that, sleeps some, and finally gets up several hours later. He dresses and goes downstairs for breakfast. The hotel puts on an excellent selection of breakfast foods, fruits, and the usual, strong, café con leche. He watches the crowd, mostly tourists, some with children, and some businessmen and women. *A harmless bunch*, he decides, and he focuses on his breakfast.

Back in his room, he empties his backpack and checks that everything has arrived safely. He turns on the small radiation detector. A series of slow, erratic clicks demonstrates the typical, weak background radiation. He turns off the sound and then turns off the detector. He places it and his other equipment back into his backpack. Nothing has gone missing from his baggage during the connection in Mexico City. He calls Carlos Bellido.

"Carlos! Peter Binder."

"Peter! You in Lima?"

"Yes. Got in just after midnight this morning. You have any updates on Cerro Nublado?"

"You're going ahead with the consulting job for Mandrake?"

"Yes," Peter says. "You heard any bad news lately?"

"It's been pretty quiet, but they're not doing much. I did talk to a couple of geologist friends who were consulting for Mandrake before Russo-Perú came along. They continued working for Russo-Perú for a while."

"What did they tell you?"

"Well…" Carlos hesitates. "They said community relations were kind of under control with Mandrake. Not ideal, but acceptable. Let's put it this way, they weren't afraid to be in the camp when Mandrake was still in charge."

"And when Russo-Perú arrived? Things changed?"

"Nothing happened right away," Carlos says. "Then the narcos began showing up in camp on a regular basis. Never more than three or four at a time. Usually they stayed the night. Always with assault rifles, pistols, big knives. One of my friends says they didn't do anything to harass the geologists, they just sat there, played with their guns, and stared at them. He says he's never been so scared in his entire life."

"What happened after that?"

"Not much. A few geologists quit. Russo-Perú fired the rest of them when they brought in their own people. I did talk to one of the NGOs that's working with some of the local villages. They're convinced that the narcos actually work for the Russian company now."

"You mentioned that possibility the last time we talked," Peter says.

"Now, I'm pretty sure it's true," Carlos responds.

"Not a happy thought."

They talk a little longer, and Peter suggests that they have dinner together, with Carlos' wife, Elena, if possible, at Astrid y Gastón when he's back in Lima from Cerro Nublado.

"I doubt Elena will be able to make it," Carlos says. "She's very busy with a television show about how to raise psychologically balanced children."

"We can certainly use a bit of that," Peter says.

Carlos laughs. "True enough!"

After the call, Peter looks at his watch. He calls Maria.

"Hi. You want to meet downstairs for lunch at one?"

"Sure."

"I have a meeting at three, but that should be plenty of time for a leisurely, Peruvian lunch. Then dinner at eight at La Rosa Nautica. The car will be here for us at fifteen minutes to eight."

"See you at lunch."

Peter calls a number Sir Richard gave him for a group in Lima.

"*Aló.*"

"*Soy Steinbauer. ¿La estás vigilando?*"

"*Si.*"

"*OK. Gracias.*"

Peter puts his phone down.

The watchers are already doing their job.

He closes his eyes and inhales deeply. Then he changes into shorts and a T-shirt and finds the exercise facilities for the hotel. Not much of a gym, but better than nothing.

No jogging on the streets of Lima this trip.

CHAPTER 16

Peter and Maria meet at the restaurant in the hotel. They both have simple sandwiches, though, as is sometimes the case in the local restaurants, both are best eaten with a knife and fork. They don't talk about anything of much substance.

"What two museums are you thinking about for tomorrow?" Maria asks.

"If you have to limit yourself to just two, some would say that the Museo de la Nación, the National Museum, should be one. I like two smaller museums a lot, the Museo Oro del Perú, which focuses on some of the exquisite metal works of ancient Peru, and Museo Larco, which has the largest collection of pre-Columbian pottery I've ever seen."

"Which do you want to visit with me?"

"I'd like to go to Museo Oro del Perú. The Museo Larco has a separate room, which has pottery mostly in sexual themes or showing diseases and medical issues. At one time, they wouldn't let unchaperoned women into that display. I don't think it's a problem now. I've always thought the pots showing diseases and medical themes were teaching tools, like illustrations in a medical textbook today. That's not always how the museum presents them. The amount of pottery they have at that museum is staggering."

"When do we leave the hotel?"

"They open at ten-thirty. Traffic should be okay on Sunday. We'll head out a little before ten, say quarter of?"

"Okay."

"You planning anything this afternoon?"

"I think," Maria says, "while you have your meeting, I'll sit by the pool and relax. Read one of the books I brought. It's just nice to be out of Toronto's winter."

"True. Dinner tonight is at eight. The car will pick us up at seven forty-five."

They return to their rooms a little after two-thirty.

At precisely three, Peter hears a knock on the door to the suite. As far as he can tell, with a look through the peephole in the door, it's Omar Vargas. Peter opens the door and lets him in.

Omar, as indicated by Sir Richard, is short but solidly built. Short-cropped black hair, nut-brown skin, a prominent nose, and eyes that appear both inquisitive and wary at the same time. He carries a thick, hard-sided briefcase in his left hand.

They shake hands, and Peter is not surprised by Omar's strong and solid grip.

"I'm glad to meet you, Sr. Vargus. You are exactly on time."

"My timing comes from working too long for Brits," Omar says with a slight laugh. His English carries a lilt that hints at the influence of British tutors. "Americans and Peruvians tend to be less punctilious."

Peter smiles. Omar's use of 'punctilious' surprises him. "Let's sit at the table by the window. Perhaps, if you don't mind, we can go by first names?"

"Good enough for me." Omar puts the briefcase on the table, turned for Peter to open it. "This contains the items you requested through Sir Richard. The combination is 7 3 8, but you can change it. The directions are on the inside."

Peter sets the combination and snaps the case open. The black cushioning material is cut out to hold two P229, 9mm pistols, two small belt holsters, one silencer, three loaded magazines of ammunition, fifteen rounds each, one of ten rounds, and two Canadian passports, one using the name Peter Binder and the other Robert Steinbauer. The passports appear to be well used, with the right entry stamp for Peru. There are also two Peruvian permits to carry the pistols, one for Peter and one for Maria.

"The permits are not forgeries. Not easy to get on short notice, but they're real. Just so you know."

"This looks good," Peter says. "Which clip is the special-order ammunition?"

"It's the one that's by itself. It's only ten rounds. If you take it out, you will see a small, linear scratch on the bottom, parallel to the sides. Handle that ammunition carefully. It's not quite as tough as it looks."

Peter takes the clip out of the case and examines it. "That's amazing. I think it will work perfectly."

"Don't mix it up," Omar says.

Peter smiles. "Don't worry, but I'm glad you made a small mark to help me." He puts the clip back and shuts the briefcase, as his phone indicates a text message. "Excuse me," he says. "I'll take a quick look."

The message is from the watchers. Maria took a taxi from the front of the hotel, and they are following. Peter texts, *Gracias.*

"Let's talk about how to handle things at Cerro Nublado," Peter says.

"Sir Richard is taking this job very seriously. I don't generally work in the field unless they're really worried."

"He's more concerned than I am. I can't see anything in the technical reports to raise any suspicions. And the CEO of Mandrake, Julius Grant, is coming into the camp with us. But… If Sir Richard is right, and Russo-Perú is hiding something, or maybe even Mandrake is hiding something, and it's important enough… If they think I'll find it, we're on extremely dangerous ground."

"Just for your information," Omar says, "we think the Russians have bought the local narcos, the old Sendero veterans who now provide their security, some of the ronderos, and all of the local police. We're pretty much on our own when we're at the camp."

"And then," Peter says, "there's El Come Huevos. He seems like a very reasonable fellow."

Omar laughs. "Oh, yes, very reasonable indeed."

"Okay," Peter says, "the best-case scenario is that no one is hiding anything. The Russians want a South American copper resource for the future; this is where they've landed; and Minera Russo-Perú is just their corporate vehicle for the exercise. In that case no one cares about my visit or what I might or might not find there."

"Nice concept, but I wouldn't count on it."

"If we want to be sure to survive, I agree. We should not count on that," Peter says. "The worst-case scenario is that someone is hiding something that they desperately want to keep a secret. They already know I'll find it, or they strongly suspect I will."

"If they already know, they will make an attempt on your life here in Lima. Of course, it won't look like the Russians, but if something like that happens, our risk profile goes way up."

Peter receives another text message. Maria is at the Russian Embassy in San Isidro, and someone just let her in.

That's interesting, Peter thinks. *Are they open for business on Saturday?* He puts his phone down.

"Sir Richard tells me," Omar says, "that you're traveling with Maria Davidoff."

"Yes."

"Are you going out to dinner tonight?" Omar asks.

"La Rosa Nautica at eight," Peter says.

"I'll let Sir Richard know."

They sit for a minute in silence.

"Let's talk about the worst-case scenario at Cerro Nublado, Omar. If they want to come after us, how do you think it'll go down?"

"The narcos, specifically their security team of Sendero veterans, will come to the camp," Omar says. "They'll probably shoot you, me and Julius Grant. They might leave our bodies, or they might throw us in the river. If El Come Huevos comes along, it could get truly ugly."

"You think we'll get any warning?" Peter asks.

"Most likely. Usually the local laborers will know about something like this, and they'll disappear, either into the jungle or head back home."

Peter thinks about the potential relationships in the camp. "I think I have to act as the slightly arrogant *norteamericano* geologist, and you have to play the role of the obedient, subservient, and unhappy Peruvian assistant. You have to sleep with the local laborers, ingratiate yourself with them, make damn sure they love you, and ensure that they'll let you know when you should run away."

"My thinking exactly," Omar says. "And I'm quite good at playing that role. My guess is, if they think you'll discover their big secret, that's the only way we survive."

Peter receives another message. Maria is on the move again.

"I'm taking one of these pistols and the silencer with me to the camp," Peter says. "I suggest you do something along the same lines. It doesn't even the odds if there are more of them than us, particularly if they bring along assault rifles, but it gives us a fighting chance."

"When you work out the schedule with Julius Grant, let me know," Omar says. "We probably need to leave by six in the morning on Monday to get in there by helicopter before dark."

"I'll let you know," Peter says.

Omar lets himself out the door and closes it softly.

Peter looks at his watch. A little after four.

Lots of time.

Time for a quick nap before he has to get ready for tonight. He receives another text. Maria has returned to the hotel.

Interesting. That was quick.

Peter heads downstairs a few minutes before seven forty-five. He is dressed in gray slacks. He has two layers of ballistic protection, one being the navy-blue sports coat. He also carries one of the P229's in a small holster on his belt, toward the back of his left side and well hidden by the sports coat.

He meets Maria at the front entrance to the hotel. The car from Seguridad Ejecutiva takes them the short distance to the restaurant. Peter speaks to Jesus, the driver, and tells him he'll call for their return to the hotel sometime around eleven. He and Maria turn and walk down the pier to the restaurant.

Peter reserved a table at the windows looking out over the ocean to the west. It's already dark, but the restaurant has outside lighting that illuminates the beach and the surf, such as it is.

"We should start with a Pisco sour," Peter says. "I'm not usually a fan of mixed drinks, but it is the Peruvian national drink."

Once the drinks arrived, Maria tastes hers. "Quite good."

"Easy to drink, and usually pretty strong. You want to go easy on them," Peter says.

Peter points to the people still in the water, some on surfboards in the modest waves. "I don't think I'd swim here. It's probably fine most of the time, but this is a big city, and the final treatment of sewage is a long pipe out into the ocean."

"That alters the romance of the scene a bit."

"Sorry," Peter says. "Speaking of swimming, did you have a good time by the pool this afternoon?"

"Calm. Relaxing." She smiles. "I did go to the Russian embassy, though."

"Really? How come?"

"Oh, an old friend of mine from way back when I was a teenager works there. I sort of forgot it was Saturday, but he was actually there. We'll try to have dinner sometime when I'm here alone."

"That should be interesting," he says.

"Yes, it should be," Maria says. "How about you? Exciting meetings?"

"Not particularly. I met with a guy who'll help me with the core at Cerro Nublado. Laid out some of our plans."

The waiter arrives to take their orders.

"I recommend their corvina," Peter says. "It's nicely seasoned, or it was the last time I came here. If you don't mind, I'll order some ceviche to share for starters."

"The corvina sounds good," Maria says to the waiter. "I'll have that."

Peter picks several varieties of ceviche. "I'll go with the *lomo saltado* for my main course," he says.

Maria raises her eyebrows. "No fish for you?"

Peter shrugs. "You're right. I should order fish, but somehow the lamb appeals to me tonight. We are having ceviche, so at least I'll have some fish. You have any problem with red wine?"

Maria shrugs. "That's fine with me."

Peter reviews the wine list, looks up at the waiter and orders an Italian Barolo. "And we should each have another pisco sour."

After the waiter leaves, Peter raises his glass. "You happy you came with me?" he asks.

She sips at her drink, puts it down and says, "I don't know. We'll have to see what happens. I'll know at the end of the trip."

"You have forgiven me a little for taking the job?"

She sits back. "Maybe a little, but I'm still upset that you're deliberately and needlessly putting yourself in a dangerous position."

"If you're worried that Minera Russo-Perú has something they're hiding, I think it's extremely unlikely."

"But not impossible."

"No… It's not impossible," Peter says.

"That's my point."

They sit in silence for a while.

Maria looks down at her drink. "When you were at my apartment packing," she says, "I noticed you included your radiation detector. Why pack that, to look at a copper deposit?"

Peter laughs. "It goes back to some research I did in grad school. Some of the granites that produce certain types of large copper deposits are a little 'hot', or slightly radioactive. I'm still interested in that. It might help evaluate copper potential in different groups of granites."

"What do you do?"

"Oh, I try to measure the background radiation levels in the freshest granite I can find. Then I randomly test the different zones of mineralization, to get a picture of radiation levels in the system as a whole. It's quick and easy, and I never include it in my reports. Truthfully? I'm a little embarrassed by this 'hobby' research. I rarely find anything of interest, and nobody's interested in it but me."

Their ceviche arrives, and they share the different varieties. They have their second Pisco sour, and their wine arrives. It is a good Barolo.

Before the main course, Maria says, "Time for a quick visit to the ladies' room. Be right back."

Peter watches her go, and he decides to go to the men's room. It's near the entrance to the restaurant across from the ladies' room. Before he enters the men's room, he suddenly stops. Maria is on her phone, in front of the restaurant, looking away from him toward the parking area, and gesturing with her free hand as she talks.

Who the hell is she calling?

He immediately returns to the table. He pours most of his second Pisco sour into the potted plant next to the table.

Maria rejoins him at the same time that the main courses arrives.

"Sorry," she says, shaking her head. "That took longer than I expected. I got a call from Pitcairn Gold. They're thinking of making a release, updating their drilling plans, and they wanted my comments."

As they begin on the main course, their conversation turns to small issues. When should they get up in the morning? Should they have breakfast together?

Peter gives her a piece of paper. "That's the name and telephone number for a lady who can set up a visit to Machu Picchu, if you want to go. I had her make reservations for you to fly to Cusco on Monday, train to Machu Picchu on Tuesday. Overnight in Aguas Calientes and return to Cusco on Wednesday. Back to Lima on Thursday."

"That's a lot of going," Maria says.

"Not really. Most of a day to muck around in Cusco, which is a fascinating city. Your hotel pumps extra oxygen into the rooms, and that should let you sleep reasonably well. You'll still have Thursday afternoon, and all of Friday, Saturday, and most of Sunday in Lima, before I return from the field." He shrugs. "You should see Machu Picchu, but if you don't want to go, give her a call. She can cancel it all tomorrow with no problems."

"I think I'll see how I feel about it tomorrow morning. Sleep on it," she says with a smile.

They talk through dessert. Peter drinks the wine as sparingly as he can. She goes to the ladies' room again. He pours most of his wine into the potted plant. *Probably not very good for the plant*, he thinks. *Probably better for me.*

When she returns, they talk a little longer before Peter signals for the check, pays, and calls Seguridad Ejecutiva. They stroll down the pier from the restaurant toward the parking area. They're a little early.

Peter, mostly out of habit, quickly surveys the busy scene. Nothing separates itself as an obvious threat in the confusion of taxis and private cars. Their car is already waiting for them. Peter holds the door to the car for Maria and climbs in after her. He sits, in the back, on the opposite side from Jesus, the driver.

Halfway back to the hotel, a delivery van stops suddenly in front of them, and Jesus nearly hits the van. Then a large black car hits them, quite hard, from behind. With a clash of metal, they slide into the van, completely blocked by the two vehicles.

Two men jump out of the van. One with a pistol on the passenger side. One on the driver's side with an assault rifle.

"¡*Carajo!*" Jesus shouts.

Both men open fire.

Jesus opens his door and bails out onto the pavement.

"Get down!" Peter shouts. He pulls his pistol out of the holster. The battlefield adrenaline slams into him.

Maria is already on the floor of the back seat. She's swearing loudly in English and Russian.

She's too quick, Peter thinks.

He chances a look through the back window. No shooters.

Peter opens the door on his side. He rolls out onto the pavement. The man with the pistol advances, firing on the car. He's about fifteen feet away when Peter fires four quick shots.

He hits the man three times. Right eye. Neck. Lower chest. The man drops his pistol and goes to his knees. One more shot to his head. He's down.

Peter looks back again and sees a man exit the rear vehicle, pistol raised. He's about twenty feet away from Peter when he turns and aims.

Peter fires five times. Four connect, including two shots to the head and two to the chest. The man falls flat on the pavement.

Peter looks under the security company's car. Jesus lies on the ground with his hands over his head.

"Don't blame him," Peter mutters.

The man with the assault rifle fires almost continuously into the windows and body of the security company's car. He has reloaded once. The car is not armored, and he riddles the car with bullet holes. Already the windshield is in shreds, and the back window is shattered.

The shooter stops to reload a second time.

Peter fires twice to the man's chest, and the attacker staggers back.

Before he can recover, Peter gets in three more shots. Left ear. Left side of his neck. Left elbow.

The shooter falls back against the lead car. Blood streams down his chest from his neck wound. He struggles to raise the rifle with his right arm.

Peter ducks down behind the security company's car again. He's out of ammunition.

He puts his pistol back in the holster and prepares to make a dash to grab the pistol from the dead shooter in front of him. He hears squealing tires.

Six shots ring out from the vicinity of the rear vehicle.

He looks over the hood of the car. A large, black car, with a heavy front crash bar, executes a slow-motion ramming of the lead vehicle.

The impact crushes the wounded man with the rifle. He manages three or four wild shots.

Peter crouches down again, beside the car.

Suddenly, it's astonishingly quiet.

"Jesus Christ!" Peter says. He feels his heart pounding. "Are you okay, Maria?"

"Okay? Dammit! What's going on?"

"Stay down! I'm not sure this is over," Peter says.

At that point, Peter hears another voice, in a rather posh British accent, "You folks okay?"

Peter remains crouched beside the car. "Yeah. I'm in one piece. Who the hell are you?"

"I'm part of security for the British embassy. Saw you at the restaurant. Didn't like who we saw following your car."

Peter rises up enough to look to the rear car. No sign of life. The driver is slumped against the steering wheel. That explains the shots he had just heard. Peter turns and looks forward. No obvious survivors.

Peter slowly stands up. He smiles and shakes his head. Sir Richard stands next to the black car that crushed the gunner and puts his finger to his lips. The British Embassy vehicle is already backing up.

"Is the lady okay?" Sir Richard asks.

Peter looks down at Maria, still in the back of the car. She is cursing loudly and slowly getting up on her hands and knees. "You okay?" he asks.

She looks up at him for a long moment. "I… am… fine," she says.

Peter reaches down and helps her up. "You're looking great, considering what just went down."

She speaks very deliberately. "I do not like feeling totally fucking helpless. If this is what a dinner date with you is going to be like from now on, forget it."

Peter laughs.

Maria glares at him as she gets out of the car.

"Sorry," Peter says.

"Come around this side," Sir Richard says. "We'll get you out of here."

Peter and Maria walk around the front of the lead vehicle. Sir Richard talks briefly to the apparently unharmed security service driver, telling him how to handle the situation.

Sir Richard holds the door for Peter and Maria to get into the back seat. He takes the front passenger seat. "Where are you staying?"

"DoubleTree in Miraflores," Peter says.

"Good hotel," Sir Richard says. "Bad show back there. Obviously, an attempted kidnapping. Terrible publicity for Peruvian tourism. Those guys were looking forward to a big payday, I suspect, but it went rather badly for them."

"Thanks to you," Peter says.

"You did seem to be defending yourself rather well."

"A bit outgunned," Peter says.

"Didn't seem to bother you too much."

"It would have. I was out of ammunition."

"Where did you come from anyway?" Maria asks.

"Like I said. I'm part of security for the British Embassy. We were on duty at La Rosa Nautica, and we thought your followers looked a little bit… let us say, down market."

Maria says flatly, "Right."

I don't think she buys it, Peter thinks. He can't help smiling. *I guess I don't blame her.*

"You have Canadian passports?" Sir Richard asks.

"Yes," Peter says.

Maria looks at him in astonishment.

"Good. We should be able to handle this for you with a minimum of involvement from the police, which is good. We'll coordinate with the Canadian Embassy. You do have a permit to have the pistol in Peru?"

"Yes. I do."

Once back at the hotel they ask the hotel to make copies of the front page of their passports, provide some other information, and watch Sir Richard disappear out the door.

Peter turns to Maria. "You still want to go to a museum in the morning?"

"You're joking."

"Yeah. I am. I don't want to go either." He looks at her. She looks completely disheveled. "You okay?"

"No! I am not okay. I was lying on the floor of a car in the middle of a gunfight. The car must have a hundred bullet holes in it. You roll out of the car and play hero, with a pistol I didn't even know you had. The British cavalry rides up out of nowhere and rescues us. Suddenly you, an American citizen, conveniently have a Canadian passport. It's like a stupid, poorly directed, and incredibly bad movie. And you ask me if I'm okay? Are you crazy?"

Peter shakes his head. "You are in one piece. Correct?"

"Yes, dammit."

"That's all I want to know at the moment." Peter takes several deep breaths. "There's nothing more for us to do tonight. Let's go to our rooms and try to sleep."

"Really?" Maria says. "Sleep? I rather doubt that." She glares at Peter, and then she heads for the elevator.

When Peter gets to his room, he sends a text to Sir Richard.

Peter: *That was interesting.*
Sir Richard: *You still think there's nothing to see at Cerro Nublado?*
Peter: *As you said, could have been a kidnap attempt.*
Sir Richard: *I don't think so. Too much shooting.*
Peter: *Maybe.*
Sir Richard: *Kidnappers want you alive. You want more security at Cerro Nublado?*
Peter: *Possibly. Maybe a small army? Talk tomorrow.*
Sir Richard: *Right.*

Peter sits at the table in his room and looks out the window… at nothing. He closes his eyes and focuses on his breathing. Gradually, his mind and his body calm. He is alone, in the white sea, in the emptiness.

When he opens his eyes, he takes a deep breath. He strips off his clothes. He locks the door to the room, sets the chain lock, and wedges a chair from the table under the doorknob. He drops into bed.

"Damn!" he mutters.

Maria's right. I should go home, but I won't. It's getting too interesting.

"You're an idiot," he says.

CHAPTER 17

In his dream, Peter is beside the car. The man with the pistol walks toward him. Peter tries to shoot him, but his pistol will not fire. The man comes closer. He aims at Peter's head. He pulls the trigger.

Peter wakes with a shout. He sits up in bed, panting.

"Jesus!"

After his breathing calms down, he gets up and goes to the bathroom. When he returns to the bed, he sits on the edge of it. He runs his hands through his hair. He thinks about what Sir Richard texted.

Kidnappers want you alive.

"It was no kidnapping gone bad," he says.

They wanted to kill me, or scare me so much that I'll leave Peru before I go to Cerro Nublado.

"Okay, buddy. What the hell do you do now?"

He looks at his watch. Too late to go back to bed. He returns to the bathroom to shower. Half an hour later, he is dressed and on his way down the elevator for breakfast. He grabs a copy of the Lima newspaper on the way to his table.

The story isn't on the front page, but two pages in he finds the picture of the bullet-ridden security car. The story is all about the hero driver, who fended off the kidnappers and saved two unnamed tourists.

Peter laughs. "Perfect!" he says.

He eats a hearty breakfast, skims the rest of the paper, and heads back to his room. Once there, he makes two phone calls. One to Seguridad Ejecutiva. He requests that they increase security with an armed bodyguard in their car, that they use a car hardened against small arms fire, and that a car follows with two armed bodyguards. They agree, and Peter approves a much higher charge for the enhanced security.

"Sorry about the car," Peter says.

"*OK! No hay problema.* We are happy that you and Ms. Davidoff were not harmed."

"Thanks to your driver," Peter says. He almost laughs.

"*Si!* Yes. We have given him some time off."

"Good idea," Peter says.

"Do you still want the car this morning?"

"I don't think so. I'll call you back if we decide to go to the museum after all."

"I understand."

Peter calls Sir Richard next.

"Purcell here."

"Peter Binder. We need to talk. Can you come to my room?"

"What's the number?"

Peter tells him.

"I'll be there in about fifteen minutes."

Peter sits back on the sofa. He thinks about what went down last night, and what he should do about it. He is surprised at how little the event seems to bother him. Other than the nightmare, which is unfortunately the norm, he's fine.

I'm scared, but that's healthy.

He feels no debilitating depression and no overwhelming anxiety. He doesn't completely understand why.

He retrieves a Coke from the small refrigerator, pops it open, and sits at the table to wait for Sir Richard.

He calls Maria in her room.

"You doing okay?" he asks.

"I'm doing okay. Not great, but okay," she says. "Sorry about how angry I was last night."

"No problem. It was a crazy night. I've told the security company to add an armed bodyguard to the car, and to have a second car with two armed guards following us. It's a little crazy, but it should be deterrent for any bad actors in Lima."

"Well… Do you think we could safely go to the museum this morning anyway?"

"Yeah. I think so, but you were the one in the car while they were filling it full of holes, not me. Are you okay with going out again this soon?"

"Soon or late. I've got to go out again eventually."

"I have a meeting shortly, but if we delay it to eleven, I think that will work."

"Don't you have a meeting with the CEO of Mandrake this afternoon?"

"Yeah. I'll send a message and put him off until four."

"Okay. I think we should go to the museum," Maria says.

"I'll meet you at the front at eleven."

That's a bit of a surprise, Peter thinks as he ends the call. He quickly calls Seguridad Ejecutiva and requests their car service for the museum tours, with the additional security. As he finishes with them, Sir Richard shows up.

"So, Peter, what do you think about last night now?" Sir Richard asks. He sits on the sofa, and Peter sits in the large chair on the other side of the coffee table.

"I guess I might agree with you now. It was not a kidnapping attempt. I think the objective was to either kill me or scare me so much that I get on the next plane home. They probably didn't care which."

"I think you're right," Sir Richard says. "Any thoughts about how they knew your schedule as well as they did?"

"Richard, I fully understand what you're driving at. Yes, it's a definite possibility, but it doesn't matter. I've doubled up on security. I don't think they'll come after me again in Lima, not with the increased security. Why should they? It's too difficult now to deal with me here, and they still have Cerro Nublado. Nice and isolated."

"There's always the possibility of what you Americans like to call an 'inside job', or an intimate assassination."

Peter glares at Sir Richard and shakes his head.

"Okay. I won't explore that any further. What's your added security?"

Peter tells him. "You okay with the added cost? It'll be substantial."

"Have they scared you?"

"Bloody right they have," Peter responds.

"Are you headed home?"

"I don't think so. I'm pretty sure I can handle the added risks."

"Then I'm happy to pay for the added security."

"Good."

Peter stands up. "I'm getting another Coke. You want something?"

"A bottle of water would be good. Still, if you please."

"What's the status with the authorities on last night?" Peter asks as he returns to his seat with the drinks.

"They're not too stressed about it. I talked with them last night. They want a statement from you, perhaps Maria too, but it's obvious what happened. Can you do that tomorrow?"

"That's inconvenient. I was planning to spend all day tomorrow to get to Cerro Nublado. I'll have to put that off a day."

"Does that give you enough time at the camp?" Sir Richard asks.

"Maybe." Peter shrugs. "If not, I can delay my return to Lima by a day."

"Speaking of the camp, what happened last night does, I think, affect how we approach your visit to Cerro Nublado."

"Yes, it does," Peter says. "I'm beginning to think that someone really is hiding something, and that they'll try to kill me, and probably anybody with me while we're at Cerro Nublado. That would eliminate my report and will certainly discourage anyone else."

"You want more security?"

"If you mean more people... I don't think so," Peter answers. "How many is enough, anyway? Twenty well-armed guards? Forty? It's a small camp, and those numbers aren't really practical. Carlos Bellido told me that there were never more than three or four of the narco security guys in the camp. That's who they'll use to get to me. It gives Russo-Perú a lot of plausible deniability." Peter pauses a moment. "You know a guy named Jim Blakestad?"

"I know about him and his work. Don't know him personally."

"He's an old friend of mine. I talked with him before I left Toronto to come here. I asked him about El Come Huevos. He didn't have a single good word to say about him, but he did say that he usually runs a very small organization. Three to four guys. Well armed. He relies on his reputation and viciousness to control the poor farmers."

Sir Richard remains silent and takes a drink of the water.

"I suspect they're a pretty small group, Richard. Hard pressed to come up with more than four guys with guns. Not to discount their potentially lethal capabilities, or that goof ball's reputation, with a little luck, I think Omar and I can handle this."

"I talked with Omar."

"What did he say?" Peter asks.

"Pretty much what you're saying, except…"

"Yeah. Except what?"

"Except he'd like to ramp up the artillery a little. He's fine with the P229, but he'd prefer the heavier caliber .357. He also thinks it might be good to have one more guy, someone who's good in the jungle. He suggested Steve Berner."

Peter shakes his head. "Jesus! That guy's… I've heard all sorts of stories about Steve, but I have never worked directly with him. Never really met him. I don't want to say he's crazy, but… some of my friends tell stories about him that are absolutely nuts. I have to admit, though, even when they're telling these stories about him, they all insist that he's really good at his job." Peter is quiet for a moment. "It is an interesting thought. What would he do?"

Sir Richard smiles. "You're right. Berner is strange, but some of his skills might be useful to you at the camp. From what Omar tells me, you're depending on the local workers warning him if something unpleasant is about to happen. You're assuming they'll know and leave camp. That's fine. Omar is really good at that sort of thing. Suppose our buddy, the egg eater, decides to move fast. Doesn't tell anyone. He might, if the Russians are calling the shots."

"That is possible," Peter admits.

"Berner would be a backup. Another potential source of information. I don't know exactly what he'd do. He'd be out there. Watching. That's what he does."

"Do you think I could pass him off as an eccentric field geologist?" Peter asks. "If I can, then he could pack some food and just disappear for a few days."

"Probably."

Peter looks out the window. "Right. Let's assume the three of us go to the camp. All of us need to get together with you, tomorrow sometime, to do some detailed planning. Can you set that up for some time after I talk to the police? Someplace other than here? Maria should be on her way to Cusco tomorrow with plans to visit Machu Picchu. She won't be back until Thursday, but I don't want Julius Grant to barge into our planning meeting."

Sir Richard stands up. "Okay. I'll set up a time at the embassy for tomorrow. You'll be using your added security detail, starting tonight?"

"Yes. Tonight, and when we go to a museum or two today."

Peter stands with Sir Richard. "I have to say it was a nice story that got to the newspaper," Peter says. "What should I tell the police?"

"I suggest the truth. It's what I told them," Sir Richard says. "The newspapers are another story altogether. Make sure you thank the driver, if the reporters find you and corner you. At the moment, they shouldn't know who you are, but you never know. Tell them that you were lying on the floor in the back seat, along with Maria."

"Okay. But it's a blow to my macho pride," Peter says with a smile.

Sir Richard laughs. "You'll survive it."

On his way out the door, Sir Richard turns. "By the way, that was some pretty fancy shooting last night. I was impressed."

"Not so smart, though, running out of ammunition."

"Oh, that reminds me," Sir Richard says. "I brought these for you," and he hands Peter two full clips of 9mm ammunition for the P229. "Anyway, three shooters, all dead or disabled, one with an AR15, and you did that with fifteen, 9mm shots? Not bad."

"Well, thanks for the cleanup," Peter says.

"That, my friend, is my job," Sir Richard says with a wave, and lets the door shut behind him.

Peter double locks the door after Sir Richard leaves. He looks at his watch. A little after ten. Time to get ready. He sends a quick message to Julius rescheduling their meeting to four, and indicating a probable delay of one day for their departure to Cerro Nublado. He dresses with an undershirt with the body armor in place. He carries the pistol in a small backpack.

He meets Maria in the lobby. The cars are already waiting.

Maria looks at the two cars and the guards. "This is impressive."

"A show of force is the best defense in the kidnapping business," Peter says. "I don't want a repeat of last night."

"Nor do I," Maria says. "You still planning on going to Cerro Nublado?"

"Yeah. I don't see that an attempted kidnapping has much impact on that decision."

"You're crazy."

"Maybe. You going to Machu Picchu?"

"I leave early tomorrow morning."

"You want some security from this group?" Peter asks, gesturing to the front seat.

"I don't think it's necessary, as long as you're not with me."

"Ouch! That hurts, but you're probably right."

When they arrive at the Museo Oro del Perú, Peter leaves his backpack in the car. He asks one of the bodyguards to accompany them, discretely.

"I should warn you, Maria. There is considerable controversy about this museum. It closed for a while after a scandal that many of the pieces on display were fake. It reopened, designating some pieces as reproductions. It's kind of helter-skelter, but there's some fascinating stuff here."

They spend a little over an hour and a half in the museum. They find a small café on a nearby, quiet street. They have a light lunch of *sopa criolla de bisteca* and a few wonderfully light empanadas.

"Well," Peter says, "I need to head back to my meeting with my employer. I suggest we drop you off at Museo Larco. Then they can take me back to the hotel, come back to the museum, and pick you up when you're ready."

"I could probably take a taxi," Maria says.

"I wouldn't recommend it," Peter says, "except possibly if a hotel or restaurant calls a taxi for you. As someone traveling as a single woman, you should be particularly careful. Keep that in mind on your trip to Machu Picchu."

"Don't worry about that. I have a car service to the airport. One meeting me in Cusco, and a guide with me to Machu Picchu and back. Your travel agent contact is being very careful with me."

"Good."

Maria nods her head. "Send the car back for me. I'll be a good girl and wait for it."

Peter laughs. They drop her off at the museum. Peter returns to the hotel at about three thirty. He calls Julius, who agrees to come to Peter's room at four. Peter strips off his body armor before he sits down to wait for Julius.

"Nice place," Julius says as he enters Peter's suite.

As usual, even after a long series of flights from his home in Brisbane, Australia, to Lima, Julius is fired up when he enters the room. His height, just shy of six feet, and his curly blond hair, makes him stand out in Peru, even more than most other gringos. Julius is also always in motion, both physically and mentally. Peter knows he's tougher than he looks.

"I've already held three meetings here with people who will help me in this review. I think it's paid for itself already."

"I'm not complaining, but what's this about delaying a day? It seems to me that you're already cutting it short."

"We can postpone our return if necessary. Anyway, there was a nasty kidnapping attempt on Maria and me last night. I have to talk with the police on Monday, tomorrow morning."

"Was that the one I read about in the newspaper this morning?"

"Yes."

"Looks like a lot of bullets were flying," Julius says.

"There were."

"But you're both okay?"

"Thanks to our driver from La Seguridad Ejecutiva Peruana, we're fine."

"Bloody hell. That's quite the welcome back to Peru," Julius says.

"Yes, it is," Peter says. "It seems a little abnormal to try to kidnap someone who has just arrived in Lima. Usually they want to study your movements. Carefully plan the ambush. I have been wondering if this might have anything to do with Cerro Nublado."

"I think you're letting your imagination run a bit wild," Julius says. "Why go after you? If they kill you or scare you away, they have to know another geologist will be right behind you."

"Not all things in life are logical."

Julius shrugs. "True."

"Listen," Peter says, "you should warn the camp that I'm bringing two assistants with me. One will help me go through the core. The other is a bit of a jungle rat. He'll head out into the jungle and look at all the outcrops he can find. We probably won't see him much in camp." Peter smiles. "Often, he prefers to sleep in the jungle."

"Sometimes, Peter, you seem to come up with very strange friends and acquaintances."

"Yeah," Peter laughs, "you included."

Julius shakes his head. "Ha. Ha. Ha."

"I have to ask, Julius. What's your real reason for having me do this review?"

"I assume you've seen how anxious my partners are to get this thing permitted and into production?"

"I have noticed that," Peter says.

"And I'm sure you're aware of some of the permitting hurdles, the local and NGO opposition to the property, the opposition by the narcos, and even the bloody church. And then there's the huge size of the development costs."

"I am aware of these issues."

"It doesn't make sense," Julius says. "As much as I want to see this thing in production, pushing it this hard doesn't make sense. They even have an advance contract with the North Koreans for smelting and refining. They must know something that we don't know. Maybe they've discovered some high grade that changes the economics in a major way. Maybe they've stumbled onto some other resource in the area. I don't know, but I want you to figure it out."

"If it's a new resource, a new discovery, and I don't have access to the information, I won't know anything about it."

"I understand," Julius says. "That's not really part of your job. It is something I wonder about, but it's rather unlikely."

"The feasibility study and all the supporting documents look great," Peter says. "They're well done by good solid groups and geoscientists. They didn't come up with any surprises, and there's been almost no drilling since then."

"They're all cookbook scientists," Julius says. "You know that as well as I do. They look for what ought to be there. They wouldn't see a major anomaly if it jumped out of the drill hole and bit them in the ass. You, on the other hand, are always looking for surprises. And you find them."

"It's usually pretty easy," Peter says. "In most cases, there are hints in the details of the feasibility studies. The only thing I can do is try to open my eyes to anything unusual and collect a bunch of small samples throughout the deposit. Analyze them for a whole raft of metals and trace elements, and see if we have something strange, like a bunch of rare earth elements that shouldn't be in a normal copper deposit. All those wonderful rare metals that everyone wants for super-magnets, modern batteries, and all the devices of our digital world."

"See? That's exactly what I'm saying about your thought process."

"It isn't rocket science," Peter responds. "All you need to do is take the samples and analyze them."

"But you need to choose your elements," Julius says. "You don't analyze the entire periodic table."

"I come pretty close," Peter says.

"Yeah. Well, I'm glad you're doing the review. If there's anything strange there, you'll find it." Julius says. "I'm planning for us to fly up to Piura on a charter flight. We'll have two vehicles meet us at the airport to take us to Huancabamba, where we'll meet the helicopter from Cerro Nublado. With any luck, we'll be in the camp by late afternoon.

"Now," Julius says, "to change the subject, where are we eating tonight?"

"I have a reservation for three at La Huaca Pucllana at seven tonight. Maria will join us."

"That should keep the conversation more interesting," Julius says.

"I should warn you that I've put on quite a bit of security as a result of last night. I'm not charging you for it, but just so you know."

"Like what?"

"Like two cars from Seguridad Ejecutiva, two drivers, and three armed guards."

"That's a bit of overkill, isn't it?" Julius asks. "It's only about six blocks. We could walk it."

"Not after last night. We are not walking anywhere, and two of the guards will be watching the place while we eat."

"Okay. I guess I can understand that. Meet downstairs at about quarter to seven?"

Peter smiles. "Sounds about right to me."

Later that evening, they have a delightful dinner with a good bottle of wine.

Julius is in good form, one of his better performances of his gregarious self, Peter thinks.

They return to the hotel without incident. Peter wishes Maria well on her trip to Machu Picchu, and tells Julius he'll call him tomorrow in the afternoon, when he's done with the police.

As he lies in bed, Peter realizes he's beginning to look forward to the challenges of Cerro Nublado.

CHAPTER 18

Peter wakes up to a text message from Sir Richard.

Omar will pick you up at 9. Our car. He'll make sure there are no language issues.

Peter is happy to have Omar there for two reasons. First, he doesn't want to rely on his Spanish for a police interview, and he prefers to have the translator on his side rather than rely on the police to translate. Second, he and Omar will work closely together at Cerro Nublado, and this gives Peter a chance to tell a little about himself to Omar, without really having to tell it.

Peter responds to the text that he will be ready, and he goes to breakfast. As he's eating, he checks the morning newspaper. There is no follow-up on the earlier story about the attempted kidnapping. Sir Richard is right. Such things are embarrassing to the authorities, and they do what they can to minimize them.

For the interview, Peter wears his good sports coat from his suitcase, the one without the body armor. He has his pistol, holstered in its usual spot. The British Embassy car arrives with an armed driver and a second, armed guard in the front seat. Peter joins Omar in the back.

"A bit of excitement Saturday night," Omar says with a small smile.

"Yeah. A bit."

"Sir Richard was impressed."

"So he told me," Peter says.

"He doesn't hand out compliments like that very often."

"How do we handle this interview, Omar? Sir Richard told me to tell the truth."

"That's what I'd do. You did nothing wrong. You have the permit for the pistol, and last night explained, better than anything else could, why you need it."

"I did like the story about the heroic driver," Peter says.

"But it won't hold up to any scrutiny by the police," Omar responds. "They'll probably want your pistol. Do you have it with you?"

"Yes."

"Good. Let's make an exchange." Omar reaches into a briefcase and withdraws a P229, the same as the one Peter hands to him. Peter puts the replacement in the holster.

"You'll have to leave the pistol in the car when we go into the police interview," Omar says.

"I assumed that would be the case." He takes the holstered pistol off his belt and puts it in the seat pocket in front of him.

Omar unloads and hands Peter's original pistol to the guard in the front seat. "Give this to the police if they ask for it," he says.

He then turns to Peter. "The interview will be with the PNP, the Policia National del Perú. Should be professional. Emilio Sanchez, a lawyer who does a lot of work for the embassy, will be there with us. He's young, but he is very good. You should follow any advice he may offer, and if you have any questions during the interview feel free to ask to consult with him. Sir Richard has already talked with the police and explained what happened, exactly as he saw it happen. We don't expect any problems."

"Yeah," Peter says. "I've been here before, but not in Peru."

Emilio meets them at the entrance to the police building. After shaking hands, he says to Peter, "We haven't had any time to discuss this interview, but I want to emphasize that you should stick to the facts and answer the questions as directly and truthfully as possible. From what Sir Richard tells me, this is a clear case of self-defense. Don't offer any opinions or interpretations, or make any guesses at the motives of the attackers. You understand?"

"I understand. Please shut me up if I begin to say anything stupid."

Emilio laughs. "I will tell you if you should not answer a specific question, and I will speak up if I see the interview heading into areas that are not appropriate. Your interviewer will be Sr. Arsenio Garcia. He is very good, which means you need to be careful."

The police interview turns into a lengthy ordeal. Neither Peter, nor the interviewing officer, Arsenio Garcia, trusts their fluency in their second language. As a result, the interview is a tedious, bilingual affair. Arsenio is a small, slightly balding man. He is intense, focused, and all business.

Probably fifty to fifty-five, Peter thinks.

The police have a detailed diagram of the scene and Arsenio reviews the interpretation developed by the police. He is patient, making sure that Omar can handle the translation. Peter listens but does not comment.

Arsenio asks Peter to provide a detailed description of what happened.

Peter points to different parts of the diagram as he runs through the sequence of events. A police translator patiently translates Peter's comments into Spanish.

"I engaged the passenger with the pistol from the lead car first, then the passenger from the following car. The last was the other shooter from the lead vehicle, the one with the AR15. I fired fifteen shots at the three targets. At that point I was out of ammunition."

"Did the AR15 shooter have body armor?" Arsenio asks.

"I don't know."

"Who shot the driver in the car behind yours?" Arsenio asks.

"I don't know."

"It wasn't you?"

"No. I was out of ammunition," Peter answers.

"Do you know when he was shot?"

"No. I heard shots just before the embassy car crashed into the lead vehicle. That's all I know."

"You have a permit for the pistol?" Arsenio asks.

"Yes."

"Do you have your pistol with you?"

"It's in the car. I brought it in case you need to see it."

"We can have the driver bring it in," the Sr. Sanchez says.

Arsenio nods. "Please do that." He turns back to Peter. "Why were you carrying a pistol?"

"I know that in Lima I stand out as a *norteamericano*. So does Maria. Some people think I am rich. Because of that, we're good targets for a kidnapping. I prefer to make it as difficult as possible."

"You made it very difficult for these men," Arsenio says. "The devil kidnapped all of them."

A policeman brings Peter's pistol to the room.

Arsenio looks at the pistol and laughs. "This is a very small pistol, señor. You really did what you say you did? With this?"

"Yes."

"We will keep this for testing." He places it on the table in front of him. "If you are so concerned about kidnapping, you should increase your personal security. You might not be as lucky next time."

That wasn't luck, Peter thinks, but he says, "Thank you. I have done that, and I don't think we'll have any more trouble in Lima."

"Excellent," Arsenio responds. "We want our tourists to be safe and to enjoy themselves while they are in Peru."

There is a moment of silence while Arsenio looks through his notes. He looks up at Peter. "Why are you here in Peru?"

"I'm an independent consultant, a geologist. I'm here for a very short time, a few days, working for Mandrake Minerals, a British company out of London."

"What are you doing for them?" Arsenio asks.

"I will visit their property, Cerro Nublado, in northern Peru, and review the drilling results."

The interviewer frowns at the mention of Cerro Nublado. "There have been some serious problems in that area with narcotics trafficking. I must warn you that it is not a very safe area."

"I understand it's been pretty quiet recently," Peter says. "I'm sure Mandrake has good security at the camp."

Arsenio shrugs. "Be careful. You may need more than a little pistol at Cerro Nublado. You should make sure there is sufficient, professional security there."

"Thank you for the warning," Peter says.

"When do you expect to leave for Cerro Nublado?"

"Early tomorrow morning."

"How long do you expect to be there?" Arsenio asks.

"Five or six days."

"Good," Arsenio says. "The shorter the better, I think."

"I like to be in and out before too many people know I'm there," Peter says, smiling.

Arsenio shuffles through his notes again before asking, "Do you have problems with the version of this attempted kidnapping that appeared in the newspaper?"

"You mean that the driver saved us all?" Peter shrugs. "I have no problem with it at all, as a newspaper story."

"You are a wise man."

Peter says nothing.

"Let's go back to the diagram," Arsenio says. "Indulge me. Go over your recollection of what happened one more time."

Peter repeats his explanations. Arsenio takes a few more notes.

After almost three hours, Arsenio closes his notebook. "I think we're done, señor. You are free to go. You face no charges, but please contact me when you return to Lima from Cerro Nublado. Make sure you do so before you leave the country."

Omar, Peter and the lawyer return to the back seat of the embassy car. Peter collects his replacement pistol and straps on the holster under his jacket. He turns to Emilio, "What's your opinion? Any chance I'll be facing any charges?"

Emilio shrugs. "If you were in serious trouble, you would not be sitting with us in this car. You clearly acted in self-defense, even if what you did is a bit unbelievable. Your pistol is legal. From what I understand, their crime scene investigation presented no surprises. Sir Richard's statement backs you up. They can hardly charge you with anything, and Arsenio Garcia said himself that you face no charges. They want this incident to go away as quickly and as quietly as possible. I think you're fine."

"And reporting to them when I get back from Cerro Nublado?"

"Call me when you get back. I'll check with them, and I'll go with you if they want to talk to you again."

After they drop the lawyer at his office, Omar says, "We'll go to the embassy. We'll meet Sir Richard there, and Steve Berner can meet with us a little later."

After they ride in silence for a minute, Omar turns to Peter. "Saturday night. What would you have done if Sir Richard hadn't come along?"

Peter sighs. "Well, I was ready to grab the pistol from the other shooter from the lead car."

"You would have been an easy target for the man with the assault rifle."

"He had lost the use of one arm. He was bleeding to death and struggling to aim the rifle. I figured it was the best chance I had."

"I have to tell you, Peter," Omar says, "initially I was uncomfortable with the whole concept of working with you at Cerro Nublado."

Peter raises his eyebrows. "Really?"

"Don't take offense, but so many *norteamericanos* are full of shit. They exaggerate their accomplishments. When I read a report about you, some of the things it said you had done, my reaction was, 'This is bullshit.' But after what you did Saturday night, I have… changed my opinion."

"Good, because I'm looking forward to working with you. Steve Berner? Maybe not so much, but I know he can be a valuable asset in the jungle. That guy's one tough sonofabitch."

"Yes," Omar says, "and a little bit crazy."

Peter nods. "And a little bit crazy."

Omar laughs.

They arrive at the embassy. The guard opens the tall gate for them to park behind the ten-foot masonry wall. Omar and Peter enter the embassy and go to a conference room.

"Have a seat," Omar says. "I'll find Sir Richard."

Peter sits down, facing the door. He thinks about what's coming when they get to Cerro Nublado.

Tomorrow will be a long day just getting there. Tedious, but probably relatively low risk.

He has a real job to do when he's there, and he has to do it properly, particularly with Julius Grant looking over his shoulder. Somehow, they have to keep Julius from discovering Peter's second job at Cerro Nublado. Considering his assistants, that will not be easy.

He hears Sir Richard coming down the hall with Omar. Peter notes that Sir Richard's slight limp seems to be a bit worse when he enters the room with Omar.

"Peter!" Sir Richard says, "I hear that you remain a free man after all."

Peter smiles. "So I understand. Thanks for your support."

"No problem. Now, let's talk a little about what we expect to happen at Cerro Nublado. Maybe you could tell us what you think, Peter."

Peter takes a deep breath. "I have to admit, I'm beginning to agree with you and Alden. In my mind, this latest incident strongly suggests that the Russians may be hiding something at Cerro Nublado. I don't know what it is, but I don't think I'll need any more than the four days we have on site. I'll either figure it out there, or I'll figure it out once I have the analyses for my samples."

"That's if you can get the work done," Sir Richard says.

"That's my real job on the property," Peter says. "It's what Mandrake is paying me to do, what you expect me to do, and I have to find a way to get it done. The second job is dealing with what's also looking more and more likely, an attack of some sort while we're there. It looks like it's probably from Mr. Huevos himself with two or three buddies."

"You're rather vulnerable while you're in the camp," Sir Richard says.

Peter shakes his head. "I don't think so." He gestures toward Omar. "If Omar is successful and ingratiates himself with the local laborers, we almost surely will know when something is coming down on us. The locals will know. They'll disappear. The only people in the camp will be the three of us plus Julius. Except for Julius it becomes close to a free fire zone."

"And Berner will be in the jungle to provide backup for us," Omar says.

"Look," Peter says, "this Huevos guy has survived a while. He's not stupid. He'll put one or two men, out of sight, as lookouts. I'm hoping that Berner can take care of them for us. That's what he's good at."

"You still think he'll come in with only three or four men?" Sir Richard asks.

"Why would he come in with more? He'll know that I'm a problem, but he shouldn't know the real reason why Omar and Steve are there with me. He'll think we're easy pickings. From what I've been told, he doesn't have a large group anyway. His type always relies on their big guns and intimidation."

"If you just have pistols, you will be seriously under-gunned," Sir Richard says.

"True," Peter says, "but I don't think we can walk into camp as geologists with AR15's. Chances are, everything will be close range, fifty feet or less. A slight upgrade from the 9mm, as you suggest, Omar, may be helpful, but

I'll probably stick with the 9mm. I'm used to it, and if they're well placed, those rounds are plenty lethal."

"You might not have much warning," Sir Richard comments.

Peter shrugs. "It takes a little while for people to clear out of a camp. I expect the danger time is toward the end of the day, after dinner, maybe an hour before dark, or even after dark on a clear night. The moon is nearly full while we're there. We just have to be careful to pay attention, all the time, day and night, to what's going on around us. We have to turn the tables and surprise them."

"What if he comes in with guns blazing, just shooting up the camp top to bottom?" Omar asks.

"With any luck, and if we get any warning," Peter says, "we'll be out of sight when he shows up. Anyway, the way he normally seems to operate is to capture people, torture them, and have his fun by eating their balls in front of them. Nasty guy, but he sounds predictable. That should give us an edge, unless the Russians change how he operates."

Omar shakes his head, almost shivering. "I hope you're right."

"What's the problem, Omar?" Sir Richard asks. "You're not quite ready to be a gelding?"

"¿Un castrado? No," Omar answers. "No, absolutely not."

They all laugh, including Omar.

"The key is getting Julius out of danger," Peter says. "We don't want him to get in the way and caught in the crossfire. I haven't been to the camp, but I think, from the reports I've read, that there's a footbridge of sorts from the lower camp across the river to Ecuador. If we can, we should get him into the jungle somewhere across the river. Then we have freedom of action in the camp."

"And just how do we convince him to do that?" Omar asks.

"Good question," Peter answers. "I have no idea." He shrugs. "Deal with that issue when we actually face it, I guess."

Sir Richard's phone rings. "Yes," he says as he answers it. "Thank you. I'll be right out." He stands up. "Steve Berner just arrived. I'll go get him."

When they are alone, Omar frowns and says to Peter, "We're going to need some good luck."

"Yeah," Peter says. "That never changes."

Sir Richard returns with Steve Berner.

Tall, skinny, with a wild shock of light brown hair, even when he's standing still, Steve's body is animated. Something is always moving. His eyes never settle on one object for long. Peter has heard stories about Berner that sound mythological. He can see things no other man can see. He can become invisible in plain sight. He can unerringly anticipate a subject's next move. He's deliberate in everything he does. Decisive.

I don't know what to believe, Peter thinks. *It all sounds like bullshit, but Jim Blakestad swears by him, and I trust Jim's judgement.*

They all shake hands. "Good to meet you, Steve," Peter says.

Steve smiles briefly. "Good to meet you, too."

As they all sit down, Sir Richard says, "Perhaps, Peter, you could quickly review what we talked about before Steve arrived. He is aware of the broad outlines of the project."

"Before I start that, I should give you the details for tomorrow. Julius Grant has us on an early morning, private flight to Piura. Omar and Steve, you should be at the DoubleTree hotel in Miraflores by six thirty tomorrow morning. He has two cars in Piura to drive us to Huancabamba, where we'll meet the helicopter from Cerro Nublado. I think we'll be in the lower camp, by the river. That's where they store most of the core, and where they have most of the bunkhouses."

"Security on the drive?" Omar asks.

Peter smiles. "I think it's us."

"What about our baggage? Will it be inspected?" Steve asks.

"We leave from the private FBO terminal. They have no inspection there," Peter says. "There should be no problem with our personal weapons and ammunition. Please be discrete. I don't want to have to explain our situation to Julius if I can avoid it. At least not tomorrow."

Peter provides a quick recap of their discussion. He reviews his thoughts on the project, what he needs to do as a geologist, and what they should expect from a security standpoint.

"I think, Steve, we need you most in the jungle, making sure we don't get surprised by El Come Huevos and his bunch. Omar and I will try to complete my actual geological job while keeping a close watch on the camp."

"You can't be sure the local labor will tell you when the shit is coming," Steve says.

"You're right. It's a good bet, but it's not one hundred percent," Peter says.

"If we pull this off, what do we do with the bodies?" Steve Berner asks.

Peter, Omar, and Steve all look at Sir Richard.

"Well," Sir Richard replies, "I'd prefer if there were no bodies. I suppose you could try to capture them alive. I suspect that's extremely unlikely, probably impossible, at least if you want to survive yourselves. The best bet is to make sure the bodies simply disappear."

"I agree," Peter says. "I'd prefer not to have any more bodies around me in Peru. But, and it's a big 'but', there's a bounty of ten million US dollars on Sr. Huevos. That's a lot of money."

"Your lives are worth something, too," Sir Richard says.

"The three of us who will be in the camp together have to make a unanimous decision," Peter says. "I don't think we can risk trying to take him alive, even if the opportunity presents itself. We can take a lot of high-definition photos of the body. Hope they accept the photos as enough proof of his death. At all times, we should value our lives more than the bounty."

Omar takes a deep breath and exhales loudly. "I'd love my share of that payment, but I'll risk it to stay alive. I agree. Kill him at first opportunity. Get the photographic evidence. Dispose of his body along with the others."

"Steve?" Peter asks.

Steve Berner looks at Peter and Omar. "We're all in this together, right? No matter who captures or kills the guy, right?"

"Yes," both Peter and Omar reply.

"Then I agree," Steve says. "Kill him on sight." He pauses. "Kill them all. They're all vicious narco bastards. None of them will show any hesitation in killing us. If they come into camp, fully armed, and the local workers have all disappeared, each one of us knows exactly why they're in the camp. If we play games, none of us will survive."

The room is silent until Sir Richard speaks. "I think, gentlemen, you have a working plan in place."

CHAPTER 19

The four men finalize a few items of preparation, such as the selection of weapons and ammunition. Peter and Omar both take a P229 chambered for the SIG .357 cartridges.

"I'll also take the 9mm I already have with the silencer," Peter says. "The lower sound level may be useful." He shrugs. "Anyway, it's a good round for close range work."

Steve looks at the 9mm. "Same for me, and the silencer is a must for my work."

"Okay," Peter says. "Keep the pistols well-hidden and packed away for the flight up to Piura. Once we're in the cars headed to Huancabamba, keep them handy, but not in plain sight. Same when we head to the camp. At least to begin with, close at hand if at all possible, but concealed. Clear?"

"Annoying, but clear," Steve says.

Omar laughs. "Clear."

"Either Julius Grant or I," Peter says, "will arrange one or two vehicles with drivers to get us from Huancabamba to Piura when we come out of Cerro Nublado, a charter flight back to Lima, and a secure car to bring us home in Lima."

"What's our cover story?" Steve asks. "Are we geological assistants?"

"Omar, you're my assistant in camp," Peter says. "Sir Richard tells me that you have a few geology courses under your belt, which should allow us to pull that one off. You, Steve, are supposed to be a jungle rat who will wander around the jungle looking for outcrops and signs of mineralization that others have missed."

"I don't know a thing about geology," Steve says quite seriously.

"Just be a sullen bastard. Answer questions with grunts and don't talk," Peter advises.

"That's easy," Steve says.

"That's what I thought," Peter says and laughs. "When we get to the camp, please spend most of your time in the jungle. You need to keep a watch, particularly at night. Either Omar or I will be on watch during the day, and part of the night as well."

When they are all ready to leave, Peter hands a sealed envelope to Sir Richard.

"Assuming I return alive from Cerro Nublado, this is something I need to do in Lima. I'm going to need a bit of help, but I think I'll be able to resolve a few things."

"I'm confident you'll make it back to Lima," Sir Richard says, as he takes the envelope.

"I'm glad you're confident," Peter says.

The embassy car returns Steve and Omar to their homes and Peter to his hotel. Before he goes to his room, Peter makes sure that the same room is reserved for him when he returns from Cerro Nublado. It's a little after two in the afternoon. He calls Julius.

"You had lunch?" Peter asks.

"No."

"It's a little late, but I haven't had anything to eat since breakfast. I need a little something," Peter says. "Shall we meet at the hotel restaurant?"

"Sure. I'll head right down."

As soon as they sit down, the waiter arrives at their table and leaves the menus. In a few minutes they make their decisions, order a light lunch, and each have a beer.

Julius takes a drink and says, "I've got a problem."

"What's that?"

Julius shakes his head. "Minera Russo-Perú has asked me to meet with them here in Lima. They wanted to meet tomorrow, but I told them I'm going to the project tomorrow."

"And… What did they say?"

"They agreed to put the meeting off until Friday. I'll go to the project with you tomorrow. I'll be there to make sure everything you need is available to you, and I'll work with you all day Wednesday and Thursday morning."

"You'll head back on the helicopter on Thursday afternoon?" Peter asks.

"That's the plan," Julius answers. "Overnight in Piura. Back in Lima Friday morning. Have my meeting that afternoon. I'll see if I can change reservations and head to New York City on Saturday. I'll leave the Sunday arrangements, helicopter, car, charter plane, all in place for you and your assistants."

Maybe one and a half days of peace at the camp? Peter thinks.

"That sounds like it will work. Just be sure to give me the details on the Sunday arrangements."

Their meals arrive, and they eat in silence for a while.

"I'm glad you were able to put them off a couple of days," Peter says. "I've been thinking that having you at the camp at least for the first day, will help a lot, now that I've lost a day. It should let me finish soon enough to come back to Lima as planned."

"I'm annoyed," Julius says, "but that's the best I can do."

They talk about camp security and the details of Peter's plan as they eat their lunch.

"Why don't you give me the numbers of the two drill holes you think are most important, and I'll tell the guys at the camp to lay them out for you," Julius says.

"That would be great. They're CN-48 and CN-71. If I only get through those two holes, get a good log or map of both, and get maybe fifty samples from each one, in a pinch that might be all I need."

"Those are excellent holes to look at," Julius says. "They both hit high grade. They're long. One drills across the deposit from south to north, the other from east to west. They both cut high grade copper, cross the late, barren granite, and come back into good grade copper on the other side. You'll see everything the deposit has to offer in those two holes."

"Good," Peter says. "I figured I'd spend the first day or two on those two drill holes. I've got four to six others I want to look at, only portions of them, and certainly in less detail."

Peter finishes his beer. "I know we're just finishing lunch, but you have any plans for dinner tonight?" he asks.

"I think I'll eat here," Julius says. "I've got to make a bunch of phone calls, and I want to get to bed early. You?"

"I'm not very ambitious. Might call a friend and see if we can have a drink somewhere. See what happens."

"See you tomorrow at six-thirty," Julius says.

They both return to their rooms.

Peter calls Omar.

"*¿Aló?*"

"Peter Binder."

"What's up?"

"Julius' Russian partners want him to come to a meeting in Lima tomorrow," Peter says. "He put them off until Friday. He's staying in camp only one and a half days."

"He leaves Thursday afternoon?" Omar asks.

"Yep."

"They're getting him out of the way."

"That's what it sounds like," Peter says. "We can probably relax a bit until he leaves."

"Unless the egg eater and his buddies are already there," Omar says.

"That would be a little unsettling, but I asked Julius about security. He said his partners don't use any. He said they told him they have it all under control."

"This is getting strange," Omar says.

"No. Not if they're using the narcos as security. They terrify everyone. Nobody will create problems for the Russo-Perú campsite, as long as they're involved. Not with Huevos around."

"We should stay on our toes, even when Julius is there. Maybe they're setting us up."

"I agree," Peter says, "but I don't think they're quite that smart. I bet they figure all they need to do is unleash that fucker on us, and we're history. They can blame it all on the narcos."

"Probably," Omar says. He doesn't sound convinced.

"We'll find out soon enough," Peter says. "See you tomorrow morning."

"See you then."

Peter calls a local number.

"*¿Dónde está Maria Davidoff?*" he asks.

"*Está en Cusco,*" the man answers.

"*OK.*"

Peter disconnects. *So far, so good. She's in Cusco, where she belongs.* He thinks for a minute, and then he calls Carlos Bellido.

"Carlos! This is Peter Binder."

"You still in Lima?"

"Yeah. I'm delayed a day. I head up to Cerro Nublado tomorrow. I'd like to share a good bottle of wine with someone tonight. You game?"

"Why don't you come up to my house for dinner?" Carlos says.

"Are you sure?" Peter asks. "I don't want to impose, and I just finished a late lunch."

"I'm alone until almost ten, and we won't eat until eight or later. Elena's working. I'll tell the cook to make enough for two. I don't know what it will be, but she's a good cook. I'll tell her to keep it light."

"Okay, but I'll bring the wine."

"Good," Carlos says. "Come around seven."

"I'll come with two cars from Seguridad Ejecutiva. You might warn your neighborhood watchman."

"I'll do that."

"See you at seven," Peter says.

Peter has the rest of the afternoon in front of him before he has to be at Carlos' house. He reserves two cars and armed guards for the evening. He requests that at least one of the cars stays in place while he visits with Carlos.

He brings his journal up to date. He looks back at his entry for Saturday night. Everything is falling into place.

"Just need to survive," he says softly.

He spends some time repacking. He will take only his backpack and leave his suitcase at the hotel. He puts the 9mm pistol halfway down in the backpack, wrapped in clothing, with four clips of ammunition. He loads the .357 pistol, puts it in his holster, places the pistol in one pocket of his field vest, and two clips of ammunition in another. He rolls up the vest and puts it at the top of his backpack. Easy to grab in an emergency.

He goes down to the lobby with his locked briefcase with the second 9mm P229 and the special ammunition. He asks the desk to keep it in their safe for him to pick up when he returns.

He finds the concierge at his desk.

"I need a bottle of good, well-aged, French Bordeaux wine for tonight," Peter says. "Is there some way you can arrange that for me?"

In only slightly accented English, the concierge asks, "Have you seen anything on the restaurant's wine list, Mr. Binder, that would fit your needs?"

"No, I haven't," Peter says.

The concierge smiles. "I understand. What are you prepared to spend?"

Peter makes a small gesture with his right hand. "Up to two hundred dollars?"

"That should be no problem at all, sir. How soon do you need it?"

"Let's say six, to be safe."

"Not a problem. I will personally deliver it to your room. Should I charge it to your account, Mr. Binder?"

"Yes, please," Peter said. He pulls out his wallet and takes out two twenty-dollar bills. He hands them to the concierge. "For your assistance," he says.

"Ah. Thank you, sir. For you it is no trouble at all."

Peter returns to his room. He checks his emails, deleting most. Two are of interest.

Peter:

> Good luck. Glad the incident in Lima turned out well for you. I'll be keeping a close watch on developments. Contact R if you need my help in anything at the end of your trip. Just remember, in the wilderness always leave it as clean as it was when you arrived!

Jeremy P.

The second email of interest came from Alden Sage.

Peter:

> Sorry to hear of the mess in Lima. Glad you and Maria made it out okay. I don't have to tell you, but stay alert. This is looking tougher than I expected.

Alden Sage

Peter re-reads the two emails. He finds the last sentence of Jeremy's interesting. *The network is staying well informed,* he thinks.

The two cars arrive on the street where Carlos lives a little before seven. The driver stops where the neighborhood watchman stands on the corner, to let him know that they will park on the street for the next few hours. The watchman is expecting them.

They park in front of the house next door to Carlos' home. Peter moves to get out, but the guard says, "*Un momentito, señor.*"

The guard steps out of the car, looks up and down the block, and motions for Peter to get out.

Peter walks the few steps to the heavy doorway in the ten-foot wall around Carlos's house. He presses the doorbell. Peter waves at the security camera.

The door buzzes, and Peter lets himself in. He walks the short distance to the front door of the house, where Carlos is waiting for him. Peter quickly takes in the house itself. Brick. Bars over the windows. With the high wall around the entire yard, it is a minor fortress.

"Good to see you," Carlos says. "Come in. I have a pisco sour ready for you." He shuts the door and locks it behind Peter.

Peter hands the bottle of wine to Carlos. "I've looked it up. It should be good, but I have never had this wine before."

"I'm sure it will be fine," Carlos says. "Come. We will sit and talk and enjoy our pisco sours, while Teresa finishes preparing dinner. Take off your jacket. Relax."

Peter removes his jacket. As discretely as possible, he removes his pistol and holster and places them in one of the jacket pockets and sits down.

"You have no children in the house these days, do you?"

Carlos raises his eyebrows and hands Peter his Pisco sour. "No. I'm a little surprised to see you are armed in Lima. And you come with a security company? This is a pretty quiet neighborhood."

"Did you read about a kidnapping gone bad, not far from here, a few days ago?"

"Was that you?"

Peter nods his head. "Maria and me."

"The newspaper said you had a very heroic driver. Rather unusual."

Peter laughs. "That's the story."

Carlos shakes his head. "You've never told me much about your life, but I've heard some strange rumors recently."

"Like what?"

"A friend of mine, from my time studying in Australia, told me about a tragic helicopter accident last year in Indonesia," Carlos says.

"Really?"

"He said you were working on the Endang deposit, just before independent sampling proved it was a huge fraud. On the way out from the camp to Manado, the helicopter disappeared. They've never found it, or any of the passengers. The Indonesian officials announced that you were missing and presumed dead, along with Maria Davidoff, the military pilot, and Teunis Dulaigh, the chief geologist for IndoGold. And here you are. Alive. In my living room."

"Dead to some, alive to others," Peter says.

"I have never believed the stories about you before. Now I may start to believe them," Carlos says and finishes his drink. "What were you doing at Endang anyway?"

"I was working for an investor, doing what I'm doing here," Peter says. "Right now, I really am working for Mandrake Minerals. They asked me to do an outside audit of the property. Julius Grant, their CEO, thinks Minera Russo-Perú may have screwed Mandrake in the terms of the deal. I don't think so, but we'll see."

"I think you're a little crazy," Carlos says. "Surely, you don't need this job. If you think you have to walk around Lima with a pistol on your belt and an armed bodyguard, I can't imagine what you need when you're at Cerro Nublado."

"You're not the only one who thinks I'm crazy. I'm beginning to agree." Peter plays with his nearly empty drink glass. "I've decided that this is my last hurrah, Carlos. After this job, I'm done."

"Done with exploration and geology, or done with your efforts to save the world from the devil?" Carlos asks.

Peter picks up his drink. He contemplates it for a moment and drinks the last few drops. "Both, I think."

Carlos raises his eyebrows. "What will you do with yourself? You'll be bored to tears."

"I keep telling people I'll become a farmer."

Carlos bursts out laughing. "Peter, I can just see you with a straw hat, overalls, sitting on a tractor, plowing the fields." He continues to laugh. "Not possible. Not possible at all."

"That was a good pisco sour, Carlos." He smiles. "You're right to laugh, I suppose, but I do think that's what I'm going to do. Except… it's probably a vineyard, not a hayfield."

"All right. That I can imagine."

Teresa steps into the room to tell Carlos that dinner is ready.

They talk about many things over dinner at Carlos' large table, mostly the state of politics and the economy of Peru. They do not talk about Peter's work. Peter asks about Carlos' family.

"The boys are fine. They're both grown. Out on their own. This is a big house for just two of us, but we don't want to move."

"And your work?"

"I'm doing okay, but exploration is in a bit of a downturn. The small companies are leaving again. They'll be back. They always come back to Peru. My wife and I… We're lucky. We've had good incomes, and we've been careful with our money. But I worry. I worry about my country."

"You're not the only one. I worry about the United States."

Carlos shrugs. "From far away, it seems like someone snuffed out the flame on the Statue of Liberty. It's excruciating to watch what a man like Wisser can do to a great country like the United States. We need wise, world leadership like never before, and it's not there."

When Elena comes home from her work, her presence turns the conversation back toward the family again. Peter has always admired her. She is dressed for her television show, and she is both beautiful and subdued, a perfect combination for a child psychologist. Her features are well defined, but not angular. Nothing showy, just quiet confidence and competence. Carlos, Peter knows, is another man who prefers independent, strong-willed women, women unafraid to express their views on the world.

"And how are you and Maria doing?" Elena asks.

"At the moment, not very well. She is angry with me."

"I'm sorry to hear that. I had hoped to see you with two or three children by now."

"Not going to happen right away," Peter says. He smiles at his two friends and then looks at his watch. "I have a long day tomorrow. I should be getting back to the hotel."

Peter calls the driver to warn him that he will be coming out to the car soon.

Carlos stands with him by the door. They shake hands.

"Take care of yourself, my friend," Carlos says.

"Thanks for making the time for me," Peter says. "Cerro Nublado may be messy, and I may have my hands full when I get back to Lima. I was afraid I wouldn't have time to see you."

"Call me. Tell me you have returned safely."

"I will do that. I should be back on Sunday."

On the way back to the hotel, Peter thinks about the contrast between him and his friend.

I have all the money I could ever need, Peter thinks, *and little enough to show for it. A cabin in the woods, on a lake with no neighbors, where I can no longer live, with a woman who is... whatever she is.*

He shakes his head.

Dumb.

CHAPTER 20

Peter, Omar, Julius and Steve all pile into the two cars from Seguridad Ejecutiva at six thirty. Traffic is already heavy. The FBO terminal at Jorge Chavez Airport is off by itself, and the security consists of the pilot checking identification. They take off for Piura a little after eight. Shortly after takeoff, the copilot hands out egg salad sandwiches, coffee, and soft drinks.

Peter dozes for most of the short flight. They land and pull up to the terminal about two hours after leaving the Lima airport.

By the time they climb into the two vehicles at the Piura airport, it's nearly ten-thirty. Peter puts on his field vest before he gets into one of the cars.

"We're not in the field yet," Julius says.

Peter shrugs. "Just getting in the mood."

They stop at a restaurant on the way out of town for a quick lunch. Peter has a large bowl of *sopa criolla* and some fresh bread. They eat mostly in silence. Julius tries to make conversation, but Steve Berner stubbornly grunts and otherwise refuses to respond. Omar Vargas responds in very short statements, mostly, "Yes", or "No."

Julius looks at Peter, and Peter smiles back at him. Julius gives up.

As they head east and steadily climb up toward the Altiplano of northern Peru, the towns shrink in size and prosperity. Peter insists that Omar and Steve ride in the lead car.

"If we run into a roadblock or any other problems, Omar speaks fluent Quechua," Peter says. "That alone might defuse any potential difficulties."

"I'm not sure either of them knows how to speak at all," Julius grumbles.

They climb into the Altiplano without incident. As they drive along the high and empty landscape, Peter comments, "I always wonder what potential is lost in these lands." He points at a young man plowing a field.

186

He is typically short, with an oversized chest, adapted to squeeze needed oxygen out of the stingy air. "What would he be capable of, with proper education and opportunities? What does he think about? He has some contact with the outside world. He listens to the radio."

Julius grunts. "What makes you so sure that he thinks about much of anything?"

"Well, I don't know, but they must have hopes and dreams. There must be a longing for something better, and if it's forever denied, that unfulfilled longing easily turns into anger." Peter looks out the window. "It's the same situation, in one form or another, all over the world. We have to find a way to do a better job of spreading opportunity around."

"You're getting rather idealistic," Julius says.

"Yeah. I suppose you're right, but it feels better than not caring at all."

Julius grunts again, and they fall into silence once more.

They arrive at the helicopter in a small field outside of Huancabamba, shortly after five in the afternoon. The sun is already gone from the valley, but they have plenty of time to land at the camp before dark.

Peter is happy to see another MD 500E, similar to his own. By the time they stuff their baggage into the baggage compartment, tie down the excess in the baskets on the side of the helicopter, and climb in with the pilot, it is a fully loaded machine.

The pilot quickly runs through the usual safety issues, makes sure everyone is belted in, starts the helicopter, and heads to the camp. Though it would be close to a full day's walk through rough country to get to Cerro Nublado, they arrive in twenty-five minutes. As expected, they land at the lower camp, the location of most of the buildings and core samples.

Not much is happening at the project. The most recent drilling program finished some months prior to this visit. As a result, only four Peruvian laborers remain in camp, maintaining the small cabins, most designed for four people, the larger office building, and the kitchen and dining area. A cook and his assistant provide their meals. Though a bit primitive, the camp has running water, hot showers, toilets, decent beds in each cabin, and wooden walkways to keep out of the mud. Bright orange, fiberglass tarps cover the roofs of all of the buildings to keep out the rain. The workers also maintain the trails to get to the work areas, the small group of additional structures on the top of the hill, and the drill sites that are scattered along the top and sides of the hill. The camp is really a small village, and it requires constant maintenance.

Everyone in the camp, including the cook and his assistant, comes out to meet them. Julius knows all but the cook's assistant, and he introduces them to Peter, Omar and Steve.

Peter is relieved to see that there are no Russians or security forces in sight.

When Julius introduces the oldest member of the maintenance crew, he says, "This is Bernardo. He's been here from the very beginning, even before I got involved with Cerro Nublado. He runs the camp and knows all the history, don't you, Bernardo?"

"A lot has changed from when I first came here," Bernardo says with a laugh.

"I bet it has," Peter says.

"Let me take you to your rooms," Bernardo says. "There's plenty of space. Nobody's here. You can all have your own cabin."

Omar and Bernardo have a brief exchange in Quechua. They laugh.

"Señors Binder and Grant, if you can follow me. You each get 'el quarto del jefe', a boss cabin, of course," Bernardo says with a smile.

"I haven't been anyone's el jefe for a long time," Peter says.

The boss cabins have a small desk in the corner of the room, two hard-backed chairs, and only two beds instead of the usual four of the other cabins. The small buildings are simple wood and plywood construction, with a wooden door and several screened windows that can be closed against the rain. Inside the cabins, two bare lightbulbs hang from the peak of the roof, along with their pull-chains to turn them on. Once he is alone, Peter takes off his field vest, locks it in his backpack, and places it next to the desk. He heads back to the largest building, which houses the kitchen and eating area.

The cook and his assistant are ready for them, and everyone, including the local workers, sits down to a simple but abundant meal. There is plenty of rice, a thick beef stew with root vegetables, and a green salad. The conversation is mostly in Spanish. The visitors slip back and forth between Spanish and English. The laborers slip into Quechua from time to time. They talk and joke with Omar.

Peter directs a question to Bernardo. "How's security lately? Anybody bothering you?"

Bernardo shakes his head. "Nobody's here. We're not doing anything, not even drilling. All we're doing is maintaining trails and the camps. Nobody cares. They have more important things to do."

"What do you think will happen if the government approves development?"

Bernardo laughs. "I think I'll go home."

"The Russians tell me they haven't had any security here for months," Julius says. "They say they made peace with the narcos, and they were the only dangerous group, as far as they were concerned."

"What does 'made peace' actually mean in this case?" Peter asks.

"Don't know exactly," Julius admits, "but if they haven't had any security needed here for a couple of months, it can't be all bad."

Peter isn't sure he believes Julius' explanation, but he keeps his mouth shut. He also notes that Bernardo offers little more than his initial comments on the subject of security.

"Have you laid out the drill holes I asked about?" Julius asks. "CN-48 and CN-71?"

Bernardo nods. "They're both laid out on the tables. We barely had space to lay out CN-71, but we squeezed it in. Will you want any others put out today?"

"No," Peter says. "These two will be enough for tomorrow, probably for the next morning, too. I have sections of five or six other holes I'll want to look at after that. Do you want a list now?"

"No. Tomorrow's soon enough. You'll be taking samples?" he asks.

"Very small samples," Peter says. He holds up his fingers indicating about two inches. "Do you have a rock saw?"

"Yes. You mark the samples. We'll saw them out for you."

"That will be perfect," Peter says. "Mark them with the drill number and the footage when you cut them."

As everyone stands up to head to their rooms, Julius says, "Stay here for a bit, Peter."

"Sure." Peter sits down again, across the table from Julius. "What's up?"

"Nothing. Just thought we could talk for a bit. I think I can find a couple of cold beers in the kitchen. You want one?"

"Sure."

Julius steps into the kitchen and comes back with two cold bottles of Pilsen beer.

"That does taste good," Peter says as he takes a drink. "It's been a long day of nothing. I always find getting into the field anywhere in Peru to be an exhausting exercise."

"Easier with the helicopter."

"True."

Julius plays with his beer bottle, slowly tearing at the label with his thumbnail. "You know, I never wanted to sell this thing. I wanted to develop it myself. Create a real mining company."

"Yeah," Peter says. "That's the dream of every junior company. Doesn't work very often. Why did you sell to Minera Russo-Perú, though? The Russians are not exactly well known for making great deals with small companies."

"I couldn't get any other takers. They all looked at the opposition and ran away. Particularly after those crazy bastards shot and killed one of the staff. The Russians didn't seem too interested at first, but they hired a mate of mine, a guy named Richard Mercer, and they sent him up here. He took a few samples, and I didn't hear anything for a long time."

"What happened then?" Peter asks.

"The Russians sent Richard back up here," Julius says. "He took a bunch more samples, and a couple of weeks later I ran into him at a bar in Lima. He said to me, 'You're going to get a fantastic offer from the Russians. They're already forming a company. I can't tell you anything more, but it's coming. It's going to make you a rich man.' Two days later the police found him dead in his Lima apartment."

"Jesus! How'd he die?"

Julius exhales sharply. "The autopsy said it was a heroin overdose. They found all the evidence in the apartment. I'm sure they're telling the truth about the evidence, but Richard didn't overdose himself. He never used any illegal drugs, not ever. He didn't even smoke pot."

"So… You think someone murdered him?"

"I know someone murdered him. I think it was because of this deposit. He knew something, and they didn't want anybody else to know it. They silenced him. Permanently." Julius drinks more of his beer. "And, you know, the deal the Russians offered was good, but it wasn't fantastic."

Peter says nothing.

"Minera Russo-Perú was required by our letter of agreement to give me all their assay results, prior to us agreeing to the final agreement. They gave me their copper and molybdenum analyses, some zinc and lead, but nothing else. I'm convinced they held something back."

"You think they murdered your friend because of the deal?"

"He was my friend, Peter. He had no enemies. He didn't do drugs. I want to know what's going on. I feel like I killed him with my own hands." Julius looks at his bottle of beer. He has shredded the label completely. "Besides murdering my friend, I'm convinced the Russian pricks screwed me. They stole this property from me."

Julius looks at Peter intently. "I know a little bit more about you than you probably think I know, which is why I wanted you for this job, rather than some other geologist. I've heard all the rumors. I've done a little research, too. I have some interesting contacts in London." He pauses. "You had a pistol in your field vest pocket today, didn't you?"

Peter says nothing.

Julius smiles. "I knew it. I felt it when we bumped up against each other at the restaurant. And that wasn't an attempted kidnapping the other day, was it?"

Peter still does not reply.

Julius is quiet for a moment. Then he says, "I want to know what's going on here, Peter, but I'm getting scared. Not just for me. For you, too."

"You're only here a little over one day, Julius. You'll be fine."

"You should come out with me," Julius says. "Get done what you can tomorrow and the next morning, and leave."

Peter looks away. "That's not going to happen, Julius."

"What about Omar and Steve?"

"Don't worry about them."

Julius raises his eyebrows and stares at Peter. "You know all about this don't you?"

Peter shakes his head. "Not really. I didn't know anything about your friend, which is an unpleasant surprise. I don't know what's going on here, either. But that's what you hired me to find out. Right?" Peter takes another drink of his beer. "There are other people, though, who want to know the truth at least as much as you do."

"Bloody hell!" Julius says. "Why didn't you insist that I not come with you?"

"I tried," Peter says. "I seem to remember someone said something like, 'I have a right to visit my own property!' Something like that."

"I think," Julius says, "I think I should leave tomorrow afternoon."

Peter smiles, a small smile. "Seriously, Julius, I don't think anything unpleasant will happen while you're here. I would advise you, however, not to stay any longer than whatever schedule you gave to your partners."

Julius exhales. "This is bloody crazy!"

"That it is," Peter says.

"You want another beer?" Julius asks.

"No. I don't think so."

"What are you going to do here? Do you plan on completing the technical review of the property?" Julius asks.

Peter shrugs. "Yes. I'm going to do my job as a consulting geologist. I'm going to do what you hired me to do. As far as anything else is concerned, that ball's in somebody else's court." Peter pauses. "However, for my personal safety, and the safety of Steve and Omar, I'd appreciate it if you said nothing to anyone about this conversation."

Julius stares at him. "I understand."

After a few minutes, they go to their respective rooms.

Peter sits at the small table in his room. He opens his laptop and pulls up a protected file. He writes out a summary of the day.

That was an awkward conversation with Julius, Peter thinks. *I told him too much, but even saying nothing, I was giving him the information he needed. We have tomorrow and Thursday morning. It'll all come down late on Thursday. Maybe Friday or Saturday.*

Peter gets up from the table and unpacks his large pack. He takes out a small day pack, and puts all his supplies and equipment for the day inside it. He looks at the radiation detector. He pulls it out of its case and turns it on. He notes a slightly elevated background level of radiation. He makes a note of the background reading, turns the meter off, and returns it to its case. He places the detector in a side pocket of his day pack.

Peter strips off his boots, pants, and shirt. He folds the clothes and puts them on a small table next to the bed. His boots go under the table, with his heavy socks rolled up in the top of the boots. They will keep unwanted critters from getting into his boots. He places his field vest on top of the other clothes. The pistol goes under his pillow.

To his surprise, in the darkness, he is at peace. He can hear the rushing of the river, which nearly hides the sound of the generator. Some small animal snuffles around in the darkness, outside the window.

"Tomorrow will be fun," he says softly.

He decides not to worry about the days after tomorrow until they come along.

CHAPTER 21

The day dawns with a clear blue sky, though by being in the valley, the warmth of direct sunlight takes a while to reach the camp. By the time Peter sits down to breakfast, Steve Berner has already eaten an early breakfast and disappeared into the jungle.

Peter has a quick breakfast and then he and Omar go into the camp's office building with Julius. They pull out the two cross sections that contain the two drill holes, CN-48 and CN-71.

"Did you spend much time on these drill holes?" Peter asks Julius.

"Not really. I've seen them before, but I didn't do any work on them. I was going nuts trying to raise enough money to pay for our share of the drilling program."

Peter laughs. "Sounds normal for a junior company." He spreads out the large, paper section that includes drill hole CN-48. "What I want to do here," he says, "is quickly run down the entire hole, as it's laid out on the tables in the core shed, and get a general feeling of the geology. It's over three thousand feet long, and it cuts across the deposit at a steep angle. It should show all the different zones of alteration and mineralization. Same with CN-71. I hope we can get to that today."

"You're not giving yourself much time to look at the details of the geology," Julius says. "Seems like you could miss a lot."

"You don't want to pay me to do a lot of detailed work. Besides, we're not looking for some little thing here. We're looking for something big. We're not interested in the details. What we're looking for has to be really big, big enough that it changes the whole picture and economics of this discovery. You can miss that sort of thing if you spend too much time on details."

"Still, if you move too fast, you could miss even the big stuff," Julius says.

"No. You don't need a lot of time and detail for this job. You need to step back far enough. Keep your eyes wide open. Look at the whole deposit, the big picture."

"Okay," Julius says. "Let's start looking at the big picture."

They leave the office and walk over to the core shed, really a building with no walls. The roof is over twelve feet above the ground, and it covers a series of crude tables made from sheets of plywood laid out on sawhorses. The cardboard core boxes each contain slightly less than ten feet of core, divided into five, two-foot compartments. The boxes are open and laid out in order from the top to the bottom of the drill hole. In this way, a geologist can read the record of the drill hole, almost like reading a book.

When freshly collected from the drill, the core is in the form of cylindrical pieces of rock, cut by the diamond-studded, hollow drill bit. Mandrake and Russo-Perú have sawed the core in half. They collected and sent one half to the lab for analyses, and the remaining half provides a detailed record of the geology.

The lack of sides on the building lets in plenty of natural light and shelters the geologists and the core from the afternoon rains. It's a cheap but adequate building to set up, even in a remote camp, and it serves its purpose well.

Peter begins to walk down along the core from the top of CN-48 to the bottom. Wetting the core, to make textures more visible, he moves very quickly, stopping only once or twice to look at some sections more closely. Then he does it again. He's mostly silent during this process.

He returns to the boxes of core from the top of the hole for the third time. "Okay," he says to Julius and Omar. "Let's go down this a little more slowly. Let's see what we can see."

This time, as they move along the tables, starting with the core from the top of the drill hole, Peter makes numerous brief notes and carries on a running commentary on the geology. There is an abundance of bright yellow, shiny iron sulfides in the speckled, mostly cream-colored core. He identifies lesser amounts of slightly tarnished yellow, maroon, and blue copper sulfides. He points out the relationships of the various small veins to Julius and Omar, which ones are early, and which ones are late and cut across the earlier veins.

"I can identify three or four different granites. I suspect I'd see quite a few more if I took the time. You see this speckled granite here? This is the late, barren granite, and it cuts off all the early veinlets. None of this is particularly important for my review. It might be during mining, but not now."

He points to the black, often slightly shiny, late veinlets. "I can't identify the mineralogy of these things, though the reports identify them as iron-manganese veins. I've seen no specific analyses of them. They're just about everywhere, though they're most abundant in the upper part of the deposit, the part they'll mine first. They're the latest event in the system. They even cut the barren granite in the center of the deposit. They may be totally unrelated to the copper mineralization."

"And they carry no copper, no molybdenum, no metal values of interest whatsoever," Julius says. "They're useless and of no obvious economic importance."

"I suspect you're right," Peter says, "but there are a lot of them. If those were copper veins, you'd have one of the richest copper mines in the world."

"Maybe they contain a bunch of rare earths," Julius says. "If they do, we know right now why the Russians are so interested."

Peter smiles. "Yeah. I did give that some thought when I read the feasibility study. To me, it looks highly unlikely, but there weren't any rare earth analyses reported. If this is a huge rare earth deposit, why try to hide it?"

"Simple," Julius says. "If that's the case, this is the biggest, richest, rare earth deposit in the world, and they got it for a song."

Peter shakes his head. "I wouldn't get your hopes up."

Omar had kept quiet, but now he asks, "What's next, Peter?"

"Well," Peter says, "I'm going to finish my notes on this drill hole, which shouldn't take long now, though I'll almost certainly come back to it again before we leave. Then I need to mark the samples I want. Once I do that, we'll move on to CN-71, and you, Omar, can find Bernardo and start preparing the samples."

Peter checks his notes and goes back to specific portions of the drill core. He and Julius discuss various geological features of the core. When Peter reaches the end of the drill hole, Julius looks at his watch. "Lunch time," he says.

"You guys go ahead," Peter says. "I'll be there in a minute. There's a couple of things I want to go back to while I think of them."

When Julius and Omar leave, Peter takes out his radiation detector. This personal research study is a bit out in left field, and he doesn't want to have to explain or justify it to another geologist. He switches on the meter and places it on different sections of the core. He checks the barren granite and different zones of mineralization, including the black veinlets. He notes the results, turns the meter off, and puts it back into its case. He heads off to lunch.

After lunch, they return to the core. Peter uses a black marker to identify sample sites approximately every fifty feet, for a total of sixty-three samples. Each sample will be about two inches long, sawed from the half-core in the boxes. He adds another five samples for particular areas of interest. He documents the samples with photographs.

Peter turns over the sampling to Bernardo, and the record keeping to Omar. Peter and Julius go on to hole CN-71.

The afternoon rains arrive and periodically become intense. They keep working and find no major surprises in the second hole.

Peter takes his photographs, completes his notes, and identifies fifty-one samples for Bernardo and Omar to collect from the CN-71. He adds six extra samples, three from areas of the most intense black veining, and three from the areas of highest copper values.

By the end of the day, they have completed the sampling for CN-48. Bernardo and the other laborers clear the core boxes off the tables and stack them up underneath. Peter gives them his list of sections of six other holes he wants to examine. They pull those boxes out of storage and arrange the first three drill holes on the empty tables.

Peter speaks to Bernardo late in the afternoon. "I think you can wait to sample CN-71 until tomorrow. It's all marked. I'll start on what you just laid out first thing tomorrow. With any luck, I'll finish with them about the same time you finish sampling CN-71. You can lay out the final three groups once you clear off CN-71."

"Sounds good," Bernardo says. "Time for dinner now, though. The cook does not like it if we're late for a meal."

"Have to keep the cook happy," Peter says. He looks at Julius. "I've seen about enough core for a day. How about you?"

"Yeah. Dinner and a beer sound good to me about now," Julius says.

"You guys go ahead. I'll pack up my stuff and be there in a couple of minutes," Peter says.

When he's alone, Peter pulls out his radiation detector again. He places it on two locations of concentrated black veinlets. He notes the readings. He does the same on several areas of high copper values, low copper values, and the barren granite. He hesitates a moment before he takes the detector into the core storage building to measure the background radiation there. He makes a few notes in his notebook, puts the meter away, packs up, and heads to dinner.

Steve joins them for dinner, another abundant presentation of family-style, Peruvian fare. Peter asks Bernardo about the early days of the project. Julius and Bernardo have a great time laughing at some of the crazy things that happened, and some of the strange people who worked on the property in the early days, just after the discovery.

As they continue eating, Bernardo says, "We've had some real characters here. One of the strangest ones was a gringo geologist who managed the project in the third or fourth year. I don't remember his name. He was so wound up, so nervous about making a mistake, I thought he'd explode."

"I remember him," Julius says. "I worried about him. They left him here for a very long time. He badly needed some time away. He had no one to help him with some of the management decisions, and the home office did nothing but complain."

"Speaking of being here for a long time," Bernardo says, "my crew and I have been here for over a month. With you people here to watch the camp, do you think it might be possible for us to take a couple of days off? Say, Friday and Saturday?"

I can't believe they're coming right out and saying this, Peter thinks.

"I don't know," Peter says. "We don't know much about the camp, or where things are. And I don't think any of us are good cooks."

"I can get all your sampling done tomorrow," Bernardo says. "I'll show Omar how to handle the generator and a few other things. Other than that, the camp can take care of itself for a couple of days. The cook will leave meals in the fridge, ready to cook." Bernardo smiles. "You'd have peace and quiet to do your work."

Barely able to keep from laughing, Peter turns to Omar. "You willing to be camp manager, along with what you have to do for me?"

"It's not too complicated, Bernardo?" Omar asks.

"No. If I can do it, somebody as smart as you should be able to do it in your sleep."

"I guess I'm willing," Omar says.

"How about you, Steve? Okay with you?"

Steve simply shrugs his shoulders.

"I guess you have your two days off, Bernardo," Peter says.

"Thank you. Thank you. Thank you. Our wives and girlfriends thank you, too," Bernardo says with a broad smile.

"When will you head out?" Peter asks.

"Probably late Thursday, tomorrow, after supper," Bernardo says. "That'll give us all of Friday and Saturday. We'll come back early Sunday, before the helicopter comes for you."

"We're hoping to fly out no later than nine in the morning," Peter says.

"No problem. We'll be here," Bernardo says with a nod of his head.

Julius speaks up and asks, "Peter, you sure you want to be here, the three of you, alone?"

"It's pretty quiet right now," Peter answers. "It shouldn't be a big problem. It's only two days, after all."

"Russo-Perú is happy with this?" Julius asks Bernardo.

"Oh, yes. As long as Señor Binder is willing, they have no problem. We talked it over this morning. They said they don't want to leave the camp unattended, but as long as someone is here, we can take a short break."

"I don't think you should be here alone, Peter," Julius says.

"I'm not alone. There's three of us," Peter says, gesturing toward Omar and Steve. "Let them go. I know what it's like being in a camp too long. It makes you a little crazy."

"I don't like it," Julius says.

"It's okay, Julius. Seriously. It's okay."

When they finish with their meal and Omar gets up to leave, Peter says to him, "Come see me in half an hour. You, too, Steve."

Peter remains at the table, across from Julius, after everyone else has left.

"You're crazy," Julius says. "You should get out with me tomorrow."

"I don't think I should."

"And why not? You'll have enough by tomorrow to make a report."

"No, Julius, I will not. At least not a report I'll be happy to sign. I need at least another one or two days to complete my work here."

Julius frowns. "I won't argue with you. Obviously, you've made up your mind, but I think you're wrong."

"I have made up my mind. But, Julius, I don't think you have to worry about us. We'll be fine."

"I'm not convinced," Julius says as he stands up, "but I'm heading to bed. I'll see you tomorrow morning. At least we'll have the second drill hole sampled."

Peter stands up. "Well, Bernardo and his buddies will be here until late tomorrow. We should be able to get the other drill holes sampled by tomorrow night. I'll have Friday and Saturday to tie up any loose ends."

Julius looks at Peter. He's silent for a moment. "If you say so."

They walk to their separate rooms.

Once he's back in his room, Peter sits on the edge of his bed. "I have to finish this," he says softly. "It's the only way to be sure."

They're actually leaving tomorrow. Now we know the timing.

While he's waiting for Omar and Steve, he begins to develop a plan for tomorrow night.

About twenty minutes later, he hears a knock at the door. "Who is it?" he asks.

"It's Omar and Steve."

Peter opens the door. "Let's take a little walk," he says.

The three of them walk down to a small, wooden footbridge across the river. The other side is actually Ecuador, though no one cares about the international boundary here. Peter stops in the middle of the bridge. Dark clouds race across the face of the moon. When the clouds cover the moon, they can barely see each other.

He turns to the others. "I can't believe that Bernardo actually came out and said that they'll disappear from the camp late tomorrow."

Omar says, "There's a little more to it than that."

"Really?" Peter asks.

"On the way back to my room, Bernardo stopped me. We had a little Quechua conversation. He said, 'When we leave, you leave. Get out of this camp. You don't want to be here.' He was pretty emphatic about it."

"He say why?" Steve asks. "As if we don't already know."

"I asked, but he wouldn't say. All he'd tell me was, 'If you want to stay alive, do as I say and get out of the camp.' I didn't ask any more questions and thanked him for the warning."

Steve grunts. "I think we have the timing down pretty close. Sometime tomorrow night. I'll bet it's between ten and midnight."

"I think you're right," Omar says. "Bernardo was very specific about when I should leave."

"I agree," Peter says, "but we need to be on guard starting tonight. When Julius leaves, even more so. When Bernardo and his buddies leave, we take up our defensive positions and get ready."

"And what exactly is your plan?" Steve asks.

"I think they'll wait until dark." Peter points to the camp, a rather wasted gesture in the darkness. "It gives us a big advantage. They have to come into a well-lit camp. We can turn out all the lights in the buildings, but keep on all the outside lights. I'll make up a body for my bed. I'm the primary target. I'll take cover this side of the camp near my cabin and just inside the edge of the jungle. You do the same, Omar, somewhere over by the core shed."

"I still think they'll leave one or two lookouts to block the trail. You need to take care of them, Steve."

"Do you know what all this is about yet?" Omar asks.

"Maybe… but I won't really know until I get the analyses back from the lab."

"And keeping it secret is worth killing people?"

"Possibly," Peter says.

"How many do you think we're going to have to deal with?" Steve asks.

"I still think four or five is probably the max. Three or four into the camp, we can handle with no problem. Much over six, we're in real trouble."

"Going to be a bunch of bodies," Omar says.

"Except for Sr. Huevos, I'd love to take them alive. I doubt that'll be possible. And it's probably stupid to try." Peter pauses. "What do we do with the bodies? They have to disappear."

"Throw them in the river," Omar says.

"They'll wash up on the sides of the river," Peter says. "People will find them. There'll be way too many questions."

"I know just the place," Steve says.

Peter turns to him. "Where?"

"I've scouted out the area around the camp. About half a mile up the river, I stumbled across a small cave on the Ecuador side. Dumb luck I found it. I had to climb up the side of the canyon to get past some cliffs and waterfalls. Some old stonework partially blocked the opening, but I looked inside with a flashlight. There's a bunch of skeletons and pottery in there. It looks like an ancient burial site, perfect for a few more bodies. I could seal it back up really easily. It's well hidden and far enough from the camp that no one will ever find it."

"Sounds like a lot of hard work to get them up there. Particularly if we have five or six of them," Omar says.

"Not too bad," Steve says. "You guys help me get them up the river. I'll take care of them from there. It sounds like I should have two days to get it done. I shouldn't need more than half a day. You two will have to clean up the camp."

"Yeah," Peter says with a grunt. "House cleaning."

They stand, silent, close together on the bridge.

"Okay," Peter says. "Steve, you take care of the lookouts, if there are any. When you've finished with that, come back to the camp for backup, but cover the trail to make sure there's no one else. We can't afford any surprises. Omar, whichever of us makes a positive ID of El Come Huevos, we kill him immediately. The others should be easy work after he's dead."

"Going to be a mess," Omar says.

"Yes, it will be a mess. Hopefully, it's a mess we can do a decent job of cleaning up."

"I hate to ask this," Steve says, "but what if they don't come in with guns blazing? What if they come in, with guns, but all peaceful like? What if they say, 'We're here to provide security for you, while the normal crew is out for a break.'? What do we do with that?"

"Yeah. I can imagine that happening," Omar says.

Peter isn't sure, but he thinks Omar's being sarcastic. "I don't like being an executioner," he says. "If Huevos doesn't come with them, we've got a problem, but I doubt he'll trust anyone to do this job without him. Are they clever enough to pretend to be peaceful security guards? If that actually happens, one of us has to expose himself and see what they do next." He pauses. "I guess that's my job, since I'm almost surely the main target.

"In any case, we don't let El Come Huevos get out of this alive, even if everything is quiet and peaceful. Once we kill him, I suspect all hell will break loose, regardless of how they approach the camp."

"Probably true," Steve says.

They turn and walk back to their rooms.

CHAPTER 22

The morning begins much the same as the previous day. A good breakfast of scrambled eggs, some meat of somewhat questionable origin, fruit, and strong café con leche. The Peruvians are carrying on a lively conversation, happy they are getting a break.

Peter asks Bernardo, "What are the biggest needs for the people in your village?"

Bernardo puts his fork down. "Two things. Decent jobs. A way to make a living. And decent teachers for the children. Some sort of medical services, even a regular priest, they'd be nice, too."

"How do people make a living now?"

Bernardo shrugs. "Mostly they're poor farmers. Hard to make a living from growing potatoes. That's why there's so much coca around. It's a reliable cash crop."

Peter nods. "It's a good crop, except for all the nasty people, guns, and bloodshed that come with the coca."

"Yes."

Peter eats some of his eggs. "A friend of mine in Canada told me about a really nasty guy. He said this man sometimes works in northern Peru for the narcos from Colombia. He calls himself El Come Huevos. You ever run into him?"

Peter notes that the conversation among the Peruvian laborers falls to total silence. As placidly as he can manage, Peter looks at Bernardo.

Bernardo meets Peter's gaze. Then he looks away and is silent for half a minute. He looks directly at Peter again, frowns, and says, "Yes. I've come across him. He's a murderous son of a whore. He does not deserve to live on this earth."

"I will try to avoid him," Peter says.

"You should," Bernardo says. "Or kill him before he kills you."

Peter takes a deep breath. "Okay. I guess it's time to get to work."

They have already settled into a routine in the core shed. Omar and Bernardo work on sampling CN-71. Peter and Julius look over the portions of the three holes Bernardo laid out the previous day. Peter identifies a few samples from each drill hole, sixteen in total.

At noon they break for lunch.

"You really ought to come out with me," Julius says. "All of you."

"No," Peter says. "We talked it over last night. We'll stay."

Bernardo says nothing.

A little after one, they hear the helicopter coming in for a landing. Julius picks up his small bag.

"You're sure you want to stay?" he asks Peter one last time.

"Yes. We know the risks. We're staying."

"Just remember my friend who died after working here. Be careful."

"We'll be careful, Julius. Enjoy your meeting with your partners."

Julius shakes his head. "Enjoy? That's rather unlikely." With a small shudder, he turns and boards the helicopter.

As the helicopter lifts off, Peter waves goodbye. He closes his eyes.

You're committed now... and you're crazy.

He opens his eyes again. "It will all be resolved, one way or another," he mutters, turns, and walks to the core shed to continue working.

Omar and Bernardo quickly finish the sampling of CN-71, and they pile the boxes of core for that hole under the tables. They lay out the additional portions of three other drill holes on the now empty tables.

Peter doesn't spend a lot of time on the portions of the additional drill holes. He has chosen them mostly for confirmation of observations from CN-48 and 71.

"You can leave these holes on the tables," Peter tells Bernardo. "I'll want to come back to them tomorrow." He hands Bernardo a short list of sections from four more drill holes. "If you can pull these sections out, just stack the core boxes at the end of the tables. If I have time, I'll go through them before we leave."

By the end of the day, they have all the samples bagged, tagged, and placed in four larger canvas bags. They include the samples from the six additional drill holes.

Bernardo and his crew pile the sacks inside the entrance to the core storage building, to keep them out of the rain. The small samples, in spite of the number, do not present a large volume or a major weight.

They all go in for a slightly early dinner. Tonight, there is a palpable sense of tension and uncomfortable anticipation in the room. Bernardo and the laborers sit slightly apart from Peter and Steve. Omar sits between the two groups, but closer to Peter and Steve. The cook and his assistant deliver the food to the tables in silence and quickly depart back to the kitchen. The laborers eat in silence. There is no Quechua bantering and joking between the laborers and Omar. Even Peter, Steve and Omar are largely silent, and Peter does nothing to encourage any discussion.

After dinner, the cook and his assistant clean up quickly. The cook shows Omar all the food he has prepared for them. Then Bernardo, the cook and assistant, and the three laborers, all prepare to walk up the trail to the nearest village, about ten miles away. Bernardo separates from the others and comes over to Peter and shakes his hand.

"*Lo siento*," Bernardo says. "*Yo…*"

Peter puts up his hand. "*No te preocupes*," he says. "It's not a problem, Bernardo. Go home. Enjoy your time off."

Bernardo contemplates Peter, says nothing, returns to the others, and they all disappear up the trail.

"What did he say?" Omar asks.

"He said he's sorry." Peter looks at Omar and Steve and raises his left hand. "So… Get ready. Get in position, as we discussed on the bridge. I'll set up my bed and get my backpack over to the core shed. Then I'll get into position as well. Until then, Omar, please cover my ass."

"Will do."

"Turn out all the lights in the buildings when you leave, but keep on all the outside lights."

Omar and Steve nod.

"Good luck to us all," Steve says. "Should be an interesting night."

"To say the least," Peter says.

Omar and Steve walk away to take their places.

Peter wastes no time. He takes the covers off the second bed, and arranges them to look like somebody is sleeping in his bed.

Not very convincing. It might work if someone's nervous and in a hurry. If it's dark enough.

He takes the .357 P229 out of his pack, loads one magazine, and puts the other in one of the pockets of his cargo pants. He puts the pistol in the holster and on his belt.

He takes off his bulky field vest. He removes the 9mm P229 from the vest, along with the silencer and three extra magazines of ammunition. He puts the pistol, silencer, and the extra ammunition in the largest of the right-hand pockets of his pants.

He goes back to his backpack and pulls out one of the undershirts and the body armor. He strips off his khaki shirt, puts on the body armor, and pulls the shirt over it again. Everything he is wearing is khaki or tan, his pants, his shirt, and his boots.

He stuffs his daypack with his notes and camera, and the field vest, into the larger backpack. He turns out the light, picks up the pack, and walks over to the core shed.

Peter feels extremely exposed, walking through the well-lit but empty camp. He can feel eyes watching him. *Hopefully only Omar,* he thinks. He steps into the shadows of the core shed with relief. He opens the door to the adjacent core storage building and drops his backpack next to the sacks of samples. He shuts the door softly.

He takes the time to look around the camp and listen. He sees and hears nothing out of place. The sound of the river and the generator form the main background sounds of the camp.

It seems to him that the constant jungle sounds, the soft and not so soft cries of animals, are unnaturally silent. He feels an almost overwhelming sense of anticipation. His body is already preparing itself.

He reaches down and pulls out the 9mm pistol. He screws in the silencer. He holds the pistol loosely in his right hand. Staying in the shadows, walking behind buildings as much as possible, he makes his way toward his chosen position. It's not far from the narrow trail down to the footbridge over the river.

He stops at the trail. Constant foot traffic has churned it into mud. He reaches down and scoops up a handful of mud with his left hand and wipes it across his face, neck and ears. He rubs some into his hair. He shakes off some of the mud and wipes his hand on his pants.

From his chosen position, Peter has a clear view of the trail leading into the camp from the mountains and the nearest community. He also has a clear view of the door to the cabin where he has been staying, about twenty-five feet away. The shadows and the edge of the jungle provide concealment, and the massive tree beside him will provide cover if he needs it.

He looks at his watch. It is almost eight.

We've got a good two hours, or more, to wait.

He leans back against the tree.

The time passes slowly. He grows tired of standing. He begins to lift his feet slightly, to get the circulation moving in his legs again. He tenses his muscles and rises a fraction of an inch on the balls of his feet.

Still no sign of anyone. No movement. No sound other than the animals, the generator, and the river.

He looks at his watch. Ten-thirty.

Maybe they're not coming. Maybe they'll make us wait until tomorrow.

He doesn't think so.

Half an hour passes. He looks harder at the trail into the camp. His eyes have been playing tricks on him in the darkness, but this is no trick.

Yes. There is something.

It's too dark to tell for sure.

Yes. Some movement.

He keeps watching.

One man slowly materializes at the edge of the light. He's short. He holds an assault rifle. Peter can't tell the make, but it has a long magazine.

Peter's heart rate advances.

A red bandana covers the man's face, except for his eyes, and a slightly floppy hat covers most of his forehead.

"Damn!" Peter whispers.

How do I identify the bastard if he has his face covered? He hadn't counted on that. *I'll have to see the tattoos.*

A second and a third man joins the first at the edge of the light. Faces covered. Light blue bandanas. Both armed with assault rifles. They take their time.

Peter watches as they look around the camp.

The red bandana points, and one of the other men jogs silently over to the edge of the clearing and disappears from Peter's view, not far from the core shed.

Nice! Peter thinks. *Right in front of Omar.*

The other two wait about ten more minutes. Watching. Listening. They turn and walk directly toward the cabin where Peter has been staying.

Well informed bastards, Peter thinks.

He stands motionless in the shadows.

The two men move silently. They approach the cabin door. The man in the red bandana has short sleeves.

Peter squints. *Is that a tattoo?* He's not sure.

The red bandana points to the door. The second man opens the door as gently and silently as he can. The hinges squeak slightly. Red bandana steps up into the room. An explosion of sound. He fires off an entire magazine from his assault rifle.

Peter flinches, but he doesn't move.

Silence.

The second man enters the cabin and turns on the light. A string of shouting and swearing.

"*¡Concha tu madre! ¡Mierda!*"

Red bandana comes to the door. He steps out. The second man follows.

"*¡Hijo de puta! ¿Dónde diablos está el gringo loco?*" Red bandana says. Then he shouts, "*¡Señor Gringo! ¿Dónde estás?*"

Peter sees the eagle, quite clearly, tattooed on the right side of his neck, but he hesitates.

In his anger and frustration, the man tears off his bandana. He looks around the camp. He turns and faces Peter.

Suddenly Peter sees the man's face quite clearly and fires four shots with his 9mm P229, with the silencer. Then he hears three shots, loud, from across the camp. El Come Huevos jerks in the crossfire, and he collapses to the ground.

There is a moment of silence.

The second man at the cabin is confused.

The sound of the rushing river nearly covered the sounds of Peter's shots. Omar's shots, though, were clear and loud, even from across the camp.

The man still standing in front of Peter's cabin cannot see Omar, but he fires at the sound of Omar's shots.

Peter hears rapid fire from the other side of the camp. From his position in the jungle at the edge of the camp, he can't see anything. It's from one of the higher caliber assault rifles. He doesn't hear any return fire from Omar.

Peter fires four more shots. The second man at the cabin goes down. Peter drops the 9mm and pulls the .357 from his holster. He runs out into the open and goes down on one knee. He fires ten rounds at the third attacker. He sees muzzle flashes from the edge of the jungle.

Omar!

The third attacker is down.

Peter reloads. He looks over at the entrance to the trail. Nothing. Silence except for the generator and the river. Even the jungle animals are silent.

He waits for a brief moment. Nothing.

Peter shouts across the clearing of the camp. "Omar! You okay?"

Peter sees movement. Omar appears out of the jungle. At least he thinks it's Omar.

Like Peter, he had covered his face with mud. Branches hang out of a dark brown knit cap.

"I'm okay!" Omar shouts back across the camp, and with his pistol held in front of him, he approaches the fallen man by the core shed.

Peter holsters the .357 and returns to retrieve his 9mm from where he dropped it. He reloads it, unscrews the silencer, and puts it and the 9mm back into his pocket. He steps back into the open. He holds .357 pistol at the ready. The sounds of the jungle are already rising.

He hears a long burst of gunfire. The sound is faint, but he hears it clearly. It's in the general direction of the trail.

Got to leave that to Steve.

Peter inhales deeply. He turns to examine the two men by the entrance to his cabin.

Huevos is a mess. He has one shot to the head. Peter can't tell exactly how many in the torso. He is not moving. Peter checks for a pulse. Nothing.

He checks the second man. Two shots to the head and two to the chest. No pulse.

Peter steps back and looks around the camp and up at the trail again. Omar is doing the same thing.

Nothing. No signs of anyone else. No more sounds of gunfire.

Peter can feel his heart pounding. He pushes at it, and it begins to slow. He takes three deep breaths.

"It came down just the way we expected," he says.

I wonder how Steve is doing.

Peter thinks for a moment. Well over a hundred rounds were fired by both sides.

Probably less than two or three minutes, first shot to the last, he thinks. *We need to clean up all the brass. And the bodies.*

He meets Omar by the body near the core shed.

"Thank you," Peter says.

"And you, too," Omar says. "You think there are any more?"

"I hope not," Peter says. "You hear the shooting up the trail?"

"I heard it. It was up a way."

"Hopefully, Steve has it under control," Peter says. He looks at the man on the ground. "What a waste. This crap is depressing."

"It was pretty lively here for a bit. Thanks for the support."

"Goes both ways," Peter says. He looks at the trail again. Nothing. "You must have better eyesight than I do. You fired on El Come Huevos with a long-distance identification."

Omar shrugs. "I was pretty sure. When you started firing, it was good enough for me."

"We should step back into the shadows just in case. I have to assume Steve has taken care of any lookouts or reinforcements," Peter says. "I didn't hear any response to the automatic fire."

"I might have. One shot." Omar looks at the trailhead. "I'm not sure. Too much noise from the river and the generator."

Peter shrugs. "Shouldn't be overconfident. We've been lucky so far."

"Yes. We have."

They step into the edge of the jungle to watch, and wait.

Almost over, Peter thinks, *all of it. Maybe.*

Peter sees some faint movement near the end of the trail. In the darkness he can't be sure.

"Someone's there," he says.

"Yes," Omar replies.

They wait. The sounds of the jungle mingle with the river and the generator. Peter listens intently. Hard to hear someone moving around in the jungle with the rising jungle sounds, the river, and the generator. He sees no more signs of movement at the trailhead.

Peter feels a sudden awareness.

There's something. Behind them.

He isn't sure what it is.

He turns around, and Omar turns with him.

Peter feels his adrenaline surge again. His hearing becomes acute. Selective.

Whatever it is, it stops, but he can still feel the presence.

He suddenly feels totally exposed. Even in the darkness. Even in the jungle.

"Get down," Peter says softly.

He and Omar go to the ground, their pistols at the ready.

"Relax guys," Steve Berner says from the dense growth of the jungle. "You done here?"

"Jesus Christ!" Peter says.

He and Omar stand up.

"Yeah. We're done," Peter says. He feels his heart rate begin to slow down. He takes a deep breath.

Steve appears out of the jungle. He looks more like a bush than a man. Mud, branches, and leaves cover him nearly completely.

"That's a good way to get yourself killed," Peter says, "sneaking around behind us like that."

Steve looks at him. "No. It's a good way for me to stay alive."

Omar is grinning. "You scared the hell out of me."

Peter looks at Steve. "Okay. I stand corrected. That was an excellent move." Peter pauses. "You are as scary in person as your reputation suggests."

"Thank you."

"What happened on the trail?" Omar asks.

"One guy," Steve says. "He got rather excited when he heard all the shooting down here. I spoke to him politely. *¡Suelta su arma!* But he didn't drop his weapon. Instead, he decided to empty a magazine in my direction."

Steve shrugs. "He couldn't see me. I was off the trail, at the edge of the jungle. His aim was really bad."

"And?" Peter asks.

"When he had to reload, I stepped out onto the trail. I think he thought I was an evil spirit. He started shaking so badly, I was sure he'd drop his rifle and run like hell."

"The way you look, I'm not surprised," Peter says.

"I told him to drop his weapon again, but when he began to raise it in my direction, I shot him. Once. In the head," Steve said, pointing at the trail. "He's over there, at the side of the trail."

"No others?" Omar asks.

"I jogged up the trail about a half a mile. Didn't see any. I'm pretty sure he's it." He cocks his head to the side and looks at Peter. "You were pretty accurate about the number."

Peter takes a deep breath and exhales. "I hope so."

"Sounds pretty quiet to me," Steve says. "If there are any more, they'd be here by now."

"Or they ran away," Omar says.

"Let's wait here for a while," Peter says.

After 15- or 20-minutes pass, Peter says, "I guess we can gather up the bodies. Let's carry them down by the river, next to the little bridge. Their bowels will probably empty themselves shortly. We can clean them up later.

"I have to take some photographs, mostly of Huevos. We can dispose of the bodies at first light. You guys good with that?"

"Sounds good to me," Steve says. "Then I think I'll clean up a bit."

"That's a good idea," Omar says.

"Let's get busy first," Peter says. "Clean up after we've taken care of the bodies."

They carry the bodies down to the bank of the river, near the footbridge, and lay them on the ground in a neat row.

"Let's strip their clothes off before their muscles totally relax. I'd rather have the mess on the ground than in their pants," Peter says.

Peter retrieves his camera from his backpack in the core storage building. He finds a new memory card and puts it in the camera.

I sure don't want these photos sitting in the camera.

Peter stands on a small stepladder he retrieved from the kitchen on his way back. He takes a series of flash photographs of El Come Huevos' body, front, back, and both sides. Steve and Omar rearrange the body as needed. Peter takes close-up photos of his face, the tattoos, and all the entrance and exit wounds.

Once he finishes with Huevos, they line up all the bodies again, and Peter completes the documentation.

"We need to burn the clothes," Peter says.

"I'll do it right now," Steve says. "We can do it at their little dump, where they burn their trash. One less thing to do tomorrow. All I need is some gasoline."

"I can get some gasoline at the generator," Omar says.

Peter looks at the bodies.

"The little communities are better off with them dead," Steve says.

"Perhaps for the short term, but there's plenty more to replace them," Omar says. "I come from a place just like where they come from. There's always a supply of macho men desperate for any chance at some real money and a sense of power. They think it's a ticket to a good life, but it's usually a ticket to an early death. Like this."

Peter grimaces. "How did you escape?"

"Lucky. I had a teacher who pushed me. He gave me a lot of help, too, and I got to University." He looks at the naked men on the ground. "I'm not sure my job is much different from these poor bastards."

"What the hell are you guys talking about?" Steve asks. "These guys worked for Colombian narcos. Because of them, thousands of people are addicted to cocaine. They were nasty, ruthless bastards who were part of El Come Huevos' worst atrocities. They were ready to kill all of us, probably after they had fun torturing us. You in particular, Peter. And you're feeling sad for them? You're both crazy."

"You're right, of course, but it's all about opportunity," Peter says. "These guys didn't have many choices in life… except bad ones. That includes Huevos, though I can't say I have any regrets over his death."

"Well, I'm glad we're vertical, and they're horizontal," Steve says.

"Yeah, but I don't have to be happy that they're horizontal," Omar says.

"Crap," Steve says, though with no great note of conviction.

Peter looks at the two of them. "I think the good guys won this round. Thank you. Both of you." He looks at his watch. A little after midnight. "We've got to get rid of these bodies at first light. God knows when somebody will come by, or who they might be."

Steve gathers up the clothing. "Go get the gasoline, Omar. I'll meet you at the burn site."

"I'll start gathering up all the brass shell casings I can find," Peter says. "We'll have to do a more serious search tomorrow, and clean up any spots and splatters of blood we can find."

CHAPTER 23

It is a long night. Steve burns all the clothing, carefully raking the ashes into the others already at the site. Peter and Omar search the camp and collect and bury as much of the brass as they can find. They both admit that some of their own are impossible to find in the jungle. They will try again in daylight.

The three of them clean up the worst of the blood stains on the ground, at least those most visible in the lights. Fortunately, there are none in the buildings.

They each get a flashlight and walk up the trail to where Steve encountered the lookout. They shovel out a small blood stain where the lookout fell. They can't find the shell casing from Steve's single shot. It lies somewhere in the jungle on the downhill side of the trail. They pick up all the brass they can find from the panicked attacker.

"I'll come back during the day and check for more brass and blood stains," Steve says.

"What do we do about the bullet holes in the buildings?" Omar asks, when they return to the camp. "And your bed and bedding?"

"Good question," Peter answers. "I'm not sure. I expect Bernardo would be more than happy to make the repairs. Surely it would be best for him and his community if there's no evidence of any violence here. Best if Sr. Huevos and his buddies just disappear. If we clean up well enough, and he repairs well enough, their disappearance will remain a total mystery."

"I wouldn't count on it," Steve says.

Omar shrugs. "It's a narco, and some poor peasants with illegal guns. The police don't give a damn."

"You're hiding the bodies, Steve. If the site's as good as you say it is, nobody will find any bodies to confirm what we did to these guys. Let's hope you're right about that old burial site." Peter looks at the sky. It is already getting a bit brighter. "It's time for us to deal with those bodies. If it's really a half-mile away, this is going to be a major pain in the ass."

They take a bucket and some rope and return to the bodies by the river. As their muscles relaxed with death, the four dead men emptied their bowels, as Peter predicted. They rinse the bodies off and clean them up as much as they can.

"El Come Huevos is the only heavy one," Omar says. "The others are pretty skinny. One each for those. Two of us to carry the big boy."

"Annoying," Steve says. "They're already getting stiff."

They cut a branch of a tree, and they hogtie El Come Huevos to the branch. With a rolled-up towel between the branch and their shoulders, Peter and Omar hoist up the branch. El Come Huevos' body hangs down like some sort of gruesome trophy as they carry him to his grave. Steve walks ahead of them, carrying one of the other, smaller bodies.

They walk clumsily with their burdens, in and out of the water on the side of the river. The footing is rocky, uneven, and slippery. Each of them falls several times on the journey. No injuries, though they are soaked from both their sweat and their falls into the river. Finally, after a little over half an hour, Steve stops near the base of a small waterfall.

"Damn!" Peter says. "I'm glad you didn't find this spot five miles from the camp. We need to get this done before the afternoon rains, before the river level rises."

"How high is the burial site?" Omar asks.

"About a hundred and fifty feet above us," Steve answers.

"You want us to help you with the big boy?" Peter asks.

Steve smiles. "That would be greatly appreciated."

Peter and Omar slip and swear their way to the ancient burial site. They fall multiple times, and they and El Come Huevos are covered in mud by the time they finish. When Peter sees the site, he realizes that this is truly a great location. Given a couple of afternoons of rain, the jungle will begin to cover any signs of their scramble to get up to the site. With the addition of a few rocks, the entrance will be blocked and will effectively disappear.

They all take a few minutes to catch their breath, and Peter and Omar untie El Come Huevos.

"It's a better grave than our buddy deserves," Peter says, still breathing hard.

Steve agrees. "I think you're right. I bet the earlier residents were pretty decent people. Let me show you." Steve pulls out his flashlight and beckons for Peter to come to the opening. "It's very orderly. No one has disturbed them for centuries."

Peter looks into the tomb. He can see six or eight skeletons laid out on a relatively flat floor to the cave, about seven feet below the small entrance. Most of them seem to be undisturbed. Once, they might have had cloth wrappings, but it is far too humid for any of that to survive. The funerial pottery offerings surround each of the ancient dead.

"I can lower our guys down with the rest of them, with the rope you used to bring El Come Huevos up here. Arrange them as neatly as possible near the entrance. I'll try to treat them with some respect, even if they were trying to kill us all."

Peter steps back from the opening. "Thanks, Steve. I've dumped bodies without much ceremony at times, but I've never liked doing it. This is not a bad place to be… for eternity."

"Let's go get the others, Peter," Omar says, "before someone comes into camp and finds them."

"Before you close the cave up, Steve, please come and get me." Peter looks back at the opening. "I just want to say something to send them on their way."

Steve looks at Peter. Perhaps he questions whether Peter is being serious. "Yeah," he says. "I'll come and get you."

Peter and Omar take the tree branch back with them and find some more rope. They hogtie the last two bodies to the branch and cart them up to the trail to the tomb. Steve says he'll handle them from there.

At a little before ten, Steve returns to the camp. He and Peter hike back to the tomb with the four assault rifles.

Peter looks through the opening. Steve has lined up the four new bodies in a neat row, close to the entrance. Peter nods his head. "That's nice."

They lower the guns down, inside the cave, to rest beside the four men.

Peter speaks to the four dead men. "You rest with better men who lived long before you. It will be a major task for your god, if you have one, to forgive you for your sins. But you will sin no more. My wish for you is that you lie in peace, for the rest of time."

Peter helps Steve close the entrance to the tomb.

As they walk back to the camp, Steve says, "You need to consider a change in profession."

Peter grimaces. "That obvious?"

"Yes. That obvious."

"Well," Peter says, "just so you know. This is my last job."

"Good," Steve says. "My wish for you is to live in peace for the rest of your life."

"Thanks. I appreciate that. And thank you for all your help here."

"Not a problem," Steve says.

They walk the rest of the way in silence.

By the middle of the day, Peter and Omar have searched the camp again and buried all the brass casings they can find. Peter sweeps out his old room. He folds and stacks his shredded blankets on the mattress that is also full of holes. He moves to a different room.

Steve volunteers to walk several miles up the trail. He encounters no one and cleans up a few minor drips of blood along the way. He doesn't find any more shell casings. The trail is deserted.

They each take a shower, dress in fresh clothes, and find their way to the kitchen. Each of them has their pistol in a holster at their side.

Peter looks in the refrigerator. "I'm famished. Let's see what's here for the three amigos."

Omar gently pushes him out of the way. "This is all Peruvian food. This is my job. Sit down. Have a beer. Relax. I will prepare a large, mid-day dinner."

Peter looks around the dining room. "I think I'll sit outside at the little picnic table. It's nice outside, and I'd hate to come out the door after lunch and face twenty armed men lined up in the camp."

Steve grunts. "If there are twenty of them, I'd hate to see them under any circumstances. Let us know when lunch is ready, Omar. I'll come and get it."

"Don't worry about it. I'll bring it out to you."

Omar begins to pull things out of the refrigerator. Most of them, Peter admits to himself, he would have no idea of how to cook, other than slap them in the microwave. In between Omar pulling food out, Peter finds three cold beers. He leaves one for Omar and takes the other two outside to sit with Steve.

"I'm not sure drinking a beer at this time is actually all that appropriate," Peter says.

"Look. They chose to come here," Steve says. "It's pretty clear what they were out to do. They shredded your bed with thirty, high caliber rounds without any warning at all. They knew what they were doing. They were evil butchers. They had their plan. It was a bad plan. Lucky for us. Unlucky for them."

Peter looks down at his beer. "In the last two years, someone has tried to kill me... I think it's twenty-one times. It's getting old, and I never get used to situations like this one. I don't know how many people I've killed in the same time frame. A bunch." Peter rubs his forehead.

"You're very good at it," Steve says.

Peter grunts. "I'm not entirely happy about that."

"If you weren't so good at it," Steve says, "you'd be dead long before now."

"If I weren't so good at it, no one would ask me to do it."

"True."

"I don't enjoy being judge and executioner, not even for people like El Come Huevos." Peter looks at Steve, frowning. "I hesitated before I shot him, even after I saw his eagle tattoo." Peter inhales deeply. "That is so incredibly dangerous. I'm starting to lose my edge, and I have to quit before it kills me."

"As I said, it's time for you to make a career change." Steve smiles and takes a long drink of his beer.

"You're right. I want to thank you for treating the bodies with some respect. Obviously, you are a more complex person than I first thought."

Steve smiles somewhat ruefully. "I probably do see things as more black and white than you and Omar do. Good and evil. Simple. That makes it easier for me."

"Is it easy?" Peter asks.

"Not really. You two are right about the choices those little guys had in life. Anyway, in the end, when we're dead, even if we're El Come Huevos, we're nothing but lumps of cold, useless, flesh and bones. Showing a little respect does no harm to anyone."

Omar interrupts by bringing bowls of soup with chicken and egg. "Something like *sopa criolla*," he says. "Maybe a little simpler, but it should be good." He puts the bowls down and sits at the table himself. "I'll heat up some rice in the microwave, and there's a pot full of something that looks like goat stew to go with the rice."

"Does the geologist side of you have some more work to do?" Steve eventually asks Peter.

Peter nods. "Yes, it does, if I can get my mind wrapped around it."

"I have been wondering if that was a real job or not," Steve says.

"It's a real job as far as I'm concerned."

"If you can show me a piece of rock that people want badly enough that they're willing to kill for it, I want to see it," Steve says.

Omar picks up the empty soup bowls. "I'll agree with that," he says as he returns to the kitchen.

"People have killed many times over pieces of rock, or the stuff that's found in them," Peter says. "Look at all the wars fought over oil. People have fought wars and committed genocides over gold, silver, platinum, diamonds, even copper. It's an ugly history of greed and murder."

"Do you know what's going on here?" Steve asks.

"I'm not sure," Peter says. "I'll have to wait for the analyses. Maybe they'll show something. I don't know."

And that's almost the truth, Peter thinks.

Omar returns in a few minutes with the main course. They eat, saying little.

When he finishes, Peter says, "I always like goat. I don't know why people don't eat it more in Canada and the United States. It has a nice taste."

"Goats have a bad rep," Steve says.

"I suppose that is the main reason," Peter says. "They're supposed to smell bad. Stuff like that."

Peter stands up. "I have a lot of work to do over this afternoon and tomorrow. At the same time, I'm a little worried about some sort of repeat of last night. I'd like you two to provide camp security while I focus on geology. Maybe one of you can go up the trail a bit, and the other can watch the camp itself. It's hard to focus on geology when you're worried about being shot."

"You going to need help with core?" Omar asks.

"No. Everything is either on the table or piled up one place or another in the shed. I just need to move it around and spend some more time with it. What I need most of all is to be alone, able to focus completely on the geology, and not worry about anything else for a while."

Omar takes in the plates and begins clean-up. Steve stands watch on the camp until Omar finishes. Then Steve walks up the trail.

Peter returns to the core shed and lays out the sections of the two additional drill holes that Bernardo and his crew had piled at the end of the tables.

Peter chose these particular sections of the other drill holes to give a detailed look at several locations of high-grade copper, and zones of more intense black veining. Most of the black veins are hairline in thickness, but some are thicker. Though narrow, they are abundant. As far as Peter can tell from the copper assays, they have no impact, positive or negative, on the copper grades.

At one point, the generator stops. Omar refuels it and restarts it. Other than that, it is a peaceful, though not necessarily quiet afternoon. The birds of the jungle are quite noisy. Several small mice scout out the area of the core shed, searching for fragments of bread and sandwiches left behind by the workers. They largely ignore Peter's presence. A few times, when he is very still, they scamper over his boots.

Peter notices a good deal of rustling in the jungle itself, but nothing is bold enough to come out fully into the open. He glimpses two animals, one black with a lighter brown head, and the other white. They look like fishers, or large weasels.

At the end of the afternoon, they all gather at the table outside the kitchen. Omar prepares another meal from the refrigerator.

Steve brings out two beers for himself and Peter. "How'd the geology work go today?" he asks.

Peter takes the first sip of the cold beer. "Not bad. I got a lot of work done."

"You going to keep busy with the rocks tomorrow?"

"I suppose I could leave now, but I'll go back to the first two drill holes I looked at with Julius. I want to check some of my notes. Take a few more photographs. I'll be all wound up, packed up, and ready to hop on the helicopter when it comes on Sunday."

"Good," Steve says. "I want to get out of here. This place is so quiet now, it gives me the creeps. Just thinking about yesterday, and looking around now, I'm on edge all the time."

"You're not the only one," Peter replies. "Thanks for being lookout today. It let me escape into the geology for a while. I keep thinking about that tomb. I'm going to dream about that. I know it."

"We have to take turns and keep watch tonight," Steve says.

"Yes. They didn't plan on announcing themselves last night. It was a shoot first and sort it out later approach. They obviously decided to take no chances and just kill me immediately."

Omar brings salads out and sits down. "Thought I should use up some of the fresh stuff," he says.

Peter eats a few bites of the salad. "It's good, Omar. I wanted to ask you about an animal I caught a glimpse of today. There were two. One black with a brown head, the other white. I didn't get a really good look, but they looked like fishers, big weasels."

"Probably tayras," Omar says. "You say one was white?"

"Yeah. One white, the other black."

"You do see white ones, once in a while, but it's fairly unusual."

"I'm seeing albino animals lately," Peter says. "The natives in Canada think they're powerful spirits. Ancestors coming back to warn you. I'm not sure whether they're supposed to be warning of good or bad fortune."

"I'll hold out for omens of good fortune," Omar says, "but some white spirits have been very bad news for Peru."

"Really?"

"You have heard of the Pishtacos?" Omar asks.

Peter nods. "White spirits that kill the Altiplano natives to suck the fat out of their bodies. I know a couple of gringo geologists who had to run like hell to get out of some of the tiny villages. The locals were convinced they were Pishtacos."

"You shouldn't forget. You're one of the albinos," Omar says. He looks terribly serious as he speaks.

"Am I an omen of good or bad?" Peter asks.

"That, I think, depends entirely on whom you ask," Steve says.

"The Pishtacos are an old story," Omar says. "But the Conquistadors were the first, living Pishtacos. They brought disastrous news for those who lived here before they arrived."

"I read that the Spanish used the fat from the enemy corpses on the battlefield to treat their wounds," Peter says. "That must have been more than a little shocking to the Incas."

"In the name of Jesus Christ and the Christian Church, the Spanish Conquistadors killed millions. They sucked the life out of this country." Omar shakes his head. "Conquistadors? Pishtacos? We are still living with their bad news."

Omar looks at Peter with a half-smile and shrugs. "I could say that greedy Pishtacos, pale men from North America, brought their demand for cocaine to Peru, and brought death with them." He raises his hands. "What has happened here is no more than the end product of a long history."

Peter and Omar look at each other for a long time before Peter says, "Omar, it is an ugly story, and I apologize for my role in it."

Omar offers a small, sad smile. "Don't apologize for your role. We are all tools of history. I don't think your role here is particularly evil. The results of last night will almost surely bring good, at least for the short term. Long term?" Omar gestures toward the core shed. "That probably lies with the rocks you study, and we don't know those results. Not yet."

Peter says nothing.

They eat for a while longer, listening to the language of the jungle around them, and the background sounds of the river, and of course the generator.

Later, as they eat Omar's main course, another stew of some sort with rice, Peter says, "Steve and I were talking earlier. We need to stand watch tonight. Someone has to be awake and watching the camp all night. I'm happy to do from ten to one, if you guys will cover the rest of the night."

"Come and wake me up," Omar says. "I'll take over at one."

"I guess that means you wake me at four," Steve says. "Not a problem. I won't sleep much tonight anyway." He finishes his beer. "I'll take now until ten, too. You can do some work, Peter, without worrying about someone sneaking up on you."

"You included?" Peter asks.

"Me included."

CHAPTER 24

For Peter, the evening begins quietly. Over Omar's objections, he cleans up the kitchen and dishes, and then he sits at the table outside the kitchen, alone, for a long time.

Steve moves a chair to the edge of the jungle, near the trail into camp. He sits there, perfectly still, watching.

Peter tries to focus on his next major step. Lima. Now that he has survived Cerro Nublado, Lima holds the final keys. The last test.

Maria! Maria! Where are you? He puts his head in his hands. *You are my life.*

As hard as he tries, he can't think straight. *Give it up.*

He shuts his eyes. He tries to meditate, but it's hopeless. His mind insists on churning through the events of the previous night and the morning. Conquistadors march through his brain, hacking and murdering. Gouts of blood spurt from brown decapitated bodies, and the heads with open eyes and gaping mouths roll into pools of darkening blood, as if searching for their former owner. He sees himself, pale as fresh-fallen snow. Blood spattered across his pale whiteness, he lurks in the background with a bloody sword and surrounded by a blood-red haze.

He shakes his head to rid himself of the violent visions, stands up, and walks down the trail to the footbridge. Clouds hide the moon, and he struggles to stay on the trail. He gropes his way to the middle of the bridge and leans on the railing. He can see almost nothing and hears only the river.

He feels his stomach begin to churn. At first he tries to hold it back, but he gives up, leans out over the railing, and vomits into the river. Again. And again, until there is nothing left but the dry heave of bile and bitterness. He takes a handkerchief from his pocket, wipes his mouth, and throws it into the river.

Peter stands up. He's breathing hard, and he lets the rush of the water overtake his thoughts.

An intense wave of sadness washes over him. He isn't sure exactly where it comes from. It isn't from last night. It isn't even from all the other nights and days that were so much the same.

My life is pointless. I've fought what I thought was evil. I've almost always won the day, and I've survived. But there's always another person who comes along, or an army. You never win the war. He frowns in the inky darkness. *There's just one battle left. Lima remains. Surely, they'll try one more time. Lima is waiting for me. Then I will be done.*

He steps back from the railing and carefully walks back into the camp. It is almost 10. He walks into the kitchen and rinses out his mouth. He takes a bottle of water and walks over to Steve.

"I can take over now," Peter says.

"Good. Don't let the white ones disturb you."

Peter smiles. "I think they'll help me stay awake, unless I see an image of myself."

"Ah," Steve says, "that's always the worst nightmare for all of us."

There is no more drama for this night. It is as if they are all on an island, quiet and isolated from all the troubles of the world.

After Omar relieves him, a bit less than an hour after midnight, Peter goes to bed. He tosses and turns restlessly trying to sleep, but bloody visions continue to race through his brain. He sits on the edge of his bed, then lies down again and attempts a lying meditation.

This time it works, and he falls asleep. He dreams of his great-grandfather. But instead of shouting and yelling advice, the old man works quietly in his vineyard. He beckons for Peter to join him. In his dream, Peter is a boy, no more than ten years old.

"Come. Come here, boy," his great-grandfather says.

Peter is shy. He hesitates. He is afraid of the big man and his wild, gray beard.

"Come. Come. Don't be afraid. I will show you how to prune the vines."

He comes and stands beside the old man.

His great-grandfather shows him how he cuts back last year's growth, leaving one or two buds at each node for this year's crop.

"Why do you grow grapes here?" Peter asks.

The old man gestures at the hillside. "Because this is the side of a hill. It's rocky. The water drains away. The vines must struggle, and that makes them strong."

"But wouldn't you get more grapes if you didn't prune the vines?"

"Yes, you would," the old man replies. "But they would be poor grapes. Even though they struggle and grow strong, the vines might lack the strength to ripen so many grapes. You might have to leave them to rot on the vine. Worst of all, if that happens, you will have no wine." The old man smiles and continues to prune.

Peter's great-grandfather looks at him and pats him lightly on the head. "I have seen your struggles, but you have grown strong. Prune away the waste." He smiles. "You will yield good fruit."

Peter awakens from his dream with a smile.

After breakfast, Peter works at the core shed. Omar and Steve patrol the camp while he works, but after lunch, Omar helps him with the minor amount of additional sampling.

Late in the afternoon, Omar returns from the rock saw with the last of the samples. Peter returns the remainder of the core to the box and replaces the cover.

"You are done?" Omar asks.

"Yes. We just need to pack up and be prepared for the helicopter when it comes tomorrow morning."

"What do you think?"

"What do I think? That's a good question. I don't know what I think."

"Your samples contain the answer?" Omar asks.

"It's the analyses of those samples that will provide the answer, if there is an answer to be provided," Peter replies.

"Someone could replace the samples, or steal them, couldn't they?"

"That is a concern."

"Will people be happy with your answer?" Omar asks.

Peter looks at the tables with the boxes of core. "I've done a lot of evaluations like this one, and I never manage to make everyone happy. Sometimes I can make a lot of people absolutely furious."

"And here?"

Peter continues to look down the rows of core boxes. "I don't know, but I doubt anyone will be happy. You've seen the anger of some already, and that was only the fear that I might, just might, discover something here."

"And you have?"

"I don't know, but, assuming Minera Russo-Perú is behind what happened here, they'll soon figure out what we did, though they'll have a hard time proving anything. I worry that they will be convinced that I have discovered, or will discover, something they want to keep secret." Peter takes a deep breath. "If that's true, the most dangerous time of all is yet to come."

"Are you afraid?"

Peter nods his head. "I'm always afraid of dangerous, angry, and unpredictable men. And women, for that matter."

Omar looks at the tables of core. "I'm glad I'm not you."

Peter smiles. "Soon, the 'me' you see before you will no longer exist."

"You will die?"

"I will be born a new man."

Omar shakes his head. He gives up on his questions and helps Peter pack up his tools.

By the end of the day, all Peter's samples are in the four large canvas bags. He writes out his orders for analyses. He will be ready to ship his samples to the lab on Monday. He thinks about what Omar said about the samples.

Not so sure I want to leave the samples at the lab in Lima.

That evening, after a quiet dinner, and before his turn at the watch, Peter works on a preliminary outline for his report on Cerro Nublado. He writes a brief note to Sir Richard.

Richard,

Field work is completed. I await analyses.

I have a large number of samples. Can you arrange secure transport to the ALS lab in Toronto, Ontario? I don't want to lose control of the samples here in Peru.

Also have some personal photos of some friends for you.

Sunday night?

Peter

He'll send the short note as a text message once he has a cell phone connection.

Peter packs everything for the trip back to Lima. He leaves out clean clothes for the morning and takes a shower and shaves. He retrieves the four sacks of samples and places them next to his backpack. He keeps out his 9mm pistol for his night watch and packs the other deep in his backpack.

Steve knocks on the door and opens it. "You ready?" he asks.

"As ready as I'll ever be."

It is another calm night. Shortly after he settles himself in the chair by the trail for his watch, the two tayras surprise him with a visit to the camp.

"Well, hello there," Peter says softly.

The two turn in unison and look at him, but they don't run away. They quickly return to their search for small, nocturnal mammals, drawn to the lights of the camp. They each catch several. They surprise Peter by their combination of patience and quick movement. If their prey is out in the open, it doesn't stand much of a chance.

Good hunters. I wonder how good the hunters will be in Lima.

Peter is wide awake at six-thirty on Sunday morning. He dresses quickly with his field vest, and he puts his 9mm P229 into one of the large pockets. He drops one of the extra magazines into another pocket.

He takes his backpack with him and finds that both Steve and Omar are already sitting at the table outside the kitchen. They, too, have their packs with them. Peter goes back for the samples. When he returns, he sits at the table with Omar and Steve.

"Time to get out of this place," Steve grumbles. "Past time."

Omar smiles. "I'll go cook some breakfast."

"You think we'll have any problems on the road to Piura?" Steve asks.

"I doubt it," Peter says. "With us all armed, we should be able to handle anything but a military attack."

Steve points at the trail. "Look."

Peter sees Bernardo emerge from the trail, followed by the cook and his assistant, and the three other members of the caretaker team for the camp. Peter waves.

"*¡Buenos días!*" he shouts.

The men hesitate. They're too far away for Peter to read their faces.

Bernardo walks slowly to the table, looking around the camp as he approaches. The others walk a couple of steps behind him. When he reaches the table, Bernardo stops. He looks intently at Peter.

"*Buenos días. ¿Cómo estás?* How are you?" Bernardo asks.

"We're fine," Peter says with a small smile.

"*¿No hubo problemas?*" Bernardo asked. "No problems while we were gone?"

"No problems," Peter says. "Should there have been any?" He continues to smile at Bernardo as he speaks.

Bernardo stares at him. "No. Of course not."

"We are eating eggs this morning," Peter says. "Omar is cooking them now. They're very special eggs. Perhaps the cook would like to take over?"

Bernardo raises his eyebrows in surprise. "*Huevos especiales. Si. Está bien.*"

Peter says, "*Está bien.* Yes. It is truly very good."

Bernardo turns and speaks to the cook. The cook and his assistant look slightly panic stricken, but they quickly step into the kitchen.

A few minutes later, Omar comes out to the table. "They threw me out of the kitchen. The cook wants to be sure to cook the eggs properly." Omar laughs. "He seemed to think I was cooking some other kind of eggs."

Bernardo takes a deep breath.

Peter stands up. "I do have one problem, Bernardo. I had to change rooms. Let me show you why." Bernardo suddenly looks concerned again, but he follows as Peter walks to the cabin where he first slept.

Peter goes to the head of the bed. "Let's move this to the middle of the floor," he says. The thirty bullet holes in the flooring and lower part of the wall are immediately obvious.

Bernardo's eyes widen, and he turns to Peter.

"Termites," Peter says. "Very noisy."

Bernardo turns back and studies the holes. "*Termitas gigantes,*" he says. He silently points at Peter and back at the bed.

"No, I was not in the bed. The termites ate the bedding, too." Peter picks up one of the blankets and puts his finger through one of the bullet holes. He does the same with one of the holes in the mattress.

Bernardo shakes his head. "*Termitas gigantes,*" he says softly. He looks at Peter, and he begins to laugh.

Peter says, "I think it would be best if you can fix the floor and wall."

"Yes," Bernardo says, shaking his head. "We don't want visitors to know we have termites. No. We don't want people to ask questions about termites."

"No, we don't," Peter says. "The huge termites got into a few other walls in camp, too. Not many."

Bernardo turns to face Peter. He extends his hand, clasps Peter's right hand and shakes it. "*Gracias,*" he says softly.

"*De nada,*" Peter says. "You are welcome. I hope it helps a little."

They walk back to the table by the kitchen. Their breakfast of scrambled eggs, toasted bread, and strong coffee is waiting for them.

"How was the time at home?" Steve asks Bernardo.

"It was good, except for the cook's assistant."

"What happened to him?" Peter asks.

"His girlfriend found somebody else."

"Sorry to hear that," Steve says.

Bernardo shrugs. "It happens… when you are away too long."

Peter nods. "I'm sorry. It happens to geologists, too."

They all turn as they hear the helicopter approaching.

"Time for us to say goodbye, Bernardo," Peter says.

Bernardo picks up Peter's pack. "I will carry your pack to the helicopter." He speaks to the laborers, and they pick up the sacks of samples.

Peter doesn't object, and they all head to the helipad. They load the gear, the samples, and themselves onto the helicopter.

Before he gets in, Peter turns again to Bernardo. They shake hands one more time, and Peter says, "*¡Buena suerte!* Good luck!"

Bernardo holds Peter's hand in both of his. "*¡Buena suerte!*"

Peter waves as they lift off. The helicopter turns and begins to gain altitude.

"Bernardo still doesn't believe it," Steve says. "Did you show him the holes in the floor of your room?"

"Yes. We agreed that there are some gigantic termites in northern Peru."

Omar and Steve laugh loudly. Omar cannot stop laughing for a long time.

When they land in Huancabamba at 8:30 in the morning, the two cars are waiting for them. Peter and Omar take the back seat of the lead car. Steve is in the second vehicle. As they pull out of Huancabamba, Peter sends his text message to Sir Richard.

The driver speaks to Peter and Omar in the back seat. "There's a roadblock not too far from Huancabamba. They're collecting to purchase a small tractor and plow for several local communities. We gave them some money on our way up. You should probably give them a little. It will make for less arguing and delay."

"Sounds like a job for our Quechua speaker," Peter says with a smile. He pulls out his wallet and gives Omar four fifty-sole notes.

"That's too much," Omar says.

"I know it's too much," Peter says. "It's about fifty dollars, but there's three of us. Give it to them anyway. Talk to them a little. Tell them that we wish them well."

Omar raises his eyebrows, but he says nothing.

Peter watches Omar talking with the men at the roadblock. Omar takes the time to have a serious conversation. He gives them the four notes. Suddenly the expressions change. All the men insist on shaking Omar's hand. When Omar comes back to the car, he smiles broadly.

"That was pleasant enough?" Peter asks.

"Yes," Omar says, still smiling. "They are good people."

"Like the people of your village?"

"Yes. They remind me of where I was born."

"Perhaps, Omar, we could, together, try to do something to help."

Omar becomes very serious. "The problems are enormous, endless."

"But we can make a beginning, can't we? That's better than doing nothing, isn't it?"

"Perhaps," Omar says.

The remainder of the trip to Piura is uneventful, quiet.

Peter receives a text from Sir Richard as they enter the outskirts of Piura.

Peter,

Transport arranged. Tonight will be fine.

Richard

Peter texts back that he'll call when he gets to Lima. He sends one more text.

Julius,

We're out of Cerro Nublado. No problems. Got the work done. Should have the samples to the lab soon. I should have a report to you in two or three weeks. Nothing conclusive to report to you until then.

Peter Binder

He receives a return text from Julius almost immediately.

Thank God you're out of there. I won't ask any questions. I know you won't answer them until you have conclusive results. Keep in touch.

Julius

They arrive at the Piura airport a little before noon. The plane is waiting. "Do you want to try to get something to eat before we take off?" Peter asks.

"No," Omar says. "Let's assume the copilot has some sandwiches again. I want to get back to Lima."

Steve agrees. They pile into the airplane with all their gear and samples, and they are up and on their way to Lima within a half hour. As expected, the copilot produces sandwiches, soft drinks, coffee, and beer. The sandwiches are egg salad again.

"¡Ensalada de huevo!" Steve says. He makes a face and laughs. Then he takes a large bite.

"They taste the same as they did on the way up," Peter says.

Omar smiles. "And I find that a little surprising."

CHAPTER 25

When they land in Lima, two cars from Seguridad Ejecutiva meet them. They drop Peter with his backpack and four sacks of samples at the DoubleTree in Miraflores. The bellman picks up the sacks, and, as usual, Peter hears the inevitable question.

"What do you have in here? Rocks?"

Peter retrieves his briefcase and suitcase from safe keeping and goes to his room with the bellman and the cart, with the samples and his backpack. He puts the samples in the closet, strips down, and takes a shower. He dresses with one of his undershirts with the body armor inserted. Open-neck, dress shirt. He lays out his sport coat with the body armor on the bed.

He retrieves the 9mm P229 from the briefcase, loads it with the special ammunition, and puts it in the drawer of an end table by the sofa.

He looks at the furniture in the living area of the suite.

"Have to rearrange this," he says.

At first, he isn't sure he can manage it alone, but after some effort he drags the table and chairs from in front of the window to the entrance area. He moves the large upholstered chair with its large pillow to the corner by the window, and arranges the sofa along the wall across from the chair, with the coffee table in front of it.

He sits in the chair and looks slightly to his left. He can't see the actual door to the room, but he can see the end of a short hallway into the room from the door. He turns a bit to his right, and the back of the sofa is about seven feet away. The main window in the room is behind him. He looks around. He feels behind the pillow.

"This will work just fine," he says softly. He looks at his watch. It is almost 4 PM, and he calls Sir Richard.

"Yes?"

"It's Steinbauer. I'm in my room. Back safe and sound, I might add."

"Omar told me about Thursday night. Sounded nasty."

"It was."

"And how was the geology?"

"I got my work done," Peter says.

"You solve the mystery?"

"I don't know."

"What do you mean, you don't know?" Sir Richard asks.

"I won't know anything for sure until I get the analytical results."

"You don't have any guesses?"

"If I have any guesses, I'm not going to tell you or anyone else about them," Peter says. "Legally, I have to give any report to Mandrake first. I'll tell you about anything I discover as soon as I know it and tell Mandrake. Not before then."

"You're impossible."

"No, I'm ethical. You've been waiting a long time to figure this out. Another few weeks won't hurt you." He pauses. "How do we handle the samples? I'm really worried about someone stealing them or screwing with them."

"You don't want the lab in Lima to have anything to do with them?"

"I'm worried that they're vulnerable no matter where they are in Lima," Peter says.

"When are you leaving for Toronto?"

"I was planning on Wednesday, but I think I'll try to move it up to Tuesday," Peter says.

"We can send them under diplomatic seal on your flight, or on a private flight we have on Tuesday to Toronto. Up to you."

"Can I go with them on the private flight to Toronto?"

"Yes."

"Let's plan on that, but come and get them. Put them in a safe place."

"You in the same room?" Sir Richard asks.

"Yes. And I have some photographs to show you."

"El Come Huevos?"

"Yes."

"I'll be over in half an hour."

"Call me before you come up," Peter says.

Peter takes a deep breath and calls Maria.

"Hello."

Peter responds as flatly as he can manage. "Hi. I just got back."

"You're back? In Lima? Thank God."

Does she sound surprised? Peter isn't sure.

"Safe and sound. You want to get together for dinner?"

"Ah. I'm having dinner with a Russian associate from way back, the one I told you about," Maria says.

"Okay," Peter says slowly. "Sorry that we can't get together for dinner, but have fun."

"You uncover any secrets?"

"I don't know," Peter says. "I'll have to get the samples to the lab on Monday. I won't know much until I get the results from the lab." He pauses. "By the way, I have something for you. Why don't you come by the room for a couple of minutes?"

"Same room?"

"Yes."

"Okay. I'll come right up."

Peter hears the knock on the door. He looks out the peephole, and he opens the door for Maria.

"Come on in," he says.

"You have all your precious samples well hidden?"

"Not particularly. They're in the closet," Peter says. "Let me give you something. It was pretty nasty up there, and I'm concerned for your safety." He takes the P229 out of the drawer in the end table. "I think you should have this."

Maria raises her eyebrows. "You're the one who needs this, not me."

"Except for when I'm in my room, I've got guards around me all the time. It wasn't nice at Cerro Nublado, and I'm afraid some of the issues might slop over onto you." He holds it out to her. "Take it."

She takes it and puts it in her purse. "Thanks, I guess." She smiles. "Maybe we can get together, in your room or mine, for a drink later, before I head to dinner. Would that work for you?"

"I'll get a bottle of wine," Peter suggests. "Why don't you come here for a glass of wine around seven? Can you do that?"

"We're planning on a late dinner," Maria says. "It shouldn't interfere. Maybe I'll bring my friend with me."

"That's fine," Peter says. "See you then."

Peter shows her to the door and shuts it behind her. He leans against the closed door.

A Russian associate friend coming to my room with her for wine? This is getting a little more complicated than I planned. Who's playing what part here?

Peter sits down and waits for Sir Richard. He calls when he's in the lobby, and Peter tells him to come to his room.

When Sir Richard arrives, they sit at the table near the door.

"Happy to see you," Sir Richard says. He hands Peter a small package.

Peter puts the package in his shirt pocket. "What's the range?" he asks.

"Hundred meters? No problem if we're in the hallway." Sir Richard nods. "The Canadians are on board, by the way."

"Good," Peter responds. "You're happy to see me, and I'm happy to be here. The mess with Huevos worked out about as I expected. They weren't very subtle."

"Not very careful, either, if what Omar told me is true."

"No. They assumed we were all asleep," Peter says. "They never checked anything. I think they wanted to make sure I was out of the way immediately. Take no chances. Then they'd have their fun torturing the others."

"You said you have photographs."

"Yes. They're pretty graphic." Peter opens his computer, inserts the memory card, and pulls up the photographs. He turns the computer to Sir Richard. "We stripped the bodies. The first dozen or so are El Come Huevos. You can see his two tattoos. I think there are six entrance wounds, but I'm not an expert. The one to his head must have killed him instantly."

Sir Richard begins to scroll through the photos.

When Sir Richard reaches the end of the photos of El Come Huevos, Peter says, "The next series are of the whole group, followed by some close-up photos of the individuals and their wounds."

Sir Richard takes his time, and when he's finished he looks up from the computer. "Pretty thorough, I'd say."

Peter removes the memory card and hands it to him. "Please take this. I do not want it."

"I guess I can understand that." Sir Richard pockets the card. "I think someone owes you ten million dollars."

"I don't want it."

"What do you mean, you don't want it?" Sir Richard asks. "It's yours. You earned it the hard way."

"Divide it. Half to Steve. Half to Omar. I don't want it, and I couldn't have done it without them. They deserve it just as much as I do."

"Are you sure about this?" Sir Richard asks.

"I'm sure," Peter says. "Besides, in two weeks or so, I suspect I may be able to solve the mystery of the Russian interest in Cerro Nublado. You said that's worth five million dollars for me. If I manage to explain the Russian interest it's all nice and neat. Five, five, and five."

Sir Richard looks at Peter. "All right. We can do that." He frowns. "Omar told me that the bodies are well hidden, along with the weapons."

"Yeah. Everything's in what's probably an ancient Inca burial site. Steve stumbled onto it. The old guys had pottery buried with them. The new additions have Kalashnikovs as their treasured possessions."

"Appropriate."

"I thought so," Peter says.

"You think you hid them well enough?"

"No one will find them for many years, if at all. It should present a neat puzzle for archeologists one day."

"What about tonight?" Sir Richard asks.

Peter frowns. "I don't know. I called Maria to invite her to dinner tonight. She turned me down. 'I'm going out with an old Russian friend, who happens to be in Lima,' she said. She suggested we get together in her room or mine for a drink before she heads out to dinner. She agreed to come here for a glass of wine at seven. Maybe with her Russian friend."

"That's… interesting."

"Isn't it?" Peter gestures. "I'm inclined to think it makes no difference whatsoever." He shrugs. "Except that it does raise the risk level a bit."

"I'd say so."

"The samples would normally go to the lab here in Lima on Monday. If anything's going to happen, it'll happen before then. It's almost surely tonight, either when Maria's here, or not." He gestures to the room. "This is the ideal time and place for them, now I've survived Cerro Nublado. It's nice and private, no obvious security on my side, and they're probably sure they can grab the samples at the same time."

"We'll be ready," Sir Richard says. "You want me to take the samples now?"

"Yes."

"You going to come with us on Tuesday? We'll leave around noon."

Peter thinks for a minute. "Probably. Depends on what happens tonight." He stands up. "Let's get those samples out of the closet."

"I don't want to ask this," Sir Richard says as he stands, "but what good do the samples do us, if you're dead?"

"You have such confidence in me," Peter says. "It's a little embarrassing to answer your question. If you follow my analytical instructions, a copy of which is with the samples, a reasonably well-educated child should be able to look at the analytical report and solve the mystery, assuming there is a mystery to be solved."

Sir Richard alerts his car and driver, and Peter calls the bellman to bring his cart. They deliver the samples to the trunk of Sir Richard's car a few minutes later, and Sir Richard heads back to the embassy.

Peter stops to talk to the concierge.

"How can I help you?" he asks Peter. "Do you need another good bottle of wine?"

Peter laughs. "You can read my mind. I think this time I can choose one from the wine list for the restaurant."

Peter looks at the list the concierge produces, chooses a wine, and asks that he have someone deliver it to his room with three wine glasses. Once again, he tips the concierge generously.

Peter returns to his room. He pulls the small package from his pocket that Sir Richard brought him. It holds a rather ordinary ballpoint pen. He presses the end of it to extend the tip. He places it and a small pad of hotel paper on the table next to the chair.

He retrieves his 9mm P229 and the silencer from his backpack. He screws on the silencer and checks that the gun is loaded with a full clip of ammunition. He places the pistol behind the pillow that lies against the arm on the large chair. He sits in the chair and determines that he can easily find and retrieve the pistol. Then he sits on the sofa to make sure it is not visible.

Peter frowns. "Feeling rather confident, aren't we?" he says softly.

Maybe a little too confident?

When the wine arrives, he opens the bottle and places it and two wine glasses on the coffee table in front of the sofa. He places the third glass on the end table next to the large chair.

He looks at his watch. A few minutes after six. He sets the alarm and lies down for a short nap in the bedroom.

He awakens to the alarm, refreshed. He puts on his sports coat, and he fills the wine glasses.

He opens the door to the room and lets it shut against the swinging, double bar on the door guard.

He sits in the chair, across from the sofa and tries the wine.

Not bad, he thinks. *I've had worse.*

He puts the glass back on the side table and waits. At eight minutes before seven, he hears a knock at the door.

"Come in, Maria," he says.

He hears Maria speak to someone in Russian. The door shuts with a click.

Maria is the first to come to the end of the hall.

"Hello, Maria," Peter says. He stands in front of his chair.

Behind her comes a tall, angular man, all too familiar to Peter.

Jesus! Ivan Denisovich! This is a surprise.

Ivan is, as usual, elegantly dressed in an expensive and well-tailored dark Italian suit, a crisp white shirt, and a tightly knotted red tie. His gray hair, slightly thinning, is recently cut and carefully combed. He is sporting a short beard and moustache, neither of which do much to hide his harsh, angular, and pockmarked face.

"Peter," Maria says softly, "you remember my friend, Ivan Denisovich? We met him in Zürich, if you recall."

"Oh, I… I remember Ivan… quite well," Peter says. He gestures to the sofa. "Please take a seat. The wine is surprisingly good, and I've let it breathe for a while."

They sit down. Peter notes the slight, unnatural bulge under Ivan's left arm.

Peter raises his glass and takes a drink. They do not.

"You have strange friends these days, Maria," Peter says, looking at Ivan.

"He has been my friend for a long time."

"And your boss? All these years?"

"He's just an old friend, Peter."

Peter shakes his head. "To what do I owe the pleasure of your visit, Ivan?"

"I told you, he happened to be in Lima, and we're going to dinner tonight," Maria says.

Peter ignores her comment. "You're pretty high up in the SVR, and a little old to be doing fieldwork yourself, aren't you Ivan?"

"SVR? You have a wonderful imagination, Mr. Peter Binder."

Peter smiles. "You have some special interests in Peru these days? Like Cerro Nublado, perhaps?"

"Why would you think that?"

"Let's see," Peter says, "I seem to remember that I once saved Moscow from being turned into a glowing, nuclear cinder. Your government expressed a good deal of gratitude for that, as I recall."

"As I remember it, Maria saved Moscow," Ivan says with an expression that falls well short of being a smile.

"Ah, well, a shared enterprise, at least," Peter says.

There is a short pause in the conversation.

"I've done a little research on you, Ivan," Peter says.

"And what did you find out?"

"Just, ah, that you have a remarkable history of torture and murder."

Ivan frowns. "History lies." He pauses. "How was your trip to Cerro Nublado?"

"It was very peaceful," Peter says. "I got a lot of work done. You must know that it's a very well-stocked camp. We enjoyed eating eggs for breakfast every morning. We even cooked up a few eggs late Thursday night."

"Did you uncover the 'secret' that Mr. Grant seems to think Minera Russo-Perú is hiding there?"

"So you do have an Interest? Well, Ivan, I won't know until I have the analytical results for the samples I took."

"What elements do you ask the lab to analyze?" Ivan asks.

Peter focuses on Ivan's eyes. "Most any element that has any value for a mining company, and a bunch that don't. But they still might help me understand the deposit."

Ivan and Peter stare at each other.

"Kill him, Maria," Ivan says flatly.

Maria pulls the P229 out of her purse.

"With my gun?" Peter asks.

"Of course," Ivan says with a smile.

"Really? After all I did for Moscow?"

"This world is transactional, Mr. Binder. You are unbelievably naïve. What you did for me yesterday has no value today." He turns to Maria. "Shoot him."

"You break my heart, Maria," Peter says. "I love you even now."

"They forced me, Peter. I'm sorry. I really am."

"Please don't tell me they threatened to kill your entire family." Peter clenches his jaw. "That excuse is out of fashion."

"I do love you. I do," she says.

My God! She's actually weeping. What an amazing performance!

Ivan shouts at her in Russian. *"Pristreli yego! Pristreli yego!"*

She pulls the trigger. Six times.

Peter knows she is aiming at his heart. He smiles and retrieves his pistol and silencer from behind the pillow.

Ivan reaches behind his jacket with his right hand.

Peter shoots Ivan's right arm, just below the shoulder. They are so close. It's an easy shot.

Ivan shouts a string of Russian curses. *"Grebanyy ublyndok! Poshel na khuy!"*

Maria fires again, and again. Her eyes are wide now. "What the hell?" she shouts.

Ivan struggles with his left hand to reach his pistol. Peter shoots his left arm, a few inches above the elbow.

Maria fires two more times.

Ivan struggles to rise, still swearing loudly. Peter shoots him in the throat. He immediately begins to bleed quite heavily. With a look of shock and confusion, he falls heavily back onto the sofa. He slowly slides down onto his side. His head lands next to Maria's lap.

Peter's aim moves firmly to Maria. "Are you done, Maria?" he asks softly in the sudden quiet after the exchange of gunfire. "You have no more ammunition."

Maria looks at Peter. Her eyes are huge. Tears are running down her cheeks now.

"You bastard!" she screams. She throws the pistol at him.

Peter jerks his head to the side, and the pistol misses. It hits the window behind him with a loud bang, but it does not break the heavy glass. "I'm not the bastard here," Peter says. "I still love you, and that proves that I am truly the greatest fool in this room. But I'm not the bastard here. Not here."

She glares at him.

Peter holds his aim on Maria. He pats his chest with his left hand, over his heart. "You see, true love never bleeds. Of course, it helps when the bullets are wax. Can you smell the wax in the air?"

"You fucking bastard!" She spits the words out at him.

Peter still speaks softly, but his voice now carries a menacing edge. "Why? Because I didn't trust you? I love you. I truly do, but I am not as naïve as you and Ivan thought."

Ivan's breathing is very noisy now. His blood runs down onto the leather sofa and slowly flows onto the left leg of Maria's pants.

She places her hand on the side of Ivan's head. She looks at him and caresses his cheek lightly.

"You killed him, you bastard!"

"No. He's still alive. You want me to kill him?"

Maria looks at Peter. Her hand still strokes Ivan's cheek. Her entire face contorts with hatred.

"Yes!" she says.

"Why should I? He was never merciful."

"For God's sake, do it!" she shouts.

Peter adjusts his aim.

He shoots Ivan. Between the eyes. Just below Maria's hand.

Maria jerks back her hand. She screams, a high-pitched scream. It doesn't seem possible that it comes from a human being.

She jumps up staring at Ivan. Screaming. Screaming.

"Sit down!" Peter shouts. The sharp sound of his voice cuts through the scream and surprises him.

Something breaks. She closes her mouth with a ferocious firmness. She sits down.

She glares at Peter. She is a cornered animal. Unpredictable. Dangerous. Deadly.

He waits a moment before he says, "Maria. I have negotiated three options for you. Do you want to hear them?"

Peter sees nothing but hatred.

Amazing! Where has that been hiding? Was it there the whole time?

She nods her head, but she says nothing.

"Option one, I kill you now. I don't want to, but I will if you demand it. Option two, you walk out the door to the Canadian officials waiting in the hall, and you surrender to Canadian justice. I will not be the loyal lover, Maria. I will not be there, waiting for you, when you come out of prison. Option three, you walk out the door and request repatriation to Russia. You will have to endure some serious questioning, but they will repatriate you. With both your body and your mind intact."

Maria stares at him for a long time.

"That's it?" she asks.

"That's the best I could do," Peter says softly.

"They're all the same. They are all death."

"That may be, Maria my love, but they're the only choices I can offer," Peter says.

She stares at him, and he can see nothing of the love he once saw in her eyes.

Was it all make-believe? Really? She was so good at it.

"I choose a fourth option," she says suddenly. She reaches into Ivan's jacket for his pistol.

"Don't!" Peter shouts.

She pulls out the pistol. She turns toward Peter. Her arm sweeps over to bring the small revolver to bear on Peter.

Peter fires. His first shot hits her just before she can complete her aim and fire. Because of the impact of Peter's first shot, her aim is a little off.

His shot tears into her chest. Pierces her heart.

She hits Peter on the right side of his chest.

His next three shots are a little wild and hit the wall above the sofa. He recovers enough that his last two hit Maria again, in the chest.

Her pistol falls out of her hand. It hits the edge of the coffee table with a loud clank on its way to the floor. For a brief moment, she looks surprised.

Then she falls to the side, on top of Ivan. Her eyes, wide open, stare at Peter and see nothing. Her blood and Ivan's blood begin to mingle together.

Strangely, the two delicate glasses, filled with red wine, still stand on the coffee table. Intact. Untouched.

"Jesus!" Peter says. The two layers of body armor he is wearing stop the bullet. But the impact is like being struck, very hard, with a large hammer. Peter breathes hard, rapidly.

He puts his pistol down on the table next to the chair. He forces his breathing to slow down.

He stares at Maria.

Tears run down his cheeks. They are due only partly to the pain. He gasps out, "You may as well come in now. It's all over."

He puts his head in his hands as he hears the door open. He sobs. It hurts. A lot.

He feels a hand rest lightly on his shoulder.

"Are you okay?" It is Sir Richard's voice.

"No... I'm not okay."

CHAPTER 26

The mad exit from the hotel. Down the freight elevator, supported and hurried along by Sir Richard and Omar. Out the delivery entrance. Out to the waiting car and to the clinic.

He tries to remember it, but all he remembers is pain in his chest. Each breath is pain. Each movement, every bump, every touch is pain, and then there is the ache of his loss.

Peter sits, bare chested, on the edge of the exam table in the small, private clinic, and Sir Richard sits on a plain chair, against the wall, looking at him.

"How are you?" Sir Richard asks.

"I don't know."

"That's no surprise."

"I'm a little confused at the moment," Peter says. "What the hell is going on?"

"They took an x-ray, and the doctor thinks you'll be fine. She says it's a good sign you're not coughing up blood."

Peter grimaces. "I think, if I coughed right now, I'd pass out."

Sir Richard smiles. "It was kind of close range."

"They're both dead. Right?"

"Yes," Sir Richard says softly. "They're both quite dead. I'm sorry about Maria."

Peter closes his eyes for a moment. He sees again that look on Maria's face when he shot her.

He looks at Sir Richard. "I knew it was coming. I didn't want to believe it, even tonight, even after I shot Ivan and saw the raw hatred in her eyes." Peter sighs. "I still loved her, and I hesitated. It nearly killed me."

"True," Sir Richard says.

"Second time in a week I hesitated."

"Not good."

"I guess," Peter says, "I finally resolved that relationship. Not exactly how I expected it to work out. I had hopes that she loved me as much as I loved her. There was a little love there. At least I think I'll decide to believe that. Mostly… I know it was, on her side, a job well done." He sighs again. "When I offered her the three options, I was sure she'd go back to Russia. I didn't realize how important Ivan was to her."

The doctor knocks at the door and enters the room. A very good-looking woman, tanned complexion and slightly wavey brown hair. Peter guesses her age as late twenties.

"You look much better," she says. Her English is excellent with a soft Spanish overtone. "How are you feeling?"

"More or less in one piece," he says.

She is all business. "You are fortunate. You were well prepared. Two ribs cracked, but not broken. You will have a large bruise." She looks at his chest. "Correction. You have a large bruise already," she says with a small smile. "You will have significant pain for a few days, maybe as much as a week. Try not to sneeze, but cough if you need to clear congestion. You can hold a pillow against the bruise when you cough to reduce the pain. Avoid heavy lifting, particularly with your right arm, for five to six weeks. It's a good idea to walk to prevent congestion in your lungs. You plan on traveling soon?"

Peter looks at Sir Richard.

"I'll be putting him on a private plane on Tuesday," Sir Richard says. "To Toronto, Canada. We can help him with his baggage."

"Good," she says. "Make sure you get up often on the trip and do some mild exercise. Half knee bends would be good, or rising up on your toes. Nothing strenuous."

With a sterner look than Peter expects, she says, "I've given you some Oxycodone tablets for the pain. Take no more in one day than I have prescribed. There are enough for four days. After that, over the counter pain killers should be enough. Keep the prescription with you if you go through customs or airport security. If the pain becomes severe, or if you cough up blood, get to emergency medical care as quickly as you can."

"Thank you," Peter says.

"Do you have any questions?" she asks.

"You say walk. Should I ski? Cross country, on the level, not downhill."

"I don't see why you can't. Just take it easy. No Olympic training programs."

"No problem," Peter says. "Can I have a drink?"

"No alcohol while you're on the Oxycodone, and this first dose lasts twelve hours."

"Damn."

The doctor relaxes a bit and laughs lightly. "Sorry. Any other questions?"

"I have lots of questions, but I don't think you can answer most of them."

"I'm sure there are others who can," she says. "Right now, you can get dressed and go. Just take it easy for the next five or six weeks. Maybe two months before a heavy run or full weight lifting."

The doctor excuses herself.

Peter steps down from the table, and Sir Richard asks, "How much of this stuff do you want to put on?"

"Let's just roll up the undershirt. I don't think I could get it on anyway. I'll put on the shirt and the jacket."

Sir Richard hands the clothes to Peter. "You're scheduled for another police interview tomorrow morning at ten. Omar will pick you up and attend with you."

"Was Omar with you in the hall?" Peter asks.

"Yes. And in case you're wondering, it wasn't easy for any of us to listen to what was happening, particularly the ending."

"Yeah. Thanks for all you've done."

"Not a problem. I told Omar and Steve about the reward for El Come Huevos. They were a little shocked."

"They deserve it," Peter says.

Sir Richard smiles. "I'm going to disappear. Omar will get you back to your hotel. Same hotel. Different suite. And don't worry about damages. We've taken care of it."

"I make lots of messes."

"Yes, you do," Sir Richard says, "but they seem to be successful messes." He opens the door. "Come on in, Omar. He's all yours. Handle him with care." Sir Richard waves at Peter as he leaves.

Omar looks at Peter with a small smile. "Do you know you're one crazy son of a bitch?"

"Everybody keeps reminding me."

"I have to admit that after escaping our buddy at Cerro Nublado, without a scratch, you sure set up a wild finish in Lima."

"A little wilder than I had hoped for."

Omar smiles. "You do look pretty good for a man who's just been shot eleven times."

Peter finishes buttoning his shirt. He grimaces as he tucks it in. "Only one shot counted."

"One's usually enough. You're lucky Maria didn't check the ammunition. She had enough time to do it."

Peter slips on his jacket, gingerly pulling it up over his right arm. "I never worried about that. She… and actually Ivan, too, convinced themselves that my love blinded me and completely destroyed my judgement. I don't think either of them could imagine me doing anything devious, at least nothing that involved Maria."

"Let's get out of here," Omar says.

"Lets."

They walk out of the clinic and into the night. It is a little after eleven. They get into the waiting car from the embassy with an armed driver and an armed guard.

Peter fumbles with the seatbelt. Omar helps him.

"I'll go with you up to your room," Omar says.

"I can manage by myself, Omar."

"I'm sure you can, but I won't let you. Besides, if you don't mind, I'd like to talk to you for a few minutes."

Peter looks at his watch. "Okay, but let's not make it too long. I have to be intelligent tomorrow."

Omar laughs. "You don't need to be intelligent until ten in the morning. I won't keep you up very long."

Omar gets Peter's key to his new room from the front desk. When they get to the door, he unlocks it and ushers Peter into his room. It is in another suite, only slightly different from the first one.

I'm glad it isn't exactly the same as the other suite, Peter thinks as he sits on the sofa.

"I'm getting a beer," Omar says. "You want something?"

"Yes, but I'll stick to a cold bottle of water. *Sin gas,* please."

Omar returns, hands Peter a bottle of still water, and sits down with his beer in the large chair on the other side of the coffee table.

"I want to ask you a question, Peter. Maybe this isn't the best time."

"I'm okay," Peter says. "Ask away."

"You suggested at that roadblock, on the way out of Huancabamba, that maybe we could do something to improve the lives of the rural poor in the Altiplano."

"Yes, I did suggest that."

Omar takes a drink of his beer. "Were you serious? Do it together?"

Peter nods. "Yes, I was serious, but I have no idea how to start. In my opinion, most of the NGOs don't know how to start or finish, at least not with any great success."

"You remember what Bernardo said were the biggest needs in his village? When you asked him?"

Peter grimaces. "My brain's a little fried right now. Maybe you could remind me?"

"He said, 'Decent jobs. A way to make a living. And decent teachers for the children.' I've been interested in trying to make a positive impact on these two areas for a long time."

Peter takes a moment before he responds. "You thinking of quitting your job?"

"The payment for El Come Huevos will give me a lot of freedom, and some capital to get a program funded for the poor communities of the Altiplano. Thank you for that. Education is a critical need. It's also one of the most difficult, with hurdles like pay for teachers, quality, transportation, and adequate school buildings. There's never been a real plan in this country to provide a decent education to the rural poor."

"It's a tough situation," Peter says. "That's why it's persisted so long. It's not unique to Peru."

"Yes, but as you said on the road, you start somewhere. Small. You try," Omar says. "Try to bring some income into the communities. Develop better markets for some of the stranger types of potatoes. Improve the woven products, the pottery, the other handcrafts. Right now, they're paid nothing for their work or their crops."

"How old are you, Omar?"

"Thirty-seven."

Peter smiles. "It's not a bad age. We're old enough to have some real-world experience behind us. You're smart. You have common sense. You want to do something good with your life. I'm in about the same situation. I'm willing to help, and I think we can raise some significant amounts of money, but you have to do a few things first."

"Like what?" Omar asks.

Peter leans forward. "Take a year off. Talk to all the experts in the fields of education, agriculture, marketing, social welfare. Learn what they know about these problems. Why they think they persist. Then let's figure out the best way to make a positive impact. I want to do the same thing, but I can't do it without someone like you."

Omar is silent.

"I know you want to start something right away," Peter says, "but if you don't do the research, it will almost surely fail. Take a year. Take your time. Let's do it right."

They sit in silence for a minute before Omar speaks again.

"I'm still thinking about those young men who came to the camp with El Come Huevos. I do want to do something right away, but you're right. Most programs on the Altiplano don't die. They just fade away slowly to nothing."

Omar stands up. He drops his beer bottle into the waste basket.

"You want help getting undressed?"

Peter laughs. "If you would help me get my shirt off, it would be nice."

Omar helps him slip it off his right arm.

"I can come to your room at quarter after nine tomorrow morning. If you need a little help, let me know and I'll be here. Right now, get some sleep and have a good breakfast in the morning. It may be a long day with the police."

Omar heads to the door. He looks back and shakes his head, and then he lets himself out.

Peter strips his clothes off and lies down on the bed. "I wish…" he says. He falls asleep before he can finish the thought.

In his dreams, he is a little older this time. His great-grandfather is providing occasional advice, but Peter prunes the grapevines himself.

The old man smiles and says, "You are doing a good job. Your vines will produce good grapes for you."

It is peaceful.

Peter smiles in his sleep.

Peter opens his eyes at seven in the morning.

"Man, I am hungry."

He realizes he hasn't had anything to eat since the egg salad sandwich on the plane from Piura. He lies still for a moment, on his back, and takes inventory.

I feel pretty good.

Then he moves. He cautiously swings his feet out of the bed and stands up. Each breath brings some pain. He takes a few deep breaths, grimacing each time.

"I can live with it," he says, as he looks at himself in the mirror over the sink. The bruise is impressive. While he stands there, it feels as though the explosion of his life last night rises up and slaps him in the face. He almost staggers back, away from the mirror.

"No!" he says. "It's done!" Then, more quietly as he grips the sink with both hands, he says it again. "It's done."

He collects himself and steps into the shower, but he moves a bit slower than usual through his morning rituals. Anything he does with his right hand results in a sharp pain in his chest. He dresses with his good sports coat and looks at himself in the mirror. It looks better than wearing the one with the bullet hole.

He digs through his backpack for the .357 P229, holsters it, and puts it on his belt, out of sight around the back of his left side and under his jacket. Then he texts Omar and tells him he'll be in the restaurant, if he isn't in front of the hotel waiting for the embassy's car.

In the restaurant, he orders an omelet, helps himself to bacon, sausage, fruit, and a café con leche. He sits down and addresses his hunger. He detects an increased level of attention from the cook and the waiter, but he wonders if he may be imagining things.

As he eats, he considers the aftermath of last night. He keeps seeing the image in his mind of Maria, as she dies. Suddenly a thought comes to him, and it pulls him back to the practical issues that still confront him. He sends a text to Sir Richard.

Richard,

Someone should make sure to get to Maria's apartment in Toronto before the Russians clean it out. Same with her belongings here at the hotel. Her computer, most of all.

The response from Sir Richard is almost immediate.

Done already.

Peter shakes his head and smiles rather ruefully.

At twenty minutes before nine, he pays his bill and heads out to the front entrance.

As Peter passes, the concierge calls out, "¡Señor Binder!"

Peter turns and stops by his desk. "*Buenos días*," he says.

"How are you feeling?" the concierge asks.

"Pretty good, thank you."

The concierge leans closer to Peter and lowers his voice. "You are a bit of a celebrity here, you know. At least among the staff." He smiles.

"I hope you can keep it to yourselves," Peter says.

"Oh, yes, sir. We know how to be discrete. If you need anything, just let me know, or any other member of our staff. We are happy to provide whatever you may need."

"I will. Thank you very much."

Peter waits inside the front door of the hotel. When the British embassy car arrives, Omar jumps out, and Peter goes outside to meet him.

Omar looks at Peter. "You look astonishingly well. I might become a good Christian yet. Right now, considering what happened last night, I surely believe in the resurrection of the dead."

Peter laughs. "I hate to tell you, but you have to believe a lot more bullshit than that to be a good Christian."

"One step at a time," Omar says with a smile. He holds the car door open for Peter.

Once in the car, Omar says, "The lawyer will meet us at the police station."

"Probably don't need him, but also probably a good idea to have him there."

As they ride to the police interview, Omar asks, "Seriously, though, how are you feeling this morning?"

"I feel great until I move, or breathe. I haven't taken any pain pills this morning. I want my brain to be fully operative... and I might like to have something to drink later on."

"After the interview, we'll have a good lunch. Ceviche?"

"Sounds good. Do you know who's interviewing me?"

"It should be the same guy, Arsenio Garcia. Sir Richard has given them a statement. Handle this the same as last time, and just tell the truth. My guess is that they'll ask about Cerro Nublado. On that one, hold the line at something like, 'Very peaceful visit. I got a lot of work done.' Period. That should be enough."

"They know that Maria and Ivan were Russian spies?" Peter asks. He is surprised by the emotional impact of just saying those simple words.

"Yes."

"They know why they wanted to kill me?"

"Sir Richard told them that it has to do with an operation, outside of Peru, that he cannot speak of due to international implications. Tell them, if they ask, that you are not authorized to say."

Peter reaches gingerly with his right hand and removes his pistol. He leaves the empty holster but puts the pistol in the pocket in the seat in front of him. "I assume the car will be waiting for us?"

"Yes," the driver says. "We will wait for you. You can leave anything you wish in the car. It will be safe."

"Just so you know," Peter says, "there's a loaded pistol, safety on, in the seat pocket on the driver's seat."

Omar and Peter leave the driver and guard at the front door to the police station. They find Emilio Sanchez, the lawyer, inside, waiting for them. They are all escorted to the interview room, where they wait a few minutes before Sr. Garcia arrives with an assistant and a translator.

Arsenio is smiling. "I must say you look remarkably good for a man who was shot so many times at such close range." He extends his hand.

"I hope you don't mind my left hand," Peter says. "My right side is a bit sore today."

"Not a problem at all."

They all take their places around the table. Arsenio looks at his notes and begins. "We have received a written statement from Sir Richard, and I spoke with him briefly, earlier this morning. We have examined the room and the two deceased individuals. The bodies are with the morgue, awaiting autopsies. The Russian embassy has already requested that we release both bodies to them. The situation appears to be clear cut. Two Russian spies. One, the woman, shoots you ten times, but you had arranged for her to have wax bullets. The second, the man, attempts to draw his pistol. You shoot him four times. The woman then draws the man's pistol and shoots you just as you shoot her six times. You are hit in the right chest, but two layers of body armor protect you. One of your shots pierces her heart and kills her instantly. Two others hit her but are not lethal. Three shots miss and are imbedded in the wall above the sofa." Arsenio looks up. "Reasonable summary?"

"Yes," Peter says. "That's an excellent summary."

Arsenio looks at Peter for some time. "What was your relationship with Maria Davidoff? Were you lovers?"

"I thought we were lovers."

"And Maria?" Arsenio asks.

"I don't know."

"Why did you give her the pistol? And why the wax bullets?"

Peter hesitates. "It's hard to explain. I thought she might be working for the Russians again, or maybe she had been all along. I thought something bad might happen in Peru."

"But why the pistol? And the wax bullets?"

"I wanted to survive."

"You set up a meeting. Did you expect Ivan Dinisovich to attend?" Arsenio asks.

"She said she'd bring a Russian friend. When I saw it was Ivan? He was a very unpleasant surprise."

"You knew Ivan Dinisovich?"

"Yes. I had met him before," Peter answers, "and I know a lot about him. He could be a very nasty boy."

"What made you sure Maria would not reload the pistol you gave her with real ammunition?"

Peter frowns. "I couldn't be sure, but I did believe that she thought I was a naïve and foolish lover. Just in case, though, I did wear body armor."

"And a good thing you did," Arsenio says. He looks down at his notes. "Now, I know you agree with my summary of last night, but please tell us in your own words what happened."

"When they arrived, they sat down on the sofa opposite me. I had poured out three glasses of wine. I drank some. They didn't."

"You talked?"

"Yes," Peter said.

"What did you talk about?"

"We talked a bit about Cerro Nublado. Ivan asked if I discovered some secret there."

"Did you?"

"I told them that I didn't know anything about secrets. I completed my normal project review, and my conclusions will have to wait until I receive the analyses for my samples."

"Where were the samples?" Arsenio asks.

"They were at the British embassy, but I had told Maria earlier that they were in the closet. At one point in our discussion, Ivan suddenly told Maria to shoot me. She pulled out the pistol I had given her. She shot me, six times."

"What did you do?"

"I smiled," Peter says. "Ivan moved to pull out his gun. I retrieved my pistol from behind the pillow on the chair. I shot him twice in the arms, but he still tried to get up and get his pistol. I shot him twice more, once in the neck and, as he fell, a second time in the head."

"What was Maria doing while you were dealing with Ivan?" Arsenio asks.

"She shot me four more times."

"What made you shoot her?"

"She went for Ivan's gun. I shouted, 'Don't!', but she retrieved the pistol. I hesitated. I didn't want to shoot her, but I did, a second before she shot me. Presumably, as a result, her aim was off. She always aimed for the heart, but this time I think she was going for a head shot." Peter pauses a moment. "She was a good shot."

"What happened next?"

"I don't remember much after that. I remember Sir Richard asking me if I was okay. The next thing I remember is being in the clinic and talking with the doctor."

Arsenio looks back at his notes. "I have one unrelated question. How was your trip to Cerro Nublado? You say Ivan asked you about it. Did you have any problems at the camp?"

"I got a lot of work done," Peter said. "It's quite a beautiful and peaceful spot."

"No problems?"

"No. We didn't have any problems. Even the helicopter showed up when it was supposed to be there. Some locals stopped us with a roadblock outside of Huancabamba. They were looking for donations for a tractor and plow. We made a donation. No problem."

Arsenio refers to his notes. "Do you think Ivan Dinisovich was behind the attempted kidnapping last week?"

Peter hesitates. "I don't know. It's possible, I suppose."

"Do you know why they wanted to kill you?"

"You'll have to speak with Sir Richard about that."

Arsenio nods. "Yes. I understand."

Arsenio Garcia looks at Peter for a long time. He sighs. "You have been a major problem for us here in Lima. I know Sir Richard well, and I respect him. He is well connected with our national security forces. I understand that you are involved in things far beyond the knowledge of a simple, city policeman." He looks intently at Peter. "Sir Richard tells me that you will leave tomorrow. I have no authority to keep you from reentering Peru, but I would request that you stay away for at least a year. You collect too many bodies around you."

"I can agree to that," Peter says. "I apologize for making trouble for you."

"And I accept your apology. It's not as though you're killing good citizens, but bodies are still bodies. They create a lot of paperwork if nothing else."

"I promise you, the next time I come to Peru, it will be as an ordinary citizen, as a peaceful tourist."

"Good." Arsenio stands up. Peter and Omar join him. Arsenio extends his hand to Peter. "Oh, sorry," he says, and he switches to his left hand. They shake hands. "I have your contact information for Canada. You are free to go," Arsenio says. "Just, please, go in peace."

"I'll do my best," Peter says.

"I'm sure you will."

As they leave the police station, the Emilio Sanchez turns to Peter. "Señor Binder, you lead an extraordinary life. You are now responsible for five bodies, perhaps six, in Lima, and the police show no interest in you whatsoever." He smiles. "I think you are charmed, some sort of magician."

"I hope I'm done with my magic act for this trip," Peter says.

The lawyer laughs. "So do I. You are a high maintenance client, but you pay well." He shakes hands, and departs for his car.

Back in the embassy's car, Omar says, "That was quick. We're early for lunch, but I made a reservation for us on the upper deck of the restaurant. We can sit outside and watch the hang gliders as they play in the wind on the cliffs."

Peter leans back against the seat and closes his eyes. "And a beer, I hope, or maybe a pisco sour or two."

Omar raises his eyebrows. "You are really off the narcotics already?"

"Yes. Perhaps temporarily," Peter says. He opens his eyes, leans forward, and removes his pistol from the seat pocket. As he clumsily returns it to the holster, he says, "Right now, a good drink and the company of a good friend is more important than the absence of pain."

Omar smiles. "I don't know about you carrying a pistol. After all, Señor Garcia told you to go in peace."

"You are funny, Omar. I assume the embassy car is picking me up tomorrow for the airport?"

"Yes. Our last major service for you."

"I'll give the pistol to the driver tomorrow morning."

"Do you know that Sir Richard's going with you?"

"Really?"

"Yes. I don't think he trusts you without an escort," Omar says and laughs.

"Probably wise on his part," Peter says.

CHAPTER 27

Peter and Omar have a quiet lunch, with six different varieties of ceviche, two pisco sours each, and a pleasant view of the water and the hang gliders.

"I'm sorry about last night," Omar says. "It had to be very hard for you."

"It was. It still is," Peter says. He breathes deeply and grimaces slightly at the pain. "It had to happen. Did you know that she saved my life more than once?"

Omar shakes his head. "No, I didn't know that."

"I don't understand it, not really. I don't understand what her job was. Somehow, they latched onto me. It doesn't make much sense. My ego wants to believe she was a sleeper, only called back into action very recently. That allows me to imagine that, at least for a while, she really did love me." Peter looks out at the ocean. "Logically, that's not likely."

"I'm amazed you're doing as well as you are," Omar says. "I think I'd be a total mess."

"Oh, I'll get depressed later," Peter says. "I invested a lot of myself in that woman." He plays with the glass and the end of the second pisco sour. "Now it's all gone. She's gone, and I pulled the trigger. I made it all disappear."

"No!" Omar says firmly. "I couldn't disagree with you more. She pulled the trigger. She made it all disappear. You're lucky to have escaped alive from that woman. Don't forget that. And don't forget that the only reason you did escape alive is that you were smarter and better than she was." Omar looks intently at Peter. "You are a good man, Peter Binder. Don't ever forget that."

"I don't know." Peter smiles a bit ruefully. "I've done quite a few things in my life that I know some would consider pretty evil."

"I think you're judging yourself far too harshly. Yes, we executed El Come Huevos, executed him, you and I together, but the world condemned

259

him long before we arrived at Cerro Nublado. He condemned himself by his own actions."

"Perhaps."

They sit in silence for several minutes, watching the hang gliders play in the wind.

"I will say one thing. Getting to know you, Omar Vargas, has been the great treasure of this trip."

"That goes both ways," Omar says. "I think you and I, together, will be able to do some good things here in Peru."

"I think so, too, but… right now, I know I should go back to the hotel and take a nap. Last night is catching up with me."

Peter and Omar part in the lobby of the hotel. Peter walks to the elevator. He turns to look back. Omar is still standing in the lobby, watching him. The doors close on the elevator.

Peter shuts the door to his new suite. He locks the door, and he pulls over the door guard. He walks into the living area of the suite. Though it is a different shape and arranged slightly differently than the first suite he had, it has the same black leather sofa with a coffee table in front of it. The large chair sits across the narrow room from the sofa, just as it did in the other suite last night.

He sits on the sofa, in the same position where Maria sat. He looks across at the chair, where he would have been sitting. He tries to see himself with Maria's eyes. He hears her say again, referring to his three options. *They are all death.*

"I never really knew you, Maria Davidoff," Peter says. "When were you assigned to me? Did it happen after I fell in love? Did you ever truly love me? How could you love mother Russia so much that you could turn on me with such visceral hatred? I have to believe you loved me once, at least a little. It wasn't all make-believe, was it?"

He puts his hand down to where Ivan's head would have lain, where Maria stroked the dying man's head.

"You loved him, in a far deeper and more fundamental way than you ever loved me, didn't you? What was he to you? Your father? Your lover?"

Peter looks at the chair and sees himself sitting there. For the first time, he recognizes the level of anger and hatred that drove him to murder Ivan with a shot no more than two inches from Maria's hand.

"I'm sorry, Maria. He was dying. You wanted me to end his pain and agony. I didn't need to do it that way."

Peter sits very still. "It was impossible, wasn't it? I could have stayed away from Peru, denied what I already knew, but I couldn't live that way. I had to know, and I had to come here. You did try to keep me away, but you made your own impossible choice, and I can't blame you for that. If you were still here, you wouldn't blame me for setting you up to die, to commit suicide."

He feels the tears beginning to flow again.

"You'd put your arm around my shoulder and tell me that I did what I had to do."

He wipes away the tears. "Wouldn't you?"

He shuts his eyes. He sees Maria before him, and he sees her moment of shock when his shot pierces her heart.

"I'm glad I loved you, Maria, even if it ended in pain, and hatred, and death. It was beautiful… as long as beauty was allowed to survive. I don't regret it. Not a bit of it."

He sees her again, standing before him in crisp, white pants and a dark blue shirt. The wind is in her hair. She's on the dock at the lake, smiling, laughing.

"Please… please…" he says. "Find a way to rest in peace, Maria."

He opens his eyes. The images vanish, and he stands up. The tears have stopped, at least for now.

He hurts, and he takes an ibuprofen. He lies down on his back on the bed, and he falls into a deep and dreamless sleep.

Peter awakens suddenly to his cell phone ringing on the table next to the bed.

"I knew you were supposed to return to Lima yesterday," Carlos Bellido says. "I didn't hear from you. I had to call."

"I'm sorry, Carlos. I got in late yesterday. I meant to call you, but it's been a rough return to Lima."

"You're okay?"

"I've been better, but, yes, I'm okay."

"What happened at Cerro Nublado?" Carlos asks.

"It wasn't easy, but I got my work done. Everything went smoothly."

"No problems with security?"

"No problems," Peter answers.

"You don't know how happy I am to hear your voice," Carlos says. "I was really worried about you. When do you head home?"

"Tomorrow morning."

"Would you and Maria like to come to the house for dinner? Elena will be here tonight. She'd love to see Maria."

Peter is silent.

"What's the matter?" Carlos asks. "Is there a problem?"

"Yes."

"What is it?"

"Maria's dead, Carlos," Peter says. "She's dead."

"¡Dios mío! What happened?"

"It's complicated."

"Do you want to talk about it?"

"No. I don't. I can't."

"Why don't you come to dinner? You need to be with friends."

"I'll be lousy company," Peter says.

"That's all right," Carlos says. "That's what friends are for."

"It has to be an early night."

"Come at six-thirty. We'll relax a bit, have a quick dinner, and make sure you get back to the hotel by ten. Will that work for you?"

"Okay, Carlos. Thanks. It will help being with you and Elena."

"I'll pick you up."

"No," Peter says. "That's too dangerous right now. If I can't get a car from the security company, I'll have to give it a miss."

Once he's off the phone, Peter looks at his watch. A little after four. He calls Seguridad Ejecutivo and asks if they a car available for the evening, with an armed driver and bodyguard. And a second car. They do.

He asks the concierge if he can find a large bouquet of flowers in time for his visit with Carlos. Then he goes to the hotel gym and walks on the treadmill, rather slowly, for thirty minutes.

After a hot shower, he looks at himself in the mirror. The bruise is about eight by ten inches. The center has turned a dark purple, almost black, which fades out to lighter purple and yellow edges. He lies down, naked, on the bed and rests again. He finds he is thinking about his technical work at Cerro Nublado. "That's good," he mutters.

He gets up, opens his computer, and sends an email to the metallurgist who did the work on test milling for the deposit. He asks them to do some special, additional analyses on the copper and molybdenum concentrates.

That should be interesting, he thinks.

Before he closes his computer, he sends a message to StolPort at Billy Bishop Airport in Toronto.

Please have my helicopter ready for me on Wednesday morning.

Peter shaves, puts on a dress-shirt, slacks, and his dress sports coat. "Time to live dangerously," he says and leaves his pistol in the safe in the closet.

The security company follows the same routine as when he visited Carlos the first time. Carlos and Elena meet him at the door.

"It is so good to see you," Carlos says.

"It's good to see both of you, too," Peter says. He hands the flowers to Elena. "Thank you for inviting me over."

"It sounds as though you should be with friends," Elena says. "The flowers are beautiful."

"Pardon my not shaking hands. My right side is hurting today." He smiles somewhat sadly. "Please don't ask too many questions. Your company will be my best medicine."

"It will not be easy," Elena says. "We are both worried about you, and we are so sad to hear about Maria."

"Yes. It's been very difficult for me, but... I'm not allowed to talk about it."

Carlos shakes his head. "We don't understand, but we will not ask any questions. As Elena says, it won't be easy. We care about you. We've always cared about you and Maria."

Carlos sighs. "Let's sit in the living room for a bit. A pisco sour before dinner. We are eating North American style tonight, half-past seven," Carlos says with a sad hint of a smile.

Peter sits on the sofa. "I am hard on my friends," he says.

They each pick up a pisco sour. Peter takes a small drink. "You always make a wonderful pisco sour."

"Much better than what you might find in Chile. No?"

"Of course, Carlos," Peter says. "I would never suggest anything else, except, maybe, when I am in Chile."

They all find it hard to laugh at the old, and perhaps rather labored joke, and they sip at their drinks in an awkward silence.

"There is one thing that I'd like to discuss with both of you," Peter says.

"And what is that?" Elena asks.

"I was talking with my Peruvian assistant at Cerro Nublado. He wants to start a charitable organization or a foundation, to try to address some of the issues of income and education in the small communities of the Altiplano of Peru. Do you have any ideas on how to approach that?"

"Elena can address that much better than I can," Carlos says.

"But first, we need to sit down at the table," Elena says.

As they settle into their meal, with a bottle of wine, they embark on a long discussion of all the issues related to poverty and opportunity in the almost numberless small, isolated communities in rural Peru.

At the end of the meal, Peter says, "It's hard to see where you should start."

Elena nods her head thoughtfully. "It is, but we have been making some progress. The real problems for education come from a simple lack of sufficient planning, sufficient resources, and sufficient training and pay for teachers. We need more good examples of what is possible with adequate levels of support. But this problem with education is present in almost every poor and rural area of the world. It's not unique to Peru."

As Peter prepares to return to his hotel, Elena says softly, "Make sure you get help if you need it. It is not good to suffer such a loss alone."

"I know," Peter says, "and thank you, both of you. Being with you has meant a lot to me tonight."

Peter returns to his hotel room, he double-locks the door behind him. He takes a chair from the table and jams it under the doorknob. When he looks at the black sofa again, he's back into his darkness and loss. He is tired, and he hurts. He's depressed. He gives in to the pain and takes an Oxycodone, and he lies down in bed.

He dreams of Maria. He wakes up with a start when he dreams of the moment when he shot her, but the Oxycodone helps him sleep again.

He gets out of bed at seven and prepares for the day. He's still tired, and he still hurts, but he avoids the oxycodone. He finishes packing and then has a large breakfast. He doesn't know what or when he will eat again.

Sir Richard adjusts the time for the flight. They arrive at the airport at a little before ten in the morning and load their baggage and the samples onto the British government plane.

They are "wheels up" in Lima at a little after eleven. Sir Richard and Peter are the only passengers on the plane, a Gulfstream G650FR. There is a crew of three, the two pilots plus a single cabin attendant. The plane can seat ten with work tables. It has a dining table for six, internet connection, and satellite telephone. It also has a small stateroom in the back with a twin bed.

The flight is uneventful, but nearly eleven hours long. They have a pleasant enough lunch, and an excellent dinner, with a very good Malbec from Mendoza, Argentina. Peter is poor company, and their conversation is labored at times. He spends most of his time working with his outline, beginning to put his report together. He'll fill in the details and conclusions later, after he gets his analytical results from the lab. He also spends about three hours trying to sleep on the bed, without a lot of success. The steady, small bumps are not helpful. They land at Pierson International Airport in Toronto a few minutes after eleven that night.

CHAPTER 28

Peter stays at the Sheraton Hotel, connected to the terminal at the airport. He barely notices the room. Almost immediately after the bellman leaves, he strips off his clothes, takes an oxycodone, and falls into bed.

After breakfast in the morning, Peter calls for a bellman to help him with his baggage and hires a cab at the front door. He drops the samples and instructions at the lab, located near the airport in Mississauga. He continues with the cab to the Billy Bishop Airport in downtown Toronto. He gives the driver an extra tip and asks him to help with his bags.

Once he has all his baggage loaded into the helicopter, Peter sits in the pilot's seat and does absolutely nothing for a good five minutes, letting his body calm down. With his physical limitations, he feels a little helpless.

"Time to go," he says.

He takes a deep breath, grimaces, and starts the helicopter. He takes off and heads west along the lake. Eventually he turns north toward the cabin. He feels good, even if his chest aches. He feels good, flying again on a glorious, calm, bright winter day. A lone, small cloud is all that mars the deep blue sky. He knows his pain, and his loss, will follow him, but for now he is determined to enjoy the freedom of flying.

He lands behind the general store in town to stock up on groceries. He assumes he'll be at the cabin for a week or two, at a minimum. On his way out of the store, in the pets and animal section, he sees that they have small bags of alfalfa and molasses horse treats for some of the locals who keep one or two horses. He thinks for a minute and adds one to his cart.

As he heads into his landing at the cabin, he sees the snowmobile tracks from John Williams making his daily check of the cabin. It looks like he shoveled off the helipad recently, and a path to the cabin. Peter smiles.

Just like John to think of that.

He lands and shuts down, and after a few minutes he gets out, grabs the duffel bag, and walks up to the cabin. He unlocks the door and steps inside. The cabin is dark, and it feels empty and dead. He turns up the thermostat for the furnace, starts a fire in the stove, and opens the metal shutters over all the windows. The cabin feels much more welcoming with the light streaming in through the windows.

"Have to get used to emptiness," he says. "It's your life again, bud."

He makes several more trips to get the rest of his luggage and groceries. It takes a while, carrying one bag at a time with his left arm. With considerable difficulty, he puts the covers on the helicopter.

The cabin warms up as he prepares a simple lunch and takes it to his desk. He pulls his computer out of his backpack and sends quick emails to Alden Sage, Sir Richard, and Julius Grant. The note is the same to each of them.

> *I'm back at the cabin. Dropped the samples at the lab in Mississauga this morning on the way out of Toronto. They're not too busy. Said I might have the results in a week or so. You should have my report within two weeks.*

He sends a second note to Bill Branch, telling him that he is back at the cabin. He asks Bill about the status of Maria's apartment, and if he can get in to retrieve his belongings.

He drags his suitcase and backpack into the bedroom, unpacks, and throws almost all of the clothes into the basket by the washing machine. He returns to the bedroom and collapses onto the bed.

He looks at the ceiling. "I'm alone. I'm depressed. And I've got nothing to do," he says. "Sounds like a totally screwed up life to me."

He closes his eyes and falls asleep.

When he wakes up, it's a little after three. He sees the basket of dirty clothes, throws one load in the washer, and sits at his desk. He picks up his VoIP phone and simply holds it in his hand for a long time. Then he punches in a number and waits for it to ring. His father, James Hodges Binder, answers.

"Hello?"

"Hi, dad. It's Peter."

Peter listens to the silence. When he finally speaks, his father sounds a little choked up.

"It's good to hear your voice, son. How have you been?"

"I've been okay. It's a little lonely up here right now. How are you doing?"

"Oh, I'm doing well. Ithaca is good for me, I think."

"The grapevines doing okay?" Peter asks.

"They're pretty much asleep until spring," his father answers.

"How's mom doing?"

"She's much the same. Some days when I visit, she knows me. Some days she doesn't."

"That's gotta be tough," Peter says.

"It is, but it's the deck we've been dealt. You should come down to see her. Can't guarantee it, but the good days are still fun."

"That's why I'm calling. I thought I'd come down. Is there a place where I can land a helicopter this time of year?"

"I didn't know you had your own now."

"I've had it for about six months. Even better than the motorcycle."

"You're still crazy," his father says with a chuckle. "Sure. There aren't any wires by the barn, and I can plow out a space there. How big?"

"I can squeeze into a space fifty-by-fifty feet, but it's a lot better to have eighty to a hundred," Peter answers.

"I can clear a hundred feet, and it's all level. It'll be great to see you. It's been a long time. Too long." Peter's father pauses. "I know a lot of it's my fault."

"Not really. I think we both own it," Peter says. "Sorry about my part of it. I'm ready to make a major change in my life, and…. You might not believe this, dad, but I'd like to talk to you about it."

His father laughs. "That is a surprise. Will Maria be with you?"

"No," Peter says. "That's over."

"Sorry to hear that."

They both remain silent for a bit.

"When do you expect to come?" his father asks.

"Depends on the weather. I'd like to fly down Tuesday or Wednesday next week. Stay a week or so?"

"I'll be ready," his father says. "Stay as long as you want. There's plenty of room."

"Dad, I have a question for you. Did your grandfather, the rabbi in Russia, have a vineyard and make wine?"

His father chuckles. "Yes, he did. My father said the wine was absolutely atrocious. Why do you ask?"

"Your grandfather's been teaching me how to prune grapevines in my dreams recently."

"That's interesting. You planning on becoming a vintner?"

"Thinking about it," Peter says.

"I guess we'd better talk."

"Yes, dad. I think we should. See you next week."

Peter remembers his pacifist father's anger when he enlisted, particularly when he became a SEAL. He refused to come to Peter's graduation ceremony for his successful completion of the SEAL training program. Peter knows that, in some respects, his own anger at that slight drove him to become the super warrior, the complete opposite of his father.

"Maybe I'm old enough to get over that now," Peter says. He laughs. "Ow! That hurts." He can't help it, though, and he laughs again.

He sees the bag of alfalfa treats and puts a few in a small bucket. He steps outside, sweeps the snow off the railing on the edge of the deck, and arranges some of the treats along the railing.

A little while later, as the afternoon sun is low on the horizon, Peter hears a snowmobile approaching. John Williams stops in front of the cabin, and Peter opens the door.

"Come on in, John."

Saying nothing, John reaches out to hand Peter the keys to the cabin.

"Hang onto them for now," Peter says. "I may go down to visit my parents next week. I'll let you know. You drinking whiskey or beer these days? Or are you sticking to coffee?"

"I don't drink alone, but right now I'm not alone. I'd love a whiskey," John says. "How'd Peru go?"

Peter puts two glasses on the table and a bottle of Ardbeg.

"From a geological standpoint, it was great. Otherwise, not great. Maria shot me eleven times. One of them was a real bullet. I was wearing body armor, but I have a couple of cracked ribs and a bruise that doesn't quit."

"Sorry," John says.

"I knew it was coming," Peter says. "But it doesn't change the hurt."

"Nope." John drinks about a third of his drink. "Guess the white moose was warning you about bad things."

"Maybe," Peter says, "but I'm still standing, and I'm done with that crap. Maybe it was warning me about good things."

John smiles. "The moose lets you choose."

He knows. He doesn't even have to ask me if Maria is dead.

They finish their drinks slowly, letting the strange and almost silent intimacy linger a while longer.

John gets up. "I'll head back. Thanks for the whiskey. It warms the cockles of my heart. It truly does."

"Thanks, John. Be well."

"And you, too. Be careful with your pain."

"Yes," Peter says.

Peter watches through the window over the sink in the kitchen as John heads back down the lake. "There goes a man who has found his own melancholy happiness in life."

Shortly after John leaves, Peter looks out to see the albino moose methodically eating the alfalfa treats off the deck railing.

Peter realizes he has little he must do for the next few days. He focuses on healing and takes relatively short, slow, cross-country ski hikes. By Sunday he's feeling much better physically, and his mind, too, seems to be in a better place. He looks at the weather forecast and decides to head to Ithaca on Wednesday. He calls his father and tells him that he will arrive that afternoon.

On Monday, he drives the roundtrip to Toronto and, under police supervision, removes all of his belongings from Maria's apartment. It isn't much. He would like to take a few mementos, but the police will not allow it.

He does look up the drug addict who tried to stab him on University Avenue and learns his name, Jacob Corman. They have a long conversation over a cup of coffee and a cheeseburger. Jacob looks considerably better. He's put on a little weight, is clean shaven, and no longer has the shakes. As Peter departs, to return to the cabin, he says to him, "I know more about where you've been than you might think, and I can tell you, your life really can change for the better."

On Tuesday, he takes the snowmobile, rather slowly, down to the fishing lodge. He tells John his travel plans.

"Am I going to see you again?" John asks.

Peter smiles. "You'll see me, but I don't know how often."

"Be well, Peter. I'll see if I can look after your albino moose. I don't think he'll hang around after you leave."

"Try horse alfalfa and molasses treats. He loves them," Peter says. "He follows me around now, almost like a dog. For some reason, I think he'll like you."

Peter packs for his visit to his father, adds the reports, maps, and vertical sections from Cerro Nublado, and flies out on Wednesday morning. He stops and refuels at Toronto and again at Rochester. He arrives at his father's farm a little after three in the afternoon, with more than a half tank of fuel. His father has cleared much more area than he needs to land next to the barn.

James Hodges Binder stands, rather dignified, on the porch of the house watching Peter come in and land. The rotor wash ruffles his gray hair.

Peter hardly recognizes the place. The barn looks freshly painted and appears to be set up as a tasting room. The tumbled-down outbuildings he remembers from his teenage years are all gone. The house wears its colorful paint like the old Victorian lady it is, and a new barn to the side holds the machinery of the nascent winery.

After he shuts down the helicopter, Peter walks up to the porch. He pauses at the bottom of the three stairs.

James Binder has aged since the last time they were together, but he's still the tall, thin and fit man that Peter remembers. Peter smiles at his clothes. He wears his crisp, tan pants and plaid shirt, as if he just stepped out of Brooks Brothers with a new set of clothes for a "country gentleman".

Peter climbs the stairs. He and his father embrace.

"I'm sorry it's been so long," Peter says.

His father holds him. "Don't be sorry, son. I was small and foolish."

"You're not the only one, dad."

Peter steps back. His father has tears in his eyes, and so does Peter.

After a moment of hesitation, James says, "Come in! Come in! You want some coffee?"

Peter sits at the table in the kitchen. The room has changed, yet it seems the same. Updated. Modernized. Still, it gives that same sense of warmth and comfort he remembers on the summer days, twenty years earlier.

"How's mom?"

Rather than answering immediately, James fusses with the coffee. *He's always fussed with the details of his life*, Peter thinks. It's part of what made him such a successful lawyer in New York.

His father finally answers. "She was quite good when I visited this morning. I told her that you were coming to visit. She cried, but they were tears of happiness."

"Could we visit her now?"

James brings the coffee to the table. "We could. She doesn't always hold it together for the afternoon, but if you show up, she'll probably rise to the occasion." He smiles at Peter. "You still like your coffee black?"

"Yes."

"Some things don't change."

They drive to the nursing home, where Beverley, his mother, is suffering through early-onset dementia. Otherwise, she is quite healthy. She lives in a small home, where she receives the watchful care she needs, and lives as connected a life as she can muster. She enjoys a visit from James almost every day, though she often forgets and thinks he has not visited for a long time. She sits to the side, in the sunroom, looking out the window.

In some ways, Beverley was always the strong center of the family when Peter was a boy. When James became too immersed in his legal career, Beverley always pulled him back to the family. Her independence and pursuit of her own career as a financial advisor never diminished her intense love for her husband, or her son. The brilliance of her white hair in the sun startles Peter. He is reminded of how much he has lost with his long absence.

She looks up. "Oh, James. Thank you for visiting. Have you been away?"

James bends over and kisses her. "Look at who showed up at the farm today."

"Hi, mom," Peter says.

She looks at him and begins to cry. "Peter? Oh, Peter. It's been so long." She holds out her hands to him.

Peter kneels down, and they hug.

"Oh, Peter. If you'd told me, I would have baked a pie." She smiles.

Peter remembers that smile, a smile that seems to involve her entire face.

"You always were one to surprise me. And I haven't even had my hair done."

They spend an hour with her. She does rise to the occasion. She is mostly in the present, though she spends much of the time talking about his childhood, and how, when he was a teenager, he fought being sent to work on the farm with his grandfather.

On the way back home, Peter asks, "How's old Viktor Sidorov doing? I always liked that grumpy guy."

"He's not as grumpy these days. He sold his farm to someone who's letting him live on ten acres as long as he wants. He can keep his farm stand going in the summer, and he still has a few years of Christmas tree sales." James pauses. "I wanted to buy his farm, but I waited too long." He shrugs. "He got a good price."

"Why did you want to buy it? Expand the winery?"

"That was the idea. Kind of foolish, I suppose."

"A little early in the life of the business, maybe," Peter says.

His father opens a bottle of Bordeaux for dinner. "Not mine, obviously. We might start production of the whites next year. We'll see about reds. I haven't planted for them yet. I hope to in a year or two."

Peter tastes the wine. "Nice."

"Yes. It is," his father says. "Now, what's this about a life change, and maybe becoming a vintner?"

Peter takes his time. "I've never told you, but I was in a nasty firefight in Afghanistan. In the end, I was the lone man standing. The military accused me of murdering my entire platoon. To this day I don't know what happened. I was a major mess for years. PTSD, drugs, alcohol, and lots of time in counseling. They finally completed a full investigation, and a month ago, they gave me a copy of the report. It cleared me of all the accusations." Peter sighs. "I've been in the business of fighting and killing, more or less, for most of my adult life. I can say that I'm very good at it, and I believe that most of the time I have fought for the good cause. But… I've made the decision to walk away." He stops for a moment. "I've also made a heap of money and have little happiness to show for it."

"I'm sorry," James says.

"It was mostly my choice, dad," Peter says. "I can do what I want now. I love good wine, and I thought about making wine. Then I thought about coming here and buying some land."

"There's not much good land for vineyards left near here."

"Viktor's land is good land. Right?"

James looks at his son. "You're kidding me."

Peter grins. "No. I'm not. I bought it. I didn't want you to know. I was afraid I might not survive my last job. I want to come home, dad. I want to make wine, and I think we might be able to do it together."

James sits back in his chair. He closes his eyes. Slowly a smile forms and grows. He opens his eyes again and picks up his wine glass.

"I'll drink to that, my son. I think my Cincinnatus has finally returned home from the wars."

CHAPTER 29

Five days later, late on a Monday afternoon, Peter receives his analytical results for the samples from Cerro Nublado. He holds his breath as he scrolls down the columns of analyses. Copper, molybdenum, lead, and zinc all look normal for a copper deposit. The precious metals, gold, silver, and platinum are all uniformly low, which is no surprise. Peter laughs at the low values for the rare earth elements.

"So much for that possibility."

Near the end of the long list of assays, he focuses on the uranium values, particularly for those samples with an abundance of black veinlets.

"Holy shit!"

He knew from his measurements in the field that these zones of black veinlets were radioactive, and he expected anomalously high uranium and thorium values. The analyses confirm his suspicions, but he's not all that familiar with uranium deposits and didn't know quite what to expect in the uranium analyses. The actual uranium values are much higher than he had expected.

I guess that explains the North Korea connection. Unlimited feed for their nuclear weapons program.

Cerro Nublado, as it turns out, is a large, extremely rich, uranium deposit, with potential for byproduct copper production.

I think I just earned my five million.

Peter spends an intense two days at his father's dining room table, plotting the uranium assays on the Cerro Nublado sections and interpreting the results. Then he completes his report. The main conclusions are simple.

1: Cerro Nublado presents two distinct periods and styles of mineralization. The older of the two creates a large, relatively low-grade, copper deposit. The upper portion of the copper deposit is overprinted by later uranium mineralization which produces a large, near-surface, high-grade, uranium deposit.

2: The black, late veins, previously reported as iron and manganese oxide veins, appear to be composed largely of uraninite or pitchblende, a complex uranium oxide.

3: The existing feasibility report appears to be accurate in its depiction of the copper mineralization, but it does not address the uranium mineralization and its impact on economics and the ability to permit production at Cerro Nublado.

4: Early production at Cerro Nublado will likely produce a high-quality uranium concentrate, suitable for refinement and enrichment. The enriched product should be suitable to fuel nuclear power plants and, potentially, the production of nuclear weapons.

5: Additional testing is required, but early production of copper at Cerro Nublado may produce copper concentrates contaminated with uranium and unsuitable for sale to any normal, commercial smelter or refiner.

6: Because the early production at Cerro Nublado must produce large amounts of uranium concentrates and potentially radioactive waste products, many new environmental and permitting issues must be resolved, prior to any permitting and production decisions.

On the Wednesday afternoon, the third of March and six weeks after he agreed to go to Peru, Peter fills in the blank sections of his report. He completes a final review and makes a few last corrections. He doesn't say the project cannot be permitted, but he suspects that may be the case, at least in the short term. A little after nine in the evening, he sends a copy off to Julius Grant, at his home in Brisbane.

Peter smiles as he shuts his laptop. *That will produce an interesting reaction.*

He sits down with his father to watch Rachel Maddow's evening news review. Wisser's continued efforts to destroy democracy give her plenty to shout about. No more than twenty minutes into the show, Julius sends Peter a text.

Peter:

We need to talk. Are you somewhere you can talk confidentially?

Julius

Peter tells him to call him on his cell phone, and he gets up from the sofa.

"I've got to take a telephone call. I'll be back in a few minutes."

He moves to the dining room, where all the sections, maps, and reports for Cerro Nublado are still laid out on the table. It's only two or three minutes before his phone rings.

"Good morning, Julius."

"Man, you sure know how to drop a fucking bomb."

"A nuclear one at that," Peter says.

"I don't know whether to kiss you or kick your bloody ass."

Peter laughs. "That's commonly the case with my clients these days. This report may be a bit more dramatic than most, though."

"You don't say!"

"Don't blame me. I just gave you the second ore deposit you were dreaming about when we talked in Peru. Only one or two problems. I'm not sure you can sell it, permit it, develop it, or mine it."

"I guess I know why someone murdered my friend in Lima," Julius says, "but it doesn't make a lot of sense. They didn't seriously think they could mine this and keep the uranium secret, did they?"

"They must have. Presumably they planned on getting much of the uranium to North Korea so they could build an unlimited number of nuclear bombs," Peter says. "Isn't that a lovely concept?"

"Unbelievable."

"What will you do?" Peter asks.

"I've got to release your bloody report to the exchange, and I have no idea of what that will do to our stock. I'm sure it will explode one way or the other. Then I have to sue those bastard Russians in London for breach of contract. I'll go after everything I can get my hands on, but I doubt I'll end up with much to show for my efforts. I'd love to see some of the bloody bastards in jail, but that won't happen."

"When do you plan to release the report?"

"Right after the stock exchange closes in London on Friday," Julius says. "I'm not sure I can get the release ready before then, and I want the market to have the weekend to think about it."

"You need a couple of signed, hard copies?"

"Yeah. Express them to me in Brisbane," Julius says.

"Okay. I'll get them on the way tomorrow."

"By the way, what the bloody hell went down when you were at Cerro Nublado? My partners tell me that the Policia National del Perú visited Cerro Nublado the other day. It seems three or four local villagers disappeared while you were in the camp."

"It's a big jungle, Julius."

"Yeah, but they were all headed to the Cerro Nublado camp. They never came home."

"It's a big jungle."

"Tell me they won't find any bodies, Peter."

"They won't find any bodies. I guarantee it."

"You're sure?"

"I'm sure."

"And you've nothing more to tell me?" Julius asks.

"Nope."

Peter hears Julius sigh before he says, "Okay. I'll take your word for it. Stay in touch. I may need you to testify in London."

"Just give me a call."

Peter returns to the living room to watch the end of the news show.

"Did I miss anything important?" he asks his father.

"Nope. Just more ranting about Wisser. What was the phone call all about?"

"A dose of drama related to the report I've been working on." Peter shakes his head. "I'll have another one or two calls in the next few days. Then it should die down. I hope."

Before he goes to bed, Peter sends three separate emails with a copy of his report, one each to Sir Richard, Alden Sage, and Jeremy Pritchard. He asks them to keep it confidential until the weekend.

Peter is in the same room he slept in as a teenager, when he came to work with his grandfather. He lies back on the bed and falls asleep. He dreams of working in a vineyard again. This time his great-grandfather is nowhere to be seen. Peter and his father tend to the vines together, each of them enjoying the quiet of the other's company.

"Do you fully realize what this means?" Alden Sage asks in his morning call.

"I'm listening," Peter responds.

"For a long time, the US has been working with the Chinese to try to starve the North Korean nuclear program. Between the two of us we can pretty much define what goes in and out of North Korea. It's been almost impossible for them to get the uranium to build more than a very small number of nuclear warheads. They know how to enrich uranium, but if you've got no feed, there's nothing to enrich. No enrichment means no nuclear warheads."

"So, Cerro Nublado was supposed to be their uranium supply, disguised as shipments of copper concentrates," Peter says.

"Right."

"Sounds crazy. How do you keep all that uranium production secret? The radiation levels on any bulk transport ship would be out of sight. You can't hide that sort of thing."

"Why not?" Alden asks. "Who checks copper concentrates in Peru for radioactivity? Besides, once it's on a Russian ship, a bulk carrier, and it goes to North Korea? Those are two countries very good at keeping secrets."

"With no controls, there will be a lot of premature deaths by cancer," Peter says.

"You really think the leaders of Russia or North Korea actually care about that?"

"Probably not, but it's also a hell of a lot of uranium," Peter says.

"Ah, North Korea won't get to keep it all. Russia will take a big chunk of the production, but my guess is that North Korea, if all this uranium came their way, would end up with one to two hundred warheads in two years. They already have the missile systems in place. They're capable of delivering nuclear bombs on South Korea, Japan, Guam, Hawaii, much of the west coast of the US, and most of the population centers of China and southeast Asia."

"And the leader of North Korea is crazy enough to use the damn things," Peter says.

"Exactly."

"What's in it for Russia, though?" Peter asks. "North Korea can sow chaos in the Pacific and threaten the US. Chaos and distrust are good for Russia, but how does an actual nuclear war benefit them? Besides, much of Russia is also in range of their missiles. Not nice to have an irrational and unpredictable neighbor with nuclear weapons."

"I'm sure they believe they can control North Korea," Alden says. "They're wrong. North Korea is the perfect example of a mad dog that bites anything that gets close enough, even the hand that feeds it."

After a short hesitation, Alden continues. "It's a great opportunity. If we play it right, we can strengthen our cooperation with China, support the people of North Korea, reduce the paranoia, and maybe make some real progress toward a reduction of tensions in that part of the world."

"How the hell do you manage that, when Wisser is throwing brickbats at China and pursuing a trade war with them? He's using China bashing all the time to rile up his base."

"First step is to make sure Russo-Perú can't develop the damn thing."

"I don't think that's a problem, now the uranium issue is out in the open," Peter says. "Julius told me that Mandrake will be suing them for breach of contract, to get the property back and anything else they can get their hands on. They'll have to redo all the feasibility reports and applications for permits. Just saying the words 'radioactive' and 'uranium' will stir up a pile of NGOs and the local opposition, no matter how good the mining plan. This project is guaranteed dead for at least ten years."

"Then it's a piece of cake," Alden says. "China can think on multiple levels. We explain what was planned, how we stopped it, and how we're going to convince Wisser to work with them to support North Korea and defuse the whole situation on the Korean peninsula."

Peter laughs. "You make it sound so easy, but how in God's name do you convince Wisser to take that sort of action? He's death on China these days. Besides, I'm not sure he can think clearly on one level, to say nothing about multiple levels. All he's interested in is grabbing more money and power for himself."

"Not to worry my boy. The man has an immense ego, and he's desperate for a foreign policy triumph. I think we can manufacture his support just by convincing someone on Fox News to endorse it, and they're dumb enough swallow whole most any bait we hand them. The end product, in eight or ten years, might be a peaceful and non-nuclear Korean peninsula."

"Okay," Peter says. "If you can pull that off, I guess all the pain and death was worth it."

"I believe so," Alden says. "By the way, how are you doing?"

"Physically or mentally?"

"Both, I guess."

"Physically, I'm pretty good, almost back to normal. Mentally? I'll be a little fragile on that front for a while, but it's not too bad. I prepared myself for the ending with Maria. It was a major disappointment, but it was not a huge surprise."

"I've been meaning to tell you," Alden says. "We sorted out those two guys who tried to mug you in Toronto."

"And?"

"Second generation Russian immigrants to the US. Part of the Russian mafia. We think they've done various bits of black work and maybe a couple of assassinations for the SVR. They'll spend a long time as guests of the Canadian government. They were onto this Peruvian situation really fast, and I find that a little astonishing."

"I don't," Peter says. "I think Maria was in contact with Ivan Dinisovich from the very beginning, probably as soon as she knew I was seriously considering going to Peru."

"I'm sorry to hear that."

"She worked really hard to convince me not to go to Peru, not to work on Cerro Nublado. I think she really did care about me, a little. I don't know if I could have expressed it at the time, but I think, in the back of my mind, I realized pretty early on that she was afraid of Peru. She was afraid that, if I went to Peru, she would be asked to kill me one more time, and this time she would have to obey."

Alden says nothing.

"And that, Alden, is the real reason I went to Peru and did my work at Cerro Nublado. I had to find out. I had to give her the opportunity to kill me."

EPILOGUE

Ten years later, on a beautiful, clear and warm summer day, a black car drives up to a gate. The sign over the gate reads: "Sidorov Winery". The driver stops and presses a button on a touch pad at the side of the road.

"Yes?" says a voice from the speaker.

"Alden Sage to see Peter Binder."

"Alden! Come on up. Lunch is almost ready."

The gate slowly opens, and Alden drives up the gravel road, past the dark green rows of grapevines. The bunches of grapes are mostly still green and hard, but a few are beginning to show a darker red color.

He smiles as he passes the large, barn-like structures that are the processing facilities and the wine tasting rooms. At the end of the half-mile driveway, he parks to the side of the glass and steel house. The back of the house is set into the side of a small hill, but two thirds of the house is cantilevered over a rocky ledge. The house overlooks the fields to Lake Cayuga at the bottom of the hill.

Peter welcomes him at the door. It's an upside-down house. The bedrooms are on the lower level, and the living areas are on the upper level, with the better view.

"The children can't wait to see you," Peter says.

"So... How are my precious godchildren?"

"Excited. You don't visit often enough."

"Well, you have to admit, you're not close to a major urban center."

"Ithaca is urban enough for me these days." Peter says.

At the top of the stairs, two children run over to Alden. The girl has her blond hair tied up in pigtails, and the boy has decided he wants his hair tied up in little tufts across his head.

"Uncle Alden! Uncle Alden!" they shout.

The oldest, Julia, says, "I have to show you what I coded on my computer!"

Peter laughs. "Give uncle Alden a chance to catch his breath. You can show him after lunch."

Alden hugs Julia and picks up the younger boy, John, to give him a hug. After he sets John back down on the floor, Alden produces several small gifts from his pockets.

Julia, negotiates for herself and her brother. "May we open them now?" she asks her father.

Peter nods his head with a smile. "Of course, but what do you say first?"

"Thank you! Thank you!" they both shout and run off.

"God, they grow quickly," Alden says.

Peter laughs. "Julia is eight, going on thirty-five. John is six, going on six. He's frightened by nothing, and I fear for his life if he doesn't learn to be afraid once in a while."

"Just like his father."

"Hopefully, he'll learn sooner than his father did," Peter says.

"They're both beautiful kids."

"Don't tell them that," Peter says. "Unfortunately, both of them already know that, and I don't want to reinforce it."

Mary, Peter's wife, comes to greet Alden. She is as tall as Peter. Her hair falls down gently to her shoulders. She's dressed in blue jeans and a blue and white, striped shirt. Everything about her exudes a sense of quiet strength.

"Mary, you look as wonderful as ever. Peter made a wise move to marry the farmer's daughter."

"Granddaughter, Alden. Granddaughter," Peter says, laughing.

Mary smiles. "Good to see you, Alden. You know you're always welcome here."

They enjoy a boisterous lunch, and Alden asks the children lots of questions. Peter and Mary sit back and watch.

When there is a bit of a pause in the children's chatter, Peter says "I hope you like my pride and joy," as he pours some wine for Alden. "We're not selling it yet, but it's our first bottling of Pinot Noir from three years ago. Each year the harvest is better, and the wine we produce continues to improve, but this is our very first batch. Very small. Only for special friends."

Alden tastes the wine, smiles and nods his head. "Not bad for a beginner."

"Ah, you're a tough audience, Alden. As I said, it is getting better."

After lunch, Alden gives his attention to Julia as she shows him her latest exercise in computer coding. Then he sits on the floor with John to play with a set of small cars and a racetrack.

Later in the afternoon, when the children have settled down for a bit of quiet time, Alden and Peter sit on the deck, looking out over the lake. Peter refills their glasses.

"How's the wine business these days?" Alden asks.

"We're just starting to get some real cashflow from the whites," Peter says. "We plow every cent and then some right back into the business. Thank God Mary runs the finances. My father and I would make a right mess of that on our own."

They sit in silence, enjoying the warmth of the afternoon, the sounds of the birds, the deep blue sky, and the view of green fields of grapevines and hay leading down to the dark waters of the lake.

"I see you're back in the White House again," Peter says. "You are truly a glutton for punishment."

"It's what I love, and I think I do some good in the world. President Wilton is a fine man. He's trying hard to heal the deep wounds that Helmut Wisser left behind. I want to do my part to help."

"It wasn't obvious to me," Peter says, "that Wilton would ever be able to enter the White House without a second civil war."

"Yes. Wisser did try to destroy the Capitol building, to have his own Reichstag moment, to launch his coup and become the dictator. He had almost enough of a mob to pull it off. In the end it was nothing more than the pathetic, panicked and dangerous flailing of the mad king." Alden pauses. "Neither he nor his spineless, self-serving enablers will ever accept full responsibility for what they tried to do to this country."

"Perhaps the courts will have some success," Peter says. "They can't force acceptance of responsibility, but they can force some accountability."

"Possibly, but I'm not holding my breath." Alden turns to Peter. "I hope you've noticed that, largely because of what you did in Peru, we've made some real progress with North Korea."

"I have noticed. It certainly took a while."

"Nothing in foreign relations worth doing is ever quick or easy," Alden says. "Do you ever think about your previous life?"

"Sometimes. I still have nightmares, but they're quite rare now. Occasionally I allow myself to think that some good arose from my twenty years of blood, violence, and death."

Peter swirls the wine in his glass and takes a swallow. "I still think about Maria. She's a part of me, for the rest of my life, I suppose." He shrugs. "It took me a long time to realize, and even longer to admit to myself, that I didn't know her at all. I thought I was in love, but I was in love with a mirage. I loved nothing more than the image that she chose to show me. I was a fool."

"We are all fools in love, one time or another," Alden says.

Peter frowns. "A good part of my previous life was pretty ugly. I don't necessarily regret it, at least not all of it, but I do know that I don't miss it."

He turns and smiles at Alden. He gestures at the view. "Just look out there, Alden. I have everything I could ever want. I have a wonderful wife and a loving family. My father and I work together after years of foolish separation, and we're beginning to make some good wine. I work with Omar Vargas in Peru. In small ways, he and I improve many lives of the rural poor in the Altiplano."

Peter Binder raises his glass as if to toast the entire world in front of him.

"Best of all," he says, "I finally live in peace."

THE END

Printed in the United States
By Bookmasters